LINDSAY McKENNA

BREAKING POINT

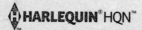

Recycling programs
for this product may
not exist in your area.

ISBN-13: 978-0-373-77867-6

BREAKING POINT

Copyright © 2014 by Nauman Living Trust

Printed in U.S.A.

HARLEQUIN®
www.Harlequin.com

To Bill Marcontell, Captain, USAF, retired,
who flew Search and Rescue helicopters for the 38th ARRS
in Southeast Asia in 1966–67. Thank you for information
involving anything and everything that has to do with
helicopters, their flight and their issues in this novel.

To Chief Michael Jaco, US Navy SEAL, retired.
I appreciate you checking the technical aspects
of all things SEAL in this book. And thank you for writing
The Intuitive Warrior. www.MichaelJaco.com

CHAPTER ONE

"Time for your trial by fire," SEAL Chief Hampton said, gesturing for Baylee-Ann Thorn to follow him out of Operations. Hampton had met her CH-47 helo from Bagram Air Base. As he walked with her from Ops toward the SEAL compound, he told her how it was always below freezing in the morning despite its being a day in June in Afghanistan.

Bay tried to quell her nervousness. They traversed deeply rutted Humvee tracks outside Operations. Camp Bravo, an FOB, forward operating base, was thirty miles from the Pak, Pakistan border. It housed all types of black ops groups. Hampton led them toward a small concrete one-story building located near the edge of the CIA and black ops complex.

The Afghan sun was rising above the sharp, high peaks of the Hindu Kush Mountains. Bay was glad for the desert cammies and her soft cap since it was so cold. She removed her wraparound sunglasses as the chief of Alpha Platoon pushed open the door for her. Bay took a deep, steadying breath, feeling as if she were about to walk into a firefight.

Inside, she halted, unsure where to go. Looking to her left, she noticed seven SEAL shooters sitting and talking among themselves. They looked as if they'd just finished a patrol, sweaty, dusty and tired-looking. She felt exactly like them, flying out of Iraq and leaving her Special Forces, a team stationed near Baghdad, for this outpost.

"Follow me," Hampton said, giving her a smile of encouragement.

Bay felt slightly better, ignoring her exhaustion and following the tall, wiry Navy chief to the front of the large room. As soon as Hampton arrived, all talking stopped and the seven SEALs sat alert and focused. There were large wooden plyboard tables pushed off to one side. To her, they looked like planning or mission tables where the black ops SEAL team would plan their patrols. The SEALs sat on a few wooden bleachers at the other end of the room.

The room quieted as three Navy SEAL officers, who ran the platoon, entered the area from another doorway. Bay stood off to one side with Hampton as Lieutenant Paul Brafford, the OIC, Officer in Command, strolled up to the center. Every man in the room wore a beard in order to fit into the Muslim culture. Two other officers followed him into the silent room.

"Gentlemen, two days ago we lost Steve, our 18 Delta combat medic and sniper." His voice turned heavy. "It's a loss we didn't want to see happen, and I know we're all upset about it." He sat down on a four-legged stool, hooking the heel of his combat boot on a lower rung. "What I'm about to tell you is top secret. And Chief Hampton is going to be passing around a paper that you will sign, ensuring that this will be kept that way."

There was a murmur among the shooters, who collectively looked at the woman standing beside their chief. They rested their safed rifles, muzzle down, across their legs or chest.

Brafford said, "Unbeknownst to us, there has been an ongoing initiative called Operation Shadow Warriors. It is an experiment created by the Joint Chiefs of Staff to see if women, who are adequately trained for combat, can be successful under combat conditions. This operation has been ongoing for three years now, in Iraq and Afghanistan. You will read and agree to what you're signing. Basically, it says you won't *ever* speak a word about having a woman assigned to our platoon."

Bay saw the collective shock on the SEALs' faces. Chief Hampton passed the papers among them. Bay was interested in how the SEALs operated. There were three SEALs on the first bench, three on the second bench. On the last bench near the rear bulkhead or wall sat one lone SEAL. She was good at interpreting facial expressions and body language. Bay noticed the anger and disgust in the faces on the first bench of SEALs. They wanted nothing to do with her. The second bench of SEALs looked surprised. Bay saw something else in the expression of the SEAL who sat by himself. Interest. Curiosity. No judgment. At least, not yet.

Bay felt her skin prickle as the lone SEAL's green eyes narrowed speculatively, assessing her. He had a square face, strong chin, wide-set eyes and was deeply tanned from being out in the elements. His black hair was dusty, longish and reminded Bay of a raven's wing. He was tall and she felt coiled energy around him. His right hand rested relaxed across the rail system on top of his M-4 rifle. Even though he appeared to be at rest,

Bay noted the tension in his broad shoulders. There was nothing casual about this shooter.

Bay was used to relying on her intuition, which was finely honed by her years of living in the Allegheny Mountains with her hill family. This man was lethal in ways she couldn't imagine. Yes, SEALs, as she understood them, were at the tip of the black ops spear. They went out on patrol or a direct action mission and moved into harm's way. SEALs were intent on taking out HVTs, high-value targets. Bullets were going to fly when they entered the picture. Still, there was something about the lone SEAL that touched Bay's fast-beating heart. If she hadn't been so tired and stressed at being thrown into this awkward and unexpected situation, she might have picked up more about him.

"Okay, gentlemen," Brafford said, "you've read it. Now sign your life away so we can move on."

Bay stood next to the AOIC, a tall, lean second lieutenant, Reed Latham. The AAOIC, an ensign, Pete Scardillo, watched and listened. The chief had told her the SEALs were instituting a new officer training template. The AAOIC was a recent graduate and officer, but he'd be going out on every mission with the SEAL shooters, learning the trade. Latham critically watched his SEAL shooters. They were all enlisted men, Bay knew. Like her. Would they accept her or not? She'd worked with Marines and Army Special Forces in Iraq over the past three years. She'd heard about the clandestine SEALs, who had an awesome reputation of being a deadly force behind the scenes. Now, for the first time, she was getting a personal and up-front look at them. There was a lot of muttering and grumbling among them.

Hampton moved through the group, took the signed papers and walked over to the AAOIC and handed the sheaf to him. The chief then came and stood at Bay's side.

The tension in the room amped up. Bay felt every pair of SEAL eyes on her. She wanted to cringe inside her cammies and hide. This wasn't going to go down well. She could feel it.

"Chief," Brafford said mildly, "would you like to finish up introducing our new doc and getting her assigned a mentor?" He eased off the stool.

"Yes, sir," Hampton said.

All three officers left through another door. Bay tried to appear relaxed, but her heart was pounding now, with adrenaline leaking into her bloodstream. She watched Hampton take the stool with accustomed ease, his hands resting relaxed on his thighs as he regarded his men.

"I want to introduce you to your newest team member, Petty Officer First-Class Hospital Corpsman Baylee-Ann Thorn. She's a combat corpsman. She's been trained for a year by the Marines at Camp Pendleton and knows the drill on being a shooter. Plus—" he looked over at her "—she's going to be one of our medics in our platoon. You'll find her competent. And I know that all of you are going to have to be flexible about having a female in our midst. I feel sure you guys can handle it. Be gentlemen and understand that because she's a medic, your life is in her hands. Got it?"

Bay saw a lot of unhappy faces in front of her. They

didn't want a woman around. She could feel their anger, surprise and distrust of her being an outsider to the tight SEAL team. Swallowing hard, Bay kept her face carefully arranged. Somehow, with the chief's help, she was going to have to make this work. The SEALs were a badass group. None of them was smiling. All but one, frowning.

"Doc, why don't you come up here and introduce yourself? Tell the guys a little bit about yourself," Hampton invited, gesturing for her to step forward.

Oh, Lord, give me strength. Doc was the nickname every combat corpsman was called in the military. Bay stepped next to the chief. "Good morning," she said, "I'm Corpsman Thorn. I know my first name is a mouthful, so most folks call me Doc or Bay." She fearlessly met their black, flat stares. "I know this is an odd situation, but I promise you, I won't become a liability. I've been working for years over in Iraq with Marines and U.S. Army Special Forces. I know the drill."

Hampton intervened. "Well, I can tell you that Doc is a very humble person. She isn't going to brag on herself." He smiled a little over at Bay and then shifted his attention to the team. "Doc Thorn is the first woman to ever be allowed to go through and graduate from Army 18 Delta combat medic training. Almost two-thirds of the Army Special Forces guys who go through this eighteen-month course fail. But she didn't. She's used her skills for the last two years in Iraq combat situations and hasn't lost a man yet."

All the SEALs looked at one another, doubly shocked. The 18 Delta combat medics were the golden hour in a field of combat. They saved lives that regu-

lar combat medics were not trained to do. Nearly all
SEALs who were medics were graduates of 18 Delta.
The looks on their faces turned to grudging respect.

GABE GRIFFIN SMILED a little to himself. Chief Hampton was smart. Bay showed her humbleness and yet
nailed the disbelievers in the team with the one thing
that counted: a damn good medic who could save their
sorry ass if they got shot out on a patrol or mission.
About half the SEALs sat back, seriously digesting
the info. Baylee-Ann Thorn's soft drawl wasn't quite
Southern, so he wondered where she was from. He
liked her husky voice, her confidence as she stood relaxed in front of the group. For a medic, she was a good
height and weight. Bay, as he decided to call her, was
probably around five feet ten inches tall. In a firefight,
this woman could haul a SEAL to safety if she had to.
Adrenaline would make up the difference.

Still, as Gabe listened to her background, he was
struck by how innocent Bay looked. She had light
brown, slightly curly hair, pulled back into a riot-
ous ponytail. With intelligent blue eyes, a nice mouth
and kind-looking face, she wasn't typical of a combat SEAL. She wasn't beautiful. Rather, natural and
at ease with herself and who she was. Gabe liked her
easygoing nature, and as he studied his team, he saw
a couple of the guys losing their bristling demeanor.

Yes, Bay certainly had a nice voice. The kind of
voice you'd want around if you were bleeding out and
going to die in two and a half minutes. You'd believe
anything Bay told you because you trusted her and
trusted her incredible training. Gabe wondered if her

personality would be able to tame the animals in this squad of eight shooters. They all sat alert on their benches, listening closely to what she had to say.

Chief Hampton looked at the team. "Thanks, Doc," he said. "I want to welcome you to Alpha Platoon. Do you animals have any questions for her?"

"Yeah, I sure as hell do," Hammer, who sat on the first bench nearest them, snarled. "Just what the hell was the Navy thinking? Putting a *woman* in our platoon? I don't care if this is some top-secret op or not. It's insane."

Bay winced inwardly at the tall SEAL's angry comment. He had disgust in his eyes. She felt his emotions strike her.

Hampton sighed. "Hammer, stand down. This is not her fault. Doc did volunteer for this experiment. Keep in mind this op has been ongoing for three years and it has been very successful."

Hammer glared at the chief, challenging him. "Have there been any other bitches assigned to a SEAL squad?"

"Knock off the disrespect," Hampton growled. "The answer is yes. And you wouldn't have heard about it through the grapevine because every man signed that waiver, promising to never speak of it to anyone. Not even to other SEAL squads or platoons."

Hammer lifted his chin. "She's going out on our patrols with us?"

"That's what a doc does," Hampton replied in a reasonable tone.

"That's friggin' babysitting, Chief!" Hammer protested loudly. "It's not like we don't have enough on our hands watchin' out for the tangos, the goddamn IEDs and the rest. Now we have to watch out for her ass, too? She's a major distraction and that can get us killed."

Bay put her hand out and briefly touched the chief's shoulder. "Chief, if you would allow me?"

Hampton shrugged. "Go for it."

Gabe sat back. Bay Thorn's blue eyes narrowed slightly and her wide, soft mouth thinned. He was surprised she'd take on a SEAL, expecting her to hide behind the chief and let him do the fighting for her. That impressed him.

Bay met Hammer's black glare. "I have never worked with SEALs, that's true. From what I've heard about you guys over the years, y'all are heroes in my eyes."

Gabe watched the team preen to a man, as if stroked by her long, narrow hand. They were warriors. And they had the confidence and training to rightfully feel that way about themselves. It was always nice to hear someone consider them heroes and tell them to their face, however. He watched Bay with fascination, wondering how she was ever going to handle this male alpha wolf team.

"The chief was right. I am trained for combat. I also have a yearlong immersion course in Pashto. I hope to be of help in different ways to you. I'd much rather be a terp, translator, for you, or another gun in the fight, than have to save your hide once you took a bullet out in the field. But I can do that, too. Like you, I'm multi-skilled and consider myself an asset."

Opening her hands, Bay said, "I come from hill people. I was born in the Allegheny Mountains of West

Virginia. I grew up barefoot, learned to hunt in the woods starting at age six with my pa. My mama is a hill doctor and she's saved many people's lives and delivered a ton of babies. I know how to track, shoot and heal. I hope you'll let me prove myself over time. I promise, I won't be a pain in your collective butt. I will never put any of you at risk for me. Instead I'm trained to take the risks for you."

The sincerity in her eyes and voice deeply affected Gabe. He looked around and saw about half his team bought her explanation. The other half didn't.

"Okay," Hammer said, "so you're a friggin' hillbilly. So what? What did you do, shoot squirrels and possum for your mama's soup kettle?"

A snicker went through some of the team.

Hampton opened his mouth to chastise the squad, but Bay cut him a glance. He closed his mouth.

Giving the SEAL a loose smile, she said with humor, "Yes, I'm hill stock, for sure. And it's true what we shoot, we eat. Squirrel ain't all that bad," she teased, dropping more into her dialect. "Tastes a little like the dark meat of a chicken or a wild turkey." She saw Hammer's eyes fill with disgust.

"We don't need no hillbilly in our squad. Hell, I'll bet you can't hit the broadside of a barn!"

Gabe roused himself. He saw Chief Hampton ready to pounce on Hammer. He didn't take guff from any of them, and Hammer was way out of line. "Hey," Gabe called to Hammer, "why don't you ask Doc what her longest shot was to kill an animal?"

Bay blinked. The SEAL in the back had a feral grin on his face as he challenged Hammer. What was this guy up to? She felt protectiveness emanating from him toward her. It was nothing obvious, but she picked up on his energy, anyway.

Hammer nodded. "Damn good question, Doc Thorn. What's your best shot out in them thar woods?"

A number of the SEALs chuckled as he mimicked her dialect.

Bay shrugged. "I bagged an eight-point buck at twelve hundred."

Half the SEALs burst into laughter, their collective guffaws echoing around the room. Bay frowned, saddened that they didn't want her in the squad. Except for the SEAL in the back and maybe three other guys who were impressed with her medical training. The SEAL in the back was looking directly at her now. Their gazes locked. She felt the intensity of his slitted green gaze, a one-cornered smile appearing on his weathered face. In that moment, she felt the full power of his invisible protection.

When the laughter died down, Gabe called, "Doc, was that twelve hundred feet or twelve hundred yards?"

Hammer twisted around. "Oh, come on, bro! You know damn well it has to be feet, not yards! What fairytale world are you livin' in?"

Bay suddenly understood what the SEAL was doing. She gave him a nod of thanks for having her back in this melee. Shifting her gaze to Hammer, who was dramatically rolling his eyes, she remained serious. "I sincerely apologize to y'all. I thought you knew I meant twelve hundred yards."

The room went completely silent. Gabe lowered his head and hid his smile. Finally, he swallowed his grin to surface and he called out, "Hey, Hammer. You got wax in your ears? Did you hear her say yards, not feet?" He enjoyed Hammer's glare as he twisted around and stared at him.

Snorting, Hammer jerked his head toward the woman standing relaxed, her hands clasped in front of her. "No friggin' way, sweetheart, have you shot anything, much less hit anything at twelve hundred yards. That's sniper-quality shootin' and I don't care how long you ran around barefoot in those woods growing up shooting squirrels out of trees—no woman can hit anything at that range. Not one."

Chief Hampton sighed. "Doc? I know you're pretty wiped out by the flight from Iraq, but are you up to a little range shooting this afternoon? You need to zero in your rifle, anyway."

"Of course, Chief. My pa began teaching me to shoot at age six. We didn't have any boys in our family, and I was the oldest girl, so I learned to do what the boys did."

Hammer shook his head. "What a load of shit."

"We'll see," Hampton murmured. He straightened and looked over the group of men. "What kind of rifle are you wanting to use, Doc?"

Bay heard the wry humor in the chief's tone. "Well, sir, if someone has a .300 Win Mag, I'd like to try my hand at that. Of course, with their permission."

Hammer howled with laughter, leaning over, his hands against his belly. Everyone in the front row joined him. The SEALs in bench two were seriously digesting her request. The Win Mag .300 was one of the rifles used by the SEAL snipers. The SEAL in the back stood up. He picked up his ruck sitting on the bench beside him.

"Chief, I'll loan her my Win Mag to settle this," Gabe called.

Surprised, Bay watched as he stood and slowly walked toward her. He had a loose kind of walk, a man with confidence to burn. There was a rifle strapped to the outside of his rucksack. This SEAL was a sniper, no question. Bay saw humor lurking in his eyes as he approached her with his boneless grace. He immediately made her think of the mountain lions she'd seen stalking prey. It was that kind of silent, lethal walk.

Gabe halted a few feet from her, set his ruck down on the concrete floor. He leaned down and pulled open the Velcro straps that held his sniper rifle in place. Pulling it out of the straps, he said, "Here you go, Doc. I'll be your spotter if you need one. I'm Gabe Griffin, by the way."

When their fingers met as he handed over his rifle to her, Bay gulped. The SEAL was tall, probably six feet or more. There was warmth in his green eyes as he smiled down at her. She took the rifle, allowing it to hang, barrel down, beneath her left arm and rest against her hip. "Thank you," she said, meaning it. "And I could sure use your help with this beautiful rifle." Her voice turned soft with humor. "I'm used to my dad's Winchester to bring down game. This one is a lot different feeling. Lighter."

Gabe turned, standing beside the combat medic. Hammer was giving him a look of utter disbelief. "Hammer, let's meet out at our shooting range, say at 1300?"

"You got it. You've picked the wrong side of this contest, Griffin."

Shrugging, Gabe said, "Hey, I was born in Butler, Pennsylvania. I grew up with a few hill people who lived up in that neck of the woods. They were all crack shots."

"A hundred bucks says she can't hit any target at twelve hundred yards," Hammer said, grinning over at his buddies.

Gabe rested his arms across the front of his H-gear around his chest. "I got a hundred that says she can nail the target dead center every time."

Hooting and hollering broke out excitedly among the team. SEALs got easily bored, and a rifle competition whetted their weapons appetites. There was heavy betting going on, mostly against the new doc. Chief Hampton raised his hands.

"You just got back off a twelve-hour patrol. Get cleaned up, eat, write up your reports and we'll meet at the shooting range at 1300." Chief looked over at Bay. "You all right with this, Doc?"

Bay kept a serious face. "Yes, sir, I am."

"I'll collect her winnings," Gabe told the chief, his grin widening. His team was in for one helluva surprise, he hoped.

"On that note," Hampton said, sliding off the stool, "I'm assigning you to be her mentor, Gabe."

More hollers and laughter broke out in the room. Hammer was gloating. "Glad it wasn't me having to train in a cherry!" he yelled at Gabe. "You poor sorry son of a bitch."

Gabe took the gibing good-naturedly. Cherry was

a slang term for the new guy coming into the squad. He saw Bay give him a confused look.

"That means," he told her, "I'll integrate you into the team. It will be my responsibility to show you the ropes, teach you how we patrol. Stuff like that."

Relief fled through her. "That's great, Gabe. Thank you."

Hampton gave Gabe a hard look and lowered his voice. "Give the team time, but don't take any shit off any of 'em, either. She's our medic. They shouldn't care if it's a man or woman saving their ass. Understand?"

"Yes, Chief, I do," Gabe replied, reading between the lines. Gabe knew half the team wasn't happy about having a woman assigned into their ranks. The only thing to do now was for her to earn their respect. Turning, he looked down into her wide, innocent-looking blue eyes.

"Can you really hit a deer at twelve hundred yards?"

Bay remained humble. She lowered her voice so only he could hear her. "Actually, I've dropped a couple of deer at fourteen hundred yards, but I didn't want them thinking I was tellin' them a big windy."

Gabe picked up his ruck and slung it over his shoulder and gave a soft chuckle. "Come on, I need to show you where our shooting range is located."

Grateful he didn't hate her as half the team did, Bay carried his sniper rifle easily beneath her left arm. The rest of the SEAL team was up, walking toward the doors with them. There was a lot of laughter and ribbing going on. Mostly about her. Bay had been hazed before and tried not to take it personally.

As they left the building, Gabe Griffin at her side,

the sun had risen more, taking off the chill. Automatically, Bay slipped on her sunglasses, just as he did. At eight thousand feet on a mountaintop, the sunlight was brutal. Without sunglasses, it would be hard to see enemy at times, especially in the glare. That could cost them their life.

"Down this unnamed street," he said, gesturing down a row of tan canvas tents sitting up on plyboard platforms.

The SEALs split up, going their separate ways. Most would put their weapons in their tents and then hit the chow hall, starved. Gabe took her over to his tan-and-gray tent he shared with Phil Baker. He decided to use the tent next to his. "Doc, this is a catch-all tent for our equipment. You'll find SEALs are real good at getting creative. I'll rustle up a cot for you after we eat."

"May I give you back the Win Mag? I want it kept safe."

"Sure." He took the weapon and placed it on his cot inside his tent. Gabe questioned why he wasn't upset about training in the newbie, man or woman. Because of his recent divorce, he'd stepped down as LPO, lead petty officer, of the team. He'd asked the chief to assign it to Philip Baker, who was content to take over the position. The chief probably figured this was a good way for Gabe to get back into the saddle as LPO at some point in the future.

Knowing Chief Hampton as he did, going on fourth deployment with him, Gabe understood he was a wily people manager, got that he was hurting. Focusing on a newbie would take his mind off his cheating ex-wife. Gabe wasn't at all sure, however, that dealing with another woman right now was a smartest decision, but Hampton had good insight into people and situations. Lily, his ex-wife, had broken his trust, broken his heart and broken any good feelings he had toward women in general.

In a way, he felt sorry for Bay, because she seemed sweet, unassuming and terribly innocent. Maybe looks weren't everything, Gabe decided. He'd fallen for Lily's blinding beauty, and look where it got him. When he emerged from the tent, Bay was waiting for him. She had an M-4 looped in a black nylon sling across his chest and right shoulder. He took her rifle and laid it on his cot next to the Win Mag. "Let's go eat," he said.

As they walked down through the avenues of tents toward the chow hall, Gabe knew Baylee-Ann Thorn had just stepped into a pack of alpha males who didn't tolerate incompetence of any kind, at any level. They were hardened warriors who knew what it took to survive, and right now half of them had their new doc in their gun sights. Could she stand the heat in the kitchen? Could she measure up or not? They'd find out soon enough.

CHAPTER TWO

"THERE ARE A LOT of women in here," Bay noted as they sat opposite from each other at a long, wooden table at the busy chow hall. The noise was high, a lot of laughter, ribbing and joking going around.

Gabe nodded, glad to get a plate of eggs, bacon, toast and grits. "You see that group of ladies over there in those tan flight suits?"

Bay looked to her left. There were at least eight women sitting together having breakfast. "Yes. Are they pilots?"

"Not just any pilots," Gabe said, savoring the salty bacon. Out on patrols, they sweated so much they lost electrolytes. Bacon helped replace the salt in his body. "They're from a black ops group known as the Black Jaguar Squadron. Been here for four years. It's an all female Apache helo combat group."

Eyes widening, Bay said, "That's terrific. How are they doing in combat?"

Gabe smiled a little between bites. People in the military usually gulped and ran. They didn't spend time lingering over a meal. She was the same.

"Let's put it this way. When our comms man calls for Apaches to come and help us out, we don't care who's flying them. All we care about is if they can hit the target." He rolled his shoulders after sitting up to take a breather. "Those gals can nail targets."

"Not even Hammer and his group are unhappy with them?" As they were unhappy with her.

"Not a peep." Gabe picked up his mug of coffee. "Hammer and a few of the other guys are worried that you won't keep up on patrols. Or you'll cost one of them their lives because they have to protect you instead of knowing you'll have a gun in the fight like them."

Nodding, Bay finished off her scrambled eggs. She reached for the strawberry jam and a knife. "That's fair."

"Since I'm going to be acclimating you to our team, can you tell me about working with U.S. Army Special Forces over in Iraq?" Gabe was more than a little curious about her background. Bay looked as though she belonged in a hospital. Maybe as a doctor or nurse. Not a woman in a combat zone.

"I ran patrols with them for six months during my last deployment. Most of the time we worked along the Syrian border area with Iraq. Sometimes we came back to the green zone in Baghdad for a rest." Wrinkling her nose, she said, "It's a terrible place, Gabe. You can't trust anyone. They all lie to you. My captain was always pulling out his hair, trying to figure out who was lying and who wasn't. One group would tell you that another group was al Qaeda. He learned a long time ago not to believe any of them. This was his third deployment and he knew the dance."

"Did you perform many walking patrols?" Gabe knew the SEALs would be out on foot patrols for up to twelve hours sometimes. If Bay couldn't, that would pose a helluva problem for all of them.

"I'm fit enough, Gabe. We'd range out on foot for eight to twelve hours. Our team was always moving along the border at night with NVGs on. That was when the Syrian smugglers would try and get past the official highway entrance gate in and out of the two countries. We'd be on patrol from dusk until dawn. Sometimes, depending upon who we ran into, we'd cover fifteen klicks."

"Any problems with those kinds of physical demands?" Gabe asked, holding her blue gaze. There was such seriousness to her expression as she considered his question. Gabe didn't want to like her, and he fought it. Hadn't he had enough woman troubles the past year?

"None. Now," Bay said, reaching for her coffee, "I treated a lot of heat exhaustion cases, muscle cramps and things like that with my team. You know how you get focused on the mission. You're chasing the bad guys and you forget to drink water from your CamelBak? Some of the strongest, most fit Special Forces dudes would keel over out there. I learned to carry a lot more IVs in my pack to rehydrate them. Otherwise, we'd be calling in a medevac every time to lift them out."

Nodding, Gabe knew the hydration problem. SEALs dealt with the same issues. "When I was LPO for my team, I was always on my guys to keep drinking water out on patrol. Everyone forgets. Especially when we're engaged with the enemy."

"Yup," Bay said, smiling a little. She liked looking at Gabe. He was rugged looking, had high cheekbones and she liked his mouth best of all. The corners moved naturally upward and his lips were even and very kissable. His beard was fairly well trimmed, unlike with some of the other guys on the team.

Bay especially liked the keen intelligence she saw in Gabe's eyes. This guy was no slouch. He had broad, capable shoulders beneath his dusty cammies. She liked his hands, now curved around the mug in front of him. He had long, spare hands, large knuckled, burned dark by the sun, a smattering of dark hair on the backs of them. They were beautiful hands for a man. Her mind turned back to their conversation about desert environs. They were out on the front lines in one of the most inhospitable climates on earth.

"Okay, so you can keep up with us," Gabe murmured, mulling over her answers. "Are you at all familiar with our patrol tactics?"

She shook her head. "Not at all."

"Then you need to shadow me. We use the L and diamond formation most of the time, and I'll show you what that means. When I get a chance, I'll lead you through what I do and what the team does if we get into a firefight."

"Sounds good. That's where I'm weak, Gabe." Bay held up her hands and laughed a little. "I can cut, operate and stitch with the best of them in a firefight, but I'm an ignoramus when it comes to your patrol methods. I know they aren't the same ones used by the Special Forces guys."

He stared at her slender, beautiful hands. Gabe could believe she was a healer. He saw a number of calluses across her palms. That was a good sign because it meant she was in top shape, was carrying fairly heavy loads out on those patrols. "You said your mother was a hill doctor?"

"Yes, my mama, Poppy, is famous for her healing abilities." Bay dug into a side pocket in her cammies and drew out a ziplock bag that contained family photos. "Here's my mama." She placed the photo in front of Gabe. "I grew up going out and collecting herbs with her, starting when I was five years old. She has taught me so much."

Gabe studied the photo of a woman down on her hands and knees weeding in a huge garden. He could see Bay's face in her mother's face. Her mother had blue eyes and crinkly brown hair sticking out from beneath the old straw hat she wore. Gabe noticed her mother wore a skirt and blouse, no shoes on her feet. "You're lucky to study with her," he said, handing the photo back to her. When their fingers met, Gabe felt the warmth between them. He walled off any reaction to the grazing touch.

"My pa, Floyd William Thorn, died when he was forty-nine," she told him, sadness in her tone. She placed a picture of her father before him. "He was a coal miner and got black lung. With the herbs she collected, Mama kept him alive many years longer than he should have lived." Her voice grew low with emotion. "I miss him so much…."

Gabe picked up the photo, studying the man with a long, unkempt brown-and-silver beard. He wore an old green baseball cap and was proudly standing with a rifle over his shoulder. Bay had his long straight nose and high cheekbones. "I'm sorry you lost him. That's too young to die."

Bay took the photo from him and carefully placed it back in the ziplock bag. "He was a good man, Gabe. He taught me how to hunt and we had so much fun together. Pa was always laughing and joking around with us. And he was very kind. There were a number of elderly folks on our mountain who needed help. Pa would go over and chop wood for them, take it to their cabins so they'd have fire to cook with and keep them warm at night during the winter. Each spring, Pa would till their gardens with our mule, Betsy, to help them get in their garden so they'd have food to eat and can in the fall."

Gabe digested her softly spoken words, saw the grief lingering in her eyes. "He sounds like a helluva good man. Responsible."

Bay pressed her lips together, feeling the loss of her father. "Hill people stick together. Sometimes we'd go out and hunt deer for these elders. We'd kill one or two, gut and skin them. Then we'd carry them back and spread the meat between these families. Pa believed you took care of your family as well as the people around you."

"And now you're taking care of people around you, too. Looks like you have the genes on both sides of your family." Gabe saw the sadness in Bay's eyes and found himself wanting to do something to cheer her up. Again, he stopped that desire. This was a dangerous edge to walk with her.

"I love helping people," Bay said, lifting her head and managing to tuck her sadness away.

"I'm blown away you're an 18 Delta corpsman. We've had SEALs go for that training and wash out. Some made it, but most didn't. From what I've heard, it's eighteen months of unrelenting hell."

"It was," Bay said. "But I loved it. I'd been a corpsman in Iraq and already been under fire, doing my job. By the time I got to 18 Delta, when they'd put you into a situation where you had to work under bullets and explosions going off, it didn't rattle me one bit. It did a lot of other guys, though. They were really great combat corpsmen, but they couldn't think through the chaos to stop bleeding or perform lifesaving field operations."

"What made you so cool, calm and collected under fire?" Gabe asked, going back and starting to spread strawberry jam over six pieces of toast he had piled up at one end of his aluminum tray.

"I don't know. My mom was always cool as a cucumber when things got tense."

"You said you were hunting with your dad at an early age? I wonder if the sound of gunfire was something you grew up with." He chewed on the toast. "I was raised near the woods in Pennsylvania. I was hunting with my father when I was your age. He was a bigtime hunter and I got used to being around gunfire."

"Maybe," Bay murmured. She watched him enjoy the toast and jam. Gabe was tucking away a lot of food, but she knew these men who were out on long patrols would easily burn through twelve thousand calories. "I find I focus so much on the guy who's wounded that I don't hear anything else around me. I've been in firefights where the guys on my team would tell me bullets were singing all around me as I was delivering medical aid to a downed soldier, and I wasn't even aware of it."

"That's a handy reaction to have," Gabe agreed. Inwardly, he began to feel some relief. Bay had the experience and calm that would be needed should they get into a firefight. And it was a given, in their business, they would.

"Why do you think the chief assigned you to me?" Bay wondered, tilting her head and holding his gaze.

Disconcerted, Gabe grinned. "You have a helluva way of getting to the heart of the matter, don't you?"

"In my business, it's always the bottom line." Bay smiled. "I'm the one who is doing the A-B-Cs…airway, breathing, circulation on a guy who's been shot. I don't have time to fool around with social niceties."

Nodding, Gabe reached for the second piece of toast. "I used to be LPO of our team until about six months ago. You probably got assigned to me because the chief trusts me. This is my fourth deployment over here with him and I'm a known quantity."

"So you were the mother hen for the enlisted guys in your platoon before this?"

Gabe chuckled. "Yeah, I was a real mother hen, for sure."

"But why aren't you LPO now?"

He stopped smiling. "A situation came up," he said gruffly.

"Hmm," Bay murmured, feeling him retreat. She saw something in his narrowing eyes, a look that warned, *back off.* Moving her fingers around the warm mug, she said, "Life sometimes kicks us in the head like a mule and it takes time for us to get back up on our feet."

Her insight stunned Gabe. For a moment, he just stared at her, and then he resumed eating. "I'm okay not being LPO. And Phil, who we call Thor, is doing a good job in my stead."

"So Chief Hampton figured if he put me with the biggest, baddest mother hen in the platoon, I'd be in good hands." She grinned.

"You need to ask the chief why he assigned you to me. I'm not in his head."

Bay finished off her coffee and set the mug aside. "I know I'm in good hands with you, Gabe. You were the only one there in that room who was protecting me against Hammer and his friends."

"LPOs always are protective of their guys. It comes with the territory. You're one of us now, and that protection is accorded you, as well."

Nodding, Bay picked up the last of a few potatoes from her tray and nibbled on them. She figured she'd stepped on a land mine with Gabe. He appeared unhappy for a moment, but then he hid his reaction with a hard, unreadable expression. A game face. Something she saw in all black ops people. "Nothing wrong with being a mother hen. I'm one. And Hammer and his friends are going to find that out big-time as soon as I get my feet under me with this team."

Gabe would bet on that. Baylee-Ann Thorn was not a weakling in any sense. She came across soft and innocent, but now Gabe was beginning to understand that sweetness could be shown or taken away, depending upon the situation. "It's the doc's job to keep the guys well." And then he remembered the photo of her father. "That was a Winchester rifle your father carrying on his shoulder in that photo you showed me?"

"Yes, a .300 Win Mag rifle."

"It looked like it."

"Why?"

"Because in a couple of hours, you'll be using my Win Mag against Hammer in the shooting competition."

Shrugging, Bay smiled a little. "So?"

"So you know how to use one."

"My pa used the civilian variety of Win Mag to bag deer and other animals. The type you guys use for sniping is a military grade and not something I'm familiar with."

"Just the cartridge is different. Stocks are made out of fiberglass because it's lighter than wood." He studied her hard for a moment. "When did your father start training you to use the Win Mag?"

"When I was thirteen."

The innocent look she gave him made him grin. "So you've been using a Win Mag for five years before you joined the Navy? And in that time, you were using it to bring down big game at fourteen hundred yards?"

"Yes."

Gabe sat up. "Has anyone ever accused you of being the mistress of understatement?"

She wiped her mouth with the paper napkin, wadded it up and dropped onto her tray. "A few times." Bay saw that dark, accessing look of his, felt it surround her. It was an intense focus a hunter would have.

"That Win Mag has a body-jarring recoil to it when

it's fired," he warned her. It would take a shoulder off a person if he didn't realize the kick of the rifle and physically compensate for that violent recoil. He wondered how she was able to handle such a weapon at such a young age.

"Oh, Pa warned me," Bay chuckled. Pushing her fingers through her curly brown hair, she said, "The first time I fired it, it knocked me on my behind. My pa never laughed so hard, and neither did I. He'd warned me beforehand about its recoil, but until you actually fire it, you don't have a clue."

Her laughter was like thick, dark honey across his wounded heart. Gabe had no defense against it. Her eyes danced with mirth. It lifted him, for no accountable reason. "Well," he growled, pushing the tray aside, "Hammer's in a lot of trouble, then."

"Ohh," Bay murmured, "I don't think so."

Gabe studied her. "Then you really don't need a spotter. You've never worked with one and you're hitting your target at fourteen hundred yards." That blew *him* away.

"My pa never called himself a spotter. He taught me about windage, wind direction, humidity and so on. I could sure use your help, Gabe. This is dry air. There's no humidity. I'm not used to firing in this kind of environment. If you could help me dial it in, I'd be grateful."

How could he refuse her? "Hammer is going to get his sails trimmed."

"All I want to do is give a good accounting of myself. Maybe then he'll get serious about me being responsible regarding my job with your platoon."

Gabe smiled wryly, picked up his tray and rose to his full six feet. Her heart opened as she regarded him standing there, waiting for her. There was an intense, quiet power around him, like that of a coiled copperhead ready to strike. She didn't see this same kind of tension in the other SEALs, although they all possessed it, more or less.

Gabe was a leader; there was no doubt. And she knew the men respected him. Why wasn't he LPO? Well, for whatever reason, Bay found herself thanking the Lord for having Chief Hampton assign her to this SEAL. He was trustworthy. And her life would be in his hands, quite literally.

Easing off the bench, Bay picked up her tray and followed Gabe to where they placed their empty trays. She noticed the women stuck together at the various benches. A number of the SEALs from Alpha were all sitting together and eating, Hammer among them. When he spotted her across the large packed room, he gave her a glare. She ignored it.

CHAPTER THREE

BAY FELT ADRENALINE leak into her bloodstream as she settled prone, on her belly. The Afghan sun beat down hard on them at the small shooting range the SEALs had created years earlier at this FOB. The wind was inconstant, blowing intermittently across the area. The range was far away from Operations. Helos were constantly coming and going, the reverberations and thumping noise pounding and chopping through the dry air.

Gabe helped her set up the .300 Win Mag because it was the sniper rifle, not the regular hunting rifle Bay was used to. The bipods were set at the front of the barrel and he made sure the fiberglass stock was settled firmly against her cheek. The entire SEAL platoon, including the officers and chief, was present. Bay didn't seemed rattled at all. She went about the business of picking up any rocks that could jam into her torso and legs when she went prone. She studied the flags waving off to one side of the square wooden targets in the distance, sizing up the wind factor and direction. The rest of the team stood behind Hammer. There was a wooden table nearby where ammo was collected.

Bay settled her cap on backward so the bill scraped the nape of her neck. She wore her sunglasses, the sun burning down on her. She felt Gabe's quiet presence as he knelt nearby with the spotter scope on a stand between his knees. There were three dials on the Win Mag, the same as she was used to using back home. Ten feet to her left, Hammer was settling down in the dirt on his belly, bringing his Win Mag into his arms. His spotter was Oz, another SEAL shooter who was his best friend.

"Okay," Gabe told her quietly, leaning toward her so that only she could hear him, "just relax."

His deep voice washed across her. The tension in her shoulders dissolved. Bay hadn't expected the officers of the team to show up. That added more pressure to her. Well, they wanted to know if she was going to be a liability or another gun in the fight on patrols. Bay couldn't blame them for wanting to know.

Listening to Gabe's direction and information, she dialed in the elevation and compensated for the wind-age. She'd lived in mountains, albeit not high ones, but the formula was the same. Mountains made their own weather, and wind was the single biggest challenge to a sniper or a hunter. The wrong assessment of wind speed could knock a bullet off course.

Bay studied the large square wooden targets that were set at twelve hundred yards. There were three red circles to create the bull's-eye. It was understood their shots had to hit the center. If they fell outside the center, then that shooter was the loser. She had three shots and so did Hammer.

Lifting her chin, Bay angled a look up at Gabe. "Hey, is Hammer a sniper like you?"

"Yes, he is. The medic we just lost was another of

our snipers. The chief's in a bind because there's no one available to come into our team who is sniper qualified. He doesn't like us without two snipers on every patrol."

"Can't blame him there," Bay agreed. That was bad news because, as she'd found out by going on patrol with Special Forces teams, those snipers were a must. There were so many situations when a sniper would make the difference between a team taking on casualties and not. Snipers were called "force multipliers" for a reason.

Gabe watched her expression. He couldn't see her eyes behind those wraparound sunglasses and wished he could. Her mouth was soft and she was relaxed. "Okay, we're taking the first shot. Ready?"

Nodding, Bay settled down into her position. This was a natural position her father had taught her. It was the rifle in her right hand, resting against her right shoulder. Her left arm was tucked in front of her chest, the bipod giving her rifle stability. The stock had to fit firmly and comfortably against her right cheek. She wasn't using a scope, rather the iron sights on the rifle itself. Hammer had insisted on iron sights only. It made hitting the target tougher. Very few ever used iron sights, the scopes superior and delivering on target all the time.

GABE GENTLY PATTED her cap, an old sniper signal that meant "shoot."

The multiple variables of the shot ran through Bay's mind as her eyes narrowed, her finger brushing the two-pound trigger, her right hand steady on the Win Mag stock. Her father had taught her there was a still point between inhalation and exhalation. It was when her breath left her body and before her lungs automatically began to expand to draw in a breath of fresh air into the body—this was the perfect time to fire the rifle.

The Win Mag bucked hard against her shoulder, the brute force of the recoil rippling spasmodically through her entire body. Gabe was watching through the spotter scope, following the telltale vapor trail of the bullet.

"Bull's-eye!" Gabe yelled, thrusting his fist into the air.

Relief sped through her. Bay eased out of the position, amazed. "Really?" she asked Gabe. He was grinning as he turned to her.

"You hit it perfect, Doc. Good going. You're dialed in." Gabe lifted his head to see Hammer snarling a curse as he settled into position. He then turned back to Bay. "What? You didn't think you'd nail it?" He laughed heartily.

Hammer nailed the first shot, too. There was a lot of clapping and cheering from the platoon as he'd made a successful shot. No one had clapped for her. Maybe, Bay figured, the guys were stunned she'd made the first shot at all. Gabe was the only one who believed in her. Knew she could do it. She felt warmth flow through her. There was an unexpected kindness to him that wasn't easily discerned on the surface, but she was privy to it. That and the care and protection she could literally feel he'd encircled her with. It was unspoken, but there. *In spades.*

"Okay," Gabe said softly, studying the flags. He watched the heat waves dancing across the flat area in front of them. They were showing a wind direction change. Leaning down, he told her to dial in to a different windage setting.

Bay settled in, focused. Her mouth compressed and she willed her body to relax. She desperately wanted to make this next shot, but the breeze was erratically shifting. It lifted several stands of her curly hair as she took a breath and let it naturally leave her body. Finger pressed against the trigger…breath out…still…fire… The Win Mag bucked savagely against her shoulder, the bark of the shot booming like unleashed thunder throughout the area.

"Bull's-eye!" Gabe hooted, pumping his fist above his head.

There was some unexpected, serious applause going on behind Bay. She twisted around and saw all three officers and their chief strongly clapping, a show of support for her. They grinned at each other like raccoons finding a bunch of crayfish in a stream. As if congratulating themselves on having the good luck to have her in their platoon. Turning back around, Bay saw the look on Hammer's face. He sneered at her and then settled in to take his shot.

Gabe patted her on the cap. "Damn fine shot. You're doing great, Doc."

"Couldn't do it without you, Gabe. You're feeding me good intel." And Bay knew that a good spotter could make all the difference as to whether the shot was accurate or not.

"Bull's-eye!" Oz shouted triumphantly as Hammer made the center circle.

More clapping, hooting and hollering erupted from the SEALs standing behind Hammer.

Bay wiped sweat from her upper lip. She could feel it running down her rib cage and between her shoulder blades. It was hotter than hell out in this afternoon sun on top of this eight-thousand-foot mountain.

Gabe's hand settled briefly on her shoulder, giving her a silent order to get relaxed back into the prone position. Bay felt less trepidation as his long fingers curved around her shoulder, as if to tell her it was all right, that she was doing fine. He appreciated her efforts.

Gabe gave her spotter info, the flags now stronger and then falling off. It was the worst kind of wind to shoot in accurately, and Bay compressed her lips, worried. She placed the stock against her cheek, feeling the perspiration between her skin and the fiberglass stock. Inhaling, she allowed her breath to escape until she was in that millisecond still point. She squeezed the trigger. The Win Mag recoiled hard, jerking her shoulder, the tremors rippling down the right side of her body all the way to her booted foot.

"Bull's-eye!" Gabe shouted, slapping her on the back, grinning.

A few more SEALs were clapping now. The officers looked elated. Chief Hampton, from what Gabe could see, appeared damn relieved. Again, Hammer cursed loudly and seemed furious. Gabe gave his teammate a wicked grin.

Bay got to her knees, clearing the chamber and safing the Win Mag in her arms. She sat down with the butt of the rifle resting on her hip and watched Hammer shoot.

"Bull's-eye!" Oz shouted.

The SEAL came out of prone position, glaring over at her, triumph written on his hard, lined face.

"It's a draw," Chief Hampton called.

"Like hell it is!" Hammer protested. He jabbed a finger toward Bay. "Let's do one shot offhand, standing." His lips curled away from his teeth. "That will separate the men from the pantywaist girls here."

Bay was startled at the dare. Standing position at a twelve hundred yards? Nothing to support her rifle but herself? Gulping, she swung a troubled gaze over to Gabe, who was kneeling at her side. He scowled hard at Hammer. And then he shifted his gaze and locked onto hers.

"Want to try it?" he asked quietly.

"I've never shot offhand at home," she admitted, worried. "I always used a tree limb or tree trunk to steady my rifle barrel if I had to stand."

Bay tried to ferret out what she saw in his narrowing green eyes as he considered her statement. Then Gabe rose fluidly to his feet, the spotting scope in his right hand.

"Hey, Hammer," he called.

"What?" the SEAL snarled, dusting off the front of his cammies, holding his rifle above the dust rolling off him.

"Tell you what," Gabe said in a reasonable tone. "Whoever gets closest to the red center is the winner."

Snorting, Hammer grinned. "Your girl ain't gonna make the grade. No one shoots a sniper rifle without some kind of bipod to steady it." He patted his Win Mag affectionately with is hand. "Me? I do it all the time."

Gabe nodded. "Fair enough. But if she comes closer to the center than you, then the money's coming her way. Agreed?"

Shrugging, Hammer laughed. "Yeah, fine, Gabe. You've always been one for dotting *i*'s and crossing *t*'s. She ain't gonna make the center. I know that. So, sure, I'll agree to it. She's gonna lose. And I'm going to shoot first."

Feeling desolate, Bay stood up after handing the sniper rifle over to Gabe. Her stomach knotted with tension. Never had she fired without her Win Mag being braced. The rifle was very heavy, and shooting without support was tough for anyone, man or woman. Bay's heart dropped.

Dusting herself off, she stood, arms crossed, watching as Hammer got into position. She had shot in all the positions at Camp Pendleton, used a number of rifles and pistols, but never standing and shooting over four hundred yards with any weapon. It was, in her mind, nearly impossible to shoot at twelve hundred yards standing.

Hammer fired. The bullet hit just outside the red center. The SEALs went crazy with clapping and yelling. Oz was slapping his friend on his meaty shoulder, yelling triumphantly.

Turning, Bay took the rifle from Gabe, feeling glum. When she looked up at him, he held her gaze.

"You can do this," he told her. "I'll talk you through it, Doc. Just listen to me and follow my directions."

His husky words flowed through her, giving her hope. Bay nodded wordlessly. She planted her feet apart. Gabe told her to shorten her stance a bit. She did. It felt more comfortable to her. Then, as she lifted the long-barreled rifle, Gabe came over and moved her right hand an inch forward. As she rested the stock against her perspiring cheek, he stood behind her and helped her adjust the stock more tightly against her face. Some of her fear dissipated as the rifle began to feel like a living extension of herself. Gabe planted the butt of the rifle deep into her right shoulder. His eyes met hers.

"Now," he told her, "it's very important to hold this exact position. It will give you the balance you need to steady this rifle." He turned and used the spotter scope one more time. She'd already dialed in, but he was double-checking. The wind was inconstant. A gust blew across the area. If she'd fired at that moment, she would have miss the target. Gabe stood beside her, talking in a low voice, giving her direction, settling her nerves.

"Now take two or three breaths. Watch the barrel move as you do. First one, find your still point and then watch where that barrel rests at that time. Then take another breath, watch the barrel move slightly upward. Make sure you have that barrel pointed at the red circle through your iron sights as you come down on the exhale. See where it rests at the still point. If the barrel is slightly off, keep breathing, keep finding your still point until you *know* that barrel is exactly where you want it on the red center. Then fire."

His words resonated. Thanks to her hunting background, Bay could focus. It was easy to listen to Gabe, fall into his quiet, low tones as he guided her, reinforced her.

It took three breaths, but as Bay reached the still point the third time, she squeezed the trigger. The Win Mag jerked hard against her shoulder. Bay was prepared for it, her slightly bent knees and legs absorbing the powerful jolt.

Gabe watched the vapor trail of the bullet. It struck just inside the red center. He gave a shout of victory, turning and slapping her on the shoulder. Bay took off her sunglasses, stared openmouthed at the target, and then up at him, feeling profound disbelief. He laughed deeply and shook his head, as if he didn't believe it himself.

Clapping and yelling broke out sporadically among the SEAL team. The officers looked at one another, amazement written on their faces. Chief Hampton stood there, grinning like a feral wolf, rubbing his hands together. No doubt about it, he'd just discovered another sniper for his platoon.

"Bull's-eye. You made it, Doc. Damn good shooting!" Gabe placed his hand on her head and patted her on the cap. "Damn good!"

Bay couldn't believe she'd hit within the target! Even better was Gabe's happy, deep, rolling laughter. It made her feel good. Equally important, Bay had proven her shooting ability to the platoon. Now they realized she was another gun in the fight. She might not know patrol tactics, but Gabe would teach her and she'd become an asset to them.

Glancing behind her, she saw the officers and chief

applauding. Was it relief she saw in their faces? Bay thought so. She was incredibly grateful that the contest was over.

Hammer cursed, slammed the toe of his boot into the dirt, raising a cloud of dust. He glared over at her.

"You just got lucky, Thorn. That's all."

Gabe took the rifle from her, safed it and rested the barrel down toward the ground. "Oh, come on, Hammer, at least be a good sport," he cajoled, grinning. He stepped over to where Hammer and his entourage stood, holding out his hand. "You owe Doc money."

Oz pulled out a wad of cash from his left cammie pocket and bitterly slapped it into Gabe's palm.

Bay left Gabe's side and walked over to Hammer. She offered her hand to him. "That was mighty fine shooting, Hammer. You're right, I just plumb got lucky. You're a better shooter than I'll ever be."

Hammer stared at her and then at her hand. Whether he wanted to or not, he reached out, grabbed her hand and shook it.

"This settles *nothing*," he growled softly. "So you can shoot at targets. Big deal. Let's wait and see how you do in the middle of a firefight." He turned and walked away, the Win Mag thrown over his shoulder.

CHAPTER FOUR

"CHIEF," HAMMER CALLED, "can we talk to you for a minute. In private?"

Chief Doug Hampton was just coming in at 0700 to his office when four of his SEALs were waiting for him. "Let's go inside," he said, opening the door and gesturing toward the planning room.

Just then Gabe arrived at their HQ. He halted just inside the entrance and watched as the Chief sat down on the stool. Four SEALs stood nearby. His intuition told him something was up. Hammer lifted his head and looked over at him.

"You might as well be in on this, too," Hammer said to Gabe. "Come and join us."

Gabe nodded and stood near the Chief.

"What's on your mind?" Hampton asked Hammer.

"That woman. We've talked between ourselves last night, and we don't want her in our platoon."

Hampton pursed his lips and nodded. "I see. Your reasons?"

"She's not a SEAL," Hammer growled, exasperated by the obvious.

"So?" Hampton murmured.

"So she's not trained, dammit! She doesn't know our tactics, our formations, if we get attacked. Hell, what are we supposed to do if we have to fast-rope out of a helo? She's not trained for that. Do we have to carry her and make ourselves targets in doing so?"

Gabe dragged in a slow, deep breath. There was genuine concern on the four men's faces. Hammer was heading up the group, but he had had similar thoughts himself. Bay wasn't trained in many of the situations where they knew what to do, but she didn't. And in a firefight, there wasn't time to teach; it was a matter of survival. He kept his mouth shut as Hammer paced the room from one side to the other. Concern and frustration were etched on everyone's face.

Hampton rubbed his hands on the thighs of his cammies. "Your points are well taken," he said. "It's a good argument except for one thing, Rettig." Pierce Rettig was the enlisted SEAL's real name and Hampton used it when things got serious.

All four SEALs had the chief's undivided attention.

"What's that?" Hammer demanded testily, jerking to a halt.

"We routinely have Navy photographers, videographers, CTT boys from the Air Force who call in the heavies and close air support for us, FBI dudes, linguists or cryptologists who are assigned to go out with us," Hampton said. "They aren't trained SEALs, either, but we need them on certain types of patrols or direct action or recon missions. You've never objected to any of them coming along. So why now? Why her?" He opened his hands, his voice remaining reasonable.

Hammer cursed. He glared at the other three SEALs and then jerked his gaze back to the chief. "You're backing her because she did sniper-quality shooting yesterday afternoon."

Hampton smiled a little and held up his hand. "Let's stay on the point, Rettig. You're pissed because she's a *woman* and not a man. You've never bitched about any guy who was assigned to your platoon before this, and you've been out on plenty of patrols and missions with non-SEAL assets."

"Bullshit!"

"It sure is," Hampton said quietly, holding the SEAL's angry glare.

"Then I want to talk to the LT about it," Hammer growled. "I'm not done with this, Chief. And I don't like that you're not handling it. That's your job."

"I did my job, Rettig. You just don't like my answer or my solution." Hampton's voice dropped. "This is bigger than you, me or the LT. This woman is highly trained in many areas, and none of us can say we don't want her and discharge her from this squad just because of gender prejudice."

"That's a bunch of crap," Hammer snarled, walking back and forth in front of the chief, his thickset shoulders bunched with tension. "I don't care what the Pentagon cooked up." Hammer stopped and jabbed an index finger at the door. "That woman is *trouble*. And I guarantee," he grated, breathing hard, "she is gonna get one or more of us killed because she's *not* a SEAL!"

Hampton straightened a little, holding the angry SEAL's gaze. "And what if I told you, Rettig, that there have been other women in other SEAL teams before this and that hasn't happened? That they've worked very effectively in those teams without causing casualties? Matter of fact, they've saved men's lives. And some of the women have lost their lives, as well, but not because of ineptitude. They're in firefights all the time right along with the men."

Shaking his head like a bull getting ready to charge, Hammer rasped, "I don't believe you."

The other three SEALs eyebrows went up collectively on Hammer's challenging grate. It was one thing to be pissed off, but you didn't call your chief a liar to his face. The three of them exchanged uneasy glances with one another.

Doug Hampton's face turned hard. Hammer was pushing his weight around. If he'd been LPO, he'd have taken him out back and pounded some sense into his head. But Hampton was the man in charge of the entire platoon and wielded plenty of power. The buck stopped with him. Gabe wondered how Doug was going to handle Hammer, directly challenging his authority, his face beet red.

"Rettig," Hampton said, standing up, "it's time you and me had a little chat outside."

Hammer scowled, no doubt because his superior was six feet three inches tall, thirty-five years old and in top shape. He had five deployments under his belt and knew more about fighting in Afghanistan than just about anyone. Hammer turned and looked at his three friends to see if they wanted to join him. They all backed off, their hands held up, a sign that Hammer was on his own.

Wiping his mouth, Hammer growled, "And if I don't?"

Hampton shrugged nonchalantly. "Then I'll beat

the crap out of you right here in front of them. Your call, Rettig, because you've outlived your welcome with me."

"Aw, dammit, Chief!" Hammer spun around and huffed and puffed around the room. He kept giving the chief furtive looks, trying to figure out what to do. How to back down gracefully and not come to blows.

Hampton was slowly rolling up the sleeves on his cammies to just below his elbows. "Ready?"

Gabe hid a smile. Doug Hampton could be a damn intimidating and dazzling manager with a recalcitrant SEAL when he had to be. Gabe was glad he'd had four deployments with Hampton to know he was manipulating the hell out of red-faced Hammer.

"Look," Hammer said, holding up his hand, "I'm not about to fight you, Chief."

"Well, then," Hampton said in his reasonable tone, "you're just going to have to make an attitude change, Rettig." His voice hardened as he strode up to the SEAL and got into his face. "Because," Hampton ground out, "you're going to work as a team. That's what SEALs are all about. You will—" he jabbed his index finger into Hammer's chest "—make every effort to get along with Doc. And I won't say this again, because next time…if there is a next time…I'll kick your ass. Got it?"

"Yes, Chief," Hammer breathed, his voice deflated, "I got it."

"Good," Hampton murmured, easing away from him. He stepped back and began to slowly unroll a cuff. "I don't know why you don't think she can't fast-rope."

Hammer gave him a shocked, quizzical look.

"As a matter of fact, I think you should get to know her a bit more. Now, I agree, Doc is a very unassuming, quiet woman who wouldn't think of bragging on herself in any way, shape or form. She *acts* like a SEAL. Humble. Never talks about herself or what she's been trained to do." Doug rolled down the other cuff. "I read her personnel file, Rettig." Hampton lifted his chin and stared hard at the SEAL. "She learned fast-roping at Camp Pendleton. The women who went through that one-year immersion combat course learned a lot of black op methods, including kill box routines and CQD, close quarters defense training. Yeah, maybe she's a little rusty on fast-roping, but she's got her special gloves, she's got the strength and I know Gabe will refresh her if that's what your team has to do on a particular mission."

Hammer scowled. "You've got to be kidding me? She can fast-rope?"

Hampton glared at the SEAL. "I wouldn't kid you, Rettig. Doc doesn't know our tactics and patrols, but she's a quick study. If I were you, I'd be thrilled pink she was assigned to us. Has it been lost on you that if your sorry ass gets pumped full of lead out there, *she's* the one who's going to try and save your sorry, prejudicial ass? And she's a linguist. Won't it be nice that you can get her to talk to the local farmers in these villages? And that she'll not only understand what they're saying, but give us accurate translation? You know how bad Afghan terps are? I find it refreshing she's here and can translate for us. Furthermore—" Hampton slowly pulled the Velcro closed around each cuff around his thick wrists "—the LT and I are jumping up and down

for joy she's been assigned to us. Right now there are
no SEALs available to fill our open slot. We're damn
lucky to have gotten her or we would be operating a
man short, down a sniper, and I damn well don't want
to go there. Do you?"

Hammer stood quiet and tense, disbelief written all
over his face. He didn't move. "No, Chief."

"Well," Hampton said, sadness in his voice, "we lost
Billy three days ago. Yesterday, Doc showed us she
can hit the broad side of a barn. Frankly, I'm ordering
Gabe to get her up to speed on sniper tactics as fast
as he can because, dammit, she can consistently hit a
target. And there are no more snipers we can get our
hands on anywhere in the SEAL community right now.
I can't even get a straphanger. There just aren't enough
of them graduating through SEAL sniper school. It's a
rough course and most are washed out in the process.
So we are looking at her as our backup sniper. I haven't
told her that yet, but the LT wants it done pronto. She's
a gun in this fight, Rettig. And you should be damn
relieved about that."

Gabe watched Hammer's face drain of color. The
SEAL knew when he had been bested. Doug Hampton
was a quiet sort, and no one ever wanted to back up
on him. He was deadly when cornered, and Hammer
had just discovered this fact. Keeping his face unreadable, Gabe saw Hammer snort and turn away, striding
toward the door.

"I didn't dismiss you," Hampton said.

Hammer halted and slowly turned around. "Yes,
Chief."

"You treat Doc like you would any newbie rotating into our platoon. Got that?"

"Yes, Chief."

"And if I have to spell that out to you again, Rettig, I'll be writing you a one-way ticket out of this platoon. Got it?"

Mouth twisting, Hammer muttered, "Yes, Chief. I got it. May I be dismissed?"

Hampton moved his shoulders as if to rid them of tautness and nodded. "In a minute." And then he looked at the three other SEALs standing in front of him. "Any of you have something to add to this little chat before chow time?"

All three shook their heads, suddenly nervous under the chief's dark, assessing look.

"I want all four of you, after chow, to take all the supplies and gear out of that tent next to Gabe's tent. Doc is going to use it." Hampton raised a finger and added, "I expect that place to be 4.0 when you're finished. She deserves a clean tent like anyone else coming into our platoon. Questions?"

They quickly shook their heads, more than ready to escape the chief's riled state.

"Dismissed."

Gabe watched the four of them quickly leave. He turned back toward Doug after the door closed. "You handled that well," he murmured, walking up to him.

"Dammit," Hampton growled. "I knew this was coming."

"You think Rettig will go behind your back and bitch to the LT?" Gabe asked, sitting on the stool near the chief.

"He'd better not," Hampton said, moving his fingers through his dark brown hair. "If he does, the LT will hand him his one-way ticket before I get a chance to do it. We can't afford this kind of divisiveness in our ranks. No way...."

There was worry in Hampton's gray eyes.

"Anything I can do other than what I am doing?" Gabe asked.

"No. Doc is safe with you, thank God. LT and the AOIC are thanking their lucky stars you intervened on her behalf yesterday morning."

Gabe chuckled a little. "Hammer was ganging up on her. I don't put up with unfair advantages."

"Nor do I," Hampton said, scowling. "But you handled it like the LPO you are. The LT was pleased."

Taking the compliment, Gabe said, "I'm happy to mentor her. She's a sharp lady."

"Far sharper than Rettig will ever be," Hampton said. "He's a damn fine SEAL, but he's too territorial. That's going to get him in deep trouble someday, and it damn well isn't going to happen on my watch."

"He's a handful at times," Gabe agreed, "but out on patrol, I wouldn't want anyone but him around. You saw how well he shot yesterday. He's sniper trained and he's a damn good shot. We need every gun we can get in those fights."

Sighing, Hampton patted Gabe's shoulder. "I know. He's a good SEAL, just misguided with his prejudices sometimes. If I hadn't landed on him with both feet, he'd have taken control of the situation."

"So, you're going to unload our supply tent for Doc?" Gabe asked, wanting to get off the subject.

"Yeah, I talked with LT about it last night. They are very impressed with her, Gabe. Frankly, so am I."

Gabe laughed again. "You three looked like an act of God had just taken place out there on that shooting range yesterday. Like a female Moses just arrived in a chariot in time to save your sorry asses."

Hampton had the good grace to look sheepish. "Who knew? In her records, she shot expert at Pendleton in all weapons—pistol, rifle and M-4 grenade launcher. None of us realized how good she was, though. It blew us away."

"Me, too," Gabe admitted. "I don't think Doc knows how talented she really is as a combat soldier."

"Yeah, she's really unassuming, isn't she? A quiet mouse."

Shrugging, Gabe said, "Well, at least she's not like ego-busting Hammer."

"You're right," Hampton said, settling his hands on his narrow hips. "We should be grateful for that. The LT has a call into the Special Forces captain she worked with over in Iraq. We want more dope on her. And once we know, I'll pass it on to you. I think she's very skilled in a lot of areas we'd never expected her to be. I'd like to know the breadth and depth of her combat experience."

"Maybe Doc is just like the other women in that top-secret op, but we've just never had the knowledge to know how they are trained. They could all be like Doc."

"I don't know, but we're going to find out. She graduated top five in her class of forty women. They're a bunch of Amazons." He grinned. "Don't tell Doc I said that. I don't want to get in hock with General Maya Stevenson. She's an Army general heading up Operation Shadow Warriors. She has a reputation of getting into your face so damn fast you won't live to tell about it."

"Not a word I'd use around Doc."

Hampton grinned. "We really don't know what Doc is made of yet, and we need to find out. The Pentagon is expecting weekly reports on her." He clapped his hand on Gabe's shoulder. "Since you're her mentor, you'll be writing up a weekly report and sending it on to me. Once I read it and make comments or whatever, I pass it up the chain of command to LT. From there, it goes into a black hole in the E-ring of the Pentagon."

Groaning, Gabe shook his head. "I don't mind mentoring, Doug, but damn, a weekly report? Can't you cut me some slack?"

Hampton smiled evenly. "No can do. It's all yours, thank God. But I am going to invite myself along every once in a while on the next few missions to make sure Hammer and those other three fall into line. I won't have him splitting the team."

"I don't know what Hammer will do," Gabe said. "One thing for sure, if he tries anything stupid out there with her, he'll answer to me. And I won't be nice and invite him outside to beat the hell out of him. I'll take him on the instant it happens."

Raising one eyebrow, Hampton nodded. "Good. She's to be treated like any newbie. Nothing more, nothing less. I don't care if they razz or tease her, but anything beyond that—"

"I have her six, Doug. Don't worry about it." Six was a term used by the military when an enemy plane flew up behind an American pilot's plane and was getting ready to shoot it down. It meant Gabe would protect Bay, should it come down to that.

Hampton gripped his shoulder. "You're in the breech, but I wouldn't have any other SEAL in that sorry position. Can you go help the guys get that tent fixed up for her today?"

Gabe eased off the stool, his M-4 in a sling across his chest. "No problem."

"You going to sit her down and show her patrol tactics and formations?"

"First thing on my list," Gabe promised. "After evening chow."

As Gabe stepped outside in the heat of the afternoon, he waffled. Should he go find Doc? Invite her to the chow hall? Part of him wanted to, but another part didn't. Still, he was her mentor and that had him walking down the dusty street between the many tents to go find her. Even after his conversation with the chief, Gabe felt nagging worry about the confrontation with Hammer. He sincerely hoped the SEAL would fall into line. Doc didn't deserve his misguided prejudice.

So far, Doc had shown all of them she could shoot. That, in and of itself, was a phenomenal shock. A good one, and Gabe grinned to himself, chuckling over yesterday's competition. Hill people might appear to be plain and unassuming, but Gabe had learned early on they were smart and possessed backwoods common sense that would dazzle everyone.

CHAPTER FIVE

BAY COULD HARDLY contain her excitement as the Chinook helicopter landed at Bagram Air Base near noon. Chief Hampton had ordered Gabe to take her to the U.S. Navy Supply Terminal to get outfitted with SEAL gear and weapons. As they disembarked out the rear of the helo into the sunlight, the heat was stifling. Bagram Air Base sat a bit north of Kabul and it was all desert. Just like Iraq.

Gabe seemed to know his way around, guiding her through the Helicopter Operations Building and requisitioning a beaten-up white Toyota pickup truck from a Marine sergeant friend of his outside the doors of the busy place. The airstrip was alive with helo activity. An enormous C-5 Air Force transport was landing at the fixed-wing operations and runway area. Apache combat helicopters were trundling toward a takeoff point with a full load of rockets and Hellfire missiles on board. The noise and activity were high and constant. It reminded Bay of a busy beehive.

They arrived at Naval Supply, a large warehouse on the other side of the base. Bay had been at Bagram only one other time, and that was the flight into Afghanistan from Iraq. The landing had been at night, so she never realized just how big this base was.

Gabe parked the truck out in front of the warehouse and climbed out. Like everyone else, he carried a weapon, an M-4 rifle he had in a sling across his chest. A SIG Sauer 9mm pistol rode low in a drop holster on his right thigh. On his left thigh was a SEAL SOF knife in a sheath. As she met him and walked into the air-conditioned building, she was proud to be at his side. SEALs stood out from other military personnel. Maybe it was the gear they wore or the confident way they carried themselves. Or both.

Gabe halted at the main counter and handed the Navy yeoman, a young woman in her early twenties, a requisition slip. She read it, looked from him to Bay.

"SEAL gear for a woman?" she asked, unsure.

"Yes," Gabe said. The yeoman frowned, scratched her blond head and shrugged. He wasn't going to tell her anything if she started to pump him with questions.

"There's no women's sizes in SEAL gear. You know what section the gear is in?" she asked him.

Gabe nodded. "I just need you to sign that and I'll take her down there and we'll collect her gear."

Bay could tell the yeoman was flustered. She was sure other women came here for military gear, too. Especially military police women. The look in her eyes, however, was questioning the SEAL gear order. Bay followed Gabe down a wide aisle where pallets of supplies were piled up nearly to the ceiling.

"You've done this a few times," she said as they walked beside each other.

"A few."

"I thought that yeoman was going to faint."

He smiled. "It's a little unusual for a female to show up needing SEAL gear—you have to admit that."

Bay nodded and scanned the area. "I didn't know what to expect when I arrived at Camp Bravo. It was nice of the chief to get me the gear I'll need in order to work with your team."

Gabe halted in the clothing section. "I just hope we can find a size that fits you," he muttered, looking through the cammies. "You're going to have to wear a man's uniform."

Shrugging, Bay moved over and looked through the sizes, her fingers moving quickly through the hanging desert cammies. "I'll survive." She grinned over at him.

This morning when Gabe had found her at the chow hall eating breakfast, he seemed subdued, preoccupied. Had something happened earlier? If so, he hadn't said anything. Still, Bay could feel the energy around him as she always felt around people, places and things.

"I think these will fit. Let me try them on." She pulled a pair of cammies off the rack and took them to a fitting room.

Within an hour, Bay had her cammies, a set of good desert boots, H-gear harness, jacket, cold-weather gear and a rucksack. Then Gabe took her over to the Navy Armory, nearby.

Bay stood looking at the rifles and pistols setting on racks behind the counter. "Why are we here?" she asked him. She patted her M-4 across her chest. "I have everything I need, don't I?"

"Well," Gabe hedged, "not quite." He turned and noticed the confused look on her face. For a second, he felt blinded by her natural beauty. It unnerved him. "The chief wants you to get a .300 Win Mag."

"What?"

He tried to get his mind back on task. "You really impressed the LT and chief out there yesterday with your shooting, Doc. We're short a sniper in our squad, and he's hoping you'll agree to train in with me on sniper ops. As a backup," he added. Her eyes widened enormously, her lips parted as she digested his words. "Want to add this to your training résumé?" Gabe sincerely hoped she'd say yes.

"But I'm *not* a trained sniper, Gabe." Bay protested quietly, keeping her voice down because the warehouse was filled with military men and women. "I haven't gone through sniper school. Won't the guys think—"

"It doesn't matter what they think," he parried quietly, holding her unsure stare. "Chief decides. If he feels you are qualified, sniper school or not, Doc, he's not going to waste whatever skills you have out there on coming missions."

It made sense to her, but it was still a shock. "Okay," she said, shrugging. "I'll try, but no promises."

"You'll be carrying the Win Mag on some missions but not all of them. It just depends on the type of op, but you'll have to carry it outside on your rucksack like I do. It's more weight."

Gazing up at the four Win Mags standing on the rack, she nodded. "It's not a problem. I carry sixty to eighty pounds of medical gear on my back already. I'm a mobile operating unit." She turned and looked up at him. His face was unreadable, those green eyes dark and thoughtful looking. "I can do it."

Gabe called over a Navy personnel man and produced another requisition slip.

Bay was excited about the Win Mag. It brought back happy memories with her father. She wondered obliquely if he was looking over her shoulder as she was given the rifle. Moving her fingers across the fiberglass stock, she heard Gabe asked for a SIG Sauer pistol. She raised her head and saw one produced by the Navy guy behind the counter. Frowning, she laid the rifle on the counter.

Gabe picked up the pistol, checked it out and was satisfied. He turned, handing it to her butt first. "You'll wear one of these, too."

Stunned, Bay stared down at the specially made German pistol. "But…" She gulped. "Oh, I can't, Gabe." She held up her hands and took a step back. "Only SEALs are allowed to wear that pistol. It's specially made for them. Even I know that."

Gabe seemed surprised at her reaction. "That's true, but you're with our team now. You need to always wear it wherever you go. It's never not a part of your daily gear you wear, Doc."

Panic ate at Bay as she stared at the pistol. She hesitated.

"What's the problem?" Gabe demanded.

Licking her lower lip, Bay said, "I want to fit in, Gabe. Not stand out. Half those guys don't want me around. I—I didn't go through SEAL training. By all rights, I haven't earned the right to wear a SIG. It just seems like a slap in their faces, to me. That I'm pretending to be something I'm not."

Gabe laid the SIG on the counter, understanding her

concerns. There was genuine anxiety in her blue eyes. He put his hand on her shoulder for a moment. "Look, Doc, what you don't understand yet is where we patrol, the missions we undertake. We're in harm's way all the time. You can't have enough weapons and ammo on you, believe me." He wanted to leave his hand on her shoulder but forced himself to release her. "You're worried Hammer and his guys are going to ride you about wearing it, aren't you?"

Nodding, Bay chewed on her lower lip. "It will be one more thing they'll hold against me. They'll accuse me of—"

"Bay," he said, purposely using her name to get her to focus, "read my lips. The chief wants you fully equipped. If you don't look like a SEAL out where we patrol, that's not good, because the Taliban we have to deal with sometimes will only respect us because we *are* SEALs. Got it?"

His logic was sound. Bay felt a shiver where he'd unexpectedly touched her shoulder. "Okay, I guess I can take it…."

Gabe picked up the black nylon drop holster and said, "Lift your arms away from your waist."

Taken aback, Bay realized he was going to place the holster around her waist. For the next few minutes, Gabe made sure the drop holster fit correctly. Pulling the two Velcro straps just tight enough around her thigh, he wanted the pistol to ride just above her knee.

"There. How does that feel?" Gabe handed her the SIG. The SEAL pistol had no safety on it.

Bay placed the pistol in the low-riding holster. "Okay," she said tentatively. "I feel like a gunfighter."

Gabe grinned. "That's what we are. Allow your hand to drop to your side. I want to see if your palm naturally comes to rest over the butt of the pistol."

Bay found his care and attention stabilizing. Intuitively, she knew Hammer and his men would say something. Probably many times over, for her to be wearing the SIG, the signature SEAL pistol. Gabe seemed unhappy with the holster position. He knelt at her side and raised the holster about an inch so that the butt was resting where her palm would naturally come to rest against her thigh. Finally, he stood back and critically studied his handiwork. Then he looked up at her.

"Okay, that feels about right to me," he murmured, gesturing toward the pistol. "Does it ride comfortably on your thigh?" She had nice legs, he'd discovered, while affixing the holster. Cammies hid a body pretty well, but working the straps, he could feel how taut her thigh was. Bay moved her hand a couple of times, her palm fitting nicely over the butt of the pistol.

"Good." He picked up a Kevlar vest, fitted it to her, got the level 4 ceramic armor plates for it and placed it over with the rest of her accumulated gear. She had to have a Kevlar helmet with a rail system, NVGs, night-vision goggles and a grenade launcher system for her M-4 rifle. Finally, they moved down the counter to where the knives were displayed.

Bay gave him a distressed look. "I have to carry one of these big knives?" She pointed toward them, disbelief in her voice.

"Yes."

"Listen, I've got plenty of scalpels in my medical

pack. I don't really think I need one more knife on me, Gabe. Do you?"

Gabe laughed as he picked up a seven-inch SEAL SOF knife and held it toward her, butt first. "Your scalpels aren't long enough, Doc. We usually wear this knife on our right outer calf if you're right-handed. Some guys like it riding low on their left thigh. Or the left outer calf. Where do you want to wear yours?"

Bay stared at the knife. The blade had tiny razor-sharp teeth beneath the lower half of it. Never mind the blade itself. Blowing out a breath of air, she said, "Okay…I guess my right calf?"

"You can start there and later, if you find out it isn't where you want it, you can move it." Gabe knelt down, attached the Velcro nylon black sheath around her lower leg, just below her knee. He tried to ignore touching her, but it didn't work. She was a large-boned woman with good muscling, and he could feel the firmness of her calf muscles beneath his fingertips. Standing up, he stood back, hands on his hips.

"How does that feel?"

Grimacing, Bay muttered, "It's okay."

"You'll get used to it. Comes in handy sometimes." He looked at the watch on his wrist. "Hungry?"

"I am."

"Okay, let's stow this gear back at Ops, put it in a locker and we'll grab some chow before we take a hop back to Bravo."

Gabe seemed to be out of his funk or whatever it was from earlier in the day. Her stomach grumbled because she hadn't eaten much at breakfast, still emotionally stressed out over some of the SEAL team not accepting her. Bay didn't want to tell Gabe, but the Special Forces guys had made her feel welcome from the beginning. They embraced her with eagerness. Here, it was like fighting every day to get a toehold of respect with everyone in the squad. SEALs were different, no question.

More and more, she oriented toward Gabe's quiet demeanor. He was thoughtful, listened closely and didn't knee-jerk on her. There was a lot to like about him. Bay saw some of the same characteristics to Navy corpsman Jack Scoville, whom she had been engaged to. The past was too painful to feel right now, and Bay tucked all those sad, traumatic memories away.

In the chow hall, Bay was amazed at how large, clean and bright it was. Hundreds of men and women were eating at the long white spotless tables. The noise level was high. One thing she instantly noticed was when they entered the chow hall, a lot of heads turned to closely check them out. Bay convinced herself it was because of the tall, rugged SEAL at her side, the M-4 hanging off a strap across his chest. SEALs were based at Bagram, but there were very few of them, and they were always a curiosity to the military people at large. As a black ops group, they were rarely seen in public.

Gabe handed her an aluminum tray as they got into line. It made him smile seeing a number of military guys gawking at Bay, who stood in front of him. He had to admit, with her height, at first glance, she looked like a SEAL. And then they would look at her a little more closely and discover she was a woman. Then their mouths dropped. If Bay saw their reaction to her, she didn't seem affected by the multitude of increasing male stares. He felt protective of her as they made it through the chow line and Gabe found a table unoccupied at the back, facing the doors.

"Sit beside me," he told her.

"Why?"

"Because SEALs always watch entrance and exit points. We never have our back to a door. We don't sit in front of windows, either."

Nodding, Bay sat down at his elbow, their backs to the light blue wall. "On-the-job training," she said in a teasing tone. "You probably feel like you're babysitting me." The food on the tray smelled wonderful. Hot food was always a luxury to those who'd lived mostly on MREs.

"I don't," he told her. "You're quick and intelligent. I like working with people like that." Gabe tried to ignore her closeness. He swore he could smell the strawberry fragrance of her shampoo. There were always soft tendrils on either side of her face even though she wore her shoulder-length hair gathered up in a ponytail. Men continued to stare openly at her. Gabe was sure sitting with him would stir up some gossip across the big base.

"I can hardly wait to get back to Camp Bravo," Bay told him between bites of her Reuben sandwich piled thickly with sauerkraut. "I've got a package coming from home. I hope it arrives today."

He smiled a little. "Never found anyone who didn't like mail call."

Picking at the French fries, Bay said, "My mama makes the best cookies—chocolate chip with walnuts from the trees around our cabin. She adds some secret ingredient she said she'd pass on to me when she died." Bay chuckled. "Does your wife send you boxes and keep you in cookies, too?"

Wincing inwardly, Gabe said flatly, "I'm divorced." He saw her expression become sad—for him. Bay was easily touched by another person's misery, he was discovering. But then again, she was a medic. Who better to be a compassionate soul?

"I'm sorry," she whispered. "How about your mom? Does she send you packages?"

"Yes, she does."

"What's her name?"

"Grace. She's an R.N. Works at the Pittsburgh, Pennsylvania, V.A. Hospital. She's a psychiatric nurse." He saw Bay react and she sighed.

"That's what I want to be when I leave the Navy. It's always been my dream to become an R.N."

"That's a dream you can reach, then," Gabe said, enjoying the big, thick hamburger and French fries.

"Well," Bay hedged, "when my pa got black lung, we lost his check from work. He had to quit his job and it was tough to make ends meet after that. I decided to go into the Navy because it would give me a paycheck and I could send most of my money home to them." She shrugged, her voice hollow. "Pa felt bad about me having to go find an outside job, but it couldn't be helped. My mama got paid for her services as a doctor with canned goods, vegetables, chickens and such. In the hills, money is scarce, so we trade."

Nodding, Gabe said, "I saw that with my hill friends I grew up with." He glanced at her. "And when you graduate from college, are you going back home?"

"I will. There's a nearby hospital in the lowlands at Dunmore, and I'll work there, but I intend to be home on weekends. That way, I can support Mama, who takes care of my sister, Eva-Jo. She's two years younger than me." Bay picked up her coffee mug and sipped from it.

"What's your sister do?" Gabe asked, finishing off the hamburger and wiping his hands on a paper napkin.

"Oh," Bay said softly, pain in her tone, "not much. My sister is mentally challenged. She has the mind and emotions of a ten-year-old." Shrugging, her voice low, Bay added, "Eva-Jo is special, Gabe. I love her dearly. And Mama is able to take care of her at home. She helps Mama in the garden, hanging the herbs out to dry and things like that. She has trouble reading and writing. It's sad…."

Hearing the concealed pain in Bay's husky voice, Gabe started to reach out and hold her hand. He wanted to take away some of her pain. His reaction shocked him enough to keep his hands right where they were. There was something kind, soft and sensitive about Bay that deeply touched him. And even more disconcerting, he had no way to armor himself against her. "I'm sorry to hear that." And he was. Her eyes widened slightly. "I don't have any brothers or sisters. I was an only child."

"I wouldn't know what to do with myself if I wasn't surrounded by my family, my aunts, uncles and cousins, my grandparents," Bay said, and smiled fondly. "Family means everything to me. When you're together, you're strong and you can weather life's storms more easily. You have support."

"The SEALs have a similar philosophy. If you consider one twig, it's easy to break it between your hands. But if you wrap a bunch of twigs together, they can't be broken. That's why the teams are so tight—they're like that bundle of sticks. The guys are close. We trust one another with our back out there and call each other brothers, and we are."

"At least you have parents," she pointed out.

Gabe shook his head. "My father's dead. All I have left is my mother. Both sets of my grandparents lived in California and Oregon, so I rarely got to see them before they passed away."

"A scattered, broken nuclear family," Bay whispered, meeting his hooded look. "Maybe the SEALs have given you back the family you lost?"

"Maybe they have," Gabe agreed. He wanted to share with Bay that he'd longed for a family of his own for a long time. He wanted children, knowing he'd raise them very differently from the way his father, Frank, had raised him. Gabe thought he'd found that dream coming true when he married Lily. As Bay said, he was part of a scattered, broken family in more ways than she would ever realize. Maybe that's why he hadn't accurately gauged Lily. He'd been driven to *want* family. *Want* that warm, loving support. Without having it as a child, how could he know which woman would be right for him to fulfill that dream with? For his vision of his future? Sometimes Gabe would feel panic in his chest, of having lost out on a very important part of life by not marrying. When he'd decided to try and capture that lost element, he'd met Lily. Marrying her five days later had been the worst decision he'd ever made. Gabe knew, without a doubt, he lacked something within himself to find the right woman who wanted to share his dream of love and having a family. A real family. Not dysfunctional like the one he'd grown up in.

To his consternation, Gabe found himself comparing Lily to Bay. There was a blinding difference. What if he'd met Bay first? God, he was so drawn to her that it scared the hell out of him. She was maternal and nurturing, unlike Lily, who was always in some kind of emotional drama. Bay was quiet and watched a lot and kept counsel to herself unless someone asked her for feedback. Lily was always telling him how she felt and usually it came out as a whining diatribe that about made him nuts.

Moving uncomfortably, Gabe was attracted to Bay's quiet strength. It exuded from her like sunlight. What man wouldn't want someone like her around him? And yet, he knew there wasn't anything he could say or do about it. He wasn't going to break Bay's trust in him by coming on to her. Gabe had to keep everything professional. Or else.

CHAPTER SIX

BAY SAT NEXT to Gabe in the small, stuffy room the SEALs used to plan missions. Chief Doug Hampton had a whiteboard set up front and was drawing a valley where they were going to pull an op tomorrow morning. He also used a PowerPoint presentation for the details. The rest of the SEALs were sitting on the other two benches. Not one of them had said anything when she'd arrived with Gabe earlier after getting off a Chinook flight from Bagram. Bay had to admit, she looked like a SEAL with all the gear she had to wear. And maybe, as Gabe had said to her, she was just being too sensitive. Even Hammer didn't say anything or give her a dark look when she'd entered the room earlier.

Doug pointed to the red oval line on the whiteboard. "This is going to be a recon mission. Alpha Platoon will go and I'll be joining you. Our assets on the ground in this valley have said that there are three villages. They're all from the Shinwari Tribe, which the U.S. has a peaceful alliance with. Assets at the Pakistan border are reporting that this valley has been targeted as new rat lines or newly created routes to get their weapons and fertilizer into the country. We have no idea when this will take place. We need to try and understand how the villagers are going to react to this new outside threat from their ancient enemy, the Hill Tribe. They're farmers and all they want to do is be left alone to go about their daily business. Unfortunately, there's a war going on around them and we don't know how they'll react to the insertion of Taliban carrying these supplies through their valley. We're going to fly in at 0600. It's an eight-hour day op, so pack your kit accordingly with first and second line gear."

Hampton looked up and pointed to Bay. "Doc, I'm wanting to use your linguistic and medical abilities out there tomorrow. Are you up for that?"

"Yes, Chief, I am."

"Good. The rest of the team is going to look around. Watch for IEDs, always. Just see how the farmers act or react to our presence. We'll also go out in teams of four to search for new trails across the area around the first village. This would tell us the shift has been made and the supplies are coming through that valley. There's a difference between a goat path and one that's being used to haul supplies. If you find a path, verify it with the kids herding the goats. Find out if they use it for the animals or not. If they don't, then put GPS coordinates on it and send it back here to the LT. When SEALs, Rangers or Special Forces have gone through the valley before these villages have offered no resistance. Maybe it's different now. We have to find out. Questions?"

Bay raised her hand.

"Doc?"

"Chief, if I'm going in as a medic, you want me to set up a clinic?"

"I do. Gabe? If you don't mind, I want you shadowing her. We don't have a familiarity with these Afghans in this shifting of routes with the Taliban. We're trying to establish some nation building with them, some goodwill so they'll trust us."

"I'll have her back," Gabe promised.

"Babysitter," Hammer muttered.

"It's better than babysitting you guys as a sniper on this op," Gabe challenged him. On many occasions, Gabe, because he was a sniper, would be ordered to high ground to have a look-down, shoot-down capability as his squad went through a village, searching for Taliban. His job was to spot a Taliban shooter and take him out before he could kill one of the SEALs. He saw the hurt in Bay's eyes over Hammer's comment. She was too sensitive to the harassment that SEALs gave one another. He'd far rather be with Bay than sitting up on a ridge if he didn't have to.

Snorting, Hammer shook his head and said nothing further.

"Chief?" Bay asked. "I'm treating women and children only? My experience over in Iraq is the men won't come to be helped because I'm a woman. Their Islamic laws decree the men can't be seen except by a male doctor."

Shrugging, Hampton murmured, "Well, we'll test that one out, won't we? We'll find the head elder of the village and depending on how bad those folks need medical help, you may find everyone lining up, no matter what their gender. You okay with that if it occurs?"

"Sure, no problem. I just need to know what to pack in my ruck, because male medical issues differ from women and children issues, is all."

Hampton nodded. "Plan for both genders, Doc. Better to be prepared than not. The Pashtuns sometimes bend rules when it suits them. If a guy has gone septic, he wants a shot of antibiotics to live. Infection is the number-one killer in this country because there are no medical services available. They die from infection, unable to obtain antibiotics, so you may well see men standing in your line as a result."

"Got it," Bay said, writing down a list of drugs to take on her small notepad. "What about food for the people?"

"This is an initial op to check them out," Hampton said. "We're going in to make first contact. Let's see what they need. Sometimes its medicine. Sometimes food. Just depends. If you can get the wives to talk, diplomatically ask them about Taliban activity through their area. See if it's happening. Maybe we'll get lucky and some woman will tell you the routes the Taliban is taking. That would be actionable intel."

Bay smiled a little. "I'm very good at getting the women to talk, Chief. Don't worry, I know how to mix business with medicine. If I get anything, you'll be the first to know. Since Gabe will be nearby, I can tell him if it's something urgent and he can pass the intel on to you."

"I like it," Hampton said, grinning. "You'll be a key player out there tomorrow, Doc."

"I'll do my best to be of help, Chief." Bay was relieved that Hammer said nothing further. With Gabe at her side, Bay felt confident that she could wrest intel from the women. They always liked talking with her in their native Pashto, were delighted she was a woman in this man's ongoing war. And they knew she could help their sick and ailing children. A trust was built quickly between women, no question.

After the planning was over, the assignments handed out by the chief, everyone left. Bay had finished up her notes, Gabe sitting nearby, when the chief ambled over to them.

"Doc?"

She looked up. "Yes, Chief?"

Hampton rested his hands on his hips. "This village is pretty safe from what our ground assets have been telling us. None of the other black ops groups moving through the area has had trouble with them. I really want you to try and ingrain yourself into these villages as we check out each one of them. Build trust with them. I want to find those Taliban rat lines through their valley ASAP." Rat lines were military slang for Taliban safe houses, villagers who were sympathetic to them or a series of new trails being created into an area by the enemy. Frowning, he added, "Now, we have no idea if this has happened yet or not. But when we go in, you know the rest of the story. You might ask the women if they've been feeding more strangers lately or not."

"Pashtun code says you feed those who ask for food," Bay said. "Okay, good to know. I'll see what I can do." If they were feeding more strangers, Bay knew it meant potential Taliban were coming through the area.

Hampton smiled a little and said, "How you getting along wearing our gear?"

Bay felt heat come to her face. "To tell you the truth,

Chief, I had a hissy fit about wearing a SIG. That's a special pistol that SEALs have earned the hard way. I haven't earned it."

Hampton pursed his lips. "I understand how you feel, Doc, but this order came directly from the LT. So, if anyone gives you any grief, you come to me. It's important you look like one of us. We can bring you up to speed on how to handle the weapons."

"I will, Chief."

"Gabe?" Hampton said, shifting his gaze to the SEAL. "I want you to take Doc out on the shooting range sometime this afternoon and get her acquainted with the SIG. She's got to know how to use it and clean it. Plus, do some rattle battle with her."

Gabe nodded. "Already figured that out. And the Win Mag?"

"Leave it here. This is a day op. We hopefully won't need it. But work in a rotation daily until she's good friends with that rifle. Have her shooting at twelve hundred to fourteen hundred yards with accuracy." Hampton looked at Bay. "You okay with filling in as a sniper trainee, Doc?"

Bay shrugged. "I'll give it a whirl, Chief. But I'm not a trained sniper."

"Gabe is one of the best in the sniping business. He'll teach you the basics." His gaze narrowed. "You okay with being a sniper?"

Bay nodded. "Chief, I was gunning and running with Special Forces over at the Syrian-Iraq border. I know I'm a medic and I'm charged with saving lives. But when my team is being shot at with the intent to kill them, I don't mind lifting my M-4 and taking out the bad guys."

"Okay, just checking," Hampton said. "You should know our LT talked to your commanding officer, Captain Morton, over in Iraq. The captain had good things to say about you. It looks like you're a solid player. You have our back and that's good to know."

Bay tried to hide her shock. Given the nature of her being an experiment, it made sense that the SEAL LT would check her out. "I'm glad the LT knows that. I'm not here to get anyone killed on my behalf."

"It's SOP to get the dope on the new guy coming into our platoon. Reputation is everything in the SEAL community," Hampton told her. "And he was calling mainly to find out your reputation among the spec op guys."

"And is the LT satisfied?" Bay wondered what Morton had said. Everyone saw her differently. Some saw her as a gun in the fight, one who could perform coolly under fire. Others saw her as a compassionate medic and trusted her with their lives.

Hampton smiled. "Yes. And so am I."

Relief trickled through Bay. "That's good to know, Chief. Thank you."

"Many guys who enter combat corpsman duty are pacifists by nature," Hampton said, assessing her.

"I don't enjoy killing anyone, Chief. But I will shoot in self-defense for myself and my team. The way I look at it, it's just another way to save a life. It's one more bad guy who isn't going to kill one of us."

Nodding, Hampton appeared satisfied with her answer. "If you haven't already got it in your notes for your medical ruck you're bringing along, put some vaccinations in there."

"Ahead of you, Chief." She saw Hampton's eyes gleam with approval.

"Can you give us a few minutes alone, Doc? I need to talk with Gabe."

Easing off the bench, Bay nodded, picked up her M-4, placed it in a harness over her chest and left.

Hampton sat down on the bench next to Gabe. "What I didn't say to her is that Captain Morton raved about her under-fire abilities. He said we don't have anything to worry about, that she's calm and thinking through the firefight. She takes orders and when she's placed in a position, she stays. She doesn't run."

Gabe placed his elbows on his thighs. "Good to know. How's it going with Hammer and his men?"

Hampton grimaced. "My threat is still working. We'll see if it lasts."

"Doc is really uncomfortable wearing that SIG."

"Yeah, I can see that."

"And the look on Hammer's face when we came in was one of fury."

"I saw that, too."

Gabe shrugged. "SEAL exclusivity can work against us at times." He gave Doug a twisted smile.

"What Hammer and those guys don't understand is that she's in combat, too, and needs that pistol to protect herself. Or them…"

"She tried to talk me into carrying a .45 instead of the SIG," Gabe told him. "I told her no. Reasoned with her that she's got to look like a SEAL whether she's one or not. A camouflage point."

"That persuaded her?"

"Enough for her to wear it, but she's unhappy about it."

Scratching his head, Hampton muttered, "Well, I hate to say it, but we're going to be in firefights sooner or later, and at that time, she's going to realize how important that SIG can be."

Gabe sat up and clipped the M-4 over his chest, muzzle down. "Bay is savvy," he reassured the chief. And then he realized he'd called her by her first name. *Damn.* He was working hard to keep distance between them. Grimacing, Gabe looked up to see Hampton grinning crookedly at him. "What?" he demanded testily.

"She's a very attractive woman."

"Not going to argue that point," Gabe growled. "But we're in combat and grab-ass isn't what you want in a platoon going into firefights, either."

"No," Hampton agreed equitably. "But there *is* a special connection between you and her. I can feel it."

Snorting, Gabe stood up. This was not what he wanted to hear. "She's a decent, caring person, Doug. Her word is her bond. There's no bullshit with her." The kind of woman he wished he'd met before marrying Lily. Gabe had discovered his idealism about women was just that: not based on rock-solid reality. And Baylee-Ann Thorn was as sincere and real as a woman could get. And dammit, that sincerity called to him. And he was struggling not to be get entangled in it. Relationships had no place out here. None.

"She's solid, no question," Hampton said, standing.

"Half the guys have bought in to her being with us. We have one half to go."

"Over time," Gabe said, heading for the door, "the other half will be convinced once they see her in action."

Hampton agreed. "Help her get her kit together for the mission. I know she's used to that length of mission, but this is Afghanistan, not Iraq."

"Roger that."

BAY STOOD WITH the SIG in her hands, firing off at a target fifty yards in front of her. The sun was low on the horizon, the heat stifling, the wind erratic. Gabe had been giving her good dope on how to use and fire the .30-caliber pistol. It packed a hell of a punch, jerking her hand hard every time she squeezed the trigger. Finally, she ran out of bullets in the mag, dropped it out of the SIG and quickly slapped another into its place and began firing again.

Gabe wanted her to be able to drop an empty mag on the run, grab another out of her H-gear harness, slap it into the pistol and keep on firing. When they got back off the op, he was going to make her run and shoot. That was rattle battle, he told her. She had to be totally at ease switching out mags and keep on firing accurately in the process while in constant motion.

Gabe seemed pleased with her progress. She hit the target every time. When she finished firing the last mag, he called, "That's enough. You're good to go."

Bay turned and smiled at him. Gabe's green eyes gleamed and he nodded in her direction. Turning, she picked up the dropped mags and placed each of them in a canvas pocket in the front of her H-gear she wore around her torso. "This is a nice pistol. Now I see why you guys like it so much," she said.

The breeze blew a number of strands of her hair across her face and she pulled them back with her fingers. For a moment, she saw something else in Gabe's face. What? As a medic, she had to be observant. Sometimes a person was in so much pain, or semiconscious, and she had to interpret his facial expressions. Did she really see what she thought she saw—longing? A man-wanting-his-woman kind of look?

Licking her lower lip, she cleared the chamber on the SIG and holstered it. There was such a powerful connection between them and it was growing stronger by the day. Bay knew it could never be spoken about. Much less acted upon.

"I'll let the chief know you're dialed in on the SIG," Gabe told her as they walked off the range. A group of Afghan boys raced forward, having waited patiently in the background. They quickly snatched up the spent cartridge shells. They would sell them and make a little money for their destitute families who lived nearby. The cartridge casings would be melted down and the metal sold to a dealer for a decent sum of money. A family could eat well for six months or more on it.

"Great," Bay said, feeling a lot more confident about carrying the special pistol. She enjoyed walking at Gabe's side. He had such an easy stride and she never heard his boots hit the ground. "Hungry?" Gabe asked. He liked the happiness he saw mirrored in Bay's face. The corners of her mouth pulled upward. A soft mouth. A damned kissable mouth. When she'd smiled at him earlier, he'd had no defense against it. Heat had flashed through his lower body, scalding and reminding him of what he'd been missing. There was such undisguised warmth in her smile, her lips lush and curved. He wondered what it would be like to kiss her, to touch those lips and feel her response. Gabe berated himself for these wayward thoughts.

"Starved."

"Good, because we'll catch an early breakfast before going out on that op tomorrow, too. You'll learn fast to bulk up on high-calorie food the night before a day mission. In these mountains and high altitude, you burn calories faster than you realize. You'll be humping in with a heavy ruck, and that will take a toll on your energy, as well."

She appreciated his experience. "You take good care of me, Gabe." Reaching out, she briefly touched his arm. "Thanks."

"You're welcome," he muttered, scowling. He wasn't expecting her fingers to brushed his arm. The huskiness in her voice, the light sparkling in her delft blue eyes, caught him off guard. Bay didn't try to hide her feelings with him at all. And yet, out on a battlefield, she'd have to sit on her emotions in order to think through the heat and haze of battle to save a man's life. So why was she sharing herself like that with him? Gabe didn't know. And he didn't like some of the possible answers.

"Sometimes," she told him, catching his gaze, "when I'm relaxed or happy, I show it." She held up her long, spare hand. "Like just now, I touched you. It was my way of saying thanks, that I appreciate you being in my life. I'm a hugger and a toucher. You'll see me out in the field tomorrow hugging all the kids, hugging the elderly. It's just a part of who I am."

Her sincerity got to him. Gabe slowed his stride and tried to think of a way to let her know he wasn't unhappy about her contact. Bay didn't realize how the gesture impacted him as a man. Looking down at her, he saw complete honesty in her expression. Bay didn't play games as Lily had. Lily was a master at manipulating his emotions, he'd found out way too late.

"That's why you're a corpsman," he managed in a gruff tone. "Touching is important when you've been shot."

Smiling a little, Bay said, "Yes, I know the healing power of touch. And when I'm in medic mode, I use it a lot."

He had so many fine, dangerous edges to walk with Bay. On one hand, Gabe *wanted* her to trust him, because once they got into a firefight, she had to trust him a hundred percent or it could cost one or both of their lives. On the other hand, he was having one helluva time personally figuring out how to interact professionally with her. It wasn't her fault.

Bay wasn't flirting with him. It was just how she was built, who she was. No, she'd reached out as a way to thank him for his time and teaching her how to use the pistol. That was all.

Gabe frowned. "You have a natural gift for healing." And then he lied. "I was just thinking about something else, so don't take my reaction personally." *Yeah. Right.* No sense in damning her with the personal problems he'd had with Lily.

CHAPTER SEVEN

BY THE TIME the squad arrived at the village, children were running around them, hands out, begging for candy. Bay walked up front with Chief Hampton. Behind her were Gabe and the other SEALs. The morning was chilly but not freezing. They were at six thousand feet and it was warmer in the valley than at the FOB. The sun was edging the mountains surrounding the long, narrow valley.

A man in his fifties, dressed in dark brown clothes, turban on his head, stood near the gate in the mud wall that surrounded the village of a hundred and fifty people. The chief glanced over at Bay. "Okay, give him the greeting and let's see what you can find out."

Bay wore a soft floppy hat like the rest of the SEALs. As she approached the elder, whose dark eyes were wary, she removed it. When his gaze settled on her, his eyes widened slightly, no doubt in his surprise that a woman would be part of this team.

Bay took the lead and halted about six feet from the elder.

"As-Salamu alaikum," she said, touching her brow and heart. "I'm Bay and we've come to offer you medical services if you need it for your people." The Pashtun rolled easily off her lips. The man's gray-and-black eyebrows rose with even more surprise.

"*Wa 'alaykumu s-salāmu wa rahmatu l-lāhi wa barakātuh,* Bay. I am Faisal, leader of our village. You are welcome to aid my people. We have many who need your help."

Bay turned and translated to the SEALs.

Hampton nodded. "Ask him permission to scout around as you set up a clinic. Let's see how he reacts to the Taliban choosing this valley to transport weapons and fertilizer."

Bay nodded, and put the questions to Faisal. She noticed the children of all ages were gathering around them, their faces upturned and mesmerized by her speaking their language. She knew, in part, it was because she was a woman, who appeared to be in charge, talking to a man, a stranger. In strict Muslim culture, a woman did not do that.

As she spoke to Faisal, she noticed a tall young woman walk up to stand beside him. She was dressed in cream-and-brown wool, a hajib over her dark brown hair. Bay gave her a greeting, also. She was Husna, wife to Faisal.

Some of Bay's worries dissolved when Faisal raised his hand and told her that the SEALs were welcome and they could go wherever they wanted. When she told Chief Hampton, he nodded and ordered the SEALs out in various directions to begin scouting the area. Gabe remained close behind her, relaxed but on guard.

Bay was surprised when Husna walked forward and gripped her left arm, speaking urgently.

"You must come, doctor. We have a very sick child. My sister-in-law, Saima, has a daughter who is dying. Will you help us? Please?"

Doug Hampton knew just enough Pashtun to get the drift of the urgent request. "Doc, go do your thing. Gabe, stay with her. I'll use my broken Pashtun and have tea with Faisal and see what else I can get. Just stay in communications."

"Roger that," Gabe murmured as he watched Bay turn and leave with Husna through the gate and into the walled village. Following about six feet behind, Gabe knew the drill. He'd been in too many villages like this. Some had mud walls four to six feet high. This one had stone-and-mud walls abut five feet high. The children tagged along, laughing and curious, like tumbling, happy puppies at their heels.

Automatically, Gabe memorized the mud homes, the streets and the egress points, if they had to get out of here in a hurry. Ahead, Husna was chatting quickly and Gabe could pick up bits of the conversation. His Pashtun was pretty much limited to orders to control a prisoner. His hands remained on his weapon, the barrel pointed downward. If he really felt threatened, he'd be carrying the weapon barrel up so he could bring it level and shoot fast. No village was safe. If there weren't IEDs planted, then they could hide Taliban inside the village from them.

Bay took off her medical ruck and set it down outside the mud house where Husna said the little girl was dying. She looked up at Gabe. "You coming in or staying out?"

"Outside, but leave the door open. You spot anything that looks out of place, tell me."

Bay had worn the radio headset just like all the other SEALs, the mike resting near her lips. "I will," she promised, nodding, then ducking low to go through the open door. Her eyes adjusted to the gloom within the hard-packed-earth room. Husna rushed forward, speaking with emotion, as she brought her to a young woman who had a girl of six in her arms.

Bay knelt in front of the distraught young mother, Saima. She quickly explained who she was. Relief in the form of tears rolled down Saima's face as she gestured to her unconscious daughter in her arms. Rahela, four days earlier, had stepped on a piece of rusted metal from a destroyed Russian shell out in one of the furrows of the field. She did not see it, and it had sliced open her right foot. The mother drew the rag that had been wrapped around her daughter's foot.

The rotting smell of infected flesh was hard to take, but Bay had seen it before. It was infection along with tetanus, more than likely. She quickly got up, excused herself and retrieved her medical pack. Bringing it in, she quickly donned latex gloves after opening the ruck and laying out the items she'd need to try and save the girl's life.

With quick efficiency, Bay examined the oozing slice across the bottom of the child's foot. She turned and asked Husna to boil hot water and bring it in, that she had to clean off the wound area. Husna quickly agreed and practically ran out of the house to do as she was asked.

"Can you help my daughter?" Saima asked, wiping the tears from her face.

Bay went to work with dressings, disinfectant and cleaned the area off. Already, pus was oozing out of the wound. "I'm going to try," she told her gently. First things first. She retrieved a syringe and gave the girl a tetanus shot in her small, thin left arm. It might be too late, but she had to try. And then a shot of lidocaine to numb the area around the wound. Quickly taking the girl's temperature and blood pressure and listening to her heart, Bay kept her face blank.

"Gabe, is it possible to call in a CASEVAC here to the village? I don't know what LT's rules are about helping out very sick Afghans that need E.R. help."

"Yeah, I'll ask. Part of nation building. If you feel the girl is critical, Hampton will make the call."

"Then do it," she whispered tightly. "What this kid needs, I can't provide." She quickly put an IV in the child's arm and asked the mother to hold the bag higher than Rahela's head so the drip would flow directly into the child's bloodstream. She also placed a syringe in the IV and filled it with as much antibiotic as the child's body could handle.

Bay was vaguely aware of the talk between Hampton and Gabe. The bottom line was a Black Hawk medevac helo from Camp Bravo was already taking off to come and pick up the little girl and take her directly to Bagram's hospital, where they had state-of-the-art help for the very sick child.

Rapidly, Bay told the mother she had to come along on the helo ride, that they were transporting her child to the American base. It was the only way to save her daughter's life. The mother's eyes went huge with fear. Saima had never left the village of her birth or flown in an aircraft. Gently, Bay persuaded her that it would be all right.

"Gabe?"

"I'm here."

"Can you come in and help me? I can carry the child, but the mother is freaking out. You escort her and I'll carry the child outside the gate and we'll wait for that helo?"

"Roger. Coming in."

Within minutes, they were outside the walled village. In the distance, Bay could see the Black Hawk with the big red cross painted on its nose coming in. No valley was safe for a helicopter to land in. They always had to watch out on landing and taking off, that some Taliban soldier wasn't hidden with an RPG, waiting to fire it into the helo. Bay asked Saima if the Taliban were around. She quickly shook her head, running to almost keep up with Bay as she carried her daughter out beyond the walls.

Gabe moved ahead, eyes down and searching for telltale signs of wires hidden by dirt to hint of an IED. When they were clear of the village and the helo could land, he set about looking for a safe landing area. Gabe tossed out a green smoke flare to show the Black Hawk, coming down the valley, where to land. Within minutes, the helo was down on the grassy area, the blades turning at nearly takeoff speed in case of attack.

Bay transferred the unconscious child through the opened door and into the arms of one of the two medics on board. She helped Husna on board, who was frightened. The air crew chief, a man in his late thirties, knew enough Pashto to convince the mother to come and sit down near her daughter. He threw Bay a thumbs-up after she told him the situation with the child.

"We'll do what we can, Doc," he called.

Nodding, she and Gabe turned and quickly moved away. The place where they landed was green with grass. For once, there were no clouds of dust being stirred up by the powerful blades.

"What do you think?" Gabe asked as they watched the Black Hawk rise and go quickly to higher altitude in the blue sky above them.

Pulling off her gloves and stuffing them into her cammie pocket, Bay said, "I don't know. It's not good. Four days, tetanus can take hold. It's going to be dicey." She glanced up at him, glad he was near. Pushing strands of hair off her face, she smiled a little. "Thanks for being there."

Gabe felt a special warmth move through his chest. He managed a lopsided grin. "Wouldn't have it any other way."

Bay looked around. Several groups of SEALs were out walking areas near the slopes of the hills. "How's it going?"

"They're finding paths. We won't know much until later whether they're rat lines or not." He met her alert blue gaze. "Come on, I'm sure Husna will have other folks who need your medical help."

"THIS WAS A GOOD OP," Doug Hampton praised his team once they assembled off the CH-47 back at Camp Bravo. His men sat on the benches, their rucks nearby. "Go get cleaned up, get some chow and I'll see you at 0800 tomorrow. Doc? Gabe? Stick around."

When the SEALs had trooped out, Hampton walked over to the bench where they remained sitting. "Good work out there today, Doc," he told her.

"Thanks, Chief." She frowned. "Husna dumped a bunch of information on me. They are aware of three rat line routes the Taliban have started creating around their village. Faisal hates the Taliban. Because he's a Shinwari tribesman, his word is his honor. When the Shinwari asked for U.S. help in building infrastructure along the villages on the border, he would back the leaders of his people."

"Did Husna tell you the location of those paths?" Hampton asked.

Rubbing her face, exhausted, Bay said, "Yes." She pulled out her notebook and opened it. "She told me about them just before the Chinook landed. I need to give you this intel."

"You do," Hampton said. He grinned a little. "Nice work. You want to get cleaned up, eat and then meet me back over here in about two hours?"

The sun was setting and Bay nodded. "I can do that."

Hampton nodded. "Gabe? I want you present."

"Got it," he murmured.

"Okay, get out of here. I'll see you two in a bit."

"NICE WORK," GABE congratulated as they sat in the chow hall, eating. He'd chosen a table at the rear. The noise was high as hundreds of men and women were coming in for their evening meal. "You really know your medical stuff."

A warmth went through Bay. She liked having

Gabe's company. Spooning in some potatoes and gravy, she savored the hot food. She hadn't eaten all day, just keeping hydrated with water and attending to over forty people in a very intense and short amount of time. "I love what I do, Gabe."

"You put what I know about combat medicine to shame. I'm like a fumbling kid with Band-Aids and you're like a skilled surgeon."

She chuckled. "You SEALs rock when it comes to field medicine, and I know it. You're all trained up to a basic EMT level, so you don't fool me." She knew SEALs were also trained to insert IVs into another man's arm to get fluids into him if necessary and that one technique could save a life.

"I was really impressed with you out there today," Gabe admitted, scraping up the leftover gravy on his tray with a piece of bread. "The people fell in love with you." He met her shadowed eyes. "You've got a great bedside manner, Bay."

He seemed frustrated with himself, probably because he'd called her by her first name. A burst of pleasure soared through Bay at how intimate Gabe sounded. But she couldn't even begin to pursue this. They had to stay professional. She pushed the empty tray away from her and picked up her coffee mug. The truth was, Gabe appealed to her. His quiet intensity drew her. It didn't hurt that she thought he was ruggedly handsome, even with a beard. There was warmth in his eyes as she met his gaze. Something happened in that charged split second. Maybe it was the slight smile tipping the corners of his sensual mouth. Or the feeling that passed between them, no words needed.

Her fingers tightened around the mug a little as she absorbed his narrowing green gaze upon her. Bay could feel him wanting her, man to woman. The discovery shook her. For so long since Jack's death, she lived in a no-man's land of numbness. Sipping the coffee, Bay suddenly felt alive again. Normal. And with normal wants and desires a woman had. Her sex drive had been nil. Until now. Until Gabe unexpectedly entered her life. Her heart pounded briefly beneath the intense, heated look Gabe gave her. It was unsettling in an exciting way, her body responding whether she wanted it to or not.

Her gaze fell to his hands wrapped around his coffee mug. She wanted to tell Gabe he had the most beautiful hands she'd ever seen on a man. There were many small nicks and scars, new and old ones. They were burned dark by the sun and time spent outdoors in the rugged Afghan climate. What would it be like to have him touch her with those long, spare fingers? She felt her breasts tighten in answer, felt her nipples harden. Even more powerful, Bay's lower body came to life, like coals beginning to glow with fire within her.

How long had it been since she felt like a sexual being? Gabe was bringing her to life whether he knew it or not. Bay closed her eyes for a moment, trying get a hold of herself. Maybe she was overtired, stressed by the patrol.

When she opened her eyes, Gabe was watching her. His intense look didn't frighten her. Just the opposite. Bay responded to that look and felt her heart opening up for the first time since Jack's death. Oh, God, what was going on with her?

"Let's mosey on over to the office," Gabe growled, getting up.

He seemed desperate to do something to break that sizzling connection that had suddenly leaped to life between them. Bad timing, wrong place to be attracted to someone. If anyone sensed what was going on, Gabe would never live it down with his team. He appeared eager to create a distance, and she did nothing to stand in his way.

"Good intel," Hampton praised, standing over the table with the map of the valley before them. Bay had used a red marker on the plastic placed over the map and drawn in where Husna had told her the Taliban rat lines were located. They'd spent a lot of time going over everything that Husna had imparted to Bay in minute detail.

"Can we get some sleep?" Gabe asked. He saw the darkness beneath Bay's eyes. She'd worked hard and she'd been smart enough to make detailed notes, even while taking care of forty people today, men, women and children.

"Yeah," Hampton said, running his hand through his hair. "This is good stuff, Doc. You did well."

Straightening, Bay moved her shoulders to get rid of the accumulated tension in them. "Thanks, Chief."

"We'll meet at 0800 tomorrow. I'm going to talk with the LT about setting up some night ops on those trails to check them out. We don't have drone capability, so we do it by sniper scope sight."

"You're going to have to go back and get GPS on them," Gabe warned.

"Yeah. We'll send out Bravo Squad tomorrow to verify locations on these rat lines for us. Then I'm sure the LT will coordinate with the other teams and some serious night ops with snipers will happen."

"Sounds like a plan I want to take part in," Gabe said.

Bay settled the helmet on her head, the NVGs on top. They'd be walking in total darkness through Camp Bravo to reach their tents. There were never any lights that could attract the Taliban's attention. Gabe put on his own helmet.

Bay was the first out the door, pulling the NVGs down over her eyes. In the distance, they heard Apache helicopters spooling up to take off, their thumping rotors a clear signature of their identification. Somewhere out there, there was a black ops team in trouble and needing their firepower. This base was operating at breakneck speed 24/7 because it was only thirty miles from the Pakistan border and in the thick of the fight to stop traffic across the Khyber Pass into Afghanistan.

"You're looking whipped," Gabe murmured, walking at her shoulder. The streets were quiet, most personnel already asleep in their tents.

"I am," Bay admitted. Everything looked green and grainy through her NVGs. The big problem on rutted areas like this, she had no depth of perception through them, so she walked slowly, making sure her boots were stable beneath her. "How about you?"

"The same," Gabe said in a low voice. The chill was below freezing now and he saw white wisps leaving her mouth as she spoke quietly with him. There was something emotionally satisfying to simply being near

Bay. Several curls peeked out from beneath her helmet and he smiled. It completely softened the military look.

"Do you think the chief was really happy with the intel I was able to provide?" There was worry in her husky tone.

"Hell yes. Those people in that village looked at you like you were an angel of mercy." He grinned unevenly as they made a left turn and went down another street. "They had nothing but respect in their eyes for you. And I've been here long enough to be able tell you they trust you. There's just something about you that opens them up. They know you really care."

This trait opened him up, too. Though he tried to suppress his reaction to her, he couldn't. Gabe had seen the positive effect Bay had on people all day long, and he was equally caught beneath her soft-spoken spell, too. Her hands were beautiful and she touched everyone so gently and with genuine care.

Gabe had seen the tender look in her eyes with every patient. He could feel her sending out her energy, her heart, to every Afghan person she treated. And he'd seen the hard faces of the men relax. The children smiled sweetly up at her, calling her Allah's angel. The mothers…well, they could only cry, hug her and profusely thank her for her compassion.

There was no doubt in Gabe's mind that Bay was going to be this team's secret weapon in the fight against the Taliban and al Qaeda. And like all her patients, he wanted to experience her touch, too. What would her fingers feel like across his chest, tangling in his dark hair? Her lips touching his mouth? He'd fought those images all day long. The ache in his chest built quickly once they arrived back to base where he didn't have to be on alert.

"Good to hear," Bay whispered, relieved. And then she gave a low laugh. "But I'm no angel of mercy. I wish I were. I want to call Bagram Hospital tomorrow morning and see if I can patch through and find out how that little girl is doing."

They halted near Gabe's tent. He shut off his NVGs and pushed them up on his helmet. Bay did the same. Eyes adjusting, he could barely see her as a quarter moon had risen over the peaks of the Hindu Kush. Her hair was mussed but beautiful around her face. Looking deeply into her darkened eyes, he made sure no one was around. The men in the tents around them were sleeping, snoring now and then. Lifting his hand, he cupped her cheek. How badly he wanted to kiss her, but that would be the stupidest thing he'd ever done. Feeling the firm warmth of her skin beneath his calloused fingers, Gabe held her softened gaze. When her lips parted over his unexpected touch, he groaned inwardly.

"Get some sleep, Bay. We're going to rock it out tomorrow. You need every bit of rest you can get. Good night...." Gabe reluctantly pulled his hand away. His roughened fingers tingled hotly and he ached to do so much more. Bay invited something he'd never been aware of before: tenderness. It was a foreign feeling. And wherever it had been hiding, she'd somehow found it and pulled it out of him. He wanted to make slow, tender love with this woman whose eyes shone like the stars above them. Whatever this was, Gabe realized he had no control.

Bay stood there, shocked by his gesture. As she watched Gabe turn and quietly disappear into the tent next to hers, she released a ragged sigh. Her heartbeat had amped up when she saw that look of attraction come to his eyes once more. When he'd moved within inches of her, reached out and cupped her cheek, she'd felt a bolt of white-hot heat sizzle through her and explode into her lower body. For an instant, she knew he wanted to kiss her.

Turning, Bay went to her tent. Her frayed emotions were beginning to unravel. As she sat down on her cot, taking off her boots and placing them beneath it, she closed her eyes and just sat there. So much had happened in such a concentrated, intense amount of time today.

Lifting her hands, Bay rubbed her face. She was filthy, feeling the grit of dust beneath her fingertips. The SEALs who had made her tent a home had thoughtfully placed a steel bowl, a towel and washcloth with a bar of soap opposite her cot. Someone had also thought about water and had stored a case of bottles next to the cabinet. Bay stood up and poured several of them into the bowl.

As she washed up, feeling the cold cloth against her gritty flesh, her heart and mind returned to Gabe. There was something good and clean shared between them. She wished they had time to explore each other, but combat ruled that out. And she couldn't afford to let her growing personal feelings for Gabe to get in the way of staying alive out here.

She inhaled the scent of jasmine soap deeply into her lungs. It blotted out the constant odor of kerosene aviation fuel polluting the air. Scrubbing her face, neck and arms, Bay felt a little cleaner. A shower tomorrow morning, a clean set of cammies, would make her feel human once again.

No one at an FOB went to sleep undressed. Just as she'd done in Iraq, Bay placed her rifle, Kevlar vest and helmet near the head of her cot. The boots were placed beneath it, within easy reach. She'd sleep in her green T-shirt, trousers and socks. The air was freezing and she snuggled beneath four wool blankets, trying to get warm. The exhaustion of the day stalked her as she closed her eyes.

Gabe… What was she going to do about him? She couldn't deny the worry over her contribution to the team. She didn't want the SEALs thinking she was a useless appendage. And she desperately wanted Chief Hampton to value her contributions, whatever they might be. Snuggling her head into the hard, unyielding pillow, Bay felt herself truly beginning to relax.

As her mind began shutting down, her last thoughts were of Gabe. Would he have kissed her out there? She'd felt his desire, seen it in his face. He wanted her as much as she wanted him.

That was what was different. Bay had lived in an emotionless vacuum since her fiancé's death. The shock must have worn off and she must be through the worst of the grief over Jack's loss. She was no angel. Her body was turning traitor on her, no matter what she did to try and stop the longing for Gabe. There was a need to be loved once again being gently suspended in front of her.

Right now Bay was being tempted and teased with

the forbidden fruit of Gabe Griffin. She couldn't blame him any more than she could blame herself. A relationship, as she well knew from experience, had no place in combat. Not at all.

CHAPTER EIGHT

"Do you think the guys are going to die laughing at my shooting of the SIG?" Bay asked Gabe as they sat on the floor of the planning room, oiling and cleaning their Win Mags. All day, Bay had been either dialing in and shooting the sniper rifle on the course or learning to shoot on the run with the SIG. The SEALs referred to this training as "rattle battle." It was late afternoon and Gabe moved her inside from the intense heat and temperature, to clean her rifle.

"When you start gunning and running, your job is to place every shot," he told her. Gabe had spread a tarp out for them to sit on and disassemble their Win Mags. He'd gotten a few of the other SEALs to volunteer to help train Bay on the SIG pistol. They'd set up an obstacle course of sorts. Having been trained during SQT, Seal Qualification Training, a year-and-a-half-long course to become a SEAL after surviving BUD/s, they had to learn to shoot on the run. They had configured a smaller course on the edge of Bravo, but nonetheless it was equally challenging for Bay. Today, Gabe had been able to get a feel for her shooting discipline. And her keen ability to focus and keep it dialed in as a combat soldier.

Bay took some of the local oil used by the Afghans

on their rifles and applied it to the parts spread out before her crossed legs. Snipers used local oil because if the Taliban walked by their place of concealment, they wouldn't smell anything out of the ordinary. If they smelled a U.S.–made oil, they would instantly knew there was a sniper nearby and start blazing away.

"It was really embarrassing."

Hearing the anxiety in her voice, Gabe raised his head. Soft curls fell around Bay's temples. She was already tanned from the Iraq sun, but sunlight at eight thousand feet on a mountaintop was more intense. Her nose was slightly red. "You should have seen me when we started the rattle battle training," he told her wryly. "I was the one who couldn't hit the broad side of a barn."

Bay's eyebrow raised. "Seriously?" At least she was hitting the target as she ran, firing off fifteen shots. She'd drop the empty mag out of the bottom of the pistol as she moved toward the next target, grabbing another full mag out of her H-gear pocket and slapping it up into the butt of her pistol. Bay had to run at least a couple of hundred feet between each of the targets the SEALs had set up for her. What was stressful were three of the SEALs were there to judge her shooting skills, off and on during the morning and early afternoon hours. They didn't laugh at her, thank goodness. But their faces were unreadable. He smiled, starting to reassemble his sniper rifle. "Yeah, very seriously. It's one thing to be lying or standing still and hit a target. It's another to be running, out of breath, your chest heaving up and down, trying to draw an accurate bead on a target. Even though you get to stop at each target and fire, your hand is moving up and down in time with your ragged breathing. It makes hitting a target ten times tougher." Gabe looked up, seeing the shadows in her blue eyes. His body instantly responded to her and he savagely tamped it down.

Last night, he'd lain awake for a long time trying to figure out why the hell he'd reached out and cupped Bay's cheek. It was a stupid, hormone-driven mistake. Sex and desire had no place out on the battlefield. And it wasn't that Bay was teasing or flirting with him. She wasn't. That made it tougher to ignore her as a woman. As a SEAL, he was taught control. Well, now he had to apply it to Bay.

"Do you think the guys are laughing at my attempts out there today?"

"No, because you were as good as they were, or better, on their first day of rattle battle. Stop worrying, Bay. You'll integrate into our team over time. You gave a good accounting of yourself out at the village. Other missions are being planned right now because of what you found out through the elder's wife. Feel good about that."

She finished oiling her piece and wiped her hands on a rag near her boot. "I'm a worrywart," she admitted. "I'm too competitive, maybe." Her heart opened as she saw him smile briefly. When Gabe allowed her to see how he really felt, a rush of excitement flowed through Bay. She couldn't explain the feeling and hadn't ever felt this way about any man, not even with Jack. She floundered over how to deal with it. Not that she hadn't liked Gabe's unexpected touch last night. He sensed her need. His sensitivity toward her was startling. Un-expected.

Gabe brought his rifle up, moving a fresh dry cloth across the fiberglass stock, careful to keep the barrel up and not pointed anywhere it could potentially do harm to someone. The weapon had already been cleared and safed, but he never took any chances. You simply did not aim a rifle barrel at anyone except with the intent to shoot him. "You have the makings of a SEAL," he told her. "We're all alpha guys who live to compete. We have the mind-set of always being a winner, not a loser. You need that drive in order to survive what we do."

"That and some serious mental toughness," Bay murmured. Her hands flew surely over the Win Mag as she quickly reassembled it. It felt good to have this rifle back in her life. She'd grown up with her father's rifle. It was now displayed on a wall at home, no longer used. She moved her fingers lovingly down the barrel, good memories rising to the surface. Her father's rifle had a wooden stock. The military type had fiberglass stock, making it lighter to carry.

Gabe eased to his feet and fitted the rifle into the canvas case and pressed the Velcro closed on it. "Mental toughness is something you either have or don't have. SEAL training brought all of us to that point and helped us recognize what we had. In my class of BUD/s, we started out with two hundred and ten guys. Hell Week sifted a lot of them out. Only thirteen graduated." He set the rifle on the planning table and stood watching her assemble the rifle. Her fingers were long, spare and graceful. There was concentration on her face as she knew which piece fit first, middle or last. And she was fast. As fast as he was. There was no question she was friends with the Win Mag.

Gabe felt his heart pound briefly in his chest. Did Bay know her blue eyes were startlingly beautiful? He remembered his mother, Grace, collected blue delft plates. Bay's eyes were exactly the same color. A man could drown his soul in them, he grimly decided.

"Wow, only thirteen graduated?" Bay said. "Now, that's a training course to kill a horse." She smiled as she stood up. Picking up the new desert-camouflaged sheath that was specially padded for the weapon, she brought it over to the table where he stood. Setting it on the surface, Bay gently slid her rifle into the fabric case and closed the Velcro on it so no dust could enter into it.

"BUD/s never killed anyone. Some guys broke arms and legs, or they picked up a bacterial infection from the polluted San Diego Bay, but no deaths." He watched Bay push tendrils away from her cheek, her grace always evident. Gabe absorbed the moment like a greedy beggar. He stopped himself from wondering a lot more about Bay's touch, those healing hands of hers slowly exploring every inch of his body. Looking down at his watch, he said, "Chow time. We've got a mission briefing in an hour, so let's get over there and get back here in time for it."

Bay picked up the sniper rifle, resting it across her left shoulder. "I want to take my rifle back to my tent first."

Gabe picked up his Win Mag, also settling it on his shoulder. "Rock it out."

AT THE CHOW HALL, they sat opposite each other at the end of a long table. Air Force PJs, parajumpers who were CCTs, communication's experts, were a couple of seats down from where they ate. Gabe pointed out the CTTs often went out with a SEAL team on a direct action mission where they expected combat. These Air Force guys were experts at calling in close air support or B-52s to drop bombs on the enemy. It allowed SEALs to focus on what they did best. Not that they didn't have communications skills—they did—but the CCTs were considered the best the military had to offer.

"I'm finding I'm eating like a horse," Bay confided, shaking her head. Her tray was piled high with meat and carbs, just like Gabe's.

"You were active in Iraq," he said. "Did you eat like that over there?"

"No, but I was equally active."

"You're training, too," Gabe said with a grin, appreciating her confused look.

"I trained with the Army Special Forces, too." She shrugged. "Maybe it's because I'm not at sea level, but at eight thousand feet?"

"Altitude does extract a lot more energy out of you," he agreed, tasting the spaghetti sauce with his meatball. "Have you lost weight yet?" He couldn't tell one way or another with all the equipment and the loose-fitting cammies she wore.

"I think I have. I know I'm guzzling water like a camel. A lot more here than in Iraq."

Gabe swirled the pasta around his fork. "Extra water rations is something you always want to pack on a mission. We drink and eat constantly. Some guys carry Gatorade plus water. There's never such a thing as having too much of it when we're out there."

"No-brainer," Bay said. She hesitated and then decided to get personal with Gabe. Maybe it would help her understand why she was so drawn to him. "You know about my family background. What about yours? What was your childhood like, Gabe?"

His mouth pulled in at one corner. "The opposite of yours."

She heard the carefully closeted pain in his voice. "What do you mean?"

Ordinarily, Gabe never spoke about his growing-up years to anyone. The care and warmth in Bay's eyes and voice broke through that barrier. "I was an only kid," he quietly admitted, cutting up the two other large meatballs on his tray. "My father was a redneck." He glanced up to see her reaction. Gabe knew hill people preferred being called hill people, not hillbillies, rednecks or yokels, as the lowlanders often called them.

"Hill people?" Bay asked.

"No, he wasn't hill people. He grew up north of Butler, Pennsylvania, where I was born. Lots of hill people around, though, but I'm making a division here between them and being a redneck."

She finished the spaghetti and took a piece of toasted bread slathered with butter and garlic. "Where I come from, a redneck is sort of a step down from the codes of conduct hill people live by." She shrugged. "Sometimes they're very coarse. And rude. They're good ole boys and not necessarily responsible toward family or the greater circle of people in their community." She frowned. "Was your father like that?"

Gabe wiped his mouth with a napkin and laid it aside. "My father was an alcoholic, which didn't help things, Bay. From the time I could remember, my mom and he were always fighting. As a kid, I was scared he was going to hit her.

Bay's heart went out to him. She could imagine him as a young boy hearing the parents screaming at each other. "I'm so sorry...."

Gabe pushed the fork around in the spaghetti, losing some of his appetite. There was just something special about Bay that made him want to confide everything to her. Damn. Yet Gabe fought it because he didn't want her to see him differently than she did right now. He had her respect. And he didn't want to lose his reputation with her by talking about his sordid past.

"Your poor mother, Grace," she whispered. "How did she take it?"

"Not well. My father was a closet drinker because, I guess when he married her, she didn't know about it."

"Was he able to hold down a job?"

"No. He was a construction worker and lost his job because he was caught drinking. It was several months before he landed another job, but not having his paycheck really put us in the hole financially. My mother had to work twelve-hour shifts at the V.A. hospital to try and make up some of the difference."

"How old were you when this happened?"

"Six."

"And he was verbally abusive to her?"

Gabe grimaced. "Yes, but she wouldn't take it and

fought back. He was at home all day, babysitting me when I wasn't at school. He'd drink. By the time I got let off the bus, he was angry and stalking around the house, looking for a fight."

Bay cringed. "Sounds like a really bad drunk." She watched him nod and saw the darkness in the his eyes. "He took it out on you?"

"Yes."

Bay drew in a deep breath. "That's awful. Did your mother find out?"

"Finally. But it was years later."

"Why didn't you tell her?"

"Because my father threatened to beat me sense-less if I said anything to her. I'd already got a taste of his hand and fist, and I knew he'd make good on the threat."

Bay's heart crumpled with pain for Gabe. She sat there trying to digest all of it. "Yet he took you hunt-ing, taught you to track…."

"He liked escaping into the woods and getting back into nature. I think that was his Cherokee side. He was always happy when we were going to hunt in the woods on a weekend. We'd stay out for two days, camping, hunting or fishing. I really liked those times with him. He was happy out there and so was I. He never drank when he was out in the woods. Just at home and on the job."

He was a child torn in two by his father's dark moods, Bay thought. "You said the other day when you were ten years old, your father died?"

"Yeah, not a stellar year for me. Or for my mother. Or him." His mouth flattened, his appetite gone. Gabe put the tray aside and picked up his coffee cup, wrapping his large hands around it. Just the tender look Bay gave him pushed him to tell her the rest of the story. "Everything came to a head when I was ten. My father lost another job because he was found drinking at a power company that was being built nearby. My mother had the night shift at the hospital. I'd just come home from school. My father had been drinking all day and my mother woke up early and caught him with a bottle. Things escalated and my father lost his temper and slapped my mother. She called the cops and filed assault charges against him."

Gabe took a deep breath. "It was the cops who started asking me questions. I tried to lie, because I was afraid my father would kill me when he got out of jail. But my mother read me right. My father had taken his leather strap to me that morning. My mother had been asleep at the time. The one cop was very nice and I guess I trusted him over the fear of telling the truth. When my mother lifted up my T-shirt and saw the red welts across my back, she about lost it."

"Oh, God, Gabe, that's terrible. I didn't realize…" Bay reached out to touch his hands wrapped tightly around the mug. And then, when she realized what she was doing, she quickly pulled her hand back. Seeing the sorrow in his eyes, Bay felt badly for him. She had never meant to stir up this kind of sadness for him. "What happened next?" she asked, her voice soft.

"My father was taken to jail. Two days later, he got into a fight with some of the guys in jail and was killed." His voice went flat. "It shook us up. We never expected that. But my father had an uncontrollable temper and even though my Mom felt guilty about sending him to jail, I didn't. I felt relief, if you want to know the truth. I never told her how I felt and I think I should at some point. Maybe when I get rotated back to the States, we'll sit down over coffee and have a talk that's been a long time in coming. It was just too painful for me to talk about until recently."

"She thought that your father's dying took him out of your life?"

"Yeah," Gabe said, shaking his head. "She doesn't know to this day how many years my father made a punching bag out of me. If I tell her, she'll probably feel guilt. And I don't want to pile more on than what she's got already. I'm still not sure I'll do it or not." Stunned that he'd told her everything, Gabe looked at his watch. He was blathering like a fool and he needed to put a stop to it. "It's time to go."

Nodding, Bay gave him a strained smile and eased off the bench.

On the way back to the SEAL headquarters, the evening cooling rapidly, Bay walked at his side. Gabe had become withdrawn. "I feel badly for stirring up a hornet's nest for you," she admitted, catching his gaze. "I'm truly sorry, Gabe." Opening her hands, Bay added gently, "I guess my curiosity about you, what made you the man you are today, got the better of me. I sincerely did not mean to make you rehash all that suffering and pain." If they had been any place else, Bay would have thrown her arms around him and just held him. While Gabe told her the story, she could see the frightened ten-year-old little boy in the recesses of his eyes. Yes, holding was what Gabe needed. He still needed it, Bay realized.

Gabe slowed his pace. They were moving through tent city toward HQ. "In a way," he admitted, "it felt good to get it off my chest, Bay. I've never told anyone about it. Ever." He managed a one-cornered smile, absorbing her tender look. "You are definitely a doc. You know how to pull out the toxic infection a person carries. By getting it out in the open, maybe they can heal up then?"

How badly Bay wanted to stop and show him how much she cared. Gabe needed nurturing, tenderness and some long-overdue TLC. She could see the need in his expression, in the set of his mouth. Disappointment flowed through her over not being able to give him what he needed. At least not here. And probably never. "There's all kinds of infection, that's for sure," she whispered, regret in her tone. "I just never realized how terrible your growing-up years were."

She tilted her head and gazed deeply into his dark eyes. "And you're so kind and caring toward others, to me. I saw it at the village. You had candy in your cammie pockets and you were handing it out to all the kids. I saw you help that old Afghan man who was hobbling around on a crutch. He dropped his bag and you went over and picked it up for him. You're not your father's son, Gabe."

"I take after my mother's side, thank God."

"That's right, she's an R.N.," Bay murmured as they turned the corner. A number of other SEALs were trekking through the entrance into the planning room.

"I'm sure she is a healer. I'm sure she helped you after your father died?"

Gabe slowed his pace. "Yes, I became the total focus of her world after that. And looking back on it, it was the best thing that could have happened to me. She's a good person, Bay. I hope someday you get to meet Grace."

"Why?"

He smiled slightly and opened the door for her. "I think you'd see a mirror reflection of yourself in her. You're a lot alike."

"Another me?" She laughed. "Oh, Lordy!" Warmth stole through her as he really smiled at her for the first time, most of the suffering dissolving in his green eyes.

They made their way inside the mission planning room. She and Gabe took the last bench near the bulkhead or wall. The rest of the SEALs sat closer to Chief Hampton, who was standing at his whiteboard with eraser and colored pen in hand. The PowerPoint on the laptop sat on the planning desk and would be utilized later in the workup on the mission.

Gabe left plenty of room between them because he didn't want talk starting among the team. There were enough innuendos being hurled his way by Hammer and his group, accusing him of being Bay's full-time babysitter. What Hammer failed to understand was that his job entailed getting her trained to be of help on a mission, not a problem thrown into the mix.

Still, as Gabe sat listening to the mission briefing by Doug Hampton, another part of him, his heart, was feeling lighter. Maybe even happy. Bay had a helluva way with questions, he'd just discovered. It was as if she had all-terrain radar that could home in on the wound or infection inside a person, ask just the right questions to expose it and then help discharge it by being a good listener. She'd done that for him whether she realized it or not.

Giving her a sideward glance, Gabe saw her dutifully taking notes about the mission. Her lips were pursed, her brow knitted, intently writing in her notebook. What made her beautiful were those soft brown curls at her temples. He ached to tunnel his fingers through that silky, thick mass. It frustrated him that he found himself wanting Bay even more than before. What had their intimate talk unhinged in him? Gabe didn't know. But he had to get a handle on it damn quick.

CHAPTER NINE

BAY TIREDLY PULLED strands of her hair away from her face. She wove her way through the busy FOB, having served over at the medical dispensary for the first half of her day. Chief Hampton had told her word was getting around they had an 18 Delta combat medic among them. The Navy commander running the medical dispensary had asked for her assistance when two medevacs flew in carrying six American casualties on board. They didn't have enough personnel and a call went out to her for help. She had aided in saving three men's lives, working frantically with the other doctor and two nurses at the unit. The dispensary was badly understaffed in Bay's opinion.

The sun was beating overhead when she got back to her tent. There, she found a cardboard box sitting on her cot. Brightening, Bay knew it was from her mother, Poppy, and it contained those delicious cookies she'd baked. Her exhaustion dissolved as she unclipped the M-4 off her chest, cleared and safed it and set it in the corner. Then she sat down on the cot and opened the cardboard box.

"Hey, you in there?" Gabe called, sticking his head between the flaps.

"Yes, come on in." Bay hadn't seen him since the

briefing yesterday. Smiling, she held up a plastic bag. "Look! My mama sent me those incredible chocolate chip cookies I told you about."

Gabe stood at the opening. Grinning, he said, "Where have you been?"

"Working over at the dispensary. Didn't Chief Hampton tell you?"

"No, but that's all right. We're getting ready to set up for that sniper op tonight."

Opening one of the bags, Bay eased to her feet, walked across the plyboard floor and offered him some of the cookies. "You have to try these."

Inhaling the odor, Gabe smiled and reached into the bag. "They smell great. Thanks."

She saw he took only one. There were two dozen cookies in the bag. "Why not take more?"

"You know, the team might appreciate you sharing them." Gabe took a bite of the cookie. It melted in his mouth. "It would be a nice way to break some of the tension with Hammer and the other guys."

The idea wasn't lost on Bay. "Okay," she said, handing him two more. "How do I do it?"

Gabe had his mouth full of cookie. "When any of us get a package from home, we usually set it on the planning board desk at HQ. That way, as the guys drift in, they see it and can take what they want."

"What if they know it's from me?" she asked, worried as she walked over to the cot. She picked up her weapon, clipped it across her chest, grabbed her boonie hat and threw it on her head. As she took the box, Gabe opened one flap so she could step out. Bay felt that special connection that was always simmering between them.

"They won't care one way or another," he said. "They're animals and they like anything homemade."

Yesterday's discovery of his abusive young childhood had softened her toward Gabe even more. As tough and hard as he was, she'd never forget he'd been harmed by his own father. Bay was mystified why any parent would beat up his child. She wondered how it had played out in Gabe's life. Maybe that was why he was closed up tighter than Fort Knox. There was drive, far more than curiosity, pushing her to know him on a deeper personal level.

Stepping into HQ, Bay noticed most of the SEALs sitting on the benches talking with one another. The coffeepot was in here and she'd discovered that the guys, once they had cleaned their weapons, tended to migrate to the planning room. They all looked up in unison when she entered.

"What's in the box?" Hammer called.

She grinned. "My mama's world-famous chocolate chip cookies. Gabe said you guys share your boxes when they come in, so I'm sharing mine." Bay set it on the planning board and opened it up. Almost instantly, the other SEALs surrounded her, eyes on the prize.

"Chocolate chip?" Hammer said, leaning over her shoulder, peering into the box.

Bay smiled and pulled out the three plastic bags that had two dozen cookies each in them. "The best you ever tasted," she promised. She'd no more than set them at various points on the long table when the men's hands were diving into them, grabbing a many as they could.

Getting out of the way, Bay watched the seven SEALs stuff their faces with her mother's cookies. The looks of sheer pleasure, surprise and glee were written clearly across all their features. She stood near Gabe and watched.

"Hey," Gabe called, "leave some for the LTs and the chief or shit is gonna rain down on you animals."

Chuckling, Bay hid her smile behind her hand.

Hammer stood there, chewing and smiling. "First come, first served, bro. It always pays to be a winner. These are good, Doc. Thanks."

Bay felt relief as she stood there watching Hammer close his eyes and simply enjoy the cookie. Maybe… just maybe…they could move their tense relationship to a better place?

"Hey, what smells good?" Hampton called, coming out of his office, sniffing the air.

All the SEALs' heads popped up in unison and looked as the chief sauntered over to the planning table. All appeared guilty, each with at least half a dozen cookies or more in his hands.

Bay watched the unfolding drama. Hampton peered into the box.

"This is empty. What did you animals do with 'em?" he demanded, scowling at the team.

"Hey, first come, first served," Hammer mumbled, words barely distinguishable as he crammed the last of his cookies into his mouth. That way, the chief wasn't going to make a grab for it. Ownership was nine points of the law.

Hampton quickly perused the three emptied plastic bags lying on the table.

The SEALs all had their mouths full, beatific looks written across their faces.

Snorting, Hampton growled, "You bunch of animals. Didn't your mothers ever teach you to share?"

Bay chuckled. Gabe laughed. All the other SEALs just looked at Hampton, huge grins spread across their faces. Each man looked like a chipmunk, cheeks stuffed with cookies.

Throwing his hands on his hips, Hampton read the label on the box that said "cookies" on it. "Oh," he said, looking across the table at Bay, "this explains it."

"Gabe said to bring the box over and share with everyone, Chief," Bay said, unable to hide her smile any longer.

"Yeah, well, Griffin forgot to tell you these guys don't share."

Hammer lifted his hands, feigning surprise. "Hey, Chief, all's fair in love and war…and this is war. Or," he postulated, placing an index finger on his chin, "only winners win…losers lose.…"

Snorting again, the chief picked up one of the bags and inhaled the flavor of the cookies still in it. In the SEAL world, it always paid to be a winner. No one wanted to be the loser. "Damn, these smell good.…"

Wiping his hands on his thighs, Hammer grinned wickedly. "Best chocolate chip cookies I've ever had."

Hampton glared at him and threw the bag into the box. "Well, thanks for sharing, Hammer."

The SEAL gave him a wide-eyed innocent look.

The men snickered collectively, exchanging evil grins.

Gabe held up his hand, offering his last cookie to the Chief. "I've got one left, Chief."

Hampton's dark looks dissolved as he raised his head. "Yeah?"

"Yeah, I know how to share," Gabe said, smirking as he handed the cookie off to Hampton.

"Suck-up," Hammer called, grinning wickedly over at Gabe.

"Yeah," Gabe growled. "And what's it gonna get me? You out on that sniper op with me tonight? You'll be out there farting all over the place because you made a pig out of yourself eating a dozen of those cookies. The Taliban won't have any problem finding us, will they? They'll smell you a mile away."

Laughter erupted in the room. Bay rolled her eyes as the men started gabbing. Hampton laughed with them.

Bay placed her hand over her mouth. SEALs were just as coarse in their horseplay as the Special Forces teams were. Nothing changed between black ops teams, Bay realized. With the stresses on them continuous and severe, black humor was the natural fallback position to alleviate some of that pressure and threat of dying.

Hampton's eyes gleam with humor as he studied the team around the table. And then he turned and met Bay's laughter filled gaze.

"Damn good cookie, Doc. Your mother is one helluva cook. Tell her thank you."

"Anytime, Chief. Sorry you didn't get more."

"Did you get any?" Hampton asked, concerned.

"I'm taking the Fifth on that one, Chief."

"Uh-oh," Oz chirped up. He gave the guys a triumphant look. "You know what that means, don't you? That means Doc has a stash of those cookies in her tent."

Bay grinned. "Yes, and I've got them counted, Oz. And if any of them disappear, I know where to come to find the culprits."

The SEALs each feigned innocence, sporting their "Who? Me?" expressions.

Hampton said, "You'd better keep them on you, Doc. These guys are well known for filching goodies from everyone's boxes. They go into SEAL stealth mode into the tent and take 'em. You've been warned." He laughed, turned away and went back to his office.

As the team began to wander back toward the coffeepot, mugs in hand, Gabe watched the enjoyment on Bay's face. She was so open and readable. Whether she knew it or not, this was a great ice breaker between her and them. Teams shared everything. Especially a box coming from home. She'd shown her capacity to be a team member, even if they gobbled up most of her cookies like starved wolves.

"You up to some more rattle battle?" he asked Bay.

"Yeah," she grumped. "I suppose."

"Gotta get you to a point where it's muscle memory and automatic," he told her, turning and holding the door open for her. Calling over his shoulder, he asked for three volunteer SEALs to join them. One of them was Hammer.

BAY WORKED FOR an hour out on the range. She was sweating and dirty, and her hands slipped on the butt of the SIG as she ran up the hill toward the next target. The ground was rocky, uneven and filled with potholes here and there. Breathing hard, still acclimating to the altitude, she released the empty mag, leaped over a rut, slammed another mag into the pistol. Her palm was bruised, her fingers aching.

Hammer was there, waiting to count her shots into the target. There was a SEAL by each position. Bay knew they would convene after this last run and she'd get their experienced feedback. Would Hammer hassle her? Coming up to the target, breathing hard, she held out the pistol with both hands, placed her feet apart to give her some steadiness. She fired off fifteen shots and then turned and headed downhill toward the last one.

Gabe convened the other SEALs in the shade of one of the large targets as Bay approached. Her face was flushed, perspiration making her flesh gleam as she walked up and holstered her SIG. Like them, she had her boonie hat on and wore wraparound sunglasses on this bright, sunny day. She plopped down, grabbing a bottle of water he handed her.

Hammer crouched opposite of her. The other two SEALs, Sax, who was twenty-five and engaged to be married when he got off rotation and Shadow, a twenty-seven-year-old who was married, squatted with the group, notebooks in hand. Gabe joined them.

"Okay, how'd she do out there?" Gabe asked them.

Sax, who stood at the first target, said, "Twenty-five yards, ten in the red center and five out."

"Any comment about her stance or how she was holding the SIG?"

Sax shrugged and said, "It's learning to control your breathing." He gave Bay a slight smile. "You're better this time than last time, so you're improving, Doc."

Bay nodded. "That's good to hear. Thanks, Sax."

Gabe nodded toward Shadow.

"At fifty yards, eleven in the red center, four out. I have the same critique. It's about controlling your breathing." His brown eyes held Bay's. "I know you're still adjusting to this elevation. It was hell on all of us the first month. You're doing well."

"Hammer?"

He rubbed his chin. "If I hadn't seen it with my own eyes, I wouldn't have believed it." He held up his notebook. "Fifteen shots in the red circle at seventy-five yards. Not bad, Doc."

Bay felt as if she could have been knocked over by a feather with Hammer's assessment of her shooting skills. "Thanks, Hammer."

"You're obviously getting your breathing under control," Gabe told her. "You were improving at each station. And at the longer ranges you were putting more lead consistently into the center."

She wiped the sweat off her brow. "I think that comes from making long shots at squirrels back home."

The SEALs all regarded her with light and easy expressions, as if they were starting to like her. It made Bay feel good. She could feel the cohesiveness beginning to build between them. It took away her anxiety and worry of not fitting into the group.

"Was your father in the military?" Hammer asked, tucking his notebook away in his left cammie pocket.

Bay nodded. "He was in the Marine Corps for four years. A corporal."

Hammer frowned. "The way you shoot, I'd bet he was a Marine Corps sniper."

Bay wiped her mouth after slugging down more water from the plastic bottle. "Yes, he was."

Gabe allowed his surprise to show. "You never said anything about that to me."

"I didn't think to tell you," she said, giving him a wry look. And she hadn't. Looking around at the tight circle of SEALs, Bay figured out that she should have because the looks on their collective faces turned to sudden respect. She shrugged her shoulders. "I figured my shooting skills would speak for me. Why is important that you guys know that my pa was a sniper?"

Gabe shook his head, wiped the sweat off his temple. "It helps us understand why you're so damn good at shooting, Doc. That's why."

"Oh…" She finished drinking the last of the water and capping the emptied bottle. "Sorry. Where I come from, your reputation is based on how you live your life on an everyday basis. It doesn't matter what my mama or pa do. It matters how I conduct myself with others. What I do." She looked at each man's face. "Isn't that a better way to assess an individual?"

Gabe conceded she had a point. He was watching Hammer's face, the SEAL in deep thought about Bay's words. "You're right," Gabe admitted. "But among us, it helps us put you into perspective. And maybe, for some of the guys who were questioning whether you had the goods or not, knowing your father was a

Marine Corps sniper could have swayed them a little sooner into trusting you as a shooter."

Bay rubbed her gritty, damp face. "Y'all are right," she muttered with apology. "Where I come from we know people by their acts and actions. My pa can't give me his sniper talents. I have to earn the skills through training and hard work."

Hammer chuckled. "Yeah, that's basically true, Doc. But you got a mean eye for a target. You have your pa's genes in you. If I'd known what I know now, I'd never have bet that hundred bucks against you."

Feeling grateful that Hammer wasn't poking fun at her or being rude, Bay felt another level of anxiety dissolve. The red-haired SEAL was regarding her with newfound respect. "Squirrels are mighty hard to shoot," she said, smiling a little and sifting the dirt through her hand. "My pa taught me the basics of tracking, camouflage and shooting, but the rest was up to me." Her smile faded as she assessed the team. "You guys need to understand, we ate what we shot. If I couldn't hit what I was shooting at, there was no food for the table that night."

Hammer stood, pulling the boonie hat a little lower on his brow. "When you going to get her dialed in on CQD, Griffin?"

Gabe stood up. "When we get time."

"Well, I'd like to help train Doc in. I'm really good at close-quarters defense." He held up his meaty hands, calluses on the edges of each of them.

Bay stood with the rest of them. "CQD?" She turned and looked up at Gabe. "Hand-to-hand combat?"

He nodded, picking up his M-4. "Yeah, it's called

Close Quarter Defense, something you need to know. Did the Green Berets ever train you up on that?"

"No."

Hammer shook his head and muttered, "Sissies."

The rest of the SEALs chuckled and they all walked off together toward the camp.

Bay strolled at Gabe's side, watching her step and where she was going. The earth was chewed up badly because sometimes the Taliban would send mortars flying into the area in the dead of night. "Why do I need to learn that?" she demanded.

"In our business, we're often outnumbered. We can't get good ground asset intel of how many Taliban are in a given area. Sometimes we're searching through houses in a village and things turn bad. We try not to shoot and kill someone if we can take them down with our other methods. We call it controlled violence. If a woman, child or elderly person is in the room, but un-armed, we don't shoot. We're looking for the bad guy with a weapon. Them, we will shoot."

Bay grimaced. "Am I going to be clearing rooms?"

"You will, in time," Hammer said. "Not right now, because you don't know our methods or how we work as a team when we do it."

"I think I'd like to just be a medic."

Hammer snickered and looked back at her. "Doc, you're on the front lines with SEALs. There is no safe place. You need to know how we operate so you don't get shot in the process. We can't protect you out there if we're doing a house-to-house search for an HVT. We want you alive, not dead."

Grinning, Bay said, "Hammer, the only reason

you're concerned is that you wouldn't get any more cookies that my mama made."

The team erupted into good-natured laughter. A new sense of camaraderie was born.

CHAPTER TEN

"BE CAREFUL OUT there tonight?" Bay asked Gabe as he got ready to board the Night Stalker piloted MH-47 Chinook helicopter winding up on the apron at Ops. It was already dark and the sniper op with Hammer had been given authorization. The chief felt Bay needed more time to acclimate to the platoon before being thrown into a sniper mission. She knew the two SEALs would be dropped below a ridge far above the village where the three new Taliban rat lines had been discovered. The villagers didn't want the Taliban in their valley; all they wanted was to be left in peace to farm and survive.

Gabe heard the worry in her tone as he straightened from tightening the knife sheath containing a SOF knight on his left thigh. They stood just outside Ops, waiting for the crew chief of the Night Stalker helo to give them the signal to board. There were no lights and he couldn't see as well as he could hear her tone. "We'll be okay."

Tucking her lower lip between her teeth, Bay suddenly felt anxiety. She knew Gabe was a good sniper and had four deployments under his belt. She worried about Hammer, too, who was running to make the helo, having gotten delayed by the Chief Hampton back at

HQ. The smell of aviation kerosene fuel was in the air as the MH-47 spooled up. Reaching out, she gripped his left arm. "Just be safe, Gabe. Okay?"

Gabe gazed down into her deeply shadowed face, her eyes fraught with fear. His arm tingled where her fingers touched the material of his cammie sleeve. When she removed her hand from his sleeve, Gabe felt as if he'd lost something special. Unquantifiable.

He sought and found her fingers, squeezing them. "You worry too much. It could be a quiet night out there. We never know...."

BAY SAT IN Chief Hampton's office with him, listening to the radio chatter. It was 0200 and she was fighting dropping off to sleep, her head resting on her arms at the corner of his desk.

"Why don't you go hit the sack?" Hampton said to her.

Rousing herself, Bay pushed strands of hair off her face. "If I'm going to be doing this work, I want to understand how you guys operate."

Hampton pulled over another report to read it. "Okay, but you're going with us tomorrow morning to that village. I'd like you sharp, Doc."

Bay sighed. She didn't want to tell the chief that she was personally worried for Gabe's safety. That comment had no place here. Rubbing her hands on the thigh of her cammies, she pushed the chair back. "Okay..."

"Blue Bird Main, this is Blue Bird Actual. Over."

Bay stopped breathing for a moment as Gabe's low voice came over the radio.

Hampton answered, "Blue Bird Actual, this is Blue Bird Main. Over."

"Two tangos coming down the northeast rat line carrying sacks. Probably fertilizer. Am I authorized to take them out? Over."

Bay released a breath as Hampton's face went expressionless. Her fingers curved into her palms. Two Taliban had been spotted coming down the rat line. If they were carrying large bags, it was usually fertilizer, which was used to create IEDs. Her heart began a slow pound.

"Blue Bird Actual, can you wait to see if there's anyone else coming down that trail? Over."

"Roger, Blue Bird Main. They have half a mile before they reach the bottom and are in the valley. Over."

"Blue bird Main, let's wait and see."

"Roger."

Hampton scowled and put the radio down on his desk.

"Do you suspect others?" Bay asked.

He rubbed his face. "Usually, when the Taliban is bringing in loads of fertilizer, there's a group of them. Not just two. And usually it's on a caravan of camels or donkeys. Sometimes on the backs of men instead. Just depends."

"So you're wanting Gabe and Hammer to wait and see?"

"Yeah. Because if there's more coming over that ridge, they're all armed. If Gabe and Hammer shoot those two, it can create a hornet's nest with the ones they don't see. We have no idea of what kind of force is out there and what they might be up against."

He picked up another radio and called for a Predator Drone to be sent to the GPS coordinates where the two snipers were in their hide, concealed from the enemy's view.

Bay heard the CIA guy on the other end who handled the drones out of Camp Bravo. One would be sent on station in thirty minutes. The crew was outfitting it with missiles right now. There was worry in the chief's eyes as he ended the transmission.

"What does that mean?"

"It means—" Hampton sighed "—that the drone isn't going to be on station soon enough to be eyes in the sky to help us out. I want to know if the rest of this Taliban group is on the other side of the mountain. If Gabe fires, they'll spot the muzzle flash."

"And that's not good," she whispered, her heart beating harder. "How close to that path are they?"

"A thousand yards," Hampton muttered.

Just then, LT Paul Brafford popped into the office. Brafford was barely six feet tall, black hair and blue eyes. He was married with three children, Bay had found out the other day. Brafford carried photos of his three kids and his wife in the upper Velcro pocket of his Kevlar vest. She was touched to hear that.

Bay stood to give the officer the chair, hoping he'd let her stay.

The LT gestured to the chair. "Keep sitting, Doc. I can hear standing up." He smiled a little.

"Thank you, sir." Bay sat down, the officer next to the desk, arms against his chest, talking with Hampton.

"We got close air support nearby, Doug?"

Hampton nodded. "Yeah, we have a B-52 circling on a racetrack at thirty thousand feet."

"Okay, call it in and tell it to stay on the racetrack. If we can't have a drone on station, they've got to have some kind of protection if the rest of the Taliban force is on the other side of the mountain."

Some relief flowed through Bay. A racetrack was a term used to mean a bomber or fighter jet was loitering in an oval flight pattern at high altitude above the area in question. That way, they were quick enough to respond with rockets, bombs or missiles if the SEALs were threatened.

The B-52 pilot came up on transmission and Brafford spoke directly to the pilot, apprising him of the situation. Were there more Taliban coming over that ridge? Bay tried to sit quietly and not show any emotion. Right now the two SEALs were speaking in low tones, as if nothing were out of place; as if they did this all the time. It was routine.

"Blue Bird Main, this is Blue Bird Actual. We've spotted ten more Taliban on the upper portion of the path. Over."

It was hard for Bay to breathe. Gabe and Hammer were three thousand feet away from this heavily armed group of Taliban! Even though they were well hidden, if things went south, the whole mission could erupt into one hell of a firefight. She glanced up at LT, who was scowling. Brafford took the radio from Chief Hampton.

"Blue Bird Actual, this is Blue Bird Main. How close to the valley floor are the first two? Over."

"They've got about five hundred feet until they reach the valley. Over."

Brafford pulled over the satellite map that had the three newly discovered rat lines outlined in red. "You're situated above the path closest to the most southern village? Over?"

"Roger."

Hampton shook his head. "That's not good. What if those guys get too close to that village?"

Brafford nodded, his expression deeply pensive. "Make a call to the Apaches over at the Black Jaguar Squadron. Get two of them out there pronto. I don't want to drop five-hundred-pound JDAMs on that group. It's just too close to the village. It will scare the hell out of everyone, and that's not want we want if it can be avoided."

Bay knew the village was pro-American. She understood the LT's wise decision. Apaches could go in and perform microsurgery, take out the bad guys and not cause havoc or destruction to the friendly village. The people would be banged out of their sleep, for sure. And probably badly scared, but .50-caliber bullets instead of five-hundred-pound bombs going off this close to their homes were a better choice. Plus, it would keep the two snipers from danger close drops of bombs, if they had been were used. And Bay knew from experience that many men were killed by "friendly fire."

Brafford got on the radio to Gabe and gave them orders to remain where they were, be eyes on the ground and follow the movement of the Taliban and not to engage the enemy at this point. They had range-finding Night Force scopes that could see through the dark and GPS so that the intel could be fed directly to the Apache helo's avionics that would be coming on station shortly. It was a quick ten-minute flight across a mountain ridge to that valley. Bay drew in a slow breath, glad that Brafford wasn't going to have them engage the large force of Taliban. It would be two against twelve.

"Blue Bird Main, this is Blue Bird Actual. We've now got twenty Taliban coming down that path. All carrying heavy loads. Got three donkeys loaded with sacks. Probably all fertilizer. Over."

"Roger, Blue Bird Actual. Apaches on the way. Switch comms so we can hear you talking them into the target. Over."

"Roger, Blue Bird Main. Switching over now...."

Bay remained glued to the chair, barely breathing, for the next half hour. The snipers had coordinated the entire dance between the Apaches and the Taliban. She sat riveted as the women pilots from Black Jaguar Squadron came online, speaking directly to Gabe. Their transmissions were short and to the point.

As soon as the Apaches arrived, they had thermal avionics capability to spot human body heat down on the ridge below. In a matter of minutes, the Apaches moved in like a wolf pack and destroyed the line of Taliban strung along the rat line. Even more surprising, Bay heard the one pilot report fifteen more Taliban coming up on the opposite ridge slope. All told, thirty men were using the path. If Gabe had fired that one shot at the first two leaders, there were twenty-eight other Taliban who probably would have dropped their bags, pulled out their AK-47s and gone out to hunt those two SEALs down and try to kill them.

Wiping his mouth, Brafford said, "Good night's

work, Doug. Get the Night Stalker in there to pick them up."

Hampton nodded. "Yes, sir."

GABE WAS WALKING through Ops, carrying his sniper rifle over his left shoulder when he saw Bay walk in. It was 0340 and his heart unexpectedly opened. There was a serious look on her face. Hammer was at his side.

"Hey," Hammer called, "by any chance are you meeting us to give us some more of your mother's cookies?" He grinned widely.

Bay laughed and shook her head. "Nah, but I wanted to meet you guys and see if you were okay." She saw the heated look Gabe gave her. Instantly, she felt a deep relief within her. Both SEALs had green-and-black face paint on so that they would blend seamlessly into the night around them. She walked out of OPs with them into the freezing night air, hands stuck in the pockets of her winter jacket.

"What did you think?" Gabe asked as they walked toward the SEAL compound.

"Riveting. Scary as hell," she admitted. "Did you guys know there was that many Taliban coming up the opposite ridge?"

"No," Gabe admitted.

"Not good odds," she muttered.

Hammer said, "The LT and Chief aren't going to throw us under a bus out there, Doc. We know when the Taliban are bringing in fertilizer to restock their bomb makers in this country, they usually pack it in on camels or donkeys. Sometimes, like tonight, human pack animals bring it in."

"You were the eyes out there on the situation," she agreed.

"Helluva light show. Those Apaches whaled the tar out of those guys," Hammer said, impressed.

"We'll be going back out at dawn," Gabe warned her, glancing down at her. Bay was somber, her lower lip thinned. "I'm sure the whole squad will go out." He looked over at Bay. "It's called a sensitive site exploitation, a fancy description for the fact that we're going to search every body to try to find identification, maps or any other intel they might have been carrying on them."

"Gruesome work," Bay said, not excited at all about the prospect.

"You ever done it?"

She shook her head. "No."

"I'd eat a light breakfast, then, tomorrow morning," Gabe advised.

Bay remained with the two SEALs through the entire debriefing process after they returned. She saw how tired they were, but they had to file individual reports, write them up out in the planning room and give them to Hampton, who read them and asked more questions. By the time they were done, dawn was crawling up on the horizon. Hampton was busy getting the entire squad ready to fly out at first light on a CH-47 Chinook.

Gabe walked with her over to the chow hall. He was starving. She seemed pensive. "You okay?"

"Yes. It was tough to be in the chief's office listening to you."

He snorted softly as they entered the chow hall, the line already getting long for those wanting breakfast.

"Hammer and I weren't exactly thrilled with the prospects of JDAMs being dropped dangerously close to us if the LT decided to use the B-52. I'm glad he opted for the Apaches instead. They're hell on wheels."

Bay picked up a tray and handed him one. The odors of breakfast made her mouth water. Yet she remembered Gabe's warning. "I'm just glad you two were all right."

He saw some of the usual glimmer she had in her blue eyes returning. "You're a worrywart, you know that?" He smiled down at her. Her cheeks flushed pink. Gabe might not be able to do anything other than appreciate her as a woman right now, but this still fed him and he felt his heart opening powerfully toward her.

Bay thanked the cook behind the counter who ladled some biscuits, gravy and grits onto her tray. Hampton had warned her they would be out on that ridge all day. They quickly passed through the line and found a table where the rest of the SEAL team was chowing down.

As she and Gabe took the last two chairs opposite each other at the table, Bay felt relief. Deep relief. It bothered her that she was becoming emotionally involved with Gabe. Hadn't she learned her lesson in Iraq? She'd fallen in love with Jack Scoville, another medic, over a nine-month period. And she'd resisted him, too. But to no end.

As she ate, Bay told herself she couldn't lose another man she loved to war. Her heart simply couldn't take the trauma. Yet, as she glanced over at Gabe, his face now free of the dark green, gray and black face paint, his five-day growth of beard on his face, her heart contracted painfully with need of him.

Bay tried to find something to dislike about Gabe. It was impossible. The SEAL team looked to him for experience, and even though he wasn't the official LPO, he was, in fact, the squad LPO whether he wanted the duty or not. He was a good leader, solid, steady and he never lost his temper. Sighing inwardly, Bay knew she had to sever the connection between her and Gabe. It just wouldn't work. It couldn't.

Gabe moved his emptied tray aside and picked up his cup of coffee. Bay's face was serious looking, and she wasn't saying much of anything. Had the night spent in the chief's office, listening to what really went on in a sniper op, sobered her on their type of missions? He wasn't sure. And he'd have to find out sooner or later, because he knew the LT wanted her as his backup partner. And with the other SEALs sitting with them, he couldn't open up a private conversation with her. Frowning, he sipped his coffee, feeling tiredness work its way through his aching joints. In another hour, they'd be up on that ridge at nine thousand feet again, rummaging through dead, torn bodies, trying to find intel that could save others from dying.

The team was in ready mode; Gabe could feel it. They were scarfing up food, tanking up, knowing they would be freezing their asses off all day long on that rocky ridge. He and Hammer would probably be sent out as lookouts, just in case. Taliban rarely moved in daylight. Like the SEALs, they used the night to their advantage. The night was their friend, but thanks to Apache thermal avionics to detect body heat and drone eyes, the enemy no longer would remain hidden in the night.

Worried, Gabe saw Bay's face close and he could no longer read her as he usually could. He recognized it as a game face. Everyone in combat put one on when the chips were down, hiding their emotions in order to do the work demanded of them. The other SEALs were talking. She ate in silence. Bay was usually engaged with the squad. *Not now.*

So, what had changed? Gabe wondered. Was Bay upset? Not wanting to take part in the work up on the ridge? Gabe knew medics usually had a more peaceful outlook on life, saving lives, not taking them. Saying nothing, he would observe her through the day's morbid activities and just see where she was. His heart, if he allowed it into the equation, clamored that she needed to be held. But then, he scoffed at his own projection on her. Bay had combat experience under her belt, that was clear. She didn't need handholding.

Sipping the last of his coffee, he called, "Ready to exfil?"

She nodded. "Yes."

Outside as they walked toward the SEAL compound, and they were alone, Gabe slowed his pace. "Something's bothering you, Bay. What is it?"

"Nothing," she assured him. It was something, but she couldn't tell him. She didn't dare.

"Last night," he murmured, keeping his voice low, "at the Operations Building, you touched my sleeve. You were worried."

Grimacing, Bay said, "I shouldn't have done that, Gabe. I'm sorry. I was out of line." And she hotly remembered him finding her fingers, squeezing them with his roughened hand. She had felt her heart wrench with fear and she'd wanted to throw her arms around him, kiss him and try to protect him.

"You cared and I appreciated that."

Pushing the boonie hat back on her head, she turned in the middle of the dirt path between the tents. "Look, Gabe," she whispered, emotion making her voice husky, "I fell in love with a medic over in Iraq." Bay heard her voice quiver, desperation thrumming through her. "I didn't want to. It just happened. Jack Scoville was an 18 Delta corpsman like me. I fought loving this guy for nine months." She met his darkening gaze, her voice shaking with the memories. "I learned *not* to mix my personal feelings with anyone after that. Jack died in my arms during a firefight. I couldn't save him...." She touched her brow, feeling the sadness and pain rise in her.

Taking a step back from the SEAL, Bay forced herself to hold his gaze that burned with unknown reactions. "We are at war. Love has no place here, Gabe. None. I learned that the hard way." Her mouth contorted and she felt herself unraveling within her heart because Gabe was a hero in her eyes. He was all the things she'd ever wanted in a man. Someone she could easily love. And yet it was the wrong time, wrong place. Opening her hands, her voice lowering with anguish, Bay whispered, "I can't take a loss like that again, Gabe. I just can't.... I hope you can understand."

Grimly, he nodded. His hand tightened on the M-4 in the sling. "Okay, I hear you. Don't worry. Whatever happened last night, outside Ops, is the end of it." The raw suffering on Bay's face tore him up. His mind spun with the information. The man she'd fallen in love with died in her arms in Iraq. That was a hell of thing to happen to Bay.

"I had a very good friend of mine die in my arms, too, Bay." Gabe felt very old and tired in that moment. "I understand, somewhat, what you're going through. I couldn't save him no matter what I did. I'm sorry for your loss. I really am." He checked the urge to reach out and touch her pale cheek, her eyes wounded with grief. He hadn't helped the situation last night by holding her hand in that moment, either.

Understanding she was drawn to him, that she had already lost someone she loved on the battlefield, Gabe felt a deep sadness overwhelm him. Until that moment, he didn't realize just how much he was wanting Bay on a personal level. Wanting her in every imaginable way. Swallowing hard, he forced his voice to sound normal.

"Come on, time to saddle up. We have a job to do."

Relief drenched Bay as she saw him change. Gabe understood. It was bittersweet. Pushing back tears that wanted to fall, Bay rallied. "Okay," she whispered, gathering her strewn emotions, "let's rock it out."

CHAPTER ELEVEN

"Doc, if you find anyone alive, you render aid to them and let me know," Chief Hampton told her as they left the area of the CH-47 that had dropped them on the eastern side of the ridge with half the platoon. "ROE, rules of engagement, say we must aid anyone we find, enemy or not."

"Yes, Chief," Bay said. Gabe was at her side. Hampton had sent Hammer with a sniper rifle to higher ground to be the eyes and ears to protect all of them. On missions where dead Taliban would be searched for intel, a sniper always watched through his Night Force scope for any movement. If there was, he alerted the team on the ground because they could be shot. She felt tension running through her as they stood on the rat line trail.

Gabe could see and feel Bay's reaction to the human carnage caused by the Apaches hours before in the darkness. Most of the Taliban carrying the sacks of fertilizer were on this side of the mountain. Bay gulped. Bodies were scattered and strewn everywhere. It was grisly work. He saw Chief Hampton give the signal to start the search.

Bay had mixed feelings about it, but she reminded herself these men were bringing over fertilizer from the plants in Pakistan to create IEDs that would kill American men and women in Afghanistan. Mouth tight, she walked down the trail, Gabe in the lead. The wind was cold and sharp, below freezing. The sun had just crested the highest peaks to the east of them. Like the rest of the SEALs, she wore winter gear, a dark blue knit cap on her head, a radio headband with a microphone near her lips. They were all in touch with one another.

"Who are those two guys?" she asked Gabe, coming up and walking on the path with him.

"Spooks, CIA agents," he said. And then he grinned and said, "Christians in Action, a real righteous group. They're here to take home the intel we find on the bodies."

"They stand out like sore thumbs. I've never worked with CIA dudes before."

He smiled a little, his M-4, muzzle up, the butt resting on his hip, prepared in case Hammer saw some movement. "The redheaded dude is in charge. He's a field agent by the name of Curtis Granger."

"I don't like him. It's just a feeling." Bay was looking around. So far, her medical skills weren't needed. Hampton had ordered them down to the end of the trail, a good thousand feet below. They were to start there and work their way back up. Another group of SEALs were at the top, working their way down. They'd meet somewhere in the middle.

"Granger's good at getting the drones up," Gabe said, swiveling his head from right to left, watching for movement of any kind. "He's rough on prisoners, though. Not my kind of guy."

Bay slid him a glance. "What? He doesn't follow the Geneva Convention when it comes to taking a prisoner?" Right now she was seeing Gabe alert and on guard. Even on the rocky path, she couldn't hear his boots coming down on the gravel. He walked like a boneless cougar, his gloved hands on his M-4, ready to fire at a moment's notice. She, too, had her M-4 up but was devoting her time to seeing if anyone was left alive.

"Yeah, you could say that. I don't like the guy's methods. He thinks waterboarding is the first thing you do to squeeze intel out of a prisoner."

Waterboarding was torture, pure and simple, in Bay's mind. She wrinkled her nose, which was going numb in the air. Their breath was nothing but white vapor every time they spoke. She tried to keep her heart out of the mix as they searched. This morning, just as he'd promised, Gabe kept his poker face. No longer could she read his expression as she had done before. It shook her how swiftly their budding relationship had occurred. Never again could she fall in love with a man in the military. *Never.*

"Gabe?"

Gabe halted, hearing Hammer's voice. "Yeah?"

"Got some movement at three o'clock. There's a bunch of bushes on your right, about fifty feet down in that wadi. Something's in there. Check it out? I'll keep a bead on it."

"Roger, out."

Bay's heartbeat took off. Everyone had heard the transmission, including the two CIA types who had trotted down the trail to begin searches at the other end with them. She quickly looked down at the thickets in a small wadi.

"Do you see anything?" she asked, her voice a whisper.

"No. Follow me…." He unsafed his M-4 and moved slowly down the slope toward the wadi, rifle aimed.

Bay felt fear move through her. She couldn't walk quietly as he did. His total focus was on the brush that was about six feet high and twenty feet wide. He gave her a hand signal to go around the brush, on the other side of it. Nodding, she went that way, M-4 ready, the butt tight against her shoulder as she moved to keep up with him. The closer they got to the wadi, the faster her heart thudded in her chest. She was scared, but she didn't let that interfere. Gabe was her partner and he needed protection by her.

Bay reached the south side of the brush and rounded it, weapon aimed, finger on the trigger. Gabe came around, his position the same. Her eyes widened. Jerking to a halt, she lowered her weapon. There in the wadi was a young girl, perhaps thirteen or fourteen years old, with a young man, perhaps a bit older than herself. The girl had long black hair, the most startling green eyes Bay had ever seen. Her face was dirty, bloodied, tear tracks down her drawn face. She was holding the boy in her arms, rocking him and softly sobbing.

Gabe quickly moved in.

"Talk to her," he ordered Bay.

Bay didn't see any weapons on the girl. the clothes she wore were men's. "Don't move," she called to the girl in Pashto.

The girl's eyes widened.

"Help me! Help me! My brother is dying! Have mercy upon us. Help him!" She sobbed, rocking her brother.

Bay reached them as Gabe stood guard. "Do you have any weapons?" she demanded.

"N-no…please, help us!" Her mouth contorted in a cry as she touched her brother's bloodied face with her shaking fingers.

"Search her," Gabe ordered.

Bay clipped her M-4. "Stand up. I need to make sure you aren't carrying weapons."

The girl sobbed and gently placed her unmoving brother, dressed similarly to her, on the rocks. Standing, she stared fearfully up at her. Bay had performed hundreds of searches on women in Iraq. Very quickly, she moved her hands around the girl's thin body. Trying to ignore the shock in her eyes, the tears smearing the dirt across her cheekbones, she completed the search.

"Clear," she told Gabe.

"Okay, check him out."

"Roger."

Bay told the girl to stand where she was. Very quickly, as she felt for weapons on the boy, who was probably in his late teens, she saw he was dead, his face grayish looking. "Clear. This kid is dead," she muttered.

"Okay, get the girl to sit down, render her first aid if she needs it. If she does, she's your patient and you're in charge of her."

Bay smiled a little and held out her hand. "My name is Bay. What is yours?"

The girl sniffed, her gaze never leaving her brother

who lay unmoving on the rocks. "I—I am Asifa." She pointed down. "That is my brother, Raouf."

"Good to know." She curved her fingers. "Come here. I want you to sit down. You're hurt."

Asifa was wearing men's clothes, but Bay couldn't understand how the young girl had managed to survive the carnage. Further, she wore sandals made of tires, which had been cut up, on her small, dainty feet. She had no socks, no jacket. The girl's teeth were chattering, her arms wrapped around herself. Bay quickly shrugged out of her medical ruck, laid it on the ground and opened it up. Asifa came and meekly sat down in front of her, her knees drawn up, arms around them, shivering.

Gabe came and stood nearby, watchful as Bay went to work. He sent the info back to the chief about their discovery. Bay carefully felt Asifa's head, moved her hands knowingly down her neck to her shoulders, seeking signs of injury. Asifa sat there, head bowed, trembling, tears falling from her eyes as she continued to stare over at her brother.

"Are you hurt anywhere?" Bay asked, catching Asifa's tear-filled eyes. She was filthy, blood everywhere.

"I—I don't know. It was terrible. The noise. The screams…" She took her hand, which was shaking badly, and tried to wipe the tears from her face. All she managed to do was smear them into mud, mixed with blood.

Moving quickly, Bay stood up, took off her warm down coat. "Here, put this on. You're going hypothermic." She helped Asifa pull on the coat. As she felt along the girl's torso, Asifa flinched. She tried not to cry out.

"Hurt?"

"Y-yes. Last night." She gulped. "The helicopters came. My beloved brother was near an explosion. He was thrown into me and we were both knocked off the path into this wadi." She pointed above to the path. "I—I grabbed him because he cried out." Sniffing, she whispered, "We landed here. I was so frightened. All I could do was hold Raouf and pray to Allah...."

Moving her hand gently, Bay said, "I'm sorry. Your brother is dead. There's nothing I can do to help him, Asifa." The girl's face wrinkled up, her wide mouth opening in a silent scream. Moving her hand over the girl's dirt-encrusted, uncombed hair, Bay whispered, "I'm so sorry...."

Gabe swallowed hard as he watched Bay work with the injured girl. Her long, spare hands were incredibly gentle, supportive. Asifa responded in a positive, trusting way toward her. Bay listened to her heart and lungs with the stethoscope and took her pulse. There was worry in her eyes. Bay finished her examination and looked up toward him.

"I need a CASEVAC called, Gabe. She's got at least four fractured ribs. I'm worried she has a punctured lung, which makes her CASEVAC status."

"Roger, will call," he told her, switching channels to the chief, who would decide whether to make the request or not.

"I—I'm so cold," Asifa chattered.

Bay nodded. "I know you are." The girl's bare feet and lower legs were grayish-blue looking. She had another pair of socks in her pack. Getting them out, Bay helped pull them over Asifa's feet. "There, that should help." She got out her canteen and handed it to her. "You need to drink as much as you can."

Grateful, Asifa took it in her shaking hands, gulping down the water, nearly emptying the canteen.

Bay said nothing, her mouth grim. Asifa was near starvation. She could feel every rib protruding from the girl's body. Her cheeks were high, but sunken, indicating starvation. Her brother didn't look very healthy, either. He, too, was very thin.

"Thank you," Asifa whispered, handing the canteen back to Bay.

"Why were you here, Asifa?" she asked, placing the canteen back on her web belt.

Sniffing, she whispered unsteadily, "Our parents are starving to death in a U.N. camp in Pakistan. We were told that if we would carry a load across the Khyber Pass, we would be paid well. Raouf persuaded me to come. He said we could earn twice as much." She sobbed, her hands against her mouth. "I—I wanted to help. I love him so much. He's my only brother who is left. The other two younger ones have already died because there was no food to feed them. Now…" she wept, "Raouf is dead!"

Bay slid her arm around her thin shoulders. Asifa leaned against her, her bloody hand gripping her Kevlar vest, hiding her face against it, weeping because she'd lost everything in her world. Bay held her carefully, watching and hoping one of those broken ribs would not puncture her lung. Her breathing was shallow and she couldn't cry without wincing from the pain.

Bay heard a commotion above her and twisted a look toward Gabe. The two CIA guys were sliding down, in a hurry to reach them. Automatically, Bay became protective. The red-haired guy with blue eyes, Granger, reached them first.

"A Taliban girl," he said, surprised. And then his face changed and became hard. He walked around Bay and reached out to grab at the jacket Bay had put on Asifa.

"Stop!" Bay growled, grabbing his wrist. She glared up at Granger. "She's badly injured. Don't touch her. We've got a medevac coming in to take her to Camp Bravo." The man's face went icy.

"You have no authority here, doll face," he said, jerking his wrist out of her fingers. "She's ours now."

"Like hell she is," Bay said, holding his glare. "I'm the medic. I'm in charge here, not you."

The second CIA guy, blond hair and hazel eyes, shorter than Granger, came around and stared at his boss and then at Bay. "Hey, let's take her and get the hell out of her. It's ass-freezing cold up here on this ridge," he grumbled.

"You're not taking this girl anywhere," Bay told him. She felt Asifa stiffen in her arms, her eyes growing huge as the two large men hunkered threateningly over them.

Granger snarled, "She's *ours,* doll. Now remove your arms and stand aside. We're taking her for interrogation. She's the only one left alive in this group, and we need to know what she knows."

Bay stood, moving in front of Asifa, her hand closing over the butt of the SIG. "That's not going to happen. She's *my* patient. And until I release her to a doctor at Camp Bravo, you're not going to do anything. She's got life-threatening injuries." Bay saw Granger get angry, his hands ball into fists.

Gabe came around to shield Asifa. "Okay, Granger, stand down. A medevac's on its way and you can wait until the doc at Bravo approves of you interrogating her."

Granger gave him a hard look. "Griffin? Right?"

Gabe smiled a little. "Want me to spell it for you?" He knew what Granger was implying. He'd remember his last name and the next time he was on a patrol and needed a drone, it would somehow, inconveniently, be slowed down in coming on station to help them. That's how people like Granger got even when someone pushed into their little fiefdom.

Bay felt the tension grow. She heard Asifa sniffing, fear in her eyes. Her disgust over Granger's behavior made Bay angry. Gabe was calm and collected, standing near her shoulder, relaxed.

"She's Taliban, dammit!" Granger suddenly shouted. He made a move to pass between them to grab the girl.

In one swift movement, Gabe lifted his M-4 and poked the barrel into Granger's chest. The CIA agent made a grunting sound, knocked backward, nearly losing his balance. He instantly grabbed at his sternum beneath the Kevlar vest he wore.

"She's Doc's patient," Gabe said quietly. "Now respect it."

Cursing, the CIA agent snarled, "You're in trouble, Griffin. *Big-time*."

Shrugging, Gabe glanced over his shoulder. He

could hear the medevac coming in. He looked over at Bay.

"Is she ambulatory?"

"Yes," she breathed softly, moving behind him to gently bring Asifa to her feet.

Gabe watched the CIA agents back off. Granger's face was crimson and it made his freckles stand out even more. Gabe turned without a word, placed his arm around the girl's waist opposite Bay and helped her slowly up the rocky slope to the path.

The medevac landed below the ridge, and as Bay helped the girl climb into the helo, she felt Gabe's hand on her shoulder. The blades were whirling nearly at takeoff speed, the wind buffeting them. She turned, looking into his eyes.

"Go with her. Make sure she gets put into the dispensary system, and stay with her. Don't let her out of your sight, because Granger will try and grab her. Chief Hampton is calling it all in right now. When we get done here, I'll come over to get you and see how she's doing."

Giving him a tight smile of thanks, Bay nodded. The air crew chief held out his hand to her and hauled her into the medevac. The door closed. Bay focused on Asifa, who was lain down on the litter, the other medic covering her with a number of blankets to keep her warm. Bay hooked into the inter cabin system and gave the other two medics Asifa's medical condition.

The gravity pushed them downward as the medevac quickly lifted straight up and then banked, moving rapidly down across the slope, quickly gaining altitude.

The shaking and shuddering felt calming to Bay as she placed an IV in Asifa's left arm after cleaning it off.

She could tell how scared the girl was. She'd never ridden in a helo before. The other two men were strangers and in Asifa's culture, men did not touch her; it was forbidden. Bay took over any tasks that were needed because she was a woman and Asifa would be more trusting of her and less frightened.

Within ten minutes, they were landing at the dispensary in the center of Camp Bravo. Two orderlies and a gurney were brought up and Asifa, under many blankets, was gently transferred to it. Bay hopped out, her medical ruck slung over her right shoulder, the M-4 across her chest. She kept a hand on Asifa's blanketed arm, the blades whipping gusts of wind around them. She was glad she had the knit cap on her hair or it would have flown all over her face.

Moving through the doors and into the dispensary, Bay saw a woman doctor approach, a U.S. Navy lieutenant commander. As they wheeled Asifa into one of the curtain cubicles, Bay gave her all the information.

"Commander Johnson? This woman is to be treated as a prisoner," Bay told her. "The CIA wants to talk to her."

Johnson, who wore a white lab coat, in her forties, smiled kindly over at Asifa, who was looking around, frightened. "This girl was found out there from last night's attack?" she demanded.

"Yes, ma'am," Bay said, remaining at Asifa's side. "I have orders from my chief to stay with this woman. I speak Pashto, and I can help translate."

"Good to know," Dr. Johnson murmured. "I speak

enough to get into trouble. So Granger is out there snooping around? Causing trouble as usual?"

"Yes, ma'am."

The woman's face grew grim. She moved the flashlight beam across Asifa's eyes. A nurse placed an oxygen mask across the girl's face and Bay explained to her that it would help her breathe easier.

"Well, Doc," Dr. Johnson muttered in a warning, "you will remain with this prisoner at all times. Those spooks think they can do anything they want around here and get away with it." Her mouth thinned as she placed the flashlight in the pocket of her lab coat. "But not in my dispensary."

CHAPTER TWELVE

BAY REMAINED WITH Asifa throughout the examination process. The young girl was emotionally spent, dehydrated, starved and distraught by the loss of her brother. Bay felt very sorry for the Pakistani girl. Dr. Johnson looked at the X-rays and said, "Can't tell if she's got a punctured a lung or not. My guess is she does, but we need an MRI to prove it and we don't have that kind of equipment here. We'll tape them and keep her on an IV of nutrients, Ringer's lactate, oxygen and let her get some sleep. She's exhausted."

Bay nodded. "And where will she be taken, ma'am?"

"We have a room over there." Dr. Johnson pointed out beyond the closed blue curtains. "I've had the nurse inform the Marine detachment here. They'll be guarding her twenty-four hours a day."

"And then what?" Bay was worried that Granger would take things into his own hands. She was horrified at the thought of Asifa being waterboarded. She was no terrorist. Not Taliban, either. All she was doing was trying to make money to buy food for her starving family.

"She's under my orders and command," Dr. Johnson said, looping the stethoscope around her neck. She smiled a little. "Get your chief or LT to give you permission to keep yourself here with her at all times. I'm going to do some finagling and call a surgeon at the Bagram Hospital. I want her transferred there immediately. An X-ray won't always show a punctured lung, but her breathing and her oxygen levels are down, indicating a lung rupture."

Relief moved through Bay. "But she'll still be treated like a prisoner of war?"

Nodding, Johnson pulled the curtain aside. "Yes, but we have a professional interrogation unit at Bagram who, shall we say, plays gentle with someone like this girl. She's no terrorist. She's just caught up in something she didn't fully understand. More than likely, they'll let her go once she recovers."

Unlike Granger's heavy-handed methods, Bay thought. "You're her guardian angel, ma'am."

Dr. Johnson chuckled, her eyes sparkling. "No, Doc, you were. I heard the radio transmissions out there on that ridge after your chief called for a medevac." Her lips twitched. "You're just what this girl needs—a big, bad 18 Delta guard dog combat corpsman. Nice job protecting your patient out there. Stay close to her, okay, Doc?"

Managing a grin, Bay nodded, relief flowing through her. She stepped out of the way as two orderlies got ready to release the brakes on the gurney and take Asifa to the private room across the way.

Bay told Asifa what was going to happen. The girl was dazed and in shock. She licked her lips and nodded, her eyes closing. The nurses had done a good job of cleaning Asifa up, but her hair was filthy. Bay asked for the equipment to wash her hair for her once they got her to the security room. It was the least she could do for the grieving young girl. Asifa had no idea how much trouble she was in. Bay made the call to her Chief Hampton and received permission to remain with the Pakistani girl.

GABE ARRIVED AT the dispensary near dusk. He'd been told Bay was with the young girl they'd found on the mountain this morning. He saw two Marine guards at the door. After Gabe gave his name and unit, the guards stepped aside. Opening the door, he walked in. The young girl slept on the bed, an IV in each arm. Bay sat nearby in one of two chairs.

She looked up, happiness brightening her face as she saw him quietly enter the room and shut the door. Gabe smiled a little hello, moving to her side. Taking the M-4 out of the sling, he set it nearby and pulled up the other chair. He made sure the chair wasn't too close to Bay. She looked tired.

"How's Asifa doing?" he asked quietly, gazing over at the girl.

"Okay. Dr. Johnson, who took care of her, has been pulling all kinds of strings to get Asifa taken to Bagram for care."

Nodding, Gabe rubbed his eyes, weariness stalking him. "Good, because I've been hearing those two CIA guys are raising hell back in Washington about that little incident out there on the mountain slope this morning." He wiped his dirty hands across his cammies. Giving her a concerned look, Gabe added, "They're pissed."

"Is this going to blow back on you and me?" she

asked. Bay stared at his mouth, which sparked her own desire. Gabe was emotionally scrambling, unsure of how to stop his feelings from reacting to her.

He shrugged. "Oh, this isn't the first rodeo we've had with these two spooks." His mouth curved ruefully and he held her worried gaze. "This is a game to them. Chief Hampton knows this girl isn't Taliban. I told him what she'd said to you out there on the slope. She's just a kid caught up in something way over her head. Her reasons were okay, but the group she picked to carry them out with wasn't."

"That's true. I talked to her earlier here in the room. She's so naive. She didn't know her brother was carrying fertilizer or that it was used to make bombs."

Nodding, Gabe leaned his elbows on his thighs, his hands clasped between them. Just being with Bay was filling him with a joyful, light feeling, erasing his exhaustion. She'd done nothing to make him want more. "Did you ask if she was carrying one of those bundles of fertilizer?"

"Yes, I did. She wasn't. She tried to carry a bag, but it was too heavy for her, so she came along to keep her brother company. He's the one who carried the bag."

Nodding, Gabe said, "That's what I thought. Damn, she's skinny."

"Starved," Bay said softly. "They're starving to death in those U.N. camps."

"War's a bitch, isn't it?" Gabe twisted a look toward her. Bay's eyes were dark with concern and he could hear the emotions in her voice. His gaze fell to her lips. She had a beautiful mouth, and sadness moved through him. He'd never get to kiss her, to taste her mouth beneath his.

"I've gotten so I hate war," Bay said, strained. "War never decides who's right or wrong. It only decides who is left to remember the atrocity of it."

Rubbing his bearded chin, Gabe nodded. "But we stop the bad guys. And that's what counts."

Bay suddenly heard men's raised, angry voices outside the room. She instantly tensed and sat up. So did Gabe.

He rose. "Stay here." He held out his hand toward her to indicate she remain seated. He walked over and picked up his M-4 and opened the door.

Bay saw Granger and his buddy trying to threaten the two Marine guards standing in front of the door. The rage was evident on Granger's face. He wasn't hiding it from anyone.

"Now, you let me in there, goddammit," he breathed in fury at the Marine sergeant in front of him.

"No, sir, I cannot," he growled back, glaring at the spook, his rifle up and across his chest.

Gabe came and stood between the two Marines. "What's your problem, Granger?"

Eyes turning black with fury, Granger snarled, "Go to hell. I've got authorization from Langley to interrogate that Taliban girl. Now let us through!"

Gabe moved his M-4 from his right hand, unsafed it and put a bullet in the chamber and held it across his chest in an unspoken "no."

Granger huffed and puffed. He was a good six feet three inches tall, heavily muscled and knew how to intimidate. The only problem here was he knew he was intimidating the wrong person.

The Marines held their ground, unimpressed. Gabe smiled a little. "As I understand it, Granger, you have no authority in a hospital matter. Dr. Johnson is the person you ought to talk to, not us. Asifa is her patient. Why don't you take her on?"

Granger's nostrils quivered as he glared at the guards and then at him. "This isn't over, Griffin. Not by a long shot and you know it! You and these jarheads are assholes."

Gabe calmly watched the two CIA dudes spin around on their heels and go hunt up Dr. Johnson. He was surprised their heads didn't start rotating three hundred and sixty degrees, too. He grinned a little at the Marines, who grinned back. Gabe walked back into the room. Asifa had slept through the whole thing. He wasn't surprised; the girl had almost died out there on that mountain last night and was still in deep shock over the horrific experience.

"Wow, that dude is out of control," Bay murmured after he quietly closed the door. "What's going on between the two of you? It looks like you have some history with each other?"

Sitting down, he cleared and safed his M-4 and said, "Granger and I go a long way back. It's nothing personal. He thinks because he's the head spook out here at this FOB, he should be treated as the head god of Bravo in general. LT Brafford routinely puts him in his place and Chief Hampton has tangled with him a couple of times, too. Granger isn't well liked by anyone stationed here. He's arrogant, pushes his weight around and tries to intimidate everyone that gets in his way. He's a tiger without teeth."

Grinning, Bay chuckled over the picture Gabe drew of the CIA agent. "A toothless tiger. Could have fooled me. Out there this morning, I was sure he was going to push me out of the way to get to Asifa."

"Yeah," Gabe said, watching Asifa sleep, "he was going to do that and that's why I stepped in." He gave her a sideward glance, his mouth hitching upward into a feral smile. "Granger doesn't respect women."

"No kidding. I was facing him. I saw it." She rubbed her brow. "I wasn't sure what to do, Gabe. He's a bully."

"If there's ever a next time, just pick up your M-4 and punch the bastard in the chest like I did. Hit him in the sternum because there's a mass of nerve endings there, and when you get punched there, it can take you down to your knees, screaming, in a heartbeat. That's why you need to learn CQD. He got my message. If nothing else, Granger does respect power."

"Great, we have a war going on between them and us. Isn't one war enough for everyone?"

Chuckling darkly, Gabe said, "The CIA thinks they own everything. They can't help it. You have to pity the poor assholes. Granger is a field agent, which is bad news for everyone. CIA field agents are pretty damn squared away and we work well with them most of the time. Granger is an exception."

Bay tried to keep her laughter quiet. When she dropped her hand, she said, "I'm starving to death. Is there any chance you can stay here while I run over to the chow hall? Maybe bring you some food back, too? Plus, those Marines out there haven't eaten, either."

Warmth moved through his chest. Bay always thought about others. He held her soft blue gaze and felt his heart pound to underscore just how badly he wanted her in every way. "Yeah, grab me half a pizza? I've got water on me. That's all I need." *I need you.* The words damn near flew out of his mouth. Stunned, Gabe compressed his lips, in shock. How easily Bay reached out and touched him.

Rising, she pulled on her knit cap and hoisted the M-4 over her shoulder. "I'll be right back...."

THEY HAD JUST finished eating dinner when Dr. Johnson entered the room. She didn't look happy. The doctor shut the door and grimaced.

"Doc Thorn, I need a big favor from you." And then Johnson shifted her gaze to Gabe. "You, too, Griffin."

"Yes, ma'am?" Bay said, standing up. Gabe remained sitting but alert toward the doctor.

"Griffin, call your LT and ask if I can have the two of you fly this girl to Bagram right now. I got those two spook jerks trying to run my show, and it isn't going to happen. They get more joy out of screwing over their own people than sending up those drones to kill our mutual enemy."

Gabe raised his eyebrows. "You need us?"

"Damn straight I do." Johnson nodded toward the door. "I don't put anything past them. I want an armed guard with this girl from beginning to end."

"Then, ma'am, you'd best call LT Brafford, because he has to authorize it. I can't make that decision."

"Understood, Griffin." She sighed loudly and then

looked over at the monitors next to Asifa's bed where she slept.

"She's doing okay," Bay reassured the doctor.

"Good." She turned toward Gabe. "I'll call your LT. One of my nurses will get back to you with his decision. I've got a medevac on standby right now. I want this kid out of here. Rock it out, Griffin."

"Yes, ma'am," Gabe said, somber.

There was grit in the doctor's tone. She was upset and angry. Bay wondered how Granger had threatened her. They would probably never know. "I'll get her prepared for transport, ma'am."

"Yes, thank you."

Gabe followed her out and the doctor made the call to the LT. Bay was fairly sure that the LT would not want them at Bagram. That was a couple of hours of flight time and night was falling. It would mean staying over on temporary duty, at the air base. She'd never stayed overnight, so she had no idea where to go. There was most likely a woman's enlisted barracks on the huge air base, and she'd have to find it.

Gabe sauntered back into the room later, a humored look on his features.

"What now?" Bay asked. She saw Asifa begin to awaken, her eyes looking much clearer than before.

"LT is giving us a thumbs-up on this unexpected guard dog op." His grin increased. "Apparently, Granger went over earlier, screaming at our LT about my behavior and punching him in the chest with my M-4. Granger is threatening to level charges at me for doing it."

Bay's hands stilled and she looked in horror at him.

Gabe seemed nonchalant about the whole thing. "What happened?"

"LT told him to get his ass out of his office or he'd take his M-4 and do worse than what I did to him," he said. "A little interagency dustup. Nothing to worry about."

"This is truly a frontier FOB," Bay muttered, placing her hand on Asifa's gowned shoulder.

"More like Dodge City," Gabe agreed dryly. "Tell the girl what's going down. Try to act like this is a normal course of action, because we don't want her stressed out any more than she is already."

Nodding, Bay turned and quickly told Asifa what was going to take place. At the knowledge that they would be flying into Bagram with her, Asifa seemed grateful, her eyes misting over. She reached out with her cut, bruised fingers and gripped Bay's hand.

Gabe kept the door open and saw two orderlies with a gurney coming their way. The Marines stepped aside to allow them in and traded fist bumps with them. Gabe moved out into the E.R. area, keeping watch.

Granger was known to be an ass about things at times like this, and Gabe put nothing past the agent. Granger liked high drama. Gabe hated it. SEALs were professionals and conducted themselves as such. He couldn't say the same for these two CIA nut jobs.

He kept one ear on the transfer of Asifa from the bed to the gurney and one on the sliding-door entrance. Moving his M-4 into a comfortable position in his arms where he could get to it if necessary, Gabe ambled out to the doors of the dispensary. The night had fallen, the wind cold and freezing. The stars above were huge, as if he could reach out and pull one out of the black velvet sky.

Bay relaxed as the medevac headed out into the night. She sat next to Asifa's gurney on the deck, monitoring her and the IVs in her arms. Gabe sat in the back, M-4 resting between his legs, his one arm resting across his raised knees. As the helicopter moved close to nine thousand feet to crest the highest Hindu Kush mountain, she saw him close his eyes to sleep.

Weariness hit her, too, but she had to remain alert for Asifa's sake. Her oxygen levels were still not good, and it did, indeed, indicate a tear or leak in her left lung where one of the ribs had punctured it. She was in a lot of pain, could only breathe shallowly and wouldn't move much because of the broken ribs. Bay had given Asifa just enough morphine to dull the pain but not interfere with her breathing ability. Bay was glad they were taking her to Bagram. There, they had a state-of-the-art hospital where Asifa would get the best of care.

She had washed Asifa's hair earlier today and gently threaded her fingers through the teen's dry, dark strands, smiling reassuringly down at her. Asifa's stress disappeared beneath her ministrations. Touch was everything. As Bay sat cross-legged next to Asifa's gurney, facing toward the rear of the helo, the dull green light in the cabin revealed the shadowed faces of all aboard.

With a helmet on, she heard all the intercabin talk. The two pilots were wearing NVGs and flying through the black night, focused on their task. The chief air crewman had lain down on the metal deck parallel to Asifa's gurney, his arms wrapped around his chest, catching a few minutes of sleep. The other air crew-man on her side of the helo was scrunched up in a cor-ner, awake and alert.

Sleep was rare and always needed out here, Bay knew. She wished she could sleep. Lifting her gaze, she looked back in the deep shadows of the shudder-ing, shaking cabin, the hypnotic thumping of the blades overhead. Gabe's head was tipped back. He wore a helmet just as she and the other crewman did. Now she could openly stare at him with impunity. He was not pretty-boy handsome, but ruggedly appealing. Yet his wide-spaced eyes, that deep green color in them, moved her body and soul. It was his mouth, full and expressive, that drew her. There was nothing weak about his face. The beard gave Gabe an even more le-thal look. His brow was broad and lined. The crow's-feet at the corners of his eyes hinted at time spent out in strong sunlight. That, or they were laugh lines; she wasn't sure. Gabe had a wry sense of humor, black humor for sure, but he never smiled much. She won-dered, with an ache, if it was because of being abused by his father for so long. There wasn't much in his growing-up years to make him smile.

Her mouth moved into a soft line as she allowed her-self to simply absorb Gabe as a man. His hands were large and square with long fingers. There was a quiet, coiled tenseness that existed in him even as he slept, as if always, on some level, he was automatically on guard. She wondered how he stood the stress of what the SEALs did. They were an amazing lot of men, she conceded, thinking back to her year with the Special Forces team in Iraq. Here at Camp Bravo, things moved at lightning speed, everything dependent on what was coming across that Pakistan border into Afghanistan. Every day was stress, unlike in Iraq.

For just a moment, Bay allowed herself the secret pleasure of wondering what it would be like to glide her mouth against Gabe's. She felt undeniable warmth pooling in her lower body, desire. And yes, it was a completely selfish want on her part. What would Gabe look like without clothes? Her womanly senses told her it would be a lavish pleasure of her five senses to move her sensitive fingers up across his body, explore him, feel his strength inside and outside her. No man had ever affected her like this. And they'd done nothing, at all, except share space and time together. *Amazing*. Giving a shake of her head, Bay returned her attention to Asifa, who slept.

Would Asifa stop being hounded by those two CIA dudes? What if Granger made a call to the CIA group at Bagram? Worried, Bay placed her hand gently on Asifa's small, bony shoulder. She was relieved Gabe was allowed to go with her. He knew how to handle trouble.

CHAPTER THIRTEEN

GABE JERKED AWAKE. Something was wrong! He quickly sat up. The cabin was dark. Bay was sitting next to Asifa, who slept. Scowling, he quickly looked around. The air crew chiefs heard it, too.

"Bay?"

She snapped up her head, her eyes drowsy looking. Hearing Gabe's concerned voice, she saw him tense and alert in the rear of the helicopter. "What? What's wrong?" Something was by the look in his face, his gaze moving up toward the ceiling of the shaking, shuddering helo.

"Rotor assembly problem," he growled.

Frowning, Bay, who like all the others, had helmets on to stop the massive sounds pummeling their eardrums that the helo created, looked up at the ceiling. "I don't hear anything...."

Suddenly, there was a grinding, shrieking sound throughout the cabin. Even with her protective helmet on, it hurt Bay's ears.

Dammit! The helo lurched and began to lose altitude. Gabe saw the horrified expression on Bay's face. Instantly, he got his radio out, looked at the GPS of their present location and called into SEAL HQ at Bagram, reporting the issue and their location. This was going to be a major problem.

"Bay, get those IVs out of Asifa's arms. We're going down!"

Terrorized, Bay moved into action. She felt the medevac waffling, the shrieking whine continuing. Asifa was awake, her eyes wide with fear. She had no helmet on her head and she was stunned by the earsplitting sounds. Bay made sure the gurney was locked to the deck. The only problem was, there were no safety straps to keep Asifa in the gurney if the helo suddenly lost all power and started flopping around in the black sky. Quickly, she removed the IVs, explaining the problem to the girl. Asifa's eyes turned to horror. Bay felt the same way.

"Where are we, Gabe?" she asked, grabbing for her medical rucksack and her M-4.

"Going into hell," he warned her grimly. He'd already slipped into his ruck and tightened the straps, leaning against the wall as the helo began to flounder, the metal screaming above them. "Probably ball bearings in the rotor assembly cracked and broke. We're going down into a pro-Taliban valley. This isn't going to be pretty. Get your gear on. We're going to need every gun we got for this fight."

Bay looked forward. The pilot gripped the cyclic and collective. The copilot was on the radio with Bagram. Mouth dry, she shrugged into her ruck. Half of it contained medical supplies; the rest were things she'd need out on a patrol. Most important were the magazines for her M-4 rifle.

"How many mags have you got?" Gabe demanded,

counting his across his H-gear harness around his chest.

Her heart was beating harder in her chest. "I've got twelve. You?"

"Twelve. That's three hundred rounds for each of us."

"What about the pilots?"

"Only a pistol on each of them."

"The crewmen?"

"Same thing. There's an M-16 above the egress door. They don't carry many weapons onboard a medevac. Usually just one pistol each."

She heard the calm acceptance in his deep voice. She stared over at Gabe for a moment, scared. "I've never been in a helo crash. Have you?"

"Too many," he said wryly. "You need to put yourself across Asifa. Kneel on one side of the gurney and place your hands on the other side of the railing if the pilots can't get this bird under control. Otherwise, she's going to fly about the cabin, and that can kill her. Okay?"

"Got it." Bay's mind began to work furiously and rise above her initial terror over their situation. She heard all the talk on the radio comms between the pilots and Bagram. Gabe was on his radio, on another channel. Probably calling Chief Hampton back at Camp Bravo. There was a QRF, quick reaction force, available on patrols, composed of other SEALs who would run to an MH-47 Night Stalker and race to where the downed SEALs were. They never left a man behind.

Asifa gripped her hand and Bay devoted her attention to soothing the young girl.

"No QRF," Gabe warned her. "This was supposed to be a simple medevac night flight, was all."

Her mouth fell open, her eyes going large as she stared through the cabin at him. "What, then...?"

"LT's on it. They're scrambling. They know we're going down into that valley."

Suddenly, the screeching sound stopped. The helicopter immediately dropped like a rock out of the sky. Bay's hands were ripped off the litter. She was thrown toward the ceiling. So was everyone else. She landed hard against the door as the helo violently shifted. Everyone was scrambling. Asifa managed to cling to the rails as the bird began to whirl around in a wide circle, gravity pinning everyone.

Fighting to her hands and knees, Bay struggled over to reach Asifa. She had managed to grab the metal rails on the sides of the gurney and not allow her to fly out of it. The young girl's face was stricken with terror.

Just as Bay lunged for the railing, the medevac sheered off and banked sharply to the right. Gravity grabbed her. Hands tightening on the railing, Bay managed to press her body across the gurney. It stopped Asifa from being thrown out. Bay hunkered down, Asifa's only protection.

Gasping, terror racing through her, Bay heard the pilots yelling, trying to regain control of the helo. They were whirling around and around, dropping down, down, down.

Bay's throat tightened with terror as the gravity pulled hard at her. Her knuckles whitened around the metal bars, and her sweaty hands slipped. Asifa grabbed on to her, screaming. The helo was heading down, dropping silently out of the night sky.

"Bay."

She heard Gabe's calm, deep voice in her helmet.

"The pilot is going to let this bird fall. He has no choice. About a hundred feet above the ground, he's going to try and pull up the bird's nose."

Bay felt Gabe come up behind her. He was large and his long arms moved around her, his hands closing over hers, anchoring her to the rails. Literally, Gabe was protecting her and Asifa with his much larger, wider body. She felt tears come to her eyes for an instant, realizing what he was doing. Gabe was using his own body as a shield to protect them. "Okay…what do you want me to do?"

"Hang on. This is going to beat a Six Flags ride by a mile…."

She managed a choked laugh. His voice had a droll edge of humor to it. His long fingers moved over hers, curving around the bars of the gurney, anchoring her. The silence in the cabin was scary. She could hear the wind whistling outside the helicopter, the erratic thunking of the rotor blades above her. Jerking a look out the window, she saw only blackness. Bay had no idea if she was flying upside down or right side up. The sensation terrified her. Gabe's large, calloused hands remained firmly over hers, holding her securely. It stopped her from being jerked and yanked around as the helicopter spun in slow, wide, floundering movements as it headed toward the black, unseen earth somewhere below.

Bay felt they were going to die. Licking her lower

lip, she tried to halt the fear from overwhelming her. "H-how many crashes have you been in?"

Gabe heard the raw terror in Bay's voice. He felt the jerk and pull of the spin as the helo sank rapidly earthward. "Too many. I could write a book about it."

His black humor broke Bay's terror. "Gabe, you're certifiable, you know that?"

"Yeah," he said, amusement in his tone. And then the humor left his voice. He continued to monitor the movement of the helo. "The pilots are good. They know what they're doing. The worst problem is where we're going to land. It's Taliban central, Bay."

"Okay, what do I do? Tell me." His warm, strong hands fed her strength. Even Asifa had calmed, seeing him protect both of them.

"When we crash-land, it's imperative we egress immediately. Get everyone out of this bird as soon as possible. The Taliban are going to hear the crash. There's going to be fire on this bird because we're carrying a heavy load of fuel. We need to exfil pronto. I'll get the girl and carry her out. You get my rifle and yours. We'll need to find cover."

"Do you have NVGs on you?"

"Yes. You?"

"Yeah, in my pack."

"We're good to go, then. We swapped out scopes on our M-4s before we left, so we'll see the Taliban coming." He didn't tell her hundreds of them would pour out of nearby villages, AK-47s in hand, ready to kill every one of them.

The medevac lurched violently to the left.

Bay bit back a scream, hanging on. Asifa did scream.

She heard the other two air crewmen thrown up into the air, crashing into the side of the bird. Only Gabe's heavier body, his incredible strength under pressure, held her and Asifa right where they were.

Gabe tensed and prepared, glancing at the dials illuminated on the cockpit. The intercabin lights began to dim. He could feel Bay beneath him, tensing, as well, her knees spread wide to take the coming impact of the crash.

At the last moment, the pilot hauled back on the cyclic and collective, jamming his boots down hard on the rudders.

The medevac's nose sluggishly rose.

Asifa screamed as the copilot yelled to prepare for crash.

Oh, Lord, let us live!

The medevac's nose pulled up, the rotors flopping loudly around and around like a bird trying to fly with one wing broken. They picked up the air on the wide, flat blade surfaces, the helo slowing its descent as it moved almost vertically on its tail for a moment.

"Hold on," Gabe growled into her ear, hunkering down, waiting for the wheels to catch the earth.

Bay shut her eyes and held on as tightly as she could. The medevac seemed to hover in the sky for a moment. And then the wheels slammed into the earth.

Everyone was thrown forward. Bay was crushed into the railing by Gabe's body, but he held her and they kept their position over Asifa. There were screams. Grunts. Curses. The two air crewmen were flung forward. A boot struck her helmet, stunning her for a moment. Gabe winced and groaned as the helicopter plowed into the earth, the grating sounds of rocks ripping open the thin aluminum skin beneath them, shrieking throughout the dark cabin.

And then the medevac skidded into something big and unseen. Bay gasped, feeling the bird strike it on the port side. Metal crushed, shrieked and ripped open. It was so dark she couldn't see anything. The entire cabin went black. She heard Gabe's heavy breathing beside her helmet. Felt the painful grip of his powerful hands across hers.

The helicopter continued to slide on its port side, still hurtling forward, plowing up the soil. The blades snapped, flying off in all directions, razors slicing through the night air.

Finally, the medevac came to an abrupt stop. Bay gasped for breath, her heart pounding.

Instantly, Gabe released her and jerked off his helmet. He lunged for the sliding door, but it refused to open. Cursing, he took his boot heel and slammed it into the handle area again and again. The door finally gave, and Gabe hauled it open so that everyone could escape.

"Exfil!" he roared into the cabin.

Bay helped Asifa sit up, telling her Gabe would carry her out. She could smell wiring and other metallic odors burning. Gabe returned to her side, and she moved into medic mode. The SEAL easily removed Asifa from the gurney, lifting her into his arms and quickly slipping out of the Black Hawk. Bay's mind gyrated. What about the pilots and crew? How were they?

She fumbled forward toward the cockpit, yanking

off her helmet. She saw the two crewman in the rear of the cabin exfil. "Hey! Are you guys all right up there?"

The two pilots were trying to get their harnesses unsnapped in order to escape. The left side of the bird's nose was caved in, although Bay couldn't see it. The pilots were cursing, jerking at their harness straps that kept them trapped in their seats. With a shaking hand, Bay reached into her pocket and pulled out her pen flashlight. She then went for the SOF on her lower leg.

"Hold on, I'll cut the straps," she yelled, pushing forward into the cockpit, turning the light in that direction. Her fingers fumbled as she sought and found the straps trapping the pilot on the right side of the aircraft. She sliced them open and freed him.

Bay pushed back on her knees to get out of the way so he could exit the cockpit. The pilot squeezed by her and exfiled. Bay struggled up into the cockpit once again.

"Dammit!" the copilot hissed, trying to get free, yanking on the twisted metal. "It won't budge!" he yelled.

"Hold on," Bay gasped. "I've got a knife. Sit still!" She flashed the light on it and quickly sawed through the nylon harness with the SOF. Instantly, the copilot was freed. He gasped with relief and pushed awkwardly out of the mangled chair. Moving out of the way, Bay leaned to one side and shoved the knife back into the sheath. The copilot grabbed the M-16 over the door, carrying it out with him. Now she needed to exfil!

Bay grabbed the two rifles and leaped out of the smoldering helo. She pushed off the lip and fell face-forward onto the churned earth. Above her, she heard shots being fired. Behind her, the helicopter erupted into a whoosh of flame, the cockpit where the pilots had been seconds before, on fire. Sobbing for breath, Bay crawled away, the light of the fire helping her to see where Gabe and the rest of the crew were.

As she crawled forward, Bay heard the yells of the Taliban coming toward them in the distance. Her mind began to work like a steel trap. Up ahead were a group of boulders at least ten feet high and about a football field in length. She could see Gabe settling Asifa in between some rocks, trying to give her as much protection as possible. The other four men of the medevac were spreading out along the boulder perimeter under Gabe's direction.

Once she made it to Gabe's side, Bay thrust the M-4 into his hands. He'd put on his Kevlar helmet, the NVGs in place. Her heart was pounding hard in her chest, her breaths coming in ragged gasps. They'd survived the crash!

Gabe gripped her by the shoulder and drew her down next to where he crouched. They had their own comms earpieces, and relief flowed through her as she heard his calm, low voice.

"I need a shooter opposite these boulders. We can't assume they're going to attack us from only one direction. Go out there." He pointed. "About a hundred yards beyond the helicopter. Prone. Keep watch through your NVGs. If you see a bunch of them coming at you, start firing. I'm going to get these Air Force guys to create a diamond pattern around these boulders. That way, no matter which way the Taliban comes at us, we'll be able to defend our space and position."

Gasping for breath, Bay said, "They don't have NVGs. They aren't going to see anything."

"They'll see muzzle flashes." His mouth turned grim as he looked toward the two pilots. "We've got a lot of problems. First, they'll fire wildly and they'll all go through their ammo in a heartbeat. That means you and me are the workhorses. Conserve your ammo as much as possible."

Nodding, Bay shrugged out of her ruck, located her NVGs. She quickly put them on the rail system on the helmet and locked them into place. The firelight from the helicopter would make the NVGs useless until she got out beyond it. Then Bay would have good vision through the goggles.

Gripping her shoulder, Gabe ordered, "Stay far enough away from that helo. They're gonna start firing RPGs into it, thinking we're hiding in there. Stay safe!" He released her shoulder.

Bay moved quickly around the helo. The instant her back was behind the flames shooting into the sky, she could see clearly through her grainy green NVGs. Hunkering down on her belly, her legs spread wide, she quickly shifted her gaze from right to left in a one-hundred-and-eighty-degree arc. Gabe was right: the Taliban were coming. A lot of men were coming from about five hundred yards away. With shaking hands, she pulled out four mags from her H-gear and laid them out in a line in front of her. They would be easier to get and slap into the rifle after ejecting the emptied mag.

Hauling the M-4 to her shoulder, Bay opened the covers on the Night Force scope, pushed her NVGs up on her helmet and began to target the closest enemy.

She gave Gabe the intel on her radio, the mike close to her lips. She was already hearing the pop and bark of weapons behind her, bullets snapping and singing into her area.

Bay drew a bead, allowed her breath to move to still point, and then fired. The sound of Gabe's M-4 roared in her ears. A man went down, the rifle flying out of his hand. Gulping, she knew the suppressor on her M-4 would not draw immediate attention. The Taliban charging toward their position were wildly firing at them. The dirt exploded in geysers all around her.

Would help arrive in time? At least fifty Taliban were running hard toward her. And how many were coming from the other directions in this valley? Bay focused on her breathing. She had to stop them. Three hundred rounds of ammunition and she had fifty men running full tilt in her direction. The only question was: Would she be able to shoot fast enough, accurately enough to get them before they reached her position and breached it?

CHAPTER FOURTEEN

BAY FELT THE world slowing down. She knew that strange sensation occurred when adrenaline shot heavily through her bloodstream. It was also the feeling she might die. She continued to methodically fire at the enemy hurtling toward her. They were in open fields, and while it was easy to sight and fire, there were more and more running toward their other positions. She heard the slow, continuous firing of Gabe's M-4 behind her. The pistols the Air Force crew had sounded like firecrackers, fast and wild compared to their deeper-throated rifles.

The sound of Gabe's voice was nearby. He spoke on the comms, directing the Apaches. Would the combat helicopters get here in time? Or would they find all their bodies in the morning? *Dead.* Her field of fire was wide. A thumping noise came from the east. The Apaches had a familiar sound as they raced through the night toward the firefight. They would never be seen by the enemy, but Bay was sure the Taliban heard them because some were halting in the field, looking up and pointing toward the dark sky.

Bay struggled to remain focused. The men who didn't stop were racing toward her, firing their weapons. She kept expecting to be hit, more than glad she was wearing the sixty-pound Kevlar vest on her upper body. Her mind raced as the M-4 bucked against her shoulder, jerking her hard every time, with every shot. Her world was slowing down. Off to the left, she heard a new sound.

As she lifted her head, Bay's eyes widened. Two Taliban soldiers had sneaked up out of her range of vision. They were less than twenty feet away from her, rifles raised and pointed at her. She rolled over on her back, wrenched the M-4 around and fired. The men screamed, both yanked backward by the power of the bullets. Gasping, she rolled back over on her belly, re-sighting on the main force.

Suddenly, the night sky lit up like the Fourth of July. The puncturing growl of the .50-caliber Gatling gun sounded beneath the bellies of at least four unseen air wolves above them. They looked like red arcs of tracers slamming into the fields. There were screams and shrieks. The whumping sound of the blades reverberated like rolling thunder through the area as the Apaches arrived with a vengeance. Gabe kept talking to them, his voice calm and unruffled. Her respect for him rose a thousand percent because she knew she would never sound that cool under fire.

Some of the Taliban escaped the Gatling guns and continued to hurtle toward her position. She released a spent mag, dropping it into the dirt in front of her, slapping another one into the M-4 with the palm of her aching hand. Behind her, above all the roar and noise, someone screamed. It sounded familiar, one of the crew. But who? She couldn't just get up and leave her position; that would be unforgivable. She had to remain where she was. Her mind began to unravel between wanting to save a life and staying put.

The Apaches were like a pack of invisible predators in the dark, spewing out their death as they circled the area around the crashed and burning medevac. Soon, Bay saw the last of the Taliban fall in the field. Gasping for breath, she called Gabe. "I don't see any more enemy out here. Who's hit?"

"One of the pilots," Gabe returned.

"Can I come in and help?"

"Yes," Gabe answered.

Shakily getting to her knees, Bay found her legs weak. She shut off her NVGs and pulled them around her neck. Sweat was trickling down the sides of her face. Adrenaline made her shaky. She raced around the end of the still-burning medevac, the flames leaping twenty to thirty feet into the sky.

"The Apaches are hunting for stragglers," Gabe said, watching Bay run around the end of the tail rotor assembly of the burning medevac. Out of the corner of his eye, he saw a Taliban soldier leap out of nowhere, his knife drawn, lunging at Bay. She didn't see him. In one, swift movement, Gabe shouldered the M-4 and fired a few inches off her right shoulder. The bullet hit the Taliban in the head just as he was bringing the knife down to strike her in the back.

Stunned, Bay jerked to a halt, no doubt misunderstanding why he was firing directly at her. And then the man screamed right behind her. She whirled around, off balance, her eyes widened. The Taliban was falling forward, a knife dropping lifelessly out of his hand.

Giving a cry, Bay stumbled and fell backward, slamming into the ground.

"Get up!" Gabe snapped. He remained on one knee, M-4 scanning behind her as she struggled to her feet. He saw the terror in her eyes. That had been so close! *Too damn close.*

Bay ran toward the protection of the boulders. All around them, the noise of the hunting Apaches drowned out everything else. The whumping sounds were sending earthquake vibrations through their bodies; they were that close, somewhere up above them, unseen. The copilot lay to the left, unmoving. The pilot was leaning over him, his face tense.

Bay dropped to her knees on the other side of the copilot. The flames from the medevac were giving her just enough light. Their field of fire was clear; no more enemy were hunting them. Quickly, she assessed the unconscious copilot. He was in his late twenties and she noticed the blood on his upper thigh. Instantly, she took her SOF from the sheath and slit open his one-piece flight uniform from his knee to hip. Gabe had been right: she did find a use for this big knife. A bullet had hit the man in the center of his thigh.

Dropping her medical ruck, Bay calmed herself. She went to work to stop the squirting arc of the blood from a torn artery pumping out of his wound. He would die in two or three minutes if she didn't stop it.

GABE SLOWLY GOT to his feet. Staying on comms with the Apache pilots, he held the barrel of the M-4 upward, walking toward the huddled group of Air Force crewmen. They were all gathered around the wounded copilot watching Bay work quickly and efficiently to stabilize him. Gabe moved past Asifa, pained by her fate. She had been killed in the melee, a stray bullet striking her in the head. There was nothing he could do about it. Gabe continued around the perimeter, staying in touch with a Night Stalker M-47 Chinook helicopter coming their way to pick all of them up. They'd be flown into Bagram. Already the hospital had been notified that one wounded and one dead were coming in.

Warm blood dripped off his fingers from a flesh wound he'd received in his lower arm, but he kept up his slow, vigilant walk. Other Taliban in farther parts of the valley could be coming their way. He'd alerted the Apaches, and already three of them were heading north to engage the approaching enemy.

One Apache continued to fly on a racetrack above where they'd made their stand. They were their eyes in the sky to keep them safe from further attack. Gabe walked around the front of the boulders that had protected them. There were hundreds of white nicks on them, showing the fierce gunfight the Taliban had thrown at them.

Rolling his shoulders, Gabe felt the stiffness caused by the crash. His mind slid back to Bay. She'd more than proved herself. If the SEAL team had any misgivings about her in combat, they'd be laid to rest now. He wondered how she was doing. She would be devastated by Asifa's unexpected death.

Gabe forged ahead, never taking for granted that they were safe. Up north of them, he saw the red tracers of the Apache Gatling guns, hearing their staccato growl echoing down the narrow valley past them. Yeah, more Taliban were coming their way, just as he figured.

Feeling sudden urgency, Gabe asked for an update on the MH-47 coming to pick them up. It couldn't be too soon. They were in a helluva bind. Taliban would come pouring down the valley and try and kill them, too. Wiping the hard line of his mouth, sweat glistening across his face, his eyes slits, he continued to guard the group by exposing himself.

BAY FELT RELIEF as the Night Stalker MH-47 landed just outside the group of boulders. She'd finished placing a tourniquet on the copilot's wounded leg, stopped the loss of blood before it landed. The powerful gusts of rotor wash hammered the group. After getting an IV going, pouring fluids into the downed copilot, Bay asked one of the shaken medevac crewmen to hold the bag above the copilot's head. The pilot and crew chief picked up the unconscious copilot, heading quickly for the M-47.

Bay turned and headed back toward the other end to find Gabe. She met him halfway, his face grim. He'd pulled down the NVGs and they hung around his neck. His face was gleaming with sweat and was unreadable, the M-4 held high in his hand. As she raced up to him, breathing hard, he reached out and gripped her shoulder, stopping her.

"Asifa is dead," he told her, holding her startled gaze. "She got hit right after the firefight started. I'm sorry."

Bay's mouth fell open. She felt her heart crash and fall through her. "N-no…" She gulped, feeling his hand tighten on her shoulder, as if to try and steady her from the shocking news.

"Take my M-4. I'll carry her to the helo. Cover us?"

Too stunned for words, Bay felt tears flood her eyes as she followed Gabe to where he'd tried to keep the girl safe. As he leaned down, slipping his arms beneath her thin neck and lower legs, Bay gulped back a sob. Gabe was incredibly gentle with Asifa. Once she was gathered in his arms, he balanced her against his body and knee, pulling the blanket over her body.

Bay fought her emotions as she watched the area around them. Gabe came up to her shoulder and walked past her. Turning, Bay kept his back, watching the rocks that had saved most of them. Above, to the north, the Apaches continued to hammer the Taliban. The whumping sounds of the unseen Apache above them kept guard as they hurried toward the rescue helicopter.

On board, Bay had other duties. The Night Stalker pilots from the Army lifted off, heading up as fast as the double-rotor Chinook could grab air. Gabe placed Asifa's body in the back, the blanket covering her. He remained beside the Pakistani girl, on one knee, his M-4 in his right hand, guarding her.

Bay's focus was on keeping the copilot stable. They'd placed him on the metal floor. The pilot had taken off his jacket to provide a pillow for his partner's head. Bay was always touched what men would do to help a fallen comrade. The other two air crewmen sat nearby, ready to assist if she needed them.

Bay could see the exhaustion and shock in all their faces. It had been a close call. As she adjusted the flow of the IV after listening to the copilot's heart, she happened to glance toward the rear of the MH-47. Gabe was hidden in the shadows, the sparse green light only enough to see where a person could walk without running into something.

Gabe's eyes glittered like black obsidian in the low light. His face was completely unreadable, mouth pursed, his attention focused on her. Bay felt her heart writhe in her chest over Asifa's unexpected death. She wanted to cry for her, for the terrible jam she'd gotten herself into without realizing it. Wiping moisture out of her eyes, Bay returned her attention to the copilot, who was remaining stable. Oh, Lord, she could hardly wait to land at Bagram.

Gabe moved near Bay after the MH-47 landed and cut the rotors to idle. The hospital orderlies with a gurney, lifted the copilot out of the rear of the Chinook at Bagram. They'd landed at the hospital instead of at the Operations Helicopter Terminal. He reached out and gripped her arm.

"Are you okay?" he asked.

She absorbed the strength of his hand around her arm. Greedily, Bay sponged in the concerned look Gabe gave her. The air crewmen were climbing out of the helo, the medevac pilot following. "Yeah, fine…I've got to go with the copilot. The doctors need to know—"

"I'll wait for you in the E.R."

Choking back a sob, Bay nodded. Gabe's voice was husky and she saw something in his eyes—care for her. He knew how upset she really was. Grabbing her ruck, she whispered, "Asifa?"

"I'll take care of her," he gently reassured her. "You

take care of the copilot. Meet me in E.R. when you're done."

His words were like a blanket of balm soothing her growing grief over Asifa's unexpected death. Swallowing hard, Bay nodded jerkily, not daring to look into his eyes again. If she did, she'd start to emotionally unravel. She wanted to wail out her animal-like grief over the unfairness of such a young life being taken. Moving out of the helo, her ruck over her shoulder, M-4 in her left hand, Bay followed the orderlies and gurney into the E.R. Above her were the cold white stars blinking silently in the sky. They had witnessed all of this. What did they think? Her mind was turning cloudy, no doubt from shock. Battle induced it. She was no stranger to it. Only this time, she'd almost died. This time, it was different.

GABE WATCHED AS Bay emerged from the elevator into the E.R. about an hour later. Her face was dirty and blood streaked, and strands of her hair, caught up in a ponytail, stuck to the sides of her temples. He quickly assessed her from where he stood near the sliding doors that led out of the hospital. Her beautiful blue eyes were raw and shadowed. Her mouth, usually soft and full, was thin and pursed. She moved stiffly and he knew the crash was really beginning to affect her. When she spotted him, her eyes widened for a moment, her lips parted. It sent a good feeling through him as he waited, the M-4 safed and lying across his left shoulder.

"How's the copilot?" he asked as she drew near.

"Going to be okay. A torn artery. The ortho surgeon said the bullet missed his femur, which is good news. It could have cost him his leg instead." She stood there, a few feet between them. "You seem so calm."

He gave her a slight, one-cornered smile. "I'm at my best in a gunfight. I live for it."

Nodding, she pushed some of her dirty strands off her cheek. "You SEALs are amazing."

"Let's go outside," Gabe urged, nodding toward the glass doors.

Bay walked out into the night with him. It was much warmer at Bagram than at Camp Bravo. The base sat on the desert, north of Kabul, the capital. She saw the silhouette of his powerful body, his broad shoulders, and followed him out until they were swallowed up by the shadowed side of the building. Where was Gabe going? Her mind was still foggy and exhaustion stalked her in earnest. All the adrenaline had left her system. Now the adrenaline crash would come, shakiness and bone tiredness setting in.

Gabe halted by the corner and pulled her into the shadows where they could not be seen. He kept his hand on her upper arm. "Listen, I have a good friend who has a villa near Kabul. I'm always welcome there. I want to get you off this base, Bay. Give you some time to collect yourself. There are two bedroom suites. Each has a bath and shower." He looked into her widening eyes, seeing utter fatigue in them. "This is on the up-and-up," he told her. "I'll be near enough if you call me and need help. Okay?"

The words barely sank into her. She frowned and looked deeply into his darkened eyes. Gabe's hand was stabilizing, and right now she needed that. "It sounds wonderful. But how?"

He smiled a little. "I'll tell you after you get a good hot bath, get some sleep under your belt. Okay?"

Too tired to resist, she nodded. "It sounds too good to pass up. Let's go." She had no idea where the women's barracks was located on this huge Army base. His plan sounded much simpler and she trusted Gabe with her life. Literally. "I'll be all right," she assured him, following him toward an area unseen ahead of them.

"I know," he said, looking down at her as they walked at each other's shoulder. "You were good out there tonight, Bay. We wouldn't be here right now if you hadn't held your position in that gunfight."

Shrugging, she said, "I didn't like the alternative."

Gabe's mouth hooked into a grin. "You gotta love a woman who can shoot straight and has a dark sense of humor...."

Bay knew between the two of them, they had fought off the majority of Taliban. It was sniper-quality shooting on both their parts. They could have been overrun. The only reason they weren't was their professional calm and collective focus. It had saved most but not all the people tonight. Without Gabe's experience at calling in for air support and directing the Apaches, they'd be dead. She'd never been this close to her own death before.

CHAPTER FIFTEEN

BAY STUMBLED INTO the villa owned by Captain Khalid Shaheen and his American wife, Emma Trayhern-Shaheen. The villa sat on a hill, ten-foot-high walls with razor-sharp concertina wire on top. As she emerged from the car driven by the Afghan driver who worked for the military family, Bay saw alert Gurkha Indian sentries at strategic points within the fortified compound.

It was dark and she felt Gabe's hand against the small of her back, guiding her up the walk lined with fragrant jasmine vines. Inside, a shy Afghan house-keeper greeted them, never meeting their eyes. She showed them to the two suites down one wing of the massive home.

Gabe opened the door to her suite. "Everything you need is in there," he told her, holding her darkened gaze. If you can just drop your dirty clothes on the bed, I'll come by later and pick them up. The housekeeper will wash them tonight and we'll have clean ones to wear tomorrow morning."

Nodding, Bay looked around, standing in the door-way. "It's…beautiful. I feel like I've stepped back into the 1930s in America." There was a colorful quilt on the large bed.

Gabe said, "Khalid went to a university in America. He loves quilts and the Depression-era period antiques of our country."

"My mama makes beautiful quilts," Bay murmured, looking at the immaculately appointed room. There was a flowery-covered couch, an overstuffed chair and a small coffee table in one corner. To her right was a large bathroom.

"Khalid's a good guy," Gabe assured her. He saw the exhaustion in every line of Bay's body. "Look, get undressed, take a shower or bath and then hit the rack. Sleep in. The housekeeper will make you breakfast whenever you get up." He smiled a little. "Khalid has taught her how to make a good cup of American coffee, too."

Pushing some strands of hair off her brow, Bay said, "What about you?" She lifted her gaze, meeting his eyes. "How are you doing?"

"I'm good."

She shook her head. "I don't believe it. I feel like I've got a mountain of reactions and they're just hanging over my head and they're going to explode any minute in me." She was finding that SEALs always said they were good, even if they weren't. What was it about them to not show weakness or admit fatigue?

Gabe kept his hands at his sides, remembering that he'd promised to keep things clean between them. Though it was obvious that Bay needed his care. Just the weariness and grief on her face tugged powerfully at his heart.

"Listen," he said gently, "you went through a lot tonight. If you can cry, do it. It helps clean out the soul a little. If you need anything, I'm right across the hall from you." He pointed to the door opposite of where they stood.

"I always have a letdown after a firefight, so don't mind me. I'll be okay. Good night, Gabe.…"

"Good night." God, the last thing Gabe wanted to do was leave her alone. Bay looked stricken and the shock appeared to deepen in her by the second. Whether she knew it or not, she needed some help, some human support. And he wanted to be there for her. Reluctantly, Gabe turned away and opened the door to his suite.

SOMEHOW BAY PULLED off her Merrill boots, shucked off the dirty cammies and dropped them all on one corner of the bed. Looking at her naked body, she saw the many bruises and scratches. Her major joints ached because of the helicopter crash. Bay shuffled into the bathroom, in pain. The shower stall was huge, all glass.

She picked up a bar of soap. It smelled like the jasmine blooming along the walk outside the villa. There was a pink washcloth and a bath towel large enough to wrap around her body twice. A second, smaller towel was folded next to them and she imagined it was to dry her hair.

Inside the cream-color-tiled shower, Bay found shampoo products on a small ledge. She was glad that the housekeeper had been so thoughtful. All Bay wanted to do was get clean. She could smell the fear sweat on her body and she wrinkled her nose.

The glass-enclosed shower was large enough for two people. The water coming out of the large overhead round nozzle resembled soft raindrops. Within moments, Bay stood in the heat and gathering steam, allowing the rivulets to move across her hair, face and body. A ragged sigh slipped between her lips as she scrubbed her skin free of tonight's memories.

The shampoo was jasmine scented, too, and it felt so good to scrub her hair free of the dirt and sweat from the firefight. The perspiration peeled away, but the flashes of trauma wouldn't leave her. Bay sat on the tile bench, the shower enclosing her in its liquid warmth as she scrubbed her feet and between each of her toes. It felt delicious to be really, truly squeaky clean.

Bay had no idea how long she was in the shower. Her skin was free of the experience. She looked at her trembling hands, the small bruises and cuts across the backs of them. Closing her eyes, she let the water stream over her head, plastering her shoulder-length hair against her neck and shoulders.

But then, in the peace, she was caught off guard as violent, sheering emotions erupted from deep within her. Reeling with exhaustion, she leaned against the warm tile wall, her hands covering her face, the streams of water falling gently around her.

Asifa's face appeared before her tightly shut eyes. Bay's lower lip quivered and she fought against the grief welling up within like a relentless fist shoving up through her chest and into her throat. Gulping several times, she tried to tamp it down, but it was impossible. Somewhere in her faltering mind, Bay knew she was in deep shock. And shock always played tricks on the mind and the emotions of a person. With a groan, she slowly slid downward and sat on the tile floor, pulling her legs up against her chest. She wrapped her arms around them and rested her cheek on her knees.

The first sob ripped out of her. She couldn't stop it. Her body shook from the release. Water trickled around her, keeping her warm as the icy coldness swept through the center of her body. The second sob sounded like an animal wailing to her ringing ears. Her hearing was dulled because of all the explosions and gunfire. Bay lifted her face, eyes closed, her mouth contorted as more sobs wrenched out of her.

Overwhelmed by the crash, the firefight and finding out Asifa had been killed, Bay finally gave in to the churning mix of virulent emotions. She allowed herself to cry, to feel. The water provided her a little bit of protection in a world where there was none.

ALREADY SHOWERED, GABE knocked firmly on Bay's suite door. He waited, a thick white towel wrapped around his waist, another one across his shoulders. Barefoot, he'd walked across the tiled hall to pick up her dirty clothes for the awaiting housekeeper to wash.

"Bay?" he called.

No answer.

Figuring she was still in the bathroom and couldn't hear his call, Gabe eased the door open. And then he heard her sobs. Frowning, he looked toward the bathroom, the door ajar. On her bed were the filthy cammies.

"Bay?" he called more strongly. "Are you all right?" Gabe hesitated. Her weeping continued. *Damn.* He was torn. Bay needed help. He understood better than most what had happened. Bay was crying now because of everything she'd experienced tonight.

Moving toward the open door, Gabe saw the steam was so thick he could barely make her out on the floor. Grabbing the huge pink bath towel from the counter, he opened the door. The steam escaped, revealing Bay naked, her legs drawn up against her body, her face buried in her hands. Her dark hair was wet and ropy around her face, her naked shoulders hunched and shaking.

"Hey," he murmured, "Let's get you out of here." Gabe turned off the faucets. Leaning down, he placed the towel around Bay, covering her so she wouldn't be embarrassed. Her skin was slick and wet, turned pink by the heat of the shower. When Bay lifted her face, her eyes widening with realization he was crouched down in front of her, she blinked and stared at him in disbelief. Her lower lip trembled. Tears mingled with the water from her wet hair.

"Come on, I'm getting you out of here, Bay."

She felt as if she were in a slow-moving nightmare where pieces of her reality were separating and spinning out of control around her. Bay had never experienced this before, and it frightened her. Only Gabe's concerned face before hers, his strong, caring hands wrapping her snugly within the plush towel, registered. She felt him pull her to her feet, an arm around her waist to steady her.

A ragged sigh escaped her as Gabe guided her out of the shower. Her feet wouldn't do what she wanted them to, and she leaned heavily on him for support. He smelled clean. She weakly rested her head against his chest, feeling the warm hardness of his muscles beneath her cheek. Closing her eyes, Bay wanted only to be held by him.

Gabe slowly guided her to the bed. Holding her and the towel with one arm, he leaned down and pulled back the sheet and covers. "Come on," he rasped, "you need to sleep, Bay. You'll feel better in the morning."

Dream or nightmare? Bay's mind stopped functioning. She had no more tears left to cry for Asifa as Gabe guided her into the bed and pulled the covers up to her shoulders. Just having him near helped her whether he knew it or not. Turning onto her side, drawing her legs up into the fetal position, Bay felt a helplessness she'd never before encountered.

Gabe walked into the bathroom, retrieved the smaller pink towel and brought it out. He slid his hand beneath Bay's neck, gently lifting her head off the pillow and placing it beneath her damp hair. He crouched down, aching to comfort her. "Go to sleep, Bay."

Gabe watched her lashes close, her hands tucked against her chest beneath the covers. God, how he wanted to slide into that bed next to her. It wasn't about sex. It was about holding her safe because she'd been through so much in so short a time. Resting his hand on her blanketed shoulder, Gabe whispered unsteadily, "You'll be okay, baby…."

Bay barely raised her lashes, pulling her hand out from beneath the covers. She fumbled awkwardly, seeking and finding his hand on her shoulder. "Th-thanks…." And it was the last thing Bay remembered as the horror of the night spiraled her into a deep, healing sleep.

GABE WAS EATING breakfast in the dining room the next morning when he saw Bay slowly emerge from the hall. She was dressed in her clean cammies, her curly hair pulled back into a ponytail. Her eyes looked lifeless as she walked over to the table. He got up and pulled out a chair next him.

"How you feel this morning?"

"Like hell. How about you?" Bay sat down and thanked him. She eyed him with curiosity, maybe because he hadn't had the same reaction as she had. The housekeeper came over.

Gabe sat down. "She doesn't speak English."

Nodding, Bay switched to Pashto and greeted the small woman who wore a set of brown slacks, a white blouse and comfortable sandals.

"I just need some coffee, please?" she asked the maid.

"Of course," the housekeeper said, bowing and turning away.

"Nothing to eat?" Gabe asked, finishing off a plate of a dozen eggs, a dozen pieces of bacon and six pieces of toast.

Rubbing her face, Bay shook her head. "N-no. I'm afraid if I eat, I'll throw up."

Gabe kept his hand where it was. "Yeah, it hits all of us like that sooner or later."

She snorted softly. "I'm glad to know I'm not the only one that has that kind of reaction." Being with Gabe made her feel stable and protected. Last night, he'd protected all of them. Her heart opened up with a fierce emotion she could only identify as love for this man. Gabe was truly a hero. To look at him, his demeanor, he seemed unaware of the vital part he'd played in rescuing so many. First, on the battlefield, and then rescuing her from the shower last night.

"We all do, Bay. It's just a question of when it's going to hit us, is all. It happens sooner or later." Gabe finished off the eggs.

The housekeeper brought over a cup of coffee, and Bay thanked her. She felt chilled and wrapped her slender fingers round the warm cup. "I've never felt this way, Gabe. Not ever. I've been in any number of firefights before."

To hell with it. Gabe reached out and pulled one hand gently away from the mug. "Listen to me, will you?" He held her cloudy blue eyes. "You forget we had three things in a row hit us last night. You've never been in a helo crash. Then our lives were on the line with the Taliban coming to finish us off." His hand tightened around her icy fingers. "I did the best I could to hide Asifa." Gabe shook his head, his voice lowering with emotion. "There was so much lead flying last night, Bay, I didn't think she'd make it. Hell, I didn't think we'd make it. It was dicey. And while you functioned just fine in combat, something this intense is bound to hit you sooner or later when it's over."

She turned her hand, lacing her fingers through his. It was so hard to speak. She felt her throat closing up with tears once more. "When you put it like that, it is a lot," Bay admitted hoarsely. "I just feel so torn up inside, Gabe…."

"It's about Asifa," he said, wanting to hold her hand forever.

Bowing her head, Bay pushed the cup away from

her. "It's more than that, Gabe. My little sister...well, she's almost a spitting image of Asifa. I couldn't believe it when we found her out there on that mountain yesterday morning. I thought I was looking at Eva-Jo." Taking in a deep, serrated breath, Bay forced herself to hold Gabe's green gaze. The game face he wore, the one of confidence and nonchalance, was gone. There was care burning in his eyes for her, and she felt it in the way he gently cradled her hand in his. "Asifa was so young and beautiful. She was pathetically thin, starved. It was like looking at my sister. It tears me up to see children hurt. It doesn't matter what country they're from, Gabe." Bay pressed her hand to her heart. "I love children. I want to see them thrive, be happy and healthy. Finding Asifa holding and rocking her dead brother out there just got to me. It's a visceral reaction, I can't explain it."

Gently, Gabe released her hand and moved a few curled strands away from her pale cheek with his index finger. "You'll make a good mother someday, Bay. Above all, you're a medic and your heart and soul are bound into saving lives. There's nothing you can do to shield your heart from who you are, baby. Not ever. It's how you're built."

The grazing touch of his fingers against her temple sent a warm, steadying sensation throughout Bay. When he called her *baby,* it was as if warm, golden honey coated the insides of her grieving heart and shattered soul. And as Gabe whispered that endearment she saw heat, need and hunger in his eyes—for her. Just the attention he was infusing her with right now was helping her feel far more emotionally stable. Giving him a wry look, she whispered, "How did you get so good at knowing me?"

Gabe set his plate aside and rested his arms on the table. "You're easy to read, Bay. There's no games, no pretense with you. What you see is what you get."

Drowning in his warmth, she felt stronger. It was him. Gabe's ability to be vulnerable when she needed him to be, stunned her. And as Bay held Gabe's calm, caring gaze, she felt new feelings taking root in her heart for him. Whether she wanted it to happen or not, she was falling in love with this man. Gabe carried the weight of so many lives last night on his shoulders as if it were a normal course of action. He wasn't devastated by it, but she had been.

Swallowing, her voice tremulous, Bay said, "Thank you for being who you are, Gabe…."

They shared a smile before Gabe turned back to the mission at hand. "Listen," he murmured, "I called Chief earlier this morning. I got up early and checked in with the team by sat phone."

Bay took a deep breath. "I wish we didn't have to go back right now." She felt too vulnerable, not ready to hit the ground running once they landed at Bravo. All Bay wanted was some time to get herself back together.

"You got your wish." Gabe grinned a little. "I told him there was a lot of paperwork to fill out on the copilot being wounded. It was a partial lie to buy us some downtime." He straightened and moved his stiff shoulders. "The chief told us to be back at 0800 tomorrow. We have all day here to ourselves."

CHAPTER SIXTEEN

BAY HAD JUST finished breakfast when the owners of
the villa arrived. Khalid Shaheen, dressed in a dark
blue flight suit, came over as she and Gabe rose out
of his seats.

"Stay put," Khalid told Bay, coming over to shake
her hand after introductions were made.

"Thanks for letting us stay here, Captain Shaheen,"
Bay said.

"This is where we get our sanity back," he said,
smiling. "Here's Emma, my wife. Emma? We have
company."

A tall, red-haired woman in a dark blue flight suit
entered the villa. Bay instantly liked the woman.

"Gabe, good to see you!" Emma said, throwing her
arms around him. "Long time no see."

Gabe had the good grace to flush. "Emma, meet my
partner, Bay Thorn. She's an 18 Delta medic."

Emma's eyes widened as she came around the table.
"Hey, I've got just the job for you! Nice to meet you,
Bay." She leaned over and embraced her.

Bay's emotions were raw, but the warmth and sincerity of the owners made her feel good. "Nice to meet
you, Emma. Thank you so much for letting us stay
here. It was a godsend last night."

Emma set her helmet bag on a nearby buffet and smiled. "Like Khalid said, it's here where we retrieve our sanity. I'll be right back. Haven't you eaten breakfast yet?" She pointed toward her coffee cup.

"No," Bay murmured. "I don't have any appetite right now."

The woman gave her a long look and then she nodded. "We just flew in from the border. We're starved." Emma turned and walked into the kitchen, where her husband and the housekeeper were talking.

Bay flashed Gabe a concerned glance. "Should we leave?"

"No. They're in and out of here all the time. If they invite you here as a guest, you're considered family." He regarded her with concern. "Sure you can't eat something?"

She shrugged. "I am a little hungry, but I still don't want to chance it."

"These two people would understand exactly what you're going through, so no worries. How about some scrambled eggs? That should sit light on your stomach."

His care made Bay felt less raw. Gabe was like an oak in the storm. And right now he was affording her his protection. "Okay...no promises, though."

Gabe pushed the chair back. "Good. I'll be right back." He turned and walked into the kitchen.

Picking up the cooled coffee, Bay sipped it tentatively. The nausea came and went in unexpected waves, but the coffee actually tasted good to her now. Maybe, she thought, she'd just needed to talk it out with Gabe. Sometimes talking helped her get rid of whatever was eating at her.

"So," Emma said, sitting down next to Bay with a plate full of eggs and bacon, "you're an 18 Delta corpsman? I didn't know the Army had opened it up to women."

Bay sidestepped the top-secret reasons and said, "I just got lucky, was all."

"I hear you were in one hell of a firefight last night."

"It was bad," Bay conceded softly, moving her fingers around the cup. "So, Gabe said you were an Apache combat pilot?"

Emma nodded. "Was. I got kidnapped by the Taliban a year ago, held prisoner and got pushed around." She held up her left hand. "I was kicked in the left shoulder and it damaged nerves in this hand. I still have two fingers that are numb and I can't feel them. And when you fly an Apache, you have to have feeling in all ten, so the Army released me."

Khalid joined them, sitting opposite of Emma and Bay, "My lovely wife was down, but not out." He gave Emma a warm, loving look.

Gabe brought over a plate of scrambled eggs and set them front of Bay. She managed a small smile of thanks.

"Even though you have a permanent injury, you're able to fly, Emma?" Bay asked.

"Khalid has a charity program set up for the Afghan children along the border area. We fly in books, desks and teachers to the villages who want our help." Emma smiled over at her husband. "He doesn't care if I have two fingers that are numb. I can fly a CH-47 with the best of them."

Bay tasted the eggs with trepidation. Surprisingly,

they were delicious. Her stomach growled its appreciation. "I think it's wonderful you two are helping the children. This country has so little…."

Khalid nodded, spooning the eggs into his mouth. After swallowing, he said, "The only way our country is going to lift itself out of this abject poverty is to educate the children, both boys and girls."

Bay smiled over at the tall, lean pilot. "I think it's a wonderful gesture."

Emma lifted her head and directed her attention to Gabe. "Hey, are you two hanging around today by any chance?"

"Yes. Why?" Gabe asked.

Emma reached out and touched Bay's hand. "We've got a medical clinic set up for an orphanage in Kabul this morning. Bay, would you like to come over and help us? We've got a doctor coming but no nurse. Do you feel up to it?"

"Children?" Bay asked.

"Yes, all ages," Khalid warned with a smile. "We go over once a month. The nurse can't make today because she's sick."

"I'd love to help," Bay said, feeling her spirits lift. She saw Gabe give her a softened look. Her heart opened even more toward him. "Gabe? Is that all right? Can you come along?"

"The day's all yours. I have to get back to Bagram shortly. Chief Hampton wants me to get some supplies at Bagram. We'll fly back to Bravo tomorrow morning. I'll catch up with you at the orphanage later in the day."

Emma rubbed her hands. "Excellent! Thank you, Bay. You're practically a doctor, so we're all in your good hands. Wait till you meet these children! They're so beautiful and they just make you smile."

As Gabe sat there watching the emotions in Bay's face, he saw the sadness finally dissolve in her beautiful blue eyes. Providence had a way of stepping in to help her, he realized. And he was grateful because Bay was special. Her suffering tore him up inwardly. He couldn't tell her that. Gabe cared deeply for this hill woman, who had absolutely no protection against her too-generous heart.

GABE WALKED QUIETLY into the orphanage near 1600. He spotted Bay sitting in a rocking chair in one corner, a newborn in her arms. She was feeding the tyke a bottle of milk. A number of children sat around her feet, just happy to be near her. Gabe leaned casually against the doorjamb, smiling to himself. Emma was over in another area of the room, helping the women who cared for the older orphans.

Amazed at the change in Bay's face, Gabe allowed himself to remain undetected and simply absorb the moment. No longer did he see tension in Bay. There was a soft smile on her lips as she gently rocked the baby in her arms. Every once in a while, she'd lean down and place a small kiss on the baby's black hair. The baby would lift its tiny hands, waving them around, and then go back to suckling strongly on the bottle of milk. The other children, all two, three and four years old, played quietly around her feet. Gabe understood why. There was a warm, nurturing energy that always exuded around Bay. He'd noticed it from the day he'd met her. She was very maternal and the children gravitated to her like plants to sunlight.

Her light brown curls lay against her flushed cheeks. Though he wanted badly to walk over, lean down and kiss her lips, Gabe remained where he was. Last night, she'd been key in their surviving the Taliban attack. This afternoon, he was witnessing her vulnerability with the children. His throat tightened, and Gabe couldn't ignore his need for her. The promise he'd made her, however, had to remain enforced. More than anything, Gabe wanted Bay's continued trust. That was more important than stealing a kiss from this woman of the earth.

Bay looked up, as if sensing him nearby. As she lifted her chin, her blue eyes met his.

Easing away from the door, his arms dropping to his sides, Gabe walked over to where she rocked the baby. "Looks like you're having a good day."

She watched as he drew over a chair and sat down a few feet opposite her. "Is it that obvious?" Bay looked down and smiled at the infant in her arms.

Gabe removed his cap, running his fingers through his black hair. The older boys were now gravitating toward him, curious about who he was. "You look beautiful with that baby in your arms," he said.

A powerful sensation of love for Gabe moved through Bay. It was the expression burning in his eyes, the rasp in his low tone that moved her.

"I love newborns. They smell so sweet and fresh." She leaned down and pressed a kiss to the little girl's brow. She had finished the bottle and was now sleeping. Bay placed the bottle on the floor next to the rocker, sliding her arms around the baby.

"They're like newborn pups," Gabe agreed, feeling his entire body tighten with desire for Bay. The openness of her expression, the joy shining in her blue eyes, touched him as no other woman ever had. He wanted to love her, hold her and love her all over again. For a moment, Gabe wanted her to carry his child. It was a primal, powerful feeling of wanting to claim her for his own.

For once, Gabe didn't fight his feelings toward Bay as he met and held her radiant gaze filled with joy. The change in her was startling. Breath stealing. This morning, she had been grieving and depressed, with good reason. Now there was nothing but warmth and contentment on her face. And something else… Gabe knew when a woman wanted her man. And if he wasn't mistaken, that was the look in her blue eyes right now—for him. He felt aroused and instantly controlled his body. *Wrong time and place.*

"Puppies smell wonderful, too," she agreed, fond memories from her own past making her smile. How happy Gabe made her feel by his presence alone! She couldn't ignore him as she had before. What had changed?

Swallowing hard, Bay blamed her rocky emotional state for these thoughts. Right now she felt needy and susceptible to him. She knew Gabe would hold her, love her and she'd be happy every minute in his arms. They had four months before his team was rotated out of Afghanistan. And she might well be reassigned elsewhere. Her life was not her own. All she could do was love him from a distance. *Look, but don't touch...*

GABE SAT WITH Bay out in the living room near midnight in the villa. He'd come out from his suite to get some water from the kitchen tap and seen her sitting on the couch, staring off into space. Emma had loaned her a set of Levi's jeans and a green tank top so she didn't have to wear her cammies. He sauntered over to the living room with a glass of water in hand.

Bay roused herself from her introspection. She was sitting in the corner of the couch, her feet bare, legs against her body, her arms wrapped around them. Gabe had come to the kitchen without her even hearing him until he'd turned the on tap. There was one lamp on in the living room, the shadows deep. He wore a tan T-shirt that outlined his powerful chest and shoulders, cammie trousers and boots.

She was struck by how athletic he was. It was a pleasure to watch the play of muscles in his arm as he lifted the glass and drank deeply from it. Right now Bay didn't feel the coiled tension she normally felt around Gabe. He settled in an overstuffed chair opposite the couch, the coffee table between them.

"How are you feeling?" he asked her quietly, holding her gaze.

"Just thinking," Bay admitted softly, appreciating how ruggedly handsome he was. Gabe settled back in the chair, his long legs splayed out in front of him. There was a naturalness to him. And right now he seemed unguarded, his hair mussed, giving him an air of relaxation instead of that constant tension he carried on duty.

"Thinking about what?" he wondered, setting the emptied glass on the lamp table next to his chair. "The last two days."

"What? Heaven and hell?" He grinned mischievously.

"Something like that." Bay pushed curls away from her brow and then laced her fingers together in front of her knees. "So much has happened. I'm trying to process it all, but it's not happening very fast."

"Don't try to rush it," Gabe advised. "Trauma is like a deep splinter in your finger," he told her. "It works its way out over time. The good news is, it will come out."

Snorting, Bay said, "Yeah, but where are my tweezers? I don't like suffering, Gabe. I want the pain *gone*. Now. Not later. I've never handled pain well. That's why I cry. It's a relief valve for me and it reduces the pain."

"It doesn't happen that way for me. I wished it did, but that's not my experience." Gabe felt tired in a good way, at ease, resting his head against the overstuff chair. Just getting this kind of intimacy with Bay was more than he'd ever dreamed would happen. It was rare, and tomorrow morning, they'd be thrown back into the mix-master of patrols and ongoing, continued danger. It made their time together excruciatingly special and he felt like a dry sponge absorbing every second.

Licking her lower lip, she asked softly, "Is there a trick to it?"

He shook his head and opened his large hand. "Bay,

you've been in firefights before when you were in Iraq. How did you handle them?"

"Good point," she murmured. "I did handle them. It didn't get to me like this time did." Her brow furrowed. "I don't know why...."

He saw the longing in her eyes for him. It was almost palpable to Gabe as he held her tenuous gaze. "Maybe you're changing. We're not static beings. We're like trees, always putting out new growth."

"I like that picture," she whispered, smiling tentatively. "Maybe I am. I don't know. I just feel—" she groped for the words "—just different." She shook her head. "I wish I knew how to work through combat."

Gabe sobered. There was such nonverbal desire burning between them. It was a special kind of hell. "Hey," he teased, trying to lighten her mood, "I've got my hands full with myself. I won't ever pretend to know how another person needs to work through trauma."

She sat back. "I'm just glad you're there, Gabe." Turning her head, Bay met and held his gaze. "You are an incredible person. I—I've never met anyone like you. Ever..."

He saw the raw need in her eyes, heard it in her husky voice. He felt the same and it hurt a lot. Oh, God, he ached, feeling his lower body hardening, needing her. Last night he'd dreamed of loving every inch of her body. Touching her velvet, warm skin, kissing it, moving his tongue across it, feeling her tense and moan with pleasure. They were adults and Bay had a maturity way past his.

"From the moment I saw you, Bay, my world changed," Gabe quietly admitted.

Her eyes widened for a moment, her lips parted. There, he'd said it. Now she knew without a doubt that what they were both feeling was mutual.

"What are we going to do, Gabe?"

Slowly easing into a sitting position, his hands clasped between his open thighs, he studied her in the gathering silence. "We're going to have to gut it out, Bay. It won't do us any good to start something here, and we both know that whether we like it or not." His mouth twisted into a wry line. "Our platoon rotates out of here in four more months. We'll be going back to Coronado. I have a condo on the island. Maybe, if things work out, we can move forward at that time when you get home and explore what we have?"

He held her gaze, waiting for her reaction. It was a bold move on his part, and Gabe surprised himself. And obviously, his suggestion surprised Bay by the look on her face. He'd never wanted anything more than her. Bay was different. She was honest, caring and there was a simplicity to her that called to the depths of his heart. Most of all, he found himself wanting to love her as he'd never loved another woman. He went hot and hungry with need of her. What would she say to his brazen offer?

Bay held his burning gaze. "I'd like that but I don't know what my orders will be, Gabe. I'll have two more months to fulfill in Afghanistan before I can be rotated stateside. I'll probably be assigned somewhere else, but I have no idea where that might be." She saw his brow furrow.

"If you had a chance to get leave, would you?" He held his breath, waiting.

"In a heartbeat."

Relief tunneled through him. "Then we'll just have to figure out a way to make this happen."

"Easier said than done," she whispered.

"Easy is done by the common man. SEALs are used to completing the impossible," he said with a smile.

CHAPTER SEVENTEEN

THE SEPTEMBER HEAT was stifling even at 1900. Bay wearily lugged her sniper rifle and ruck back to her tent. Where had the months gone? Her being an 18 Delta corpsman had spread quickly throughout Camp Bravo. If she wasn't out with her SEAL team, there were requests for her medical help at the dispensary. Or she was asked to hold a women's clinic in another Afghan village in one of the valleys by the Special Forces teams stationed at Bravo. She didn't want for work.

After dropping her ruck on the plyboard floor of her tent, Bay placed the Win Mag in a corner, making sure the protective sheath was closed to prevent dust and sand from getting into it. The evening was squalid with hundred-degree temperature even at eight thousand feet. Perspiration ran down her temples as Bay sat on her cot and removed the heavy Kevlar vest.

Her thoughts turned back to Gabe, as they always did in rare quiet moments. Their secret had remained just that. They worked hard not to allow anyone in the team to think they had a personal connection. It was hell, as Gabe had said months earlier, when they realized they were powerfully attracted to each other. Bay rubbed her face, feeling the grit on it. She wrinkled her nose, got up, walked over to the basin and poured water into it. There were hot showers available, and she was going to get to one soon. Right now she just wanted the grit off her face.

"Bay? You in there?"

She lifted her head, hearing Gabe's voice outside her tent. Instantly, her heart pounded. "Yes...hold on just a sec," she called back.

Quickly sloshing water across her face, she picked up a towel. She went over to the open flaps and stepped outside. They made sure he would never be seen inside her tent. He was still in his patrol gear. Why? The team was standing down for five days after the last patrol.

"What's up?" she asked, wiping the last of the moisture from around her eyes and nose.

"Chief Hampton wants us to fly into a Shinwari village three valleys over and take a pregnant Afghan woman to Bagram. She's the wife of one of the leaders and requested our help." Gabe smiled, his hands resting across his M-4 slung horizontally across the front of his body. "Want to?"

"In a medevac?" Bay saw his eyes were shadowed.

"I know what you're thinking," Gabe said wryly. "Last time we were in a medevac, it crashed."

"Yeah, no kidding." Bay sighed, utterly spent from a night patrol hunting Taliban. At dawn, they'd been airlifted to another Shinwari village to conduct medical clinics during the daylight hours. It had been fourteen hours on the ground, and all she wanted right now was sleep.

Nodding, he said, "The doctor's worried about the woman, thinks she might need a Cesarean to deliver her baby."

"Okay," she said with a grimace. "Chief Hampton asked for both of us?"

"It's routine—if one member of a team is on a medevac, if possible, another team member goes along. I just happened to be the last guy left in the HQ when the call came in. Hampton told me to find you and ask if you're up for it. He said if you were, I was to go along."

Gabe saw the weariness on her face. He also saw yearning—for him. He could relate to any concern she might have that something might happen on that medevac flight. Hampton had asked him upon their return from the first crash if anything had happened between them that day they'd spent at Bagram. One thing a SEAL did not do was lie to another team member. Ever. Gabe could honestly tell Hampton that nothing had happened. And it hadn't. It would remain that way. But each time together was going to be a special torture for them.

"This is a pro-American village?" Bay asked.

"Yes, but it's in an area where we've been rooting out Taliban who want to create rat lines and take it over. That's why I'm coming along. Hampton doesn't think anything will happen, but you need a big, bad guard dog."

"Hold on, let me get my medical ruck and I'll be right out."

Gabe stood waiting. He took special care not to give her any more attention than any other SEAL member on the team. He didn't want Bay's career or his own destroyed by their desire to be with each other. That didn't mean he didn't dream of meeting her in San Diego after his team rotated back Stateside. He'd have time to be with her, explore her, share with her. That was worth waiting for.

Bay slipped between the flaps, the medical ruck slung over her right shoulder, her M-4 and SIG in place. "Okay, let's rock it out."

He smiled a little, seeing the warmth in her eyes for him alone. "This should be routine," he assured her, walking at her side. And maybe, just maybe, they could spend some quality time at Bagram before hitching a chopper ride back to Bravo. It wouldn't be much, but it was a moment to steal a little privacy with her.

THE MEDEVAC LANDED outside the village at dusk. Bay and Gabe hurried out of the sliding door of the Blackhawk and walked toward the gate to the small village. A tall man dressed in white-and-cream robes, a white turban on his head, stood near the gate, his hands clasped in front of him.

Gabe looked around. He was tense because the medevac was on the ground and, therefore, a target. The village was small, maybe a hundred people who lived at the far end of this narrow valley. The mountains and hills were shadowed around the oval valley, night coming on quickly. The medevac was equipped for night flight, but the two pilots and the crew chief weren't happy about having to sit and wait. Gabe couldn't blame them.

As they approached, the forty-year-old chieftain, named Taher, seemed upset. After giving him the greeting, Bay asked to be taken to his wife, Razia.

Gabe increased his stride to catch up with the leader and Bay. Everything looked normal, the shadows running deep. He could feel the chill and gusting winds coming down off the mountains at this time of the evening. The village appeared almost deserted, but at this time, families were inside eating. He could smell the wood smoke and spices used for cooking their meals in the air.

Taher led them down one of the main streets. They barely saw the outline of a two-story mud and stone house at the end of it. This village did not have a wall around it to protect it from intruders. The slope of the mountain was literally about a hundred feet away, providing some protection for the village.

Taher stopped outside the door. "My wife is in there. You must hurry. She's in great pain." He opened the wooden door. "Please, both of you go in."

Gabe looked around, his hands on the M-4. Taher appeared nervous, but Gabe wrote it off to the fact that his wife was in labor. Bay went in and he followed.

Just as they made it inside the house, Gabe heard a horrifying sound. It was the hollow thunk of an RPG being fired.

They saw the pregnant woman sitting in the corner, on the floor, surrounded by pillows. Her face was sweaty, her eyes wide with fear. She was holding her large belly, gasping for breath. When Bay heard the sound, she froze in the middle of the room.

As the explosion hit, the house shuddered. Instantly, Gabe called it in on his radio. His eyes were narrowed as he brought the M-4 up, ready to fire.

"Bay, *exfil!*"

She hesitated only a second. Turning, she lifted her

M-4, her heart pounding. Had they been set up? Who was attacking them?

Gabe pushed the door open. Taher was nowhere to be found. Gabe called the medevac, hearing more RPGs being fired. No answer. *Damn!*

"Stay close," he growled to Bay.

Fear rolled through her. The night was almost complete. She could see fire and dark, thick black clouds rising in the air. "It's true. We've been set up!" she gasped.

"Get your helmet on. You need NVGs," he rasped.

Gabe had worn his Kevlar helmet into the village, his night-vision goggles already in place. Dropping her pack, with shaking hands, Bay pulled the protective helmet out of her ruck. Her NVGs were next. Breathing hard, Bay quickly pulled the ruck back over her shoulders and picked up her M-4. "What are we going to do?"

"Get the hell out of this village," he snarled, angry at himself for not paying more attention. "Follow me!"

Gabe ran for the slope of the mountain. As a sniper, he knew to take high ground. It meant safety. He had seen a wadi, a ravine, about two thousand feet above them. The Taliban could be hiding in there. Best to avoid it entirely.

"What about the medevac?" Bay rasped, following on his heels.

"They're dead."

Oh, God... Tears filled her eyes for the three-man crew. "We were suckered in," she cried, stumbling and digging in on the rocky slope.

"Yeah, dammit."

"You've contacted the chief?"

"Yes. Come on, we've got to hide. We have no idea how many Taliban are around here. Or where they are." He scrambled up the steep slope like a surefooted mountain goat. The rocks were many, gave way and began to tumble down past him.

Her lungs began to burn as they faded into the night. They climbed a thousand feet up the slope. Bay turned once, gasping for breath, seeing the medevac helicopter enveloped in flames. She pushed up her NVGs up because bright light of any kind would destroy her night vision. The flames had spread out, an orange dancing circle around the destroyed helo.

Gabe halted, breathing hard himself. The village sat at eight thousand feet. Now they were close to nine, and he was laboring, too. Grimly, he watched the helo burn. Three good men had just died. And for what? Anger roared through him.

They knelt on the mountain side, using some small bushes to crouch behind. He called in their GPS position, requesting a drone. There was one coming on station as he spoke. Cursing, Gabe wished there had been a drone active over the valley before they'd flown in. It could have picked up the hidden Taliban in the hills above the village. And saved the lives of four men.

Bay knelt at his shoulder. "How many mags you got on you?" he asked.

"Twelve. You?"

"Same. Pistol?"

"I got four mags."

"Good. Water?"

Bay knew how important water was out here. "I've got a full CamelBak and six bottles in my ruck."

"I've got the same." He looked around, keying his hearing. Below, he could see at least twenty Taliban approaching the helicopter, AK-47s in their hands. "Damn, that's a big group," he muttered.

"They were waiting for us." She wiped tears from her eyes, her heart broken. Bay worried about the pregnant woman, but there was nothing she could do to help her now. Had the leader and his wife been threatened by the Taliban? Had they threatened her life if they didn't call in for American medical support to lay the trap? The Taliban knew they would respond. And they'd fallen for it.

Gabe reached out and gripped her shoulder. "Come on, we've got to find a hide."

"I wish I had my Win Mag," she gritted out, rising the turning to follow him up the mountain. The night air was freezing, the wind blowing in gusts across the ridge above them.

"Makes two of us," Gabe said. Pulling down his NVGs, he studied the wadi a thousand feet above them. The snow line was at the top of it. Would the Taliban be using in it? He had no way of knowing.

"I hope we find out how many Taliban there are," Bay huffed, following at his heels.

"We'll know shortly when Hampton calls us."

Once they reached the lower end of the wadi, Gabe stopped at the edge of the thickets and crouched. Bay moved next to him, alert, looking around. They were high enough now that they couldn't hear the burning of the helicopter anymore. The village looked far away.

She quickly took a drink from her CamelBak, glad she'd filled it before they'd left.

Gabe spoke quietly on another channel on his radio. Unable to hear, Bay continued to scan the area. She saw nothing on the slopes on either side of the wadi. Maybe this one was too high and too damn freezing for the Taliban to use. Shivering, she hadn't packed her winter gear. Her hands were numbing around the M-4. She hadn't brought gloves, either.

Gabe scowled as he completed the transmission to Hampton. He reached out, touching Bay's sleeve. Tugging on it once, she moved closer to him to hear his lowered voice. "Hampton says the drone is picking up approximately two hundred Taliban on the hills to the east of the village."

"Two hundred?" The disbelief in her voice was a whisper, but Bay felt terror work through her. "They must have planned this for a long time?"

"Yeah," Gabe whispered, drinking water. Wiping his mouth, he pushed up his NVGs and took his binoculars out of his ruck. He focused on the burning helo below but couldn't see the enemy. The Taliban would know the Apaches would come and hunt them down. Most likely, the enemy was already scattering throughout the hills to avoid retaliation. The enemy could be coming their way, too. "Bastards," he snarled.

Bay nodded, still trying to catch her breath. According to the Geneva Convention, no one was allowed to shoot at a medevac helicopter, no matter from what nation. It had a bright red-and-white cross painted on its nose, easy for anyone to see. "I feel horrible about this."

Gabe lowered the binos and put them back into his

ruck. "Don't. We had no idea. The Taliban is smart and they know we'll come to an aid of a woman in labor." He pulled his NVGs down, gazing around the area above, beside and down below them.

"Do you think they know we've escaped?"

"I'm sure of it. They're probably going house to house right now searching for us."

Fear twisted in her gut. "How are we going to get out of here?"

"Hampton's working on it with the LT." Gabe wiped the sweat off his temple. "We need to go into sniper mode, Bay. We'll work our way quietly off to the left of this wadi. Once the Taliban don't find us in the village, the next place they'll think we've hidden is in this wadi." Snipers never chose obvious cover to set up their hide.

Nodding, Bay knew his logic was sound. "Yeah, thank God for sniper training. Never hide under a tree, a bush or in a ravine because it's the first place the enemy will look."

"Right." Gabe studied the slope above them. He pointed upward. "Those boulders at the snow line should do it. Let's hoof it up there and check it out."

Bay slowly eased from her crouch. She was freezing but didn't say anything. They'd been working in high desert, not in the mountains. "I wish I had my winter gear on me," she said, following him.

"Makes two of us. We can't carry everything in our rucks."

Wasn't that the truth? Bay could feel fear eating at her. In the black ops groups, they never left a man behind when they were in trouble. She was sure Hampton and the LT were working at light speed to figure out a way to drop a Night Stalker helicopter in to pick them up. As she watched where she was putting her boots, Bay knew it wasn't as simple as she made it out to be. There could be other Taliban around. They might be hidden up among the boulders, where they were heading. A group of unknown size might be on the other side of the mountain ridge. It would take time for the drone to fly around the mountain and send back live video feed into the SEAL compound at Bravo.

Gabe halted about five hundred feet away from the boulders. He crouched and so did she. Breathing hard at his shoulder, Bay studied the monoliths that resembled a string of stone pearls halfway around the mountain.

He received another call. She waited, her heart pounding, her hands now numb.

Gabe hissed a curse after signing off. Twisting around, he rasped, "Bad news. There's about fifty Taliban on the other side of this ridge where we're located. And they're coming directly at us."

CHAPTER EIGHTEEN

FEAR GALVANIZED BAY as she followed Gabe higher.
The gusts sliced across the ridge, about five hundred
feet below where they wanted to hide. The stars were
bright, huge and close. If she hadn't been so scared, she
might have appreciated their beauty at this altitude. The
good news was, there were no clouds, which meant no
snow or sleet would fall to make their situation even
more miserable.

Gabe walked quietly, M-4 in his right hand as he
chose a lay up between where the drone had spotted
the Taliban coming over the ridge and the wadi. They
had some luck as he discovered a depression of rocks,
a vertical slit that would fit both of them into it. The
rocks surrounding it weren't very high, but they would
conceal their presence from anyone walking nearby.

Using hand signals, he ordered Bay down into the
depression. Moving around the area, Gabe hunted to
make sure there were no goat paths near it. If there
were, it would be the wrong place to wait because the
Taliban used these paths to traverse an area. He saw
one about one hundred feet away, but it wasn't close
enough for them to be spotted in the depression.

Bay quietly moved some rocks out of the way, making it a bit deeper as well as easier for them to lie on their bellies.

Gabe clicked the radio once. It told her he was returning to the layup. Any time the enemy was near, SEALs relied on radio clicks to communicate. No voices were ever utilized, because they could give away their position. The wind gusted above them and she was grateful to avoid some of it in their hiding place.

Slipping quietly into their spot, Gabe was breathing hard. He sat down and contacted the chief once again, giving their GPS position in a low voice. Some communications could not be clicks, and with the enemy still not in sight, it was safe enough to speak.

Bay continued to watch the ridge above them and to her right. Her mouth dry. She tried to slip her one numb hand into the pocket of her cammies, hoping to warm it up.

Gabe lay down next to her. He moved his head near hers, his voice low. "Chief said the Taliban on the other side of the ridge will crest in about five minutes. There's a goat path the drone spotted. That path comes a hundred feet from our layup. We're going to have to be quiet and not move."

"Okay. What should I do?" Their layup was short and narrow. It was barely long enough for Gabe's body. It was about four feet wide and ten feet long and eight feet deep. They wouldn't be able to spread out, severely limiting the arc of their shooting. Just having his body against hers gave her a sense of safety. There was nothing safe, however, and she knew it. Gabe was calm, seemingly unruffled by the situation. Bay found his reaction amazing because she was scared to death, adrenaline flowing strongly through her.

Gabe whispered, "No choices. We'll lie together, aim our M-4s to the right and wait."

"That's what I thought."

His eyes narrowed. "Taliban…"

Dragging in a ragged breath, Bay saw the first of the fifty of their enemy emerge over the goat trail. How they could see at night without NVGs and only a thin trail of moonlight amazed her. The men all carried AK-47s, some RPGs. They had several donkeys burdened with ammunition, food and water. Her mouth went even drier, and she flattened herself down into the depression, wishing she could disappear.

Gabe was glad to be on the side the Taliban were on. He wanted to protect Bay as much as possible. Shifting his M-4 so that the rifle was pointed directly at the enemy, he slowed his breathing. One of the major duties of a sniper was observation. His only worry was if the enemy picked up an odor they were unfamiliar with as they passed. They'd know the enemy was nearby. If Bay had washed her hair with that jasmine soap, the Taliban would get a whiff of it and know it was a strange scent, and it could give them away. The Taliban would stop and start hunting them. Bay always washed her hair after coming off a patrol, but thankfully, she hadn't had time to do it before they'd been ordered out to the village.

Bay forced herself to breathe through her mouth. Gabe was tightly wedged beside her. She could feel his quiet strength, his focus, his head barely above the layup. There were rocks around the depression and she wondered if his rounded Kevlar helmet looked like just another rock to the Taliban, should the enemy peer in their direction. She hoped so. Her fear amped up as the long, snaking line of silent Taliban emerged on their side of the mountain. Bay froze as the leader walked toward them on the goat path.

Gabe felt her stiffen. He forced himself to remain relaxed, the adrenaline pouring through his veins. He slowed his breathing and watched through his NVGs the grainy green shape of the leader no more than a hundred feet away from him. Wind gusted and he saw the leader draw his heavy wool cloak about him more tightly. The man wore sandals and Gabe found it mind-blowing as the temperature was well below freezing. He keyed the radio, one click, to let Hampton know the Taliban were on top of them.

The Taliban leader was so close. The last thing they wanted to do was fire and give away their position. They'd have to make a stand, and two against fifty Taliban would end their lives.

Time crawled by. The temperature continued to fall. Bay couldn't feel her hands at all anymore. She didn't move as the long line of Taliban silently walked past them. The donkeys were tired, their heads drooping. It was good news for Gabe and her because it meant the Taliban weren't as alert as they might have been. Finally, the last member walked past them.

Relief tunneled through Bay. She released a breath, resting her brow on her M-4 for a moment. Her heart was pounding like a freight train in her chest. She was sweating heavily. Fear gripping her.

Gabe clicked the radio again to let the chief know

the Taliban had passed by them without contact. When he felt it was safe, he called Hampton and reported fifty-two Taliban, the number of weapons they carried, how many RPGs and anything else that was relevant. He felt Bay move beside him, more like a slight movement of relief. He understood. His own heart was doing a slow pound in his chest.

"Chief says the Taliban is dispersing east to south of that village. This other group that just filed past us is heading directly down toward the village." His mouth flattened, his brow furrowing. "J-bad is on this. They've got B-52s coming in, but they can't just drop daisy cutter bombs on them if they're too close to that village."

Gulping, Bay nodded. "It's a Shinwari village. They can't…"

"Right." He wiped his mouth, keeping his voice very low. "The drone isn't picking up any more activity on the other side of the mountain, so we should be relatively safe here for now. They'll call us if there's any new movement."

Eyes going wide, Bay protested, "You mean we have to *stay* here?" She moved her right hand, her fingers numbed.

"Yeah, no joy." Gabe could barely see her face. "They can't risk picking us up. Too many Taliban in the area. We're going to stay put until morning. By then, this group will hopefully be south of the village and they can get the B-52s on station and drop those bombs."

"Okay," she whispered, the terror starting to abate. She did not want the Army Night Stalker pilots risking their lives by trying to rescue them. The crew of the medevac were already dead.

Gabe reached out, his hand over hers. "How are you doing heat wise? It's going to get cold tonight." Her fingers were icy feeling. He could barely feel his.

The unexpected warmth of his hand over hers made Bay feel a sense of protection. His voice was roughened, his calloused hand remaining over hers. "My hands are numb. I don't have any winter gear. At all. Half my ruck was medical supplies, not extra clothing."

Grunting, Gabe squeezed her hand and slowly got to his knees, ensuring that he made no sounds. He eased out of his ruck and placed it next to Bay's head. Slowly opening the Velcro straps so they made no noise, he pulled out two blankets and a set of gloves. He dug out some protein bars and handed them to her. After closing the ruck, he brought it slowly around and shrugged it back over his shoulders. The blankets were wool and would help protect them. The gloves would keep Bay's hands from becoming frostbitten.

He tugged at her shoulder and leaned over. "Let's quietly turn around so we're facing toward the village below. Hampton will alert us if the drone sees any Taliban coming over the ridge."

Bay nodded and dragged herself to her hands and knees. The rocks jammed into her joints and lower legs. She understood how quiet they had to be. Gabe remained in a kneeling position, helping her to turn around. Once she was on her belly, he drew two blankets across her body and handed her the set of gloves. And then came to lie next to her.

Opening the protein bars, Gabe handed her one. "Eat this. And drink plenty of water afterward."

The gloves felt incredibly warm to her fingers. They were much too large for her, but Bay didn't care. She fumbled with the protein bar between the awkward gloves. The blankets protected her and she felt her legs, which had been going numb, start to warm up. As he situated himself down into the hollow, their bodies jammed against each other, Bay frowned. "Do you have gloves on?"

"No."

"But—"

"It's okay," Gabe said, chewing on the bar, swiveling his head around the area, looking for anything out of place on the slope.

"You've got to be cold!"

"Bay, it's all right. I've done this a time or two. You're going to get colder a helluva lot faster than I will."

The Kevlar would work to trap heat in the core of their bodies, Bay knew. She finished off her protein bar, drank a lot of water and felt returning warmth seeping back into her fingers. There was so much she wanted to say to Gabe, but talking had to be kept to a bare minimum. Bay could see his shadowed profile, head barely above the depression, NVGs down, alert and watchful. Grateful he was with her, she felt the temperature dropping even lower.

Gabe lay very still, observing. He used the Night Force scope on his M-4 and followed the thermal body heat patterns of activity to the east of where they lay on the mountain. It was a 32X magnification and he could see the Taliban continuing to disperse over a large area on the hills above the Shinwari village. When he was focused, time ceased. Always sensitive to Bay, the left side of her body pressed against his, he could feel her shivering in earnest.

He glanced down at his watch and saw that it was midnight. They had a long way to go until dawn. And the coldest hours were ahead of them. He could see his breath flow out of his nose and mouth. It was probably twenty degrees now. It could easily plummet to zero by dawn.

"Bay?"

"Y-yes?" Her teeth were chattering uncontrollably. There was a gruff concern in Gabe's low voice. He had to be an ice cube himself. For the past two hours, he'd lain completely still, observing and passing on radio intel to the chief. She'd tried to sleep, but her legs were jerking and trembling, her body's core heat going deep in order to keep her internal organs alive.

"Come here." Gabe reached across her, bringing her fully against the front of his body. Their Kevlar vests met. He guided her head against his shoulder as he pushed back against the wall of the layup. "This is how SEALs stay warm in cold conditions," he told her, a hint of humor in his voice. He placed his one leg over hers, drawing her completely against him and rearranging the blankets so they were tucked tightly against her exposed areas.

Bay started to struggle. "But—"

"Hush," he said against her ear. "When SEALs go out in teams of two, they'll tuck their bodies together, not front to front like we're doing, but one will curve up behind the other's back. It can stop both of us from spiraling into hypothermia. There. Are you comfortable?"

Bay closed her eyes. The helmet acted like a pillow of sorts. Her cheek rested against his shoulder. "You're warm…."

He tucked the blankets in around her neck and shoulders, keeping out the cold. He laughed a little, a low chuckle, as he ensured that the blankets were around her as much as possible.

"Helluva an excuse to hold you, but this is damn cold weather."

"It is," Bay agreed, her words coming out in a stutter. She closed her eyes, feeling an incredible sense of safety against Gabe's long, hard body. Her gloved hands were clasped against the vest between them. Something primal flowed through her, even though her teeth kept chattering. He settled down, relaxing with her trapped against him. Gabe weighed a lot more than she did and he had a lot more muscle mass. That was why Bay felt warm almost instantly. She surrendered to him.

Gabe keyed his hearing. He kept the M-4 across Bay's blanketed body, his hand always near the trigger. Though assured of their safety, he now worried about hypothermia. He could already feel her begin to relax against him, her soft, moist breath against his neck. The teeth chattering slowed down and she stopped tensing and jerking every few seconds over the next fifteen minutes. The gusts of wind continued, but the layup protected them from the worst of it.

"You can't stay awake all night," Bay whispered, feeling warmth flooding her legs and arms.

"I'll wake you in two hours," he said.

She felt his warm, moist breath near her cheek. His voice vibrated through her like sudden, unexpected heat. His mouth barely grazed her cheek as he spoke. *So close. So incredibly close to him.*

The Kevlar vests prevented Bay from snuggling even closer, but she was grateful for his lifesaving training. "Okay…" she whispered, closing her eyes. All the fear, the adrenaline had bled out of her earlier, leaving her exhausted. She'd been weary before this mission ever started. The wind howled around them. In her mushy mind just before she drifted off to sleep, she worried about Gabe. How could he handle this kind of freezing cold? She couldn't.

The stars overhead moved like a huge, slow-turning wheel in the sky above. Bay sagged against him, her breathing softening even more. She ached to kiss him. Just being able to rest her warm cheek against his jaw helped lull her to sleep. The wind continued to shriek overhead, as if the earth were exhaling.

A SENSE OF PEACE descended over Gabe. He was holding Bay the way he'd been wanting to ever since he met her. How and where had he fallen in love with her? Gabe closed his eyes for a moment, stunned that he could fall helplessly in love with this woman. And he'd never even kissed her. That was astounding to him. War twisted everything out of proportion. Just feeling her breath, the slow rise and fall of her chest against his vest, the warmth of her breath flowing across his neck, sent a powerful emotional feeling of protectiveness through him.

He wasn't sleepy. He should have been, but Bay was in his arms. She was tall and lanky and she fit against him like some lost puzzle piece he'd always been searching for but had never found until now. Though he wanted to lean over and kiss her breathless, Gabe knew it wouldn't happen. Not here. Not now. Still, as he watched the Milky Way turn overhead, the stillness interrupted by roars of gusting wind, he had a new sense of contentment he'd never felt before.

His mind moved from listening to the sounds around them, to focusing on Bay, who slept soundly in his arms. She trusted him. He'd always known that. There had always been something strong, clean and good between them. He'd admired her from the beginning, and watching her for the past three months, he'd gained an even greater understanding of Bay's courage and her generous heart. She pushed herself to her maximum, never really getting rest in between patrols. His brow furrowed as he considered that reality. Bay was too good at her job as an 18 Delta corpsman. Everyone desperately needed her high level of skills and experience.

Mouth compressing, Gabe decided to tell Hampton about it when they returned to Bravo. She was burning the candle at both ends, unable to tell those who desperately needed medical help, no. It was her nature, a part of what he loved about Bay, but now he was going to step in to protect her.

Above where they lay, Gabe saw a meteorite arc across the sky, its yellow tail long and wide. He wondered what Bay would say about that, because she saw symbols in everything around her. Daily, he was able to devour something new she saw through her eyes or learn about her as a person. One corner of his mouth quirked inward. Maybe the Victorian Era had it all right. A long engagement, at arm's length, to get to know each other over time hadn't hurt their relationship. Nowadays, people hopped in and out of bed like frogs moving from one relationship to another. He'd been one of them where Lily was concerned.

These past three months had helped Gabe see clearly that Bay was a woman of immense strength, incredibly kind and sensitive to others. She gave new meaning to the word *compassion*. And it had opened up his scarred heart. She had breathed new life, new hope, into his soul. How badly he wanted to tell her just that.

Gabe remembered his torrid five-day affair with Lily. They'd met like two dogs in heat, spent five days in bed and decided to get married. It was the stupidest thing he'd ever done and all for the wrong reasons. He'd wanted a family—something good, clean and healthy, unlike his own upbringing. And where had it gotten him? Gabe learned his lesson. It wasn't about sex. It was about finding a partner who complemented him, who could be a friend, lover and confidante.

Bay had become all of those facets except as a lover. There wasn't a morning that went by that he didn't look forward to meeting her at the chow hall for breakfast. Sometimes they sat together but most times not. When they did, their conversations were deep and wide-ranging. She fed his soul.

Did he want to love her? *Hell yes*. In the worst of ways. But he wasn't going to go against the no-fraternization rule in the team, with women coming into their squads. Team cohesiveness was absolutely essential. He would never risk any member of his team for any reason. Not even for love. Taking a slow, deep breath, Gabe told himself their time alone would come. And then…the gloves came off. He would get to know Bay under far less threatening circumstances and not be breaking any rules that held the team together.

CHAPTER NINETEEN

"Bay?"

Gabe whispered her name softly, his lips almost brushing against her cheek. He squeezed her just hard enough to wake her without scaring the hell out of her.

Instantly, Bay jerked awake. Disoriented, she looked at the steel grip of his arm around her shoulders holding her in place. "Easy, baby…" he said reassuringly.

Starting, Bay blinked the heavy, drugging sleep from her drowsy eyes, her heart leaping into a pound, adrenaline pouring through her. But then she recognized the low, coaxing tone. They weren't in danger, but they needed to move.

"The Night Stalker helo is coming in. They'll be here in about fifteen minutes. We need to get out of this lay up and head south for about five hundred feet," he said.

"Okay," she mumbled, sitting up. Bay rubbed her eyes, trying to orient herself. She noticed a hint of grayness on the eastern horizon. "What time is it?" she whispered, looking around. The winds seem to be lower, but it was incredibly cold, her breath white vapor as she spoke.

Gabe eased up to one knee, gathering the blankets from around her. "O four hundred, four a.m."

Shoving the severe tiredness away from her, Bay got stiffly to her knees, helping him gather up the blankets. "And the Taliban?"

"All of them went south. Even the ones that came over the mountain earlier. The BUFFs, B-52s are on racetrack station above us. The Taliban are now far enough away from the village and the bombing's going to start just before the Night Stalkers pick us up. LT and Chief wanted a diversion so the helo could come in and not take fire."

Relief fled through Bay. "That's good news." She handed him one of the rolled-up blankets. "Thanks for keeping me warm."

"You kept me warm, too." He smiled a little. Bay didn't realize just how much real pleasure he'd gotten out of those four hours of holding her. "You feel warmer?"

"Much," she said, getting her M-4 and putting it over her left shoulder. "I don't remember anything. I was dead to the world."

"That you were," Gabe murmured, easing the ruck back over his shoulders. Looking in both directions, he said, "Let's get going. Follow me."

Positioning the NVGs over her eyes and turning them on, Bay watched him silently rise into a crouch and move without a sound out of their layup. She tried to be equally quiet.

Gabe took the goat trail the Taliban had taken earlier. Looking around, her rifle in her hands and ready to use, Bay realized why they were going lower. Chances were, a Black Hawk helicopter would be picking them up. The blades were long, and if it had tried to land in the hide area, they would have struck the rocks above them, splintering the blades and causing the bird to crash.

Gabe mentally counted off the elevation and halted on the trail. He knelt down and signaled Bay to come and crouch beside him. She wasn't as quiet as he was, but she hadn't been taught how to walk soundlessly, either. When she knelt down beside him, inches between them, he said into his mic, "The bombs have been dropped."

Bay heard nothing. She knew the B-52s were probably at thirty thousand feet, undetected. As she focused into the darkness south of them, she listened as the Night Stalker pilot contacted Gabe. In five minutes, they would arrive. Shivering again, she was glad to be getting off this icy coffin of a mountain.

The first bombs splashed into the earth, erupting in arcing red, orange and yellow tentacles of fire. The booming sounds rolled and reverberated throughout the valley, the thunderous sounds careening off the slopes of the mountains where they crouched. Bay could literally feel the invisible concussions of the bombs ripple through her body. She heard a helicopter nearing them.

"Exfil," Gabe told her, turning on his heel and standing up.

The Black Hawk helo rose slowly up and over the ridge above them. Gabe threw out three green chem lights to show the pilots where they could safely touch down. Then he pulled Bay down next to him and waited. The rotor wash was powerful, nearly knocking her backward if not for Gabe's hand gripping her shoulder.

Behind her, the booming sound of bombs hitting the hills continued in a rhythmic dance. The vibrations rocked through her. She watched as the Black Hawk lowered its wheels and barely grazed the rocky earth close to where they were crouched. The door opened and a crewman gave them the signal to come aboard.

Relief was sharp through Bay as the crewman grabbed her hand and hauled her upward. Gabe leaped into the doorway, rolling into the helicopter. Instantly, the crewman slid the door shut, telling the pilots to lift off.

Bay scooted to the other side of the helicopter, her rifle in her right hand. Gabe slid next to her. She pushed up her NVGs, incredible relief tunneling through her. They were safe! Through the window of the climbing, shaking, shuddering Black Hawk, she saw the bombing continue.

Closing her eyes, resting her helmeted head against the skin of the chopper, Bay felt such deep weariness beginning to sap her of the energy. *Safe.* They were safe. How she looked forward to getting back to Camp Bravo.

CHIEF HAMPTON MET with them after they'd landed, gotten out of their gear and gone to the chow hall for an early breakfast. He wanted to make sure they were all right. Bay felt as if her bones were breaking, the night spent in that rocky depression making her stiff and sore. Gabe had his usual grace, as if completely unfazed by their brutal night. It served to tell Bay how much suffering the SEALs took in stride, expecting to be in pain or discomfort when out on patrol.

Entering into the HQ near 0600, Gabe went directly to the coffee machine and poured them each a mug of coffee. Bay thanked him and they walked into Hampton's small office. The dawn was barely breaking, and she felt almost normal after nearly freezing last night. In no small part, she'd survived, thanks to Gabe. She saw his eyes were bloodshot, exhaustion lining his strong face.

"Nice job," Hampton congratulated them as they ambled into his office. He gestured to the two chairs. "We're going to send out a patrol at 0800, and you two aren't going. The drone is reporting the bombs did their work. We're going to do a sensitive site exploitation. We need to get men in there to look for identification, maps and anything else they can find on those bodies."

Bay was silently glad she didn't have to go. She gratefully sipped the hot coffee, both her hands warmed around the mug. Hampton looked absolutely elated over the developments.

"The call for a medevac," Gabe said, "was a trick to get us to fly in."

Hampton scowled and leaned back in his chair. "Yes, it was. No one could have known. It's a damn shame that medevac crew died."

"Was there *any* way we could have known?" Bay asked, her voice husky with emotion. "Five of us were put at risk. Three guys died. Could it have been prevented?"

"We're looking into it," Hampton said, his voice sad over the turn of events. "The LT and I are going into the village in a couple of hours to talk with the leader. He's the one that made the call."

"Don't you think the Taliban told him that if he didn't make the call, they'd kill his pregnant wife? Maybe kill a lot of the people in his village? He had no choice."

"Probably," Hampton agreed, frowning. "We'll get the details." He looked over at Bay. "How are you holding up?"

"I'm good," she said, lying. She wasn't sure she should tell the chief about their night in the layup. Understanding that team integrity and no fraternization was demanded of all of them, she wasn't sure Hampton would understand what Gabe had done to keep her from going hypothermic.

Bay noticed that Hampton gave Gabe a glance, but she couldn't exactly read it.

"Well, you two get back to your tents and get some well-earned sleep. When you wake up, come over and write up your reports."

Bay stood along with Gabe. "Yes, Chief."

On the way back to their area, Bay saw the light in the east becoming stronger. It was still cold at eight thousand, but nothing like the night on that mountain slope. Gabe walked at her side, his hands in his cammie pockets

"Thanks for what you did last night, Gabe. I was afraid to tell Chief Hampton we were pinned into that hide next to each other."

"Don't worry about it. He knew."

"How?" Bay frowned.

"He knows how cold it is up there. He knew we were going on a medevac call and didn't have cold-weather gear on us." Gabe saw her eyes widen with worry. "When you write up your report, avoid the details of me holding you."

"Would that get you in trouble?"

Shrugging, Gabe smiled a little. "No, but it's assumed by command we slept together because in cold-country missions, that's what SEALs do. It's not out of the ordinary, Bay. It just happens that this time, it was a man and a woman together. Not two men."

Taking a deep breath, she whispered, "Okay."

Gabe slowed as they made the turn that would take them down to their avenue of tents. "How are your hands and toes?"

"Good to go, thanks to you." She met and held his dark gaze for a moment. "There's so much I want to say to you, Gabe...." Her heart opened with powerful emotions toward him, but at that same moment his mouth compressed.

"Same here, Bay." He moved his shoulders and looked around. "Soon, we can lead normal lives...."

Understanding, she nodded. "I'm looking forward to it." Bay tucked her lower lip between her teeth for a moment. She wanted time to get to know him, kiss him and yes, make love with him. She saw all that in his eyes as he gazed at her. The hardness normally on his face had vanished. Now she just felt his desire.

"Last night, when I held you in my arms, I felt like the luckiest man in the world, Bay. I watched the stars silently turn above us, felt you breathing, your warm breath flowing across my neck. I realized that anything worth having was worth waiting for." He halted in front of his tent, a gritty warmth in his voice for her alone. "Just hold the dream of you coming to my condo. We'll talk. We'll explore each other. We'll have the time, place and space to do it. We won't be breaking any rules that way." His mouth curved faintly as he held her tender gaze. "You're worth waiting for...."

BAY WAS SAYING goodbye to all the SEALs in the platoon who were going home to Coronado. Their last month had sped by. In the cold early dawn air, the team was scheduled to leave for Bagram and then home to San Diego, California. She'd already shaken the LT's hand and saw how happy he was to be going home. Both other officers had to stay behind to brief the new platoon that was coming in this afternoon. Chief Hampton remained behind to make sure everyone got out of here on time to meet the CH-47 waiting on the apron at Ops for them.

Some of the SEALs were married. The excitement in their faces was evident. They were going home. Some of her joy for them was dampened by the fact she wasn't going home with them. Orders had come down from General Stevenson that she was to hook up with a Special Forces A team at Camp Bravo for the next two months. That was part of her commitment to Operation Shadow Warriors. Every female volunteer had to spend six months in a black ops team, depending on circumstances. And then they would rotate for six months back in the States, getting more education in her skill set area.

Her heart was heavy because as she hugged each of the SEAL shooters, telling them goodbye, they were like extended family to her. Bay considered them brothers she'd never had. Gabe had been the first to say goodbye to her and it was so hard to treat him like the other SEALs, but she did.

They exited the large planning room, heading toward Operations where a Chinook helicopter was going to carry the platoon on to Bagram. From there, an Air Force C-5, the largest transport plane in the U.S., would take them to Rota, Spain. They would land at Andrews Air Force Base near Washington, D.C., on the final leg of the trip. Another hop on a C-130 transport would land them at NAS North Island and they'd disembark and be home.

Swallowing her sadness, Bay finally walked over to Hammer, who was the last SEAL shooter to leave the place. Chief Hampton was in his office, finishing up last minute details before he left.

"Hey, Hammer," she said, throwing her arms around his meaty shoulders, "you be good when you get back to Coronado."

He grinned and hugged her hard. "Don't worry, Doc, I'll never be good. You know that." Hammer lifted her off the ground and then set her back down, releasing her. "You know what? I thought a woman coming in here would be a bitch, but I was wrong." He lifted his ruck and threw it over his left shoulder. "You're a professional, Doc. In every way." Hammer lowered his voice and whispered, "After I got over my hissy fit of you being assigned here, you've actually been a nice addition to our platoon. Take care of yourself out there, okay?" He shook his head. "SF guys just aren't as good as we are, so you gotta watch your six."

Bay chuckled and took a step back. "I hear you, Hammer. Bye..." She lifted her hand, her heart breaking with sadness. She'd come to love these SEALs. Every man was a hero. They'd eventually accepted her, making it far less stressful on her. For that, Bay was more than grateful.

The door closed after Hammer left. She stood in the silence, looking around, remembering the many good times here in this room. Good memories. Some of them funny. Some serious.

"Doc?"

She turned toward Hampton's office. He had his briefcase in hand, his M-4 slung over his left shoulder, ready to leave. "Yes, Chief?"

"Just wanted to say thank you," he said, walking over to her. "You've been an asset to our platoon in every way." He smiled down at her, searching her up-turned face. "Frankly, I was worried about fraternization."

Nodding, Bay said, "I know you were."

"You acquitted yourself well, Doc. I can speak for the officers and myself in saying we appreciated the way you conducted yourself here among us."

He didn't know the heartbreak she felt. Gabe was gone and it would be a minimum of two months before they could see each other. In a way, Bay felt tortured emotionally by all of it, but the chief didn't want to hear about her personal pain.

"It wouldn't have worked any other way," she agreed in a quiet tone. "I wanted to fit in and become a member of your platoon. I know I'll never be a SEAL, but I didn't want to cause more upset by working among you. I would never be a distraction. That can get people killed, and frankly, my conscience couldn't stand it if that happened."

He smiled. "You fit in well, Doc." Hampton gestured toward his office. "Do me a favor?"

"Of course." She saw a glint in Hampton's eyes she couldn't decipher. A slow grin came to his face.

"There's one more person you need to say goodbye to. He's waiting for you in my office." Hampton became serious and reached out and touched her upper arm. "Stay safe out there with those SF boys."

Confused by his request, Bay felt him squeeze her arm and release it. What was going on? She'd said goodbye to everyone in the team. Hadn't she? "Okay, Chief. I will. Thanks…" She watched him turn and leave the building. Bay frowned and moved toward the empty office.

Her breath caught as she saw Gabe leaning lazily against the desk, smiling over at her. "Gabe! What are you doing back here?"

Rising to his full height, he walked over and shut the door behind her. "Chief suggested I go into stealth mode in order to give you a real goodbye."

Stunned by the turn of events, Bay couldn't help the rush of excitement as he pulled her into his arms. This time, there was no Kevlar between them. This time they were alone. And then she realized what the chief had done for them, joy tunneled through her.

"Oh, Gabe!" She threw her arms around his broad shoulders, feeling his arms slide around her waist, hauling her hard against him. Gabe's mouth curved hotly against hers. It was the first time they'd ever kissed, and Bay absorbed the scent of him as a man, the strength of his mouth against her own. Bay tasted him, tasted the coffee he'd recently drunk, and moved her mouth in celebration against his. Gabe skimmed his hand down the length of her spine, his long, strong fingers memorizing every inch of her. Breasts pressed tightly against the span of his chest, her whole body tingled wildly in the unexpected moment.

Gabe couldn't get enough of her soft, pliant mouth sliding wetly against his own. Touching her tongue, he felt her tremble violently in his arms. His breathing turned ragged as she moved her hands around his neck, celebrating their union. She smelled of jasmine soap, her hair loose and free around her shoulders.

Settling his hands on her shoulders, Gabe reluctantly eased his mouth from hers. Bay's blue eyes were drowsy with desire. It made him feel powerful as a man, keen, hot hunger flowing through him. The golden highlights in her eyes sparkled with happiness. Bay smiled tremulously as he slid his fingers through her thick curly brown hair. It was silky feeling, strong, like her. Gabe ached to do more than kiss Bay right now. But time was against them and he knew it.

"Listen," he told her roughly, kissing her brow, nose and cheek, "I've got to make that helo." Gabe pulled her away just enough to hold her gaze. "Christmas, Bay. You'll be home in time for Christmas. I want you to spend it with me. You get a hop to NAS North Island and I'll be there waiting for you." He dug into her dazed eyes. "Is this what you want? Thirty days of leave with me?"

His heart bounded hard in his chest. Gabe knew she could be planning on going home for Christmas to visit her mother and sister instead. Gabe wouldn't stand in the way of that, either. He'd figure out something else because he was driven to create a space where they could have quality time to get to know one another. Without any damn rules and regulations or interruptions.

"Y-yes, I *want* to be with you. I'll let my mama know. She'll understand…." Raising her hand, Bay felt his recently shaven cheek beneath her fingertips. His beard was gone and Gabe looked even more handsome to her than before. "I'll be there. I promise," she whispered, an ache in her voice.

"Good." Gabe quickly dug into his cammie pocket, producing a rabbit's foot. "Here, my mother gave this to me when I joined the SEALs a long time ago. I wear it in my Kevlar vest and it's my good luck charm. It's saved me from a lot of bad situations." He gripped her hand, opened it and placed the rabbit's foot in it. "Wear it in the pocket on your Kevlar vest. For me."

Tears gather in her eyes. The poor rabbit's foot was pathetically hairless, but she curled her fingers around it. "I—I promise I'll wear it, Gabe." The words *I love you* were almost torn out of her. What if she was killed in the next two months? Bay knew it was better Gabe did not know she was falling in love with him; the grief would be easier for him to bear if it did happen.

Framing Bay's face, he kissed her hard, branding her. He was hers. Bay absorbed his strength and courage into that final soul-searing kiss.

As they came apart, Gabe rasped, "I'll be waiting for you, Bay…that's a promise… We'll have email…

Skype…" And he turned on his heel, opened the door and silently slipped out of it.

Her mouth tingled wildly in the wake of his last, powerful kiss. The main door opened and shut. Standing there, fingertips resting against her swollen lower lip, Bay felt her knees go weak. Leaning against the desk, her breath coming in gulps, she closed her eyes. She allowed herself to feel Gabe touching her, his hands heatedly memorizing her body, kissing her senseless. She'd never felt more hungry, more needy, than right now. Somewhere in her spinning senses, she realized belatedly that Chief Hampton knew they had a relationship, albeit a chaste one. That was why he'd arranged this unexpected meeting. Bay opened her eyes, resting her hands on the desk. Either Hampton had sensed it or Gabe had told him directly about it. She'd find out more later.

Smiling softly, Bay eased off the desk. She gently placed the lucky rabbit's foot in her cammie pocket and closed it. In the distance, she could hear a CH-47 powering up to take off. It was carrying the SEAL platoon to Bagram. The puncturing whirl of the blades reverberated throughout the camp. Her heart expanded with silent joy over being able to kiss Gabe. How long had she wanted to do that? *Four months. And two more to go.*

Bay left the now-silent building. The helicopter bearing the SEAL team was leaving, the roar covering Camp Bravo. She headed slowly toward the Black Jaguar Squadron HQ. There, she would receive her new orders. Somewhere in this camp, she'd be taking those new orders to another captain of an Army Special

Forces A team. And she'd learn to fit in again, become a team member and be support to that group, just as she had done with this SEAL platoon.

Her heart exploded with joy over being able to say goodbye to Gabe, to be held in his powerful arms and kissed until her world melted into his. Bay knew without question, it was love. She'd never before felt what she felt for Gabe. Over the next two months, they'd make their relationship work. If they could handle the past four months of looking and no touching, the next two months would be bearable. As the SEAL saying went, the only easy day was yesterday.

Christmas. Bay halted as she saw a CH-47 in the distance, moving higher into the early morning light blue sky, heading toward Bagram. The man she loved was on that flight. Pressing her hand against her wildly pounding heart, suffused with love for him, Bay stood there, watching the helicopter finally grow into a small black dot and then disappear altogether into the blue of the sky.

Christmas...

Compressing her lips, Bay forced herself to walk to the BJS HQ. Her body might be here at Camp Bravo, but her heart was held gently between the hands of a SEAL warrior who loved her with a fierceness that took her breath away. Christmas couldn't come too soon....

CHAPTER TWENTY

GABE WAS WORRIED. He stood inside Lindbergh International Airport, the main San Diego civilian terminal, waiting for the arrival of Bay's commercial airliner. Leaning casually against one of the walls off to one side of the security area, arms across his chest, Gabe absently watched people streaming from the security area. Christmas music played softly in the background. It was raining, the weather cool for San Diego. He wore a black leather jacket along with his Levi's jeans and a red, long-sleeved cotton shirt beneath it.

His gaze moved across the happy crowds, the excited people waiting on this side of security for their loved ones to emerge so they could welcome them home. His mouth compressed with long-held emotions as he waited impatiently for Bay. Gabe began to understand as never before what a family went through stateside. The tables had been turned on him. He was home, safe in the States, and Bay was in harm's way. Gabe was grateful the master chief of his platoon, Braidy Colton, was able to feed him intel, up to a point, on Bay and her whereabouts with the Special Forces A team she had been assigned to.

His brow furrowed as he thought about the last transmission from the SEAL platoon based at Camp

Bravo. Bay's team was in that same village they'd been in before, the same one where the medevac crew was killed by a Taliban RPG. After the B-52s had cleared out the Taliban insurgents, that Special Forces team went in and lived in the village, trying to stabilize it. The U.S. Army black ops group was much different from the SEALs in that they were nation builders. SEALs were not. They took the fight to the bad guys. SF teams went in, created connection with the leaders and people. They remained in the village, providing medical, food and any other type of humanitarian services they could render. Many of the team members spoke Pashto and were educated on the tribe's protocols. Bay had taken the place of another 18 Delta corpsman who was wounded in an earlier firefight with that SF team.

Gabe idly pulled his cell phone from his pocket and looked at it again. Bay had his cell number and would text him as soon as she deplaned. It was 8:00 p.m. and her flight from San Francisco was supposed to arrive any minute now. His heart soared with joy. And then it plummeted with anxiety. The master chief had called him at his condo in Coronado three days ago and told him to get into the Team HQ pronto. Colton had something to tell him that couldn't be discussed over an unsecured phone.

Gabe had driven to ST3 HQ on Coronado and seen the master chief. Colton had picked up some intel from the village Bay was in at present. The village had been attacked by Taliban. No matter what the master chief tried to do through the SEAL network at Camp Bravo, they could only get sporadic info about the firefight.

Gabe was worried about Bay's safety. Had she been wounded? Killed? He'd gone back to his condo, torn up and living in agonizing limbo.

Things were tense at Camp Bravo, the SEAL OIC had told the master chief. Usually, in the winter, all attacks ceased because of the heavy snowfall and conditions impossible for moving an army around the Hindu Kush Mountains. But this time, the Taliban was on the move, something new in their strategy playbook. The attack on the village was showing the Taliban was active despite the terrible weather conditions. It was a buildup to the coming spring offensive the SEAL OIC at Camp Bravo told the master chief. Not a welcome sign.

There was nothing on the screen of his cell phone. Gabe pushed it back into his pocket and waited. He'd gone through three days of hell of not knowing if Bay was wounded, dead or all right. Yesterday, out of the blue, he'd received a call from her. She had called him from Bagram Fixed Wing Terminal and was getting ready to board a C-5 to Rota, Spain. She would then catch another C-5 flight across the Atlantic to Andrews Air Force Base near Washington, D.C.

Gabe had felt his dread dissolve beneath her husky voice. She spoke quickly, because boarding was going to take place in a few minutes. And yes, there had been a firefight at the village. She said she was good, and that's all that mattered to him. But "good" in SEAL lingo had a whole lot of interpretations. Gabe had broken his ankle out on a mission, taped it up with duct tape and completed it. When the chief ask how he was, he'd said, "Good." His instincts told him something was wrong with Bay but she couldn't discuss it on the phone. *Damn.*

But when she'd called from Andrews yesterday, Gabe's concern grew. He heard exhaustion in Bay's voice and understood how time zones, jet lag and not getting decent sleep all conspired against a person. Plus, she was coming directly out of combat. From war to peace in a very short space of time and no decompression time.

And then, late in the afternoon, he'd gotten another call from her. She was stuck at Travis Air Force Base north of San Francisco. There were no flights into NAS North Island at Coronado. She'd have to find another way to get to the San Francisco International Airport and then grab a commercial flight down to San Diego.

Gabe knew the special pressures put on someone who'd been in combat who was suddenly thrown violently back into the civilian world. Airports were a special nightmare all of their own. The crowds, the TSA security and the holiday season meant herds of humanity. The last thing someone who'd just been in life-and-death combat situation wanted was to be surrounded by chatty people who had no sense of how the military person was feeling internally. Gabe was sure Bay needed to have silence, to be alone, to be given a chance to decompress, but none of that was happening for her. The extra emotional strain on Bay's nervous system would tear her down. The only question was: How much?

His cell phone vibrated. Gabe pulled it out and saw a text message. It was from Bay. She was deplaning. His heart rate doubled and he forced himself to remain where he was. A large crowd of awaiting, excited families gathered ten feet deep just outside security, anxious to see their loved ones to arrive. Another group, holding signs welcoming soldiers home, stood off to the left. His vantage point gave him a clear view of the narrow area between the wall and security where all passengers would flow into the terminal. The noise level grew in volumes as anticipation mounted.

BAY WALKED SLOWLY, remaining near the wall as hundreds of people quickly flowed past her. It felt good to get out of the cramped, ridiculously small coach seat of the airplane and move once again. Her body was bruised, her joints stiff. Just being active helped her feel better.

She carried her ruck on her back, her weapons stored back at Andrews Air Force Base where she'd pick them up in thirty days. Wiping her face, she felt incredibly drained but her heart beat wildly in anticipation of seeing Gabe. He would understand what she was going through. He would provide her the safety and protection she so desperately craved. And most of all, even though she was fatigued, her spirit lifted as she got through the opening and out of security area.

The noise hurt her ears and she winced. It was almost too much for her to bear. The crowds, the loud laughter, the cries of joy and celebration pounded against her oversensitized nervous system. Bay was suddenly jostled by a scowling businessman who had a briefcase in hand. He struck her left shoulder, trying to squeeze between her and the slower-moving crowd, throwing her off stride. A group of well-wishers waved a sign at a group of National Guard soldiers, men and women, ahead of her. There was a huge swell of cheers. With her ears ringing, all she wanted to do was find Gabe in this thick, milling crowd. Her senses were raw and blown. She didn't even have the necessary focus to find him. For an instant, Bay felt adrift and panicked, turning slowly around, enclosed by the crowd.

Fingers curved firmly around her upper right arm. Bay looked up. Gabe's face was dark with concern as he pulled her against him and then used himself as a shield between her and the other passengers bumping and jostling into one another. Bay gave him a strained smile of welcome, her heart opening fiercely with love for him. He was being a SEAL right now, protecting her. He understood where she was emotionally, as if she were in another kind of brutal firefight.

Gabe gently guided her off to one side, away from the milling crowds and rushing passengers. Feeling his guard dog energy, Bay released an audible sigh. He maneuvered her next to a wall where they could be alone.

Gabe helped ease the heavy ruck off her shoulders, which caused her to grimace. He took the ruck and placed it across his left shoulder. Positioning himself in front of Bay, she wearily leaned against the wall, tilting her head up to meet his gaze.

"Welcome home," he rasped, leaning down and gently kissing her. The noise swelled even higher around them. Gabe could feel her cringe with anxiety. But he also felt her warmth, her personal joy of being with him once again. He kept their kiss short, knowing Bay needed his care. As he ran his hand down her left shoulder and along her back to her waist, she flinched and her face

went white. *What the hell?* He instantly lifted his hand
away from her waist, frowning.

"What?" he demanded, searching her eyes.

"It's nothing. I'm good. Can we get down to baggage and pick up my duffel bag? I need to get out of
here before I lose my mind."

He nodded, swallowing his concern. "Let's go. I
know a less crowded way to get down there," he said,
touching her cheek. Instant relief came into Bay's face.
She was terrifyingly vulnerable. What the hell had happened out in that village? Gabe placed his arm around
her shoulders, kept her on his right side, away from all
the jostling, pushing and moving hoards of civilians.
Bay remained beneath Gabe's arm while they waited
forty-five minutes in Baggage before her green duffel
bag was spit out onto the carousel. She seemed content
to simply rest her head against his shoulder, absorb his
strong, solid body as a support for her tired one. They
didn't speak much; they didn't have to.

Gabe retrieved the eighty-pound duffel and hoisted
it easily across his right shoulder. Bay waited nearby.
She looked better, a flush spreading across her cheeks.
He'd shielded her so she could simply rest and hide
beneath his arm. But why had Bay flinched when he
barely grazed her ribs on the left side of her body? Saying nothing, Gabe guided her outside.

The rain smelled wonderful. It was light, constant,
the darkness hiding them as Gabe guided her toward
the parking lot outside the terminal. The raindrops felt
good the puddles splashed beneath their booted feet.
Rain was such a blessing, and so little of it fell in Af-

ghanistan. It was considered a rare event, one to celebrate.

Gabe halted at his dark blue SUV and opened the passenger door for Bay.

"Hop in," he told her.

She climbed in slowly, favoring her left side. Scowling, Gabe put the duffel and rucksack in the rear of his vehicle. As he closed it, he felt the rain running down the sides of his face. It was picking up, the wind beginning to blow. Once he climbed in, he could see Bay's shadowed profile. Her brow was wrinkled, her right hand resting against her ribs on the left side of her body.

"What's going on with your ribs?" he asked, shutting the door.

Bay's mouth quirked. "I took a bullet to my Kevlar three days ago. It's nothing. I'm good." She turned her head, her gaze meeting his and melting beneath it. Gabe's face was deeply shadowed, his eyes glittering with worry. "I'm okay, Gabe. I'm just—tired," she whispered,

"Got it," he said, starting the SUV. Turning on the windshield wipers, he added, "We'll be home in about thirty minutes." Bay had picked up on something a SEAL always told his buddies or the chief. "I'm good" translated: "I'm hurting like hell, but I can continue the mission." She didn't fool him, but he didn't gig her on it, either. Right now Bay needed peace, not pressure. Tenderness, not censure.

Sighing, Bay closed her eyes, leaning against the seat, feeling all the tension begin to drain out of her. "I was so looking forward to this…to seeing you…"

"I'm sorry you had such a hell of a time getting flights. You didn't need that on top of everything else." Gabe quickly guided the SUV out of the area, heading down the freeway toward San Diego and Coronado. The rain was picking up and the temperature was dropping. Worried, he would look at Bay every once in a while. She closed her eyes, her lips parted, her right hand protectively over her left side.

"You were in a firefight three days ago," he said quietly.

"Yeah...a bad one."

"My master chief got wind of it through the SEAL platoon stationed at Bravo. Can you tell me what happened?"

Bay sighed. "All hell broke loose." She opened her eyes, watching the windshield wipers move quickly back and forth. The rain reminded her of tears falling from the sky. "No one was expecting an attack by the Taliban in winter. It had snowed the night before. I was with the SF team in a home in the center of the village. We were eating our MREs when the Taliban attacked. They were sending RPGs into every house they could reach." Wiping her face, she felt the moisture beneath her fingertips.

"The captain of the group called for help from Bravo, but the Taliban were *in* the village. It came down to the ten of us facing an unknown force. There was no drone up, either. We didn't have eyes in the sky because the CIA didn't fly them because no one attacked during the winter months. Both drones were in for maintenance."

"The Taliban is forever creative," Gabe muttered,

hearing the slur of her words. His mind bounced from her receiving a hit to her Kevlar to the stress of the attack. Bay had come straight out of a firefight, stepped on a C-5 and come back to Christmas crowds at a major civilian airport. A perfect storm.

Bay managed a slight snort, but the pain in her left side amped up. Moving her fingers gently across the swollen, bruised area beneath her cammies, she whispered, "They have changed tactics."

"What happened then?" he demanded, seeing the Coronado Bridge that spanned the bay from San Diego to the island coming up. The lights along the graceful spans lit up the lowered clouds hanging just above it. Below, the lights glimmered reflectively across the dark waters of the San Diego Bay.

"It—was awful." Her voice lowered. "You know how you guys showed me how to move with a SIG in rattle battle?"

"Yeah," he said, his voice grim. It meant she was on the run with the SF team, running, firing and hoping like hell not to take a hit.

"Well, we went on the offensive. We had no idea what kind of force we were up against. We moved in twos through the village, with NVGs on, finding out where the RPGs were being fired. I was with Sergeant Hugh Cristner, and he knew what he was doing. Eventually, we ran out of ammo for our rifles and went for our pistols." Bay shook her head, her voice lowering with emotion. "I was down to my last mag in my SIG and Hugh was completely out of ammo. It was a scary situation because no one was coming to help us with any reinforcements. At dawn the next morning, after it was all over and we pushed the insurgents out of the village, we found fifty dead Taliban."

"You were on your own," Gabe growled, angry. "If you were with a SEAL team, that would never have happened. They'd have sent in a QRF to support you."

Bay saw the beautiful long spans of the Coronado Bridge coming up. The yellow lights across the bridge reflected brightly into the ocean below it. "Yeah, well, this wasn't a SEAL gig, Gabe. The SF operates differently. They're more conservative about dropping men into a firefight. Besides, we didn't have a drone up. The CIA had no other drones in the area from Bagram, either."

"Damn them," he ground out, his hands tightening around the steering wheel. "How did you get hit?" Slowing down, he guided the SUV onto the bridge, glad they were almost home. In another ten minutes, he'd have Bay safe and sound in his condo. There, he could help her. Protect her. Love her.

She rubbed her face tiredly, closing her eyes. "It wasn't pretty. I got called out to medically help one of our guys who went down. I was running across the village toward the area where he was shot and I got hit by a bullet in the left side of my vest. It sent me flying. My SIG flew out of my hand and Hugh, who was with me, snatched if off the ground and returned fire. He killed the guy who shot at us."

"I owe that sergeant a handshake," Gabe said, his voice low with feeling. "And then you got up and went and took care of the wounded guy?"

"Of course. I knew I had probably gotten a hematoma, maybe some fractured ribs out of it, but I could still do my job." Her mouth drew in. "I was able to save him. But God, it was close. Too close. They wouldn't even bring in a medevac until dawn, so we moved him to a house where I could stabilize and care for him."

"I wish I'd been there," Gabe snarled. "You'd never have waited so long."

Bay looked at the homes on either side of the short street. She'd never been to this area before. There were palm trees, luxurious tropical bushes in front of each yard. They looked as though most had been built in the 1920s or 1930s. She heard the frustration in Gabe's lowered voice, felt his helpless rage over the situation. At the end of the block, she saw nothing but darkness in front of them.

"Is that water?" she asked.

"Yes, San Diego Bay. My condo is located about a hundred feet from the ocean." Gabe tried to lighten his tone and take the anger out of his voice. "When I joined the SEALs, I put all my money into buying a six-condo unit here on this island. I felt it was a good investment because over the last decade, prices for rentals have skyrocketed. I made a good decision and I have six condo units along this side of the bay. I have one and I lease out the other five to SEALs."

"Wow," Bay murmured, giving him a look of admiration, "I didn't know you were a real estate mogul like Donald Trump."

He smiled tightly as he drove in to the last three-story building next to the blackened water of the bay.

"One day," Gabe said, putting the SUV in park in the driveway, "I knew I'd leave the SEALs and I needed some kind of income." He turned off the engine and released his seat belt. "Come on, let's get you inside. I know you're beyond exhaustion. What you need right now is a hot bath and a lot of uninterrupted sleep."

CHAPTER TWENTY-ONE

BAY STUMBLED AS she walked into his large condo on the first floor. Gabe's arm went around her shoulders to steady her.

"I can't even walk straight," she muttered in apology.

Gabe turned on the lights. "It's all right," he said, understanding the rigors and pressures that combat put a person through. He guided her through the foyer and into the living room.

"This is beautiful," Bay breathed, looking around in awe. The wooden floor was made of natural blond bamboo, the windows were floor to ceiling and overlooking the dark water of the ocean. The furniture was all rattan with jade-colored cushions. There was a minimalist quality to the condo that reminded her of Japanese design. She felt peace and more of her tension dissolving.

"Anything would be after coming out of Afghanistan," he said, guiding her down the wide hall. Gabe pushed the door to the bathroom open with the toe of his Nike shoe. "Everything you need is in there, Bay." He turned her gently to the opposite side of the hall. "Your bedroom is here, right across from it. I've got a robe in the bathroom for you, shampoo and some jasmine soap. All you need to do is walk across the hall when you're done."

Bay leaned against him, smiling wearily. "You've thought of everything, Gabe. Thanks so much." She felt his strength and was grateful for his arm sliding around her shoulders.

"Before you go to bed, I need to look at your ribs, Bay."

She heard the grimness in his tone. "It's just a bruise."

"I'll be out in the kitchen. Give me a call when you're done with your bath. I need to check it out."

She nodded. "I will."

He released her and as she looked up into his face, a powerful wave of care come over her from him. His eyes were narrowed and filled with concern. "I know I'm whipped, but I want you to know how grateful I am for you being here. All throughout the trip, you were all I could think about." Bay reached up and slid her fingers around his thick, powerful neck. "Kiss me. I'm not going to break…." She leaned up, curving her mouth against his.

Kiss me. Her words seemed to reverberate throughout his body. A jolt of heat raced through him as her soft, searching lips sank hotly against his mouth. He wrapped his arms around her, mindful of her injury. He took her lips, felt her breath mingle with his, tasted her. The kiss made him forget everything except Bay and this exquisite moment. Her mouth was pliant, giving and taking against his. Pure happiness began to replace his anxiety for Bay. Very slowly, he eased away from her glistening lips. Drowning in her dark, radiant eyes, he noticed the moisture in them. She was fragile and so damn vulnerable.

"Look, get your butt in there and take a bath or shower. You're so tired you can't see straight, Bay. I'll be nearby if you need anything." Gabe gently turned her around and led her into the large, spacious tiled bathroom. There was a chair where she could sit.

"I'll be okay," she whispered. "A bath sounds like heaven." Several jars of bubble bath sat on a ledge. Touched by his thoughtfulness, she turned and released his hand. "I'll give you a call when I'm done."

As GABE BUSIED himself with making coffee out in the kitchen, he realized there was almost a shyness between them. His emotions warred within him. They hadn't seen each other in two months. He sensed Bay's reserve with him and understood it was going to take a while to get reacquainted. She needed time to come down from the firefight. Time to adjust to civilian life where no one was throwing an RPG her way. Time for them to slowly get to know each other once again without the stress of combat threatening them. Thank God, they had thirty days. Because the last thing Gabe wanted to do was rush Bay in any way.

He'd learned the hard way about rushing into things with Lily, and he wasn't about to make the same mistake twice. Allowing Bay to set the pace, set the boundaries, was the only wise thing to do. And more than anything, Gabe wanted her to come to him. Wanted Bay to want him as badly as he needed her. It had to be mutual and it couldn't be rushed. This was one time when patience was a virtue. Being a sniper, he knew all about patience, and Bay was more than worth waiting for.

Gabe worried. He knew what bullet injuries into the vest meant. The bullet could break bones, cause internal as well as external bleeding, a hematoma, which was dangerous if not taken care of. It slugged a person with an invisible sixteen-pound sledgehammer emotionally as well as physically.

The two times he'd taken hits to his Kevlar, he'd gone through weeks of shattered emotions. Of nearly dying. Death was a funny thing, he'd discovered. SEALs were taught they were invincible. Yet, when he'd been hit and lived to tell about it, Gabe understood he wasn't invincible at all. It had changed his perspective in many ways as a warrior. And he knew without a doubt, Bay's view of dying, of living, would change, too. The only question was how.

After pouring himself a cup of coffee, he walked into the open-concept living room, the filmy cream-colored bamboo curtains drawn across the large windows for the night. Sitting down on the rattan sofa, he propped his feet up on the rattan-and-glass coffee table and waited.

Bay emerged half an hour later, wrapped in Gabe's dark blue terry cloth robe. It was so large it brushed her bare feet as she padded barefoot down the hall and into the living room. Gabe relaxed on the sofa, but his eyes, those always-alert SEAL eyes of his, were focused intently on her. She managed a slight smile. "Your pajamas and robe are way too big for me. I feel like I'm swimming in them. And I'm not a frogman."

The inside SEAL joke wasn't lost on Gabe. He

grinned and eased to his feet. "We'll get your stuff out of the duffel bag tomorrow morning. I thought you could survive one night in my sleep gear."

"They're fine. Thanks for being so thoughtful." She absorbed his boneless grace as he walked up to her. Gabe's shoulders were always proud, his carriage of a man who had absolutely confidence in himself. It soothed her raw emotions. The burning look in his eyes made her more than aware of his guardian-like energy that surrounded her. To say he was a big, bad SEAL guard dog was a gross understatement.

"Come on, let's take you down to your bedroom. I want to examine where you got hit."

"Really, it's all right, Gabe." Her heart beat faster as he gently slid his arm around her shoulders and guided her toward the hall.

"I know you know your medical stuff, but suffer with me on this, all right? I've seen a few of these and I know when one needs medical attention or not."

Bay wrinkled her nose. "And you don't trust me to know?"

Gabe nudged the door open to her room. There was a stained-glass lamp sitting on the dresser shedding just enough light. "I trust you, baby. Take off the robe. Lie down on your right side. I'll lift the pajama top and take a look at it. Nothing more."

"Okay," she said. Again, she was glad he was being circumspect. Gabe had seen her naked in the shower, but she still felt shy in his presence. "Thanks for understanding," she whispered, shrugging stiffly out of the robe and laying it across the bottom of the queen-size bed. The room was darkened except for the lamp. The bed had a rattan headboard and it curved gracefully across the width of it. She sat down on the dark green quilt and slowly lay down. The pillow felt welcoming and she sighed heavily as her head sank into it.

"I promise this won't hurt," Gabe said. He settled next to her hip. The lamp would provide enough to light to view her injury. Bay had moved her left arm so that he'd have a clear view of her lower rib cage. As he pulled the cloth away, being sensitive not to reveal her breast in the process, Gabe stared down at the massively bruised area. The bullet had struck the ceramic plate midway down her rib cage. The swelling was breathtaking and he quickly assessed the area. The dark purple and blue bruising spread out and was larger than his hand. It was worse than he expected.

"This is a bad one," he growled. He gently laid the cloth down across her covered breast. "I'm going to have to touch the area." He carefully laid his fingers across the swollen flesh. Bay flinched. *Not good.* The central area where the bullet had struck was the size of a softball. "What have you done so far about this?" he asked, lifting his head and catching her gaze. He saw the corners of her mouth tucked in, understanding even his tender examination to the area was painful for her.

"I've been taking Motrin every twelve hours."

"Did you go to the dispensary at Bravo when you got back to base? Get some antibiotics?"

"No. And you know why. If they'd seen this, I could have been held up for days and not made my C-5 flight out of Bagram on time." Her voice became more emotional. "Gabe, I wanted to come home. I wanted out of Camp Bravo." She slid him a pleading look. "You understand."

He sighed, studying the pus in the center of the hit area. It was infected. "Yeah, I do, but, baby, you *know* this should have been looked at." He carefully brought the flap of the pajama top over the injury. "Were you able to ice it down?" Ice and Motrin were the usual ways to deal with a Kevlar hit. "Did you get an X-ray to rule out broken or fractured lower ribs?"

"No X-ray, no antibiotics. I had some chemical ice packs in my medical ruck. I'd put them on every couple of hours and held them in place with some duct tape. I'm still on Motrin."

Shaking his head, Gabe studied her in the silence. He saw how exhausted Bay was. "I'm taking you to the Navy Dispensary on Coronado tomorrow morning. You need some medical eyes on this. Fair enough?"

Bay made a face. "Don't push it, Gabe. I'm whipped. Just let me sleep. We'll talk about it tomorrow morning."

Nodding, Gabe got up. She was already going to sleep on him. "Tomorrow," he promised quietly. He moved to the other side of the bed, lifted the cover and sheet and brought it over her. Making sure she was warm, he turned off the lamp on the dresser. Gabe turned around to take one last look at her. Bay was already asleep, her left hand nestled beneath her cheek, her lips parted, her damp hair was a dark frame around her face. His heart ached for her. As badly as Gabe wanted to lie down and simply hold her, it wasn't the right time.

Easing the door closed, Gabe moved silently down

the hallway toward the kitchen. It was nearly 10:00 p.m. The stress was hitting him, too. He had to be careful of making a mountain out of molehill with Bay. She was a medical corpsman, and he was sure she'd assessed her own injury. Inwardly Gabe knew he'd have done the same thing. He'd want to get home so damn bad that nothing, not even a Kevlar bullet hit would stop him. No matter how bad it was. Still… He tried to rein in his worry for her.

SUNLIGHT WAS POURING into Bay's bedroom when she slowly awoke. Though feeling as if she'd been hit by a semitruck, she luxuriated in the warmth of the covers over her. Sometime during the night, she'd turned over on her back. Moving her fingers to the bruise, she felt how tender it was. There was a lot of heat in it, too. That meant it was infected. *Damn.*

Frowning, Bay slowly sat up, the cover falling around her hips. She looked around, admiring the bedroom's tasteful décor. The rattan bed stands, dresser and mirror mingled with the rough weave of wheat-colored wallpaper. To her left were floor-to-ceiling windows. The drapes were a jade color and shielded most of the light pouring into the large room from the bay. On the dresser was a vase of fresh flowers, beautiful and exotic orchids in purple-and-white colors. Moving her fingers across the softness of the silk green quilt, Bay shook her head, feeling as if she were in some magical dream.

She eased stiffly out of the bed, her bare feet touching the cool wooden floor. Just sitting in a soft bed, feeling halfway decent and clean, she drew in deep a breath, grateful. Her ribs ached, reminding her that drawing in a deep breath made them feel cranky. She figured she had hairline fractures in a couple of them, and Gabe wouldn't be happy about it.

Just hearing the silence and seeing the dark marine blue of the bay made her relax. What a startling difference between snowy, cold, desolate Afghanistan and here. Bay's mind wasn't functioning well right now, mostly from jet lag and flying halfway around the world.

The door quietly opened and Gabe looked in.

"Hey," she called, her voice thick with sleep. "Good morning."

He seemed to watch her as an eagle would its prey. Or maybe it was really concern she saw in his eyes.

"You're up." Gabe had a cup of coffee in hand. "I was just coming to check up on you."

"Mother-henning me," she joked, rubbing her eyes.

He stood at the door, as if not wanting her to feel pressured. "SEALs always mother-hen each other when they're down," he said. Holding up his cup, he asked, "Feel like some coffee? Maybe some breakfast?"

She wiped her eyes and allowed her hands to fall to the coverlet. The sleek feel of the raw silk was such a pleasure to her fingertips. "That sounds wonderful." Bay looked around. "My duffel bag has some civilian clothes in it."

"I'll go get it," he said. "Coffee?"

"That would be great. Thanks, Gabe." Her heart expanded with joy as he gave her that careless smile. He could go from being so damn intense to boyish in a heartbeat. Fierce love for him swept through her.

She watched Gabe leave as silently as he'd arrived. Someday he was going to have to teach her how to walk like that.

GABE SAID LITTLE as he watched Bay eat breakfast with relish. He'd made her a cheese-and-bacon omelet, with a small cup of fresh fruit and sourdough toast. She looked beautiful in the pink tee, white linen pants and white sandals. Most of all, her hair curled and lay around her shoulders, a light gold and brown frame for her beautiful face. It was then that Gabe realized how gaunt Bay had become. Stress, firefights, not getting to eat as often as you would like, were all causes of weight loss. He lost twenty to thirty pounds when in combat, and only on coming home would he put the weight back on. Combat always caused him to lose his appetite. And then he forced himself to eat so he wouldn't pass out on a patrol. It was just part of combat stress for everyone and the reason why Bay was so thin.

"I've got an appointment with the Navy Dispensary for you," he finally said after she finished her meal. He watched her pick up the coffee cup, her fingers long and spare. Fingers that he wanted to touch him, love him, that he wanted to kiss one by one. How many times had he wondered what it would feel like to lie with Bay? He dreamed of loving her slowly. Thoroughly. Gabe had memorized every inch of her beautiful body. He wanted to capture her heart and breathe his life into her. And he'd inhale her sweet breath deeply into himself.

Gently, Gabe put all of those yearnings aside. His first step in getting Bay reacquainted with civilization was a trip to the doctor's office. And he could already

see her wrinkle her nose, but he said nothing as she
sipped the coffee.

"I'd really like to sidestep that appointment." She
had some antibiotic in her duffel bag and would take
them instead.

"I wouldn't." He held her gaze. "I'm not taking no
for an answer, Bay."

She managed a lopsided smile. "I can see that."
Knowing he cared, she didn't fight it too much.

Gabe rested his arm on the bamboo table. "What
would you like to do today?"

"Not go to the dispensary?"

He saw her grin. "Nice try, but no. What about afterward? Are you just wanting to be left alone here at
the condo? Some quiet downtime?"

Lifting her gaze to his, she murmured, "Just quiet.
I felt myself unraveling in the airport last night. The
noise…it felt like bombs were going off around me. I
know it's me, it's not them…."

"I knew what you were feeling." He moved his fingers around on the design carved into the bamboo.
"What about going out to the beach? Watching the
surf?"

Bay closed her eyes, her elbows resting on the table,
the cup between her hands. "That sounds perfect, Gabe.
It really does." And then she opened her eyes and met
his warm gaze. "Is that what you do when you get
home?"

Gabe was never surprised by Bay's insights and sensitivity toward others. It was one of the many things he
loved about her. And it was love. Just sitting with her
at the table, talking, absorbing her into his heart, was

an incredible gift. "Yeah, when I get off deployment, the first couple of weeks, I avoid civilization as much as possible. The noise, the crowds, the rat race, wear me down and make me emotionally raw. I get pretty irritable and cranky. I'm not someone you'd want to be around until I can sort things out in my head."

"And so you being a SEAL and your love of water, you go back into the arms of Mom Ocean to get healed?"

"Water is always soothing to me," he acknowledged. "What about you?" Gabe was hungry to get to know Bay. To discover all the little facets that made her who she was.

"I love the water, too. We have a creek out back of our cabin, and I was forever playing in it as a kid." She smiled fondly with those memories.

"Speaking of home, did you let your mother know you were home?"

"Yes, I called her while I was waiting for my flight out of San Francisco." She was touched that he would be concerned about her family. There was so much more to Gabe than she ever realized, and a new kind of excitement threaded through her. Finishing her coffee, Bay set it aside. Gabe looked so damn masculine in his dark green T-shirt and jeans. The material stretched cross his chest and outlined his incredibly broad shoulders like a second skin. It made her yearn for him all the more.

"Good." Gabe glanced down at his gold Oyster Rolex on his thick wrist. "We've got an hour before your appointment." He looked out the windows, the drapes drawn back. "Looks like the front has gone through. Blue sky out there. Lots of sunshine. Perfect for a beach lunch. You up for it?"

Was she ever! "More than ready," Bay whispered, holding his gaze. Despite his masculinity, his being a warrior, she was discovering another incredible side to this man. Gabe was far more nurturing than she ever realized. That night out on the mountain where they were squeezed together, hiding from the Taliban, should have made her realize it. But she hadn't, too scared and stressed out by the nearby danger. Now, as Gabe eased out of the chair to his full height, Bay felt joy moving through her. Was this some kind of Cinderella dream she was in?

CHAPTER TWENTY-TWO

JUST THE SOOTHING sound of the ocean waves rolling in and crashing upon the beach calmed Bay's anxiety. After seeing the doctor at the dispensary, they'd driven up the coast to La Jolla and gone to the public beach. The doctor had given her antibiotics, saying there was a slight infection in the hematoma area. Her ribs were not fractured, just badly bruised and that was good news. Otherwise, as Bay suspected, she'd have to wait until the swelling went down before she could have full use of her body once more.

The sun felt good on her, but the jacket that Gabe had brought along felt even better. The scent of salty air filled her lungs, chasing away her tension. Bay sat between his legs, leaning against Gabe, content as never before. His body curved around hers and she felt warm and protected.

In front of Bay, along the beach, a few people were walking along the damp sand at noon. The storm that had passed through last night left it chilly and the wind blowing inconstantly. Above them wheeled white seagulls, always hunting for food. Bay loved their graceful dance on the currents of the air. The sound of waves crashing their foamy lives out on the sand lulled her. She felt Gabe's cheek rest against her head.

"Better?" he asked. Bay had appeared stressed after coming out of the dispensary. He couldn't blame her. Squalling kids, children running around without proper adult supervision, the place overcrowded, all served to make her tense. He felt Bay's hand come to rest on his right thigh.

"This was the perfect call," she whispered, closing her eyes, her head resting on his left shoulder, brow against his jaw. Gabe pressed a small kiss to her brow. "Thank you…."

"I want to do more. I wish…" he said, frowning, "I know where you're at, Bay. I can feel you." Gabe lifted his left hand and gently moved some of her curly strands away from her temple. The humidity of the ocean was making her hair curl even more.

"You're doing it." Bay sighed, pressing her cheek into his open hand. The thick calluses on his palm were rough against the smoothness of her flesh, but she didn't mind. His tender care brought tears to her eyes. Bay tipped her head back on his shoulder and opened her eyes, looking up into his strong face. "I haven't had my letdown yet. I know it's coming. I can feel it."

"I remember finding you sobbing in that shower stall at the villa." Gabe took a deep breath, feeling the need to do more, but he knew reactions were different for everyone. It was like threading a needle and never being sure where the eye of it was located. Now he worked completely off his internal instincts where she was concerned. He couldn't read Bay's mind. He did know what she felt. But his finely honed military instincts would take over the job and hopefully help him guide and support her during the healing process.

Her mouth pulled into a partial smile. "I'll try not to duplicate that experience in the shower this time around."

Gabe laughed softly. "Don't worry about it. I'm just glad I was there when it happened."

She saw tenderness burning in his eyes as he regarded her. "It's so nice to be able to be with you, touch you, Gabe, be in your arms…"

"It was hell in Afghanistan," he agreed wryly. Gabe squeezed her hand gently. "But you were worth waiting for, Bay."

"Did Chief Hampton know about us?"

Shaking his head, Gabe said, "I didn't think so, but after I said goodbye to you, he met me out back. He told me to wait in his office until everyone had left."

"Then he knew."

"He must have," Gabe said, kissing her wrinkled brow. "I never said anything to him. And I know you didn't."

"He's scary smart," Bay muttered. "He could have called us on it and we could both be in trouble."

Shrugging, Gabe said, "Good chiefs know when to look the other way. Doug probably had suspicions, but that was all. And I think because we towed the line in the platoon, he gave us the gift of really being able to say goodbye to each other."

"I was in shock. I really was, but I was so grateful to him."

Gabe nodded, watching the waves rolling in. There were puffy white clouds in the noontime blue sky. "What's going to happen with you once you've had thirty days' leave?"

"We rotate six months in the U.S. and then six months deployed into combat. General Stevenson has it set up that the six months spent stateside include more training in our specialty. I have to go back East for medical refresher courses, which I'm looking forward to."

"And then you get reassigned to another black ops team?"

She nodded. "Yes."

"And those reports are collected in the Pentagon by the general?"

"Yes. In another four years, the operation will be over. General Stevenson will have seven years' worth of info on the forty women who volunteered for the program at that time."

"How many women have you lost in combat?"

"Seven so far. We're kept in the loop because we all trained together, became friends and we're tight with one another. When a woman is wounded or killed, General Stevenson lets all of us know about it. We're like a big family of sorts, kind of like you SEALs have your own version of an extended family."

"It sounds like it." Gabe saw the faraway look in Bay's eyes as she watched the ocean. "So you have one more tour in Afghanistan?"

"Yes." She smiled a little. "I've loved being a part of this operation, Gabe. I've learned so much, grown and changed. Some of it has been awful. I haven't met any of my sisters who don't have PTSD. General Stevenson is running a program on our symptoms, to see how we're dealing with it."

"Black ops guarantees you PTSD," he growled. "It's a natural part of our business."

"No question," Bay whispered. "You seem so steady and solid, Gabe. You are never rattled. I don't see the symptoms in you." She angled her head slightly to meet his eyes.

Gabe placed a light kiss on her nose. "That's because I've had two months to decompress before you got home. I was just like you when I arrived home. I hated crowds, hated the noise, didn't want to be around people. I'm glad I have my condo because I could hide there, go scuba diving, hunt for abalone, jog daily on the beach at Coronado and just let the crap slough off my shoulders." His mouth thinned and his voice deepened. "Now I know what it feels like for a wife or girlfriend who worries about her man who's in combat. I found myself worrying about you all the time. I didn't like not knowing where you were and what was happening to you."

"Yes, but you had an edge," Bay reminded him. "You could go over to team headquarters and talk to me by Skype. And we had emails. And you had the master chief who fed you info on me via the SEAL team back at Camp Bravo."

"I know, but the worry is always present, Bay. It never goes away." Gabe shook his head. "I can only imagine how a wife handles not knowing. Or a husband whose wife is in an area of combat overseas."

"It's rough," Bay acknowledged softly, content to remain in his arms. "That's why there's such a high divorce rate in the SEAL community. You don't know where your husband is. Most are out on missions and they can't email very much. I don't know how spouses cope."

"I don't, either, because I found my day consumed with worry about you," Gabe admitted.

Bay picked up Gabe's right hand and brought it to her lips, kissing the back of it and then gently turning it and placing his palm against her heart. "There's nothing easy about war, Gabe. There never will be."

"My enlistment is coming for renewal while I'm stateside," he told her, feeling the warmth of her long fingers around his hand. Every cell in his body screamed to take her and love her. Yet Gabe knew it would be at least a week before the swelling along her ribs would go away. And he had no desire to pressure Bay, because she was fragile.

"Really?" Bay sat up and slowly turned around, legs crossed, opposite him. "What are you going to do?"

Gabe picked up her hands and held them gently. "I've done four rotations. I've been hit by bullets two different times. Every time that happens, Bay, I realized I could have died and didn't. And then I go through a helluva lot of emotions about it. Death staring you in the face has a funny way of getting your attention." His mouth turned grim. "I can see you wrestling with it right now because of your own experience."

"That's true," she admitted, seeing the darkness in his eyes. "I feel like a leaf in a storm, emotionally speaking."

"I've had it happen to me twice. And I'm thinking I don't want to go through it again. I know I have my lucky rabbit's foot, but the poor thing is hairless." Gabe shared a grin with her.

"I'm sure it saved my butt out there," Bay said. "I need to give it back to you."

"No, you keep it. I'll collect it from you after you return from your last deployment."

Nodding, she could see storminess in his expression and she felt Gabe wrestling with a lot of unspoken emotions.

"Bay, I want to know what you think of me reupping or not." His hands became more firm around hers. He seemed eager to say something but bit back the words, searching her face.

"How can I make that decision for you, Gabe? I know how much you love your SEAL team." Inwardly, Bay didn't want him to go back into combat. He'd served his country with courage and patriotism. Didn't combat have to end at some point for men like Gabe? Didn't they deserve some family time? Home? A bed to sleep on, instead of a cot or out on some rocks, freezing to death?

"You're afraid if you ask me to stay home, not reup, that I'll be angry or upset with you?"

"Absolutely." Her mouth twisted with anguish. "Why would I want you in harm's way? Why wouldn't I want you here with me? You have a beautiful condo. You have an income. Is there anything else in life that calls you as strongly as the SEALs do?"

Her voice was strained and Gabe winced inwardly. "Yes, something does," he rasped. "You hold my heart, Bay. I like what we have. I have dreams, but they include both of us."

Tears jammed into her eyes. Bay wiped them away with trembling fingers. "I don't know when or how I fell in love with you, Gabe, but I did. And my love for you just grew stronger over the months. When you left, my heart broke." She sniffed. "There's just something so rock-solid about you, mature and wise, Gabe, that I felt like half of me was gone when you left." She reached out and slid her hand into his. "I love you, Gabe. I want to live life with you. Oh, I know we need more time, but there's nothing else I want. I was trying not to tell you this so soon...."

"Because?"

The tears moved down her cheeks. "I thought we needed more time."

He lifted his hand and cupped her cheek. "This is too funny," Gabe said, holding her tearful look. "I was trying not to tell you I loved you, too. I worried if I said it too soon, you'd see it as another pressure and stress on you, Bay."

Bay chuckled. "It's not a stressor, Gabe. It's just the opposite." His hand moved away and she missed the intimacy of his contact. "We never said we loved each other over in Afghanistan. I was afraid, too, for so many reasons. But it didn't mean I didn't love you or that I didn't believe we had a future with each other."

"That's all I need to know, baby." Gabe carefully gathered Bay into his arms to hold her against him once more. Nestling his jaw against her silky hair, he rasped, "I love you so damn much it hurts. I didn't know what real love was until I had to leave you alone over there in Afghanistan, Bay. I never knew the depth of worry or agony I'd feel when I was here and you were over there. I had horrible thoughts about what could happen to you." He kissed her hair. "I didn't sleep very well at night, let me tell you. It was a special hell."

Her heart pounded with relief, with joy. His arms held her warmly. She could feel Gabe being sensitive to her left side of her ribs. "I'm sorry you had to go through it," Bay whispered. "You'll have to go through it again in another six months."

"That's all right, Bay. I'll be here, stateside, with my platoon. I'll still have more contact with you than most people will ever have. My enlistment ends in about nine months and you'll be coming home. I'll be released from my obligation to the Navy in November."

"And then what?"

"Then I'll meet you at an airport and we'll work things out until I'm finished those last months. I want a life with you, Bay. And someday, maybe start a family if it feels right to you."

A soft sigh tore from her. "You'd really leave the SEALs?"

"I would."

A ribbon of relief moved through her as Gabe tightened his arms just a little more around her, as if to persuade her he was serious. "I—I was trying to steel myself for the fact that you wouldn't leave them. That I would be like every other woman, worrying about her man overseas and never knowing anything…."

He leaned down and kissed her, whispering, "Why would I throw away someone like you away for combat duty?"

A lump formed in her throat. "You're sure?"

"Never more. I'm twenty-nine. I've done and seen it all. The only thing I didn't have and was looking for was the love of a good woman. I want to have a family. I screwed that up with my first marriage. But I'm not screwing it up a second time. You and I deserve a shot at a good relationship, not one that's torn apart by me being gone all the time."

"It sounds good to me, Gabe." Bay wrapped her fingers around his arms that spanned across her shoulders and chest. "I can hardly wait until I'm all better."

He laughed a little. "Makes two of us. The wait will just make it more sweet when I can love you, Bay. In the meantime, we're together, we can hold each other, kiss each other.... And that's a helluva lot more than we had in Afghanistan."

CHAPTER TWENTY-THREE

SEVEN DAYS HAD passed and Bay checked her hematoma as she dressed after awakening. The swelling and infection were gone. Just pretty rainbow colors of yellow, green and blue, indicating the worst had passed in the area, remained. Sunshine poured through the woven drapes, flooding the bedroom. The clock read 0600.

Every day, she was waking up earlier, another indication she was over the worst of her trauma and jet lag. Never mind that three days ago, the emotional blowout she was expecting came when she was walking the beach at Coronado with Gabe. He'd held her in his arms, giving her the safety she needed as the deep sobs had torn out of her.

Today, they were buying a Christmas tree from a local vendor on the island and going to decorate it. It was something Bay eagerly looked forward to. Christmas was always a big deal in her family. After pulling on a dark red long-sleeved cotton tee, her black gabardine slacks, a pair of black, warm socks, Bay slipped into a pair of simple leather shoes.

Her heart swelled with affection when she thought of Gabe. She could hear him puttering around in the kitchen, the clinking noise of a skillet or pan, drifting down the hallway. She'd discovered another facet to this man: he was a gourmet cook. Who knew? Her hair was still damp, the brown curls beginning to form as she pushed her fingers through the strands. Walking down the hall, Bay wanted to be with him more than ever. The time of sleeping in separate bedrooms was over.

GABE LOOKED UP from the granite island where the stove was located. He saw Bay round the corner. Today, as never before, she looked whole, her eyes clear and sparkling. He loved her more every day. And now she was here, walking over to sit on a stool opposite him.

"Good morning," she said, her voice still drowsy. Gabe was frying up a pound of bacon in a large black skillet. He smiled at her, turning the bacon.

"You look good this morning." Hell, she looked good enough to eat. His body responded hotly to her presence. There was a special hell for men like himself who had the patience of Job. His master bedroom was just down the hall from the guest bedroom where Bay slept. It was tough getting to sleep knowing how close she was. Even tougher as his torrid dreams were always about kissing her, loving her, making her his own.

"I am." Bay patted her left side. "My hematoma is practically gone."

There was a wicked look in her blue eyes, something that had been missing since she'd arrived home. Oh, that look was almost always there the four months they'd had duty together. "Yeah?" he teased, moving to the counter and pulling down a couple of plates.

"Yeah," she whispered.

Gabe poured her coffee and reached across the island and slid it into her awaiting hands. His heart lifted as their fingers briefly met. The mood around Bay was remarkably different. Better.

"So," Gabe said, transferring the bacon to a plate with paper towels across it. "Does this mean what I think it means?"

He said it teasingly, always aware of not pressuring Bay. If she loved him as much as he loved her, her emergence from combat would take time. And God knew, he was a sniper and had patience to burn. It didn't mean he liked it, but he accepted it because he had no desire to push himself on her before she was ready.

"I consider this a Christmas Eve gift for both of us," she said, noticing a glint in his green eyes, wanting him, wanting to love him as fiercely as she could. She smiled a little as she sipped the coffee.

"Mmm," he said, putting the bacon aside. "You are a gift," he told her in a low, gritty tone. He saw heat and desire in her stare. "Well, then," he said, a slow smile coming to his mouth, "we're both going to need food for the long haul. How many eggs you want?"

"Good idea. I'm open to three. Want me to make toast?"

"Sure, go ahead." He watched Bay slip off the stool. The bright red tee beautifully outlined her lean, strong body. Gabe knew he'd never tire of her grace as she moved. He busied himself with cracking six eggs into the skillet. "Ready to get that tree this morning?" Gabe wanted her to choose the time and place of coming together. Hell, he'd do it right now, but it was Bay's call. There was something satisfying about waiting and knowing at some point she would approach him. Today was going to be a very special day, and Gabe was going to absorb every aspect of it as they moved toward each other's arms.

Popping two slices of bread into the toaster, Bay said, "I am."

"Are you going to call your mom tonight?" Gabe knew from talks with Bay that her family celebrated Christmas with all the trimmings. They had a baked goose with stuffing, candied yams, cranberry relish and pumpkin pie. He was going to make sure the two of them had those things this time. Cooking a goose was new to him, but he'd have her to help him figure it out.

"I will," she said over her shoulder. "Strawberry jam?" Bay asked, opening the refrigerator.

"Yes. Is there anything else you want?" He looked over his shoulder as she stood at the counter, the silverware drawer open. Her profile sent his heart sky rocketing with need. Gabe wondered for the thousandth time how someone as sensitive and kind as Bay handled combat. But she could and did. She had emotions, but she knew when to put them in a box, just as SEALs did. He was mesmerized by how her emotions would then appear afterward to scrub her soul free of the carnage and trauma she'd seen and experienced. He guessed he didn't have that mechanism.

Gabe forced himself to pay attention to the eggs in the skillet. Seeing her strength only made him love Bay more than he already did.

"You know what I want. I know what you want. I think strawberry jam tops your list of the good stuff in your life."

"*You* top my list, baby, not the strawberry jam."
Gabe kept his eye on her as she pulled a large jar of jam
from the refrigerator. She met his heated look and she
brought over the jar to the island where they would eat.

"I think you have good taste." Her heart fluttered
over the sizzling look a man gives a woman that he's
going to make love to. Never had she yearned to be in a
man's arms more than his. Her lower body clenched beneath that his gaze. It excited her. Somehow she knew
Gabe would be a considerate lover, a man who was as
interested in pleasing her as himself. Her skin reacted
to that thought, tiny tingles racing wildly throughout
her, igniting a hunger she'd had to ignore until now.

"I know I do. Butter?"

"Umm, right..."

"Now, don't get distracted," Gabe teased, flipping
the eggs over. *Distracted?* He was this close to de-
stroying the eggs in the skillet. Bay had the ability to
utterly disintegrate his focus. And as a sniper, he had
laserlike focus. This quiet, gentle hill woman could
make it so that only his body and heart survived her
smile and shimmering blue stare. Now he was getting
to see her under less stressful conditions. And he liked
what he saw.

Bay laughed softly, retrieved the butter and set it
on the island. She walked up behind Gabe and slid her
arms around his waist. "You are a total distraction of
the best kind," she whispered, hugging him with all
her strength. And then she released Gabe because he
was trying to get the eggs out of the skillet.

"You're a tease, you know that?" Gabe placed three
eggs on each plate. Her unexpected affection blew

through his carefully controlled movements. She was spontaneous and that was something new. Something good. He turned off the burner and put the spatula down on the island. Bay picked up the toast that had just popped out of the toaster. Wiping his hands on a cloth at the sink, Gabe watched her give him an impish smile. The change in her was breathtaking. Heartstealing. Once Bay had been able to cry and off-load all the dark emotions caused by combat, she'd bounced back.

Gabe walked up to where she sat waiting for him, slid his hands around her face, trapping her. He leaned down and found her smiling lips. As his mouth moved hotly against hers, he heard her moan, her arms coming around his shoulders. She tasted like cinnamon and coffee. She deepened the kiss, drawing him closer, her fingers caressing the nape of his neck, moving through his short hair.

Bay sighed as Gabe eased away, breaking their kiss. Her lips tingled wildly in the wake of his powerful kiss. She looked up through her lashes into his stormy green gaze.

Gabe grimaced and grazed his hand across her soft, slightly damp hair. "Food is energy," he gruffly agreed, and sat down next to her. "Let's eat or else I'm carrying you off to my bedroom and we won't emerge from it for the rest of the day or night."

"You're right, we have to eat, but I don't want to."

"Let's eat," he urged, his body turned into knots of fire and need. Gabe wanted this to be a perfect day for them. It was Christmas Eve. For once, he wanted to celebrate the holiday because he'd hated it as a boy with his drunken father always ruining the season for him and his mother.

As Bay sat at his elbow, the silence was broken only by soft, instrumental Christmas music from a radio.

"Who would ever have guessed you were such a gourmet cook?" she remarked.

He grinned as he sipped his coffee. "What? Men can't cook?"

"Something like that," Bay said, giving him an amused look. The salty bacon tasted delicious to her this morning. In fact, her world looked different. Before her emotional blowout, she'd felt moody and irritable at times. Gabe had taken it all in stride. "Your mom must have trained you."

"Yes, she did. She was working full-time and told me that someday I'd get married and the woman shouldn't have to be expected to be chief cook and house cleaner." His mouth drew into a grin. "I got trained real early."

"I can hardly wait to meet her," Bay said, slathering the strawberry jam across her piece of toast. "My mama believed men should help in the kitchen and do the cleaning, too."

"I'm fully trained," Gabe assured her with a chuckle. He saw the soft pink flush cross Bay's cheeks. He'd never seen her so upbeat and happy. She seemed to be decompressing, coming back to who she really was when her life wasn't being threatened daily. The change rocked his world, and all Gabe wanted to do was love her thoroughly, completely and hold her against his naked body.

"I'm so excited to be getting a Christmas tree today," she said. "Do you have any decorations for it?"

He shook his head. "No." And when he saw her disappointment, he added, "Christmas wasn't a big deal at our house, Bay. My father hated the holidays and I can't ever remember one Christmas when he wasn't angry and constantly arguing with my mother. I hid a lot during those times because I knew he'd take out his anger on me if I was around. After my dad passed, we were on my mother's income and things were tight. She saved the money for a few gifts for me, instead of buying a tree."

Bay reached out and slid her fingers across his shoulder. "That's okay. We're going to have an old-fashioned Christmas just like we have at our cabin. Are you game? It will be fun." Bay gave him a pleading look.

"Sure, I'm open to it. I want to know about you, your family and your traditions." There was an effortlessness to Bay, he'd discovered early on in Afghanistan. Anyone who was in her presence automatically felt as if they counted the most in her life. She had a nuanced ability to make everyone feel special beneath her sunshinelike personality.

Gabe felt like the luckiest damn man on the planet to have her here with him now. To be the object of her full, undivided attention. And he was lapping it up like a starving animal. Always, Gabe wondered how Bay had survived three years of combat. He also realized she had a tough, tensile inner strength that was like a GPS unit, always bringing her back into balance within herself. It made him feel so damn lucky. And he'd never had any luck in his life until she'd walked into his world that day in Afghanistan.

Rubbing her hands together, Bay whispered, "Good! You're going to love how we celebrate Christmas!"

GABE SAT AT the granite island midafternoon with Bay. The Christmas tree was standing in the corner of the living room, ready to be decorated. She had popped popcorn and brought over a huge bowl and set it between them. She'd shown him how to string the kernels on a long thread with a needle, and now he had about two feet of it snaked out to the left of him across the island. And while he was doing that, she had brought over colorful construction paper, scissors, glue and bottles of glitter.

Bay slid up on the seat beside him. "You have to remember, my family isn't well off. I grew up stringing popcorn for the tree, using construction paper to draw stars, round circles, Christmas trees and then putting glue on them and sprinkling them with glitter." She picked up the scissors, expertly beginning to cut circles to be the bulbs for their six-foot fir tree.

"This is kinda fun," Gabe admitted, watching her hands fly over the paper and producing dozens of circles on the counter.

"Me and my sister always looked forward to Christmas Eve. Mama would have all the items laid out on the table." She felt warmth watching Gabe struggle with the needle and thread. A combat medic he was not. Half the popcorn ended up broken and falling around the bowl. He had large hands and the delicate kernels weren't exactly his forte. Imagining those scarred, sun-darkened hands moving across her body made Bay's lower body burn with anticipation.

By 8:00 p.m. the paper decorations and the long white swaths of popcorn adorned the tree. Gabe had attached a paper star that had gold glitter to the top of it. Bay got her cell phone and clicked a photo of their hard work and sent it to her mother and sister. Gabe did the same and sent a picture to his mother. Their families might not be with them, but they were there with them in spirit.

The tree was adorned and Gabe seemed to enjoy every second of this special day. This evening, she'd felt caught up in the spirit of Christmas, more so because he was with her.

Bay felt him approach her from behind and she turned around. She saw the look on Gabe's face and slid her arms around his shoulder, happy to be drawn up against his body. "You know what I want as a gift for Christmas?"

"What?" he asked.

"You."

Gabe gave her a heated look, lifting his hand and smoothing a few tendrils away from her flushed cheek. "Funny," he murmured, his mouth stretching into a teasing line, "I was going to tell you the same thing." His mouth grew into a full smile, his eyes shining with love for her alone.

"We're mind readers." She laughed, sliding her hand across his jaw, the prickle of his beard sending tingles through her fingertips.

"Are you ready for this?" Gabe asked, searching her eyes.

"More than ready. "

"What about the hematoma?"

"Good as new." Bay saw his concern. Giving him a shake, she said, "Gabe, I'm not some fragile egg, you know. I'm strong now. All that's left of that hematoma is an ugly bruise." Her fingers dug into his shoulders, and her voice lowered with feeling. "How long have we waited for this?"

In one motion, Gabe picked her up into his arms. "Too damn long...."

With a gasp of surprise, Bay gave a laugh and rested her head on his shoulder as he carried her across the living room and down the hall to his room. Gabe nudged the door open. Bay had seen his room before, but tonight the lights along the edge of island were shining like small, dancing beams across the smooth ocean that surrounded Coronado. He laid her on the bed and walked over and closed the drapes. The room became shadowy and intimate.

She watched him walk with that boneless, confident grace as he came back to the bed. Her heart began to beat a little stronger in her chest as he closed the door and turned toward her. His eyes met hers. The naked desire in them made Bay's heart fly open.

Gabe crouched near her feet, a wry look on his face. "If I told you how many times I'd undressed you in my dreams while I was in Afghanistan, you wouldn't believe me." He removed each of the shoes from her feet and he leaned down, placing a featherlight kiss at the top of her right ankle, his fingers sliding between her flesh and the sock. As he eased it slowly off her foot, he kissed her here and there.

Bay smiled and closed her eyes. "You weren't the only one undressing somebody." She sighed softly. "That feels so good…" she whispered, the tiny wavelets of tingles moving across each of her feet and up her ankle.

Gabe dropped the socks on the floor. Getting up, he moved to her hips, sliding his hands slowly around her waist. "I'll bet I did it more times than you." He held her slumberous gaze.

"I lost count," Bay admitted, feeling his roughened fingers slide down between her skin and the waistband. He slowly unbuttoned her slacks. Her abdomen tightened in anticipation of his touch. The sound of the zipper came next and his hand slipped beneath the material, her flesh taut as he pulled the slacks downward off her hips. As he brought the slacks over her thighs, he stopped, brushed each one with several provocative kisses. Bay strained, her curved thighs tensing as he would lick a spot on the inside of each one and then kiss it tenderly before moving on. The slacks dropped beside the bed.

Bay's lower body grew needy and damp as his lips traced a slow, fiery path inward on each of her thighs. She ached for his continued touch, his mouth rasping across her sensitized flesh. Her fingers curled into the silky fabric and she moaned. Gabe followed the line of her silken panties, his tongue probing beneath the material. She wanted so much more of him.

He followed the curve of the cloth, pushing it aside, lips caressing her. Bay's breath jammed in her chest, her entire lower body erupting with heat, a cramping pain clenching down through her womb. She reached out, her fingers grazing his powerful shoulder.

Gabe felt her fingers dig into his flesh and he smiled to himself. He was going to please her first until she was restless with hunger, making sure she was ready for him. With his hands, he continued to kiss her and feel her tense with anticipation. All his fiery dreams of undressing her were going to come true tonight. She was incredibly responsive and his heart soared. She purred his name, trying to arch closer to his mouth teasing her. Never had he wanted to please a woman as much as he did Bay. Gabe wanted to give back all the kindness and compassion she effortlessly bestowed on others with her touch and voice. Tonight, it was her turn to receive. And he was just the man to give her that gift because he loved her more than anything he'd ever loved in his life.

Bay's breathing quickened as he lifted his head. He eased her thighs apart, settling down between them, holding her pleading, hungry gaze. His fingers slid across her sensitive skin. He leaned over, gently nipped the inside of her thigh and then used his tongue to soothe the area. Every time, he would hear her gasp with pleasure, her hands reaching out for him, gripping his shoulders. The sound of Bay's breathing, the feel of her fingers digging frantically into his shoulder, crying out for him, made him grit his teeth. The pain of his erection pressed against his jeans.

His fingers lingered and traced across the seam of her panties as they curved to the juncture of her thighs met. Her back arched as his lips slowly moved closer to her warm, wet core. She gripped his shoulder, pleading with him, wanting more of him. Just seeing Bay's eyes close, her lips parted in anticipation, made him feel good. Her breasts rose and fell sharply beneath the red tee she wore. *Dreams do come true....* He pulled away just enough to draw the silky panties downward and off her long, firm legs.

He smiled down at Bay as he eased her to the edge of the bed. He knelt down on the floor, opening her to him. Her eyes were wild-looking, hungry, and she was trembling. He whispered kisses across her belly, stopping, licking her salty flesh. Gabe felt her entire lower body contract, her strong thighs clenching at his shoulders. He could hear her breathing turning ragged, her voice hoarse, calling his name. He slid his roughened fingertips across the curve of her taut thighs, spreading her wider, leaning down and whispering kisses against her secret place. Bay uttered a distressed sound deep in her throat, pressing herself against his mouth, wanting more. Much more. He slowed and deepened his sweet, focused strategy upon her, feeling her lush body responding to his desire. The sweet, musky scent of her made him groan. He inhaled her, his erection throbbing.

Bay restlessly squirmed, wanting more of his touch, wanting him inside her. She could no longer lie still beneath his exploratory, teasing ministrations. As his tongue moved slowly in a maddening circle around her core, she cried out in frustration and need. Eyes tightly shut, her entire body convulsed with the force of those slow, wet patterns he wove with his mouth and tongue. She lost awareness of everything except Gabe cherishing her, opening her, touching her. Loving her.

And when he eased his fingers into her, she made a hoarse sound, her hips thrusting upward and enveloping him. Bay felt as if she'd lost her mind, moving restlessly, held prisoner with his strong hands holding her thighs open, holding her until she whimpered his name. Her body ached and felt as if on fire. She could feel the building orgasm as Gabe moved and rocked her with his mouth on the hardened, swollen pearl. More sounds of distress tore from her lips as he brought her to that point where her body simply imploded, contracting violently into wild, scalding ripples. Her body arched in spasms, her head rearing back, a scream of pleasure tearing out of her. Wave after fiery wave of scorching heat roared through her. In seconds, Bay felt floating in a cauldron of incredible and intense fire as it embraced her. Gabe continued to caress her, milking her body of everything it had hidden within it, widening the circle of flames throbbing through her pelvic region, her cries hoarse with pleasure as she surrendered utterly to him in every way.

Gabe watched a rose flush spread across her trembling, damp lower body all the way up to her cheeks. Easing up, he saw her breasts taut, the nipples jutting against the tee she wore. Her eyes were dazed. She was lost in the rapture he'd helped create within her. There wasn't anything more powerful, better feeling to Gabe than being able to please her. He wasn't done. He'd just begun.

Holding Bay's drowsy gaze, he smiled as he repositioned her on the bed. Although he was still dressed, he straddled her midsection, his knees against her hips. Leaning down, he whispered against her lips, "I love you, baby. And I'm going to show you just how much...." He deepened the kiss, giving her a taste of his need for her, their tongues moving and touching each other in a slow, burning dance.

Sliding his hands beneath the tee, Gabe was careful to barely skim the area of the bruise on the left side of her rib cage. Bay wore no bra, just a silky white camisole beneath the tee. He eased off the tee, then threaded his fingers through her soft hair. Gabe leaned down and began to place light kisses down the length of her slender neck. He added small nips here and there. Each time, she reacted, her hips pressing upward against his powerful erection. Arousal glinted in her eyes. Gabe lavished the valley between her breasts with his mouth and tongue. Her nipples stood hard against the silky material. How long had he wanted to touch them?

In moments, Gabe brought the camisole over her head, leaving her naked beneath him. Her breath was chaotic as he stroked her left shoulder his hands enclosed the softness of her breasts. He kissed the valley between her breasts and Gabe could feel the pounding of her heart beneath his exploring mouth. Bay gasped as his thumb moved languidly across the first harden peak.

She moaned his name, her entire body arching and pressing her hips against the rough denim enclosing his erection. Gabe placed his lips over the first nipple, teasing it. Bay cried out, her hips twisting beneath his as he suckled her. She was like hot, silky ribbons flowing in his hands as he licked the second nipple and then gently closed his teeth around it. The wetness of his mouth, the puckered tension of the nipple, made her go wild. Bay gripped his upper arms, her hips writh-ing, bucking beneath his own.

Gabe lifted his head and met her lust-filled eyes. There was silent pleading in them. She wanted him. All of him. Bay's finger dug into the tight flesh of his upper arms, lips parting, wanting him to kiss her. Gabe did not want to disappoint her and he curved his mouth powerfully against her own. They met and fused explo-sively with each other. Months of loneliness, aching for each other, fired their hunger that had waited so long to be ignited. The shattering heat rolled through both of them, melting them into each other.

Her hands shook as she forced the material of his T-shirt up across his chest and tried to get it off his shoulders. He broke their wet, clinging kiss, sat up and pulled it off. It didn't take much to stand, push the shoes off his feet, get rid of his jeans and his briefs. There was no mistaking his need of her once he was completely divested of his clothes as he came back to her side.

Bay turned, rolling to his right, her hands strong and guiding as she pulled him on top of her. With a heated smile, Gabe resisted her efforts.

"Not yet, baby. You're ready again, aren't you?"

She made a muffled sound of frustration, trying to urge him on top of her. He silenced her by taking her mouth, gently biting her lower lip and then using his tongue to soothe it. "Open your eyes," he rasped.

Bay dragged her eyes open, her body hungry and wanting Gabe, the hard gleam in his dark green eyes more animal than man. She felt his male power, ab-sorbed it and was now meeting the man whose love for her burned in his eyes and branded her wildly pounding heart.

His voice was thick, almost a growl, as he kissed her flushed cheek, her temple and damp brow. "Baby, you're coming first. You'll always be first in my life." He splayed out his hands across her shoulders, gently pushing her back into the tangle of sheets and covers. Need was clearly written in her eyes, the pout of her parted lips, her fingers gripping his thickly muscled biceps.

"Please… Gabe…I need you, oh, how I need you," she whispered in anguish.

"It's the sweetest compliment a man can ever have from his woman." His voice was roughened with hunger. "You're my woman, Bay. You were from the first moment I saw you, and you knew it, too." Gabe smiled a little, watching her wet lips part. "And more than anything, I want to give you pleasure and I'm going to do something about it right now," he growled, moving his hand down across her damp torso, his fingers spreading out across her abdomen. He slid his hand slowly downward where her thighs met, placed a tender kiss on her mouth and took her ragged breath deep into his lung. "You're mine…" he grated against her mouth.

Curving his fingers across her mound of silky hair, he eased her thighs open just enough. Every muscle in Bay's body tightened. She trembled violently as he moved his fingers until he slowly circled the slick, hot opening. He heard her give a small cry, shuddering, her hips arching against his hand, her body begging for him to explore her further once again. He felt powerful, humbled by her incredibly sensitive body against the palm of his hand. Gabe waited, wanting the need in her to double and then triple as he continued to move in gentle, exploratory motion.

He slid his other hand beneath her shoulder blades, bringing her body closer to him. Lips closing over the peak of her nipple, he teethed it just enough to bring her excruciating pleasure. A cry tore from her lips. And then he slid his fingers deep inside her. She went wild and frantic, her entire body writhing as he went deeper.

He found the sweet spot within her and an animal-like sound clawed out of her throat, her head thrown back. She was incredibly sensitive and he could feel her entire body contract around him as he gave her the pressure and the pleasure she needed.

Her cries were hoarse, her body straining against him as he continued to draw out her release. Finally, Gabe felt her sag against him, exhausted. He eased out of her, lifting his head to see Bay's cheeks were stained pink, eyes closed, a soft, trembling smile across her mouth.

Never had Gabe felt so humbled as right now. No woman had ever given the gift of herself like this unless there was something far deeper, more bonding between them than just having sex. Loving her and Bay loving him in return afforded Gabe the ultimate trust. It made him want to cry for joy. He'd never felt this before. She was his. And now he was going to brand her with his essence, take her, love her until she swooned from so much pleasure that she melted away in his arms.

Gabe eased over her, his erection pressing deeply against her belly. He made sure to distribute his weight evenly so she wasn't crushed beneath him. Looking into Bay's eyes, he saw a dreamy quality in them. Gabe caressed her gently, slid his large hand beneath her hips, preparing to enter her. As they kissed, he settled his knees between her thighs. If Gabe thought she was going to be shy about this, he was mistaken.

She thrust her hips upward, her damp, warm body surrounding him, drawing him deeply into herself. A groan rolled through him and he clenched the covers on either side of her head. Above all, he didn't want to hurt Bay. He couldn't live with himself if he hurt her in any way. He could feel the fiery beat of her heart against his. The beautiful sounds emanating from her throat increased each time he slid more deeply into her welcoming body.

"I don't want to hurt you," Gabe said raggedly, watching her, seeing the wildness starting to build.

Bay rolled her head from side to side. "Gabe, you can't hurt me. I need you. Please…stay inside me… stay…"

Gabe wasn't sure. She was so damn tight and small that he knew he could hurt her. She cried out as he held her captive, his large hand angling her hips so he could begin to move her into oblivion with him. His mouth was cajoling, giving, taking. Her breath came in shallow gasps as he went deeper, carrying her with him to exquisite worlds he'd never experienced before. Finally, their hips met, fused and burned, and he was fully inside her, a part of her. His control was shredding by the second. Could he hang on? Could he give Bay one more gift before he came?

She was insistent, gripping his hips, pulling at him

frantically, trying to urge him to move with her. Finally, once he was sure he hadn't hurt Bay, he thrust hard, stroking into her, feeling her begin to tense, her back curving into a taut bow as he plunged as deeply as he could go.

Her body suddenly spasmed and contracted around him. Bay tore her mouth from his, arching as the first rippling explosion occurred deep within her. A tearing cry spilled from her lips as Gabe increased the pressure and the pleasure for her. Bay's lashes shuttered closed and he could feel the continuing releases pulse through her, squeezing him like a fist. White-hot ripples of searing fire consumed her. His body was sleek and wet, sliding against hers.

They became this primal union, their hearts thundering against each other. Her hands opened and closed spasmodically against his tense, sweaty shoulders. And just when Gabe thought he could take no more, he released his control, gritting his teeth, straining hard against her softer, yielding body. Heat scalded him. With her hands gripping his hips, she moved fearlessly against him, his hands curling into fists on either side of the pillow where her head lay. Gabe suddenly relaxed, his weight settling against her, his brow against hers.

Hot, moist breath flowed hotly across Bay's cheek. Time ceased and she languished with Gabe in a haze of fire, pleasure and satisfaction. He came off her just enough to slide his arm beneath her neck, drawing her upward against him. Bay felt as if she had been torn loose from every earthly mooring she'd ever had. Her body glowed hotly, still rippling with intense pleasure in the aftermath, still feeling Gabe inside her, their love finally fused with each other.

Bay lingered in a boiling cauldron of intense gratification. His hand outlined her damp hip and gently stroked her outer thigh. Never had she been so well loved. And it was love, Bay realized in her wandering, ripe and fulfilled senses. Gabe had whispered that he loved her. As he eased off her, he brought her fully against him, their legs entangled with each other. Bay didn't want Gabe to leave her; the sense of joy and fulfillment still flowed through her, fueled by so many emotions she'd had to control until now. His arm came around her shoulder, keeping her in place; his other large hand splayed out across her hips, pressing her tightly against him, a prisoner to his passion.

She rested her head on Gabe's arm, feeling his heart racing against her own. Happiness flooded her being, and all Bay could do was lie along his length and simply savor him as a man who had loved her so thoroughly and completely that she continued to float in the dark, sensual magic of his arms and body.

CHAPTER TWENTY-FOUR

BAY AWOKE SLOWLY. Her nostrils flared, drawing in the musky and male scent of Gabe as she lay curled up in his arms. Her body glowed even now. Opening her eyes, Bay saw light filtering in around the drapes. Her gaze drifted to Gabe as he slept. His hair, although short, was mussed. His beard had grown, the hollows of his cheeks more pronounced, giving him a look of the warrior he was. His mouth made her lower body contract with need. Incredibly strong, beautiful lips that had loved her so thoroughly she was still floating even now. It was impossible not to touch Gabe, feel her hand move across his powerful chest, tangle her fingers slowly through the soft, dark hair. There were scars hidden beneath the hair and she could feel the ridges of old wounds beneath her fingertips. He'd suffered so much pain that it hurt her. Bay wished she could take those memories of the pain away from him. Leaning upward, she placed a lingering kiss on Gabe's chest where his heart lay.

Gabe stirred. For once, he didn't snap wide-awake. He felt Bay's long, firm body curving against his and her small but beautiful breasts pressed against his chest. As she nestled her belly against his hardening erection, her firm, slender legs tangled and captured his. Her breath was warm against his chest, feathering across it, his flesh sensitized. Her long fingers slid through his chest hair. Wasn't this what he'd dreamed about for so damn long? Exactly this kind of intimacy with Bay? *Yes*. Gabe captured her hand and laid it against his heart, letting her know he was awake. Outside, the morning was a promise of blue skies and sunshine for Christmas Day.

As Gabe pulled her more tightly against him, Bay nestled her head against his shoulder. His muscles in his chest wall tightened beneath her exploration. "Merry Christmas," she whispered near his ear, closing her eyes.

"It couldn't be better," he agreed thickly, kissing her silky, curled hair. The tendrils tickled his mouth, nose and cheek. He inhaled her feminine scent and felt himself wanting her all over again. Hearing Bay's softened sigh, her lips caressing his jaw and neck, Gabe groaned. She wanted him. It was so easy to bring her on top of him, her knees settling against his hips. Her hair was mussed, a beautiful golden-brown frame around her face. Her blue eyes were still drowsy with sleep, but he saw the lust banked in them, too.

Reaching up, Gabe drew her down to his mouth. As he grazed her lips and rasped, "I love you, Bay. I love you so damn much it hurts." She had no idea what she was doing to him, branding him with her mouth, tongue and hands, her hips moving suggestively to let him know just how much she wanted him.

Gabe's guttural voice awakened her body and senses. His mouth cherished hers and Bay felt him slip deep within her. She was more than ready for him, relaxing against him with an utter moan of pleasure. Her breasts were teased by the hair across his chest. His mouth drew fire from hers and she responded wildly to the moment, lost in the heat and haze of his thrusting body and commanding mouth.

If she thought her body had been satiated from last night's torrid lovemaking, Bay was surprised. Within minutes, Gabe had brought her to full orgasm once more. Whatever they shared, it was electric, spontaneous and primal. As Gabe's hands settled across her hips, thrusting against her, she felt a series of explosions rocket throughout her. All she could do was cry out as the scalding waves plunged outward through her like a tsunami. She was consumed by the pleasure, burned by it. Face pressed against his, her breath chaotic, Bay felt him stiffen and groan. His male body became galvanized, encompassing her as she felt him release deep within her.

Closing her eyes, Bay could do nothing but rest weakly on Gabe afterward, feeling his thudding heart against her own. She smiled tremulously, lifting her hand to caress his stubbled cheek. Words were useless. She lay there absorbing their mutual heat, their love and his hands cherishing her. Never had she experienced such happiness, such powerful love with any man.

THE NEXT TIME Bay awoke, the sun was shining brightly around the drapes. She found herself alone in the bed and still wrapped in a sensual haze created by their lovemaking earlier this morning. When had Gabe left her side? Automatically, Bay slid the palm of her hand across the sheet where he'd lain before. It was cool to her touch. The door was partially open and she could hear Christmas music wafting down the hall. Her heart filled with joy, Bay thought she might die from happiness. She heard soft footfalls coming down the hall toward the bedroom. It had to be Gabe.

Sitting up, the sheet pooling around her hips, she watched as Gabe eased the door open and looked in. He was dressed in a red T-shirt, dark green cargo pants and a pair of black boots. To Bay, he looked magnificent, the clothes simply showing off his primal, powerful body to perfection. She gave him a drowsy smile. "Yes, the dead actually do arise," she murmured wryly. He held two cups of coffee in his hands.

Grinning, Gabe sauntered in and sat down beside her. "You slept well," he teased, handing her a cup of steaming coffee.

"I had good reason to," Bay whispered, taking the cup and looking deep into Gabe's clear green eyes. She saw happiness in them. She hoped he saw the happiness reflected in hers. "Thanks...this was so sweet of you."

"I felt you wake up." Gabe enjoyed watching her sip the coffee, her upper body naked, beautiful and already making him hard, wanting her all over again. Her breasts were perfect. Her nipples rose pink. And he'd tasted them last night and this morning, lavishing his attention upon them. He wanted to taste her again and feel her nipples harden once more in his mouth.

Tilting her head, she said, "But...how?"

Shrugging, Gabe said, "Over the years I've developed a strong sixth sense. It never leads me wrong. I was out in the kitchen and I felt you stir, decided to make some fresh coffee and welcome you back into the world of the living."

Bay warmed beneath his very male smile, her body already reacting heatedly to the arousal in his eyes. "My mother had that very same kind of intuition with my father. They were so in love and in tune with each other." She sighed softly. "I always dreamed of having that same kind of magical connection with the man I fell in love with."

"You do. It just comes naturally between us, Bay." Gabe threaded his fingers through her hair, taming some of the softly curled strands and easing them away from her flushed cheek.

"Mmm," she purred, closing her eyes. "All you have to do is look at me and I want you. And when you touch me—" her eyes opened, watching him "—I just want you all over again."

His predatory look made her go hot with longing. Gabe wasn't arrogant about being a consummate lover. No, he was humble and that touched her heart. He wanted to please her. He'd controlled himself to bring her along with him. How did she get so lucky?

"I think we need a small time-out." He didn't want one, but Gabe never wanted Bay to feel pressured in any way. He always felt women were his equal, not beneath him, not secondary, as his father had treated his mother.

"Maybe you're right." She smiled a little wickedly. "Well, at least for the next hour, maybe? What time is it?"

"Ten-thirty," he said, grinning. "With the exception of making love with me twice, you probably slept a solid eleven hours." His voice lowered, his expression growing solemn. "You needed that deep, healing sleep, Bay. You still need a lot of rest to catch up in the coming weeks."

Pushing several curls away from her face, she murmured, "I feel completely rejuvenated, Gabe, not exhausted." Reaching out, Bay grazed his shaven cheek with her fingertips. "Thanks to you." She whispered, "I have never had a man love me like you did. I still feel like I'm floating in some other world." She held his narrowing gaze. "You are incredible, Gabe." She laughed a little shyly. "If I'd known how good we'd be together, I don't think I could ever have kept my hands off you in Afghanistan."

He gave an amused look and caught her hand, kissing it. "Remember? I had six months of dreaming of what I was going to do to you when you got home."

Laughing softly, Bay said, "Your dreams were far more creative than mine."

"We'll compare notes over the coming days," Gabe promised, releasing her hand. The glint in her eyes told him she was more than ready to live out her dreams with him. He'd never felt stronger or more powerful as a man than right then, drowning beneath her drowsy blue gaze. Bay was open, trusting and Gabe always knew where he stood with her. She trusted him with her life, with her body, and most important, with her huge, giving heart.

"I feel like a lazybones," Bay admitted, setting the cup on the bed stand. "I need a shower."

"Go ahead. I was cutting up some red-and-green peppers to celebrate Christmas in our omelet once you got up." He stood. "And Santa Claus left you something under the tree. So don't take too long."

There was a sparkle in his eyes, that male mouth of his twitching with humor as he stood up. "Really?"

"Uh-huh."

She felt as if she was his woman, and she loved this idea. Of being owned in a loving way by this incredible warrior and man. She saw him leave as quietly as he'd come.

Pulling the sheet and cover aside, Bay stood up and stretched. Her heart sang with joy. As she padded into the large bathroom, she felt as if she were walking on clouds, not on the cool ceramic tiles.

Half an hour later, Bay went into the living room. Gabe was in the kitchen prepping their omelets. As she stepped over to the tree, she saw a large wrapped gift and a smaller one beneath.

Turning, she said, "I have something I made for you." Moving to the living room Bay opened her dark green duffel bag. She crouched down, she rummaged through it until she found what she was looking for. "Ah, here it is!" she said triumphantly. Lifting out the huge, wrapped package, she grinned over at him.

Gabe saw the package in her arms. "No wonder your duffel felt so damn heavy." He saw her flush, her eyes dancing with happiness.

"I just got it finished two weeks before I left. I called the SEAL team chief at Bravo and asked if he had any Christmas wrapping paper. You know chiefs have everything." She laughed a little.

"Christmas wrapping." Gabe shook his head. "SEALs have two of everything," he murmured, grinning.

"That was nice of him to give it to you."

"It was," Bay agreed, setting the package beneath the tree. "He knew I'd been with your team." Straightening, she added, "He told me I was a little SEAL sister, and I thought that was so sweet of him."

Eyebrows raised, Gabe said, "That was a real compliment from him. Your reputation preceded you. We're a very small community and everyone knows everyone else. No one was supposed to talk about you, though. You were top secret."

"Well," she said with a slight smile, "he said he and Chief Doug Hampton spoke. I guess Doug asked him to sort of watch over me, even though I had been reassigned to the Special Forces team in that village. I went all mushy inside when he told me that."

Gabe gave her a steady look. "SEALs always take care of their own, their families, Bay. I'm sure that's why Doug alerted him to the fact that you were in harm's way. Top secret or not," he added with a grin. He'd have to thank Doug the next time he saw him. A good chief in a platoon made everyone rise to that bar of morals and values, and there was no one finer than Doug Hampton as far as Gabe was concerned. He had Bay's back, and Gabe was grateful.

She pushed her fingers through her drying hair, the strands beginning to curl as she looked at the two gifts he had for her beneath the tree. "I didn't get you very much, Gabe..." she called over her shoulder.

"Don't worry about it." He held her soft gaze. "There isn't anything else I'll ever want, baby. You're my gift."

Touched to almost the point of tears, Bay wandered into the kitchen, set her mug down on the island and turned to Gabe. He had a butcher knife in hand, chopping up the colorful peppers. Drawing her arms around his waist, she pressed her cheek against his back and whispered, "I love you, Gabe. I don't think I told you that last night or this morning…but I wanted you to remember that I do." Releasing him as he laid down the butcher knife and turned around, Bay caught his burning look, her body instantly responding.

Gabe eased her into his arms. He groaned as she fell against him, all her softness against his angled hardness. Nuzzling her cheek, kissing her brow and nose, he said, "I know you love me. You can't share what we had last night or this morning and not love each other, Bay. It's about trust, and trust only comes with real love."

Bay sighed, content to rest her head against his shoulder. "You're so much more than I ever realized, Gabe."

"So are you, baby. You're an amazing, angelic creature come to earth to save this sorry-assed SEAL from a life of loneliness."

She lifted her head, meeting his darkening green eyes. "Funny, I was going to say something similar to you, how you've saved me. And you have, a number of times, literally." Raising her hand, Bay grazed his recently shaven cheek. "You're a warrior, Gabe, but that's only one facet of you. You're like a diamond with so many other facets. I'm hungry to explore you, find out everything I can possibly know about you as a man, the human being…."

Leaning down, Gabe skimmed her lips with a tender kiss. "Baby, I intend to spend the rest of my life on this earth exploring you."

She trembled in his arms as his rasping breath flowed across her mouth. The man was so damn sensual and sexy. "You hid yourself pretty darn well over there in Afghanistan."

He kissed her and then released her. "I had to. There was no other choice." Gabe placed all the ingredients in an awaiting bowl of eggs mixed with milk. He walked over to the sink and washed off his hands. Drying them on a towel, he said, "You don't have that capacity to hide, Bay. You're so damn open and trusting. Everyone saw how kind you were to them, to others. The guys in my platoon saw the same thing I did—an incredible healer among us. You have no idea how your presence lifted all of us. And when you smiled, I saw all the guys melt beneath you. So did I. And there wasn't one of us that didn't want to be in the aura of your sunlight. Just by walking into the room, you made us all feel better." He lifted an eyebrow and added, "And I'm not saying that in a sexual manner, either. There are just some people in life, Bay, that have a special quality within them to lift even the sorriest son of a bitch after a rotten day. I know you're not aware of how you touch people, baby, but take my word for it, you do. My platoon is a bunch of barely tamed animals, but you tamed them with just your smile, your thoughtfulness and your ability to sincerely listen to them when they needed someone to talk with, to confide in." Gabe shook his head and finished up his duties with the vegetables. Wiping his hands, he saw tears in her eyes. "I'm so goddamn lucky, Bay, I don't know quite how to absorb it all. I often wondered what you saw in me. You could have had your pick of any man on this earth."

Bay walked into his arms, absorbing his strength and tenderness as he embraced her and gently took her mouth. Their lips lingered against each other and she closed her eyes, wanting to simply melt into this man who had made her heart and body sing. "You don't see yourself, either," she reminded him, her voice breathy. "You were the only SEAL there who saw me. Really saw me. There's something equally special about you, Gabe." Her eyes glinted. "And I'm just like you. I want to spend the rest of my life exploring every possible facet of you. I have a hunch I'll never be bored." She grinned.

Gabe eased away even though he wanted to lift Bay into his arms and take her straight to his bedroom. "What we share, baby, is special. We're lucky and we both know it."

Stepping out of his arms, Bay felt herself trembling inwardly with want of Gabe all over again. "Every day is going to be so special, Gabe." Already, Bay began to think that too soon, she was going to have to leave him. Again.

CHAPTER TWENTY-FIVE

GABE SAW BAY'S eyes grow sad, and he sensed she was thinking about having to leave him in less than thirty days. He placed his finger beneath her chin and smiled into her sad eyes. "Are you hungry for that Christmas omelet I'm making for us?"

She gave him a look of deviltry. "For you."

He poured more coffee into her cup and led her over to the island. "We have to eat earthling food, too, if we're always going to be flying in the stratosphere."

Bay nodded. "I keep forgetting that we have time. Thirty days. I don't have to get up and leave today. I'm afraid it's going to go too fast…."

Gabe placed the heavy cast-iron skillet over the flames and then poured the egg mixture into it. "I understand. Over there, time was never on our side. Not ever."

Bay simply enjoyed watching him make the huge omelet. The Christmas music in the background added to her happiness. "After we eat, I'm going to call Mama and wish her a merry Christmas."

"Makes two of us," Gabe said. "I got my mother a very fancy sewing machine she's been wanting. I want to hear what she thinks of it after opening it up this morning." Gabe grinned.

"And you're a SEAL."

His eyebrows rose. "And…? Where are we going with this statement?"

She shrugged. "There are so many other dimensions to you, Gabe."

"SEALs aren't one-dimensional," he said. "You're just seeing one facet of us—the warrior. We're a highly intelligent, commonsense bunch of men. We come from all walks of life. Our diversity actually makes our team stronger in the long run."

"But you're so much more than that. If I wasn't here…well, I'd never realize all this about you."

"We're a pretty skilled, creative bunch of guys. Don't ever sell us short, huh?" Gabe grinned as he expertly slid the omelet onto an awaiting platter.

"What else do you do? What other skills?" Bay challenged, watching him cut half of it and put it on her awaiting plate.

"I was great in woodshop in high school. I've always liked working with wood. I've made dressers, tables and bed stands for my mother. I've been carving since I was a little kid. My father taught me when I was seven years old. He bought me a nice Buck knife and showed me how to listen to the wood and let it talk to me. The wood will tell you what to carve out of it."

"Thank you," Bay said as he handed her the plate. She discovered she was starving. As Gabe came and sat next to her, she said, "You're very creative."

"I like to think so." Gabe gave her a teasing look. "But you have to tell me if that's true or not."

Bay held his teasing gaze. "Oh, you're stellar, Gabe,

no doubt about it. My body is still singing with pleasure."

"You know how to make a man feel good about himself, baby."

She met his heated smile. "So, what else do you do? What other skills? I'm on a serious hunt to know you inside and out."

Chuckling, he cut up his omelet. "I already know the inside of you. So let's talk about the outside." Getting his mind off sex with Bay was like trying to get a bee away from pollinating a flower. It just came naturally. And his protectiveness toward this sensitive, caring woman had grown exponentially from last night. She was so damn incredibly sensitive to his hands, his mouth, his…and he had to stop or he was going to drive himself crazy.

"I have an MBA," he told her.

"Are you serious?" Bay gasped, staring at him as if he had suddenly sprouted horns and grown two heads.

His mouth eased into a wicked smile. "You just thought I was some E-6 swabbie?"

Laughing, Bay shook her head. "No way, sailor. I knew you were special the moment I laid eyes on you. But an MBA? How did you do that?"

Gabe shrugged and continued to eat. "I've got eighteen months in rotation stateside, so I was always taking night courses at San Diego University. It took me six years to get it, but I wanted to have a skill that could transfer over to the civilian world once I left the SEAL community someday."

"But…you're enlisted. You could be a SEAL officer if you wanted, Gabe." Only men with a college degree could hope to attain officer status in the military. Yet Gabe was still an enlisted SEAL. She frowned. "How come?"

"Because I don't want to become an officer. They get kicked upstairs and see no action. I wanted to remain a shooter. I'm good at what I do, Bay, and I like the action. Becoming an officer was playing politics, and I'm not good at that. I'm a pretty black-and-white guy. And I call the shots as I see them, and officers need diplomacy, among many other skills, that I don't have."

"Incredible," she murmured, amazed. "You're an MBA. Wow."

"Oh," he teased. "And what is *that* going to get me with you?"

She chuckled. "You're too funny. I could give a flip if you have an MBA or not. I love you. I fell in love with the guy in Afghanistan. Okay?"

He reached over and grazed her flushed cheek. "Okay. An MBA doesn't define who I am, baby. The only person I want to define me is you."

"Do you always say the right words?" she whispered, touched.

"No," Gabe growled, and dropped his hand from her cheek. "I try, Bay, but I'm not always successful. With you, I want to always say the right things, but I know that's not realistic. I just hope you will love me enough that when I make mistakes, you'll still love me. I'll learn from them, baby. What we have is good, and I want you forever."

Tears crowded into Bay's eyes. Gabe meant every word he said. She could feel it in her heart. It burned

into her soul. Gabe was just like her, she realized: he
gave it his all. He didn't hold back. He didn't lie. He
was who she saw. "I want the same thing," she told
him, her voice trembling with emotion.

"Let's eat or all my hard work is going to waste,"
he teased, trying to lighten the mood. Gabe couldn't
stand to see a woman cry, and he could see the tears
glittering in her soft blue eyes. All he wanted was to
see Bay happy and smiling. God knew, she deserved
that and so much more.

He was bathed in warmth as they laughed, teased
and shared Christmas breakfast. When they were finished, he led her over to the tree and guided her to the
nearby couch.

"My turn first," Bay said, pushing him onto the
couch.

"You're always first in my world." He saw the suffused joy in her eyes as she turned and quickly walked
over to the tree. The package was big and odd shaped.
Her cheeks became flushed as he took it from her arms.

"What did you do?" Gabe wondered, running his
hands over the wrapping.

Excitedly, Bay sat down next to him. "I worked on
it every minute I had to myself after you left." Her
voice turned breathy. "Open it, Gabe. It's just for you."

It didn't take much to tear the wrapping off. As he
did, a soft, knitted afghan of dark blue and gold fell
across his lap. He looked over at her. "You knit, too?"

"Well—" she laughed "—if you can have an MBA,
I can be a knitter, can't I? Unfold it."

Removing the paper, Gabe sat up and found one end
of the huge wool afghan. His heart blossomed fiercely

as he opened it up. Bay had knitted the golden SEAL trident symbol in the center of it. The afghan was at least seven feet long by five feet wide. The wool was soft and thick between his fingers. It was big enough for him to lie beneath it.

"Well?" Bay demanded, holding her breath. "Do you like it? Did I get the SEAL symbol okay?"

He gently folded the afghan and set it aside. Turning, Gabe drew her into his arms. "It's beautiful, Bay. Unbelievably beautiful." He leaned down, curving his mouth against hers. She moaned and melted into his arms, her breasts against his chest, her arms sliding around his neck. He took her hotly, deeply, branding her with himself, with his love. Her breath turned ragged and Gabe felt her strain wordlessly against him, as if not able to get close enough to him.

Coming up for air, both of them breathing hard, he framed her face and drowned in her shining eyes. "You're my guardian angel, do you know that? You touch my heart and my soul. I want you to know that. Never forget it, Bay. I don't know how the hell you had the time to knit something this big for me over there in the midst of everything else." And he didn't. He knew how busy Bay had been at Camp Bravo. She rarely had an hour to herself.

Sighing, Bay reached up and grazed his jaw. "I made the time, Gabe. I wanted to make you something that on days when I wasn't here, you could wrap me around you with this afghan. It has my energy, my love knitted into it for you. As I knitted it, I dreamed of us, of our future. I saw us happy. I saw us always together. This afghan is our dreams, and I want you to hold our dreams for us while I'm away. I know there will be lonely days ahead of us. Worrisome days. But through it all, beloved, you can hold me as close as wrapping up in that afghan I knitted for you. Close your eyes and know they are really my arms around you, holding you, loving you."

Tears pricked behind his eyes. Gabe was shocked by them and fought the reaction. How easily Bay impacted him. It totaled him in ways he'd never realized could exist between a man and a woman. But she wasn't just any woman. Bay was *his* woman. His soul mate.

"You are my breath, baby. You own my heart, my soul." He grazed her lower lip with his thumb, seeing her eyes grow tender with love for him. "And you can bet, no matter where our platoon goes in training, that afghan is going with me. It isn't you, but you made it and it's a lot better than holding nothing when I'm lonely for you at night." Her lip trembled, the relief and happiness in her eyes. Gabe still didn't know how on earth Bay had time to knit this huge afghan for him. She was simply amazing.

"I'm so glad, Gabe. I really wanted you to be comforted by it because I know how lonely it can get when your loved one is gone overseas."

He kissed her gently and for a long, long time. Finally, he released Bay and said, "Now it's your turn." He stood.

"I can hardly wait!" she gushed. "I love getting Christmas presents!"

"Now, this isn't much," Gabe warned, handing her the two gifts.

Bay was thrilled and smiled up at him. "All gifts are great. Come and sit by me."

"Why? So you can slug me if you don't like them?" Gabe chuckled as he sat down, sliding his arm across her shoulders. Bay looked like a little child in that moment. Not the healer, not the courageous combat medic who was willing to give her life for another, but a little child utterly thrilled with the unexpected presents. It sent a deep joy through him.

Bay opened the large present and discovered a beautiful blue silk robe. She gasped as she ran her fingers over the smooth, glistening material. "This is beautiful, Gabe. I can feel the quality of the silk."

"You like it?"

She lifted it out of the box and held it up. It was a simple robe, but beautifully cut and long enough to hang to her ankles. "I love it. Now you can have your huge terry cloth robe back. Thank you." She leaned over and kissed his cheek. Carefully, she settled the silk robe back into the box.

"I figured when you got here, you wouldn't have many other clothes. It gets cold here in San Diego in the winter, and silk always keeps a person warm."

She laid the box near her feet. "You're right about that. My duffel bag is heavy enough as is. I usually carry two sets of civilian clothes in there. A set of pajamas and no robe. Just not room for one." In fact, she had to give away some of her clothes to Afghan women to make room for the huge afghan she'd knitted for Gabe, but he didn't need to know that.

Gabe watched her focus on the small gold-foil-wrapped box between her hands.

She gasped as she opened the box. Inside was a carved wooden heart made of golden-and-red cedar. It was no larger than the size of nickel. There was a very small gold latch on it and she pried open the red and golden wood. Opening it, she saw small letters carved on both sides of the heart. It read: GG loves BT. Tears jammed in her eyes as she carefully held the wooden heart in her fingers. Sniffing, Bay looked up at him, seeing the worry in his eyes. "Th-this is so beautiful, Gabe…thank you." She managed a partial smile, her lower lip trembling.

Relief tunneled through Gabe. She gently closed the heart as tears rolled down her flushed cheeks. He leaned forward, brushing the tears away with his thumbs. "Don't cry, baby. God, you'll rip me apart. I'll be with you when you go back to Afghanistan. Tuck it in the small pocket at the top of your Kevlar vest. That will be me being with you every second you're away from me…."

Whispering his name, Bay threw her arms around Gabe. He pulled her across his lap so she could rest her head against his shoulder and jaw. "You like it?" His heart was pounding with relief and joy.

Kissing his temple and brow, Bay whispered, "I do. I love you so much, Gabe. I don't know what I did to deserve you, but I feel like the luckiest woman in the world."

He squeezed her gently, content to have her arms around him, her brow nestled against his. "We'll work through this coming year together," he promised her. "The carved heart isn't a warm, fuzzy afghan, but the thought is the same. You'll have a little piece of me with you."

And then his heart pounded with real fear. Gathering his courage, Gabe held her a little more tightly in his arms. "Bay, I want to marry you. I know it can't be right now. I think we loved each other from the moment we were introduced." He forced himself to look down at her. What would she say? Gabe was afraid of her answer. And he wasn't afraid of much in life. Real fear snaked through him as he watched her closely for reaction.

Eyes widening, Bay sat up. She saw trepidation in Gabe's narrowing eyes. Fear that she'd say no. She leaned her brow against his, their noses touching. She whispered, "I love you, Gabe. And yes, we need time, but we have that." She lifted her head to look at him. "I want very much to be your wife, your best friend, Gabe. We worked so well together in such harsh, life-threatening conditions, I've got to think when the pressure's off, we'll have so much more to share together."

He moved his hand across her shoulder, down her arm and captured her hand, squeezing it. "Time hasn't always been on our side. We've got a year to go, and even though we'll be apart for most of it, this is an opportunity to deepen what we already know we have."

"I never thought I'd love again, Gabe." Bay drew in a ragged breath, holding tightly to his powerful hand. "Combat isn't a place to find love. That's what I learned over in Iraq with Jack Scoville. And when I met you, I felt this immediate connection with you, and it scared me to death. I tried to run from you because of it."

"You didn't want to lose me in combat like you lost

Jack," he said, understanding her reason. "When you told me about him dying in your arms, I got it."

"The four months we worked together, Gabe, showed me so much more of you as a man and a person. The longer we were together, the more I was afraid I'd lose you, too. I tried not to like you...love you..." Her mouth quirked and Bay looked up at the ceiling for a moment before training her gaze on his somber face.

"That night we spent out in that rocky depression and you brought me against you..." Sighing, Bay said tremulously, "I loved you in that moment. I'd tried to so hard to tell myself I couldn't fall in love again in a combat situation. But you were so caring, so tender toward me in that moment, I cried." She ran a hand along his jaw. "You saved my life that night. I know I would have frozen to death out there."

"Come here, baby," he rasped, taking her into his arms and holding her close. He nuzzled her cheek, feeling her hand come to rest against his chest. Gabe held her for a long time. Nowhere was as important as Bay in his arms. Her softened, moist breath flowed across her neck and chest. He could feel her grief, her struggles.

"In time you'll heal up from all the trauma you've survived, Bay. We have each other." His deep, husky words were like balm to her fractured heart. Gabe's arms were strong and caring.

Bay remained with her eyes closed, the tears slipping silently from beneath her lashes. "If someone had asked me if I'd fall in love with another man in the military, I'd have said no."

Gabe smiled, kissing her brow, her curly hair tickling his cheek. "We both tried to avoid loving each other for different reasons."

"I just never expected to be drawn to you." She shrugged. "There was just something about you, Gabe. Despite being a tough SEAL, you also had this incredible nurturing side to you that I sensed. You were always there for me, too. Every time. I often thought of you as an oak and I was the willow. When life storms hit, I knew I could always count on you, your strength and care."

"I want to be here for you, always," Gabe said.

Bay was content to be held in his arms, absorbing his barely whispered words that came out with a rush of emotion. "I've never experienced what I have with you, Gabe. A year apart seems like forever…."

Gabe cupped her jaw and brought her down to his mouth. This time, her lips trembled softly against his. He felt her love as never before as she sank against him, her mouth clinging hotly against his. Finally, they eased an inch apart from one another, breathing raggedly.

"Could we go back to my home for our wedding? Invite your mother, Grace? Mama knows the pastor and so many of my relatives would want to come and celebrate with us. I love my home so much, Gabe. I miss it. It's a part of my soul and when I go back home, the place feeds me in a spiritual sense. I can't explain it, but there've been times when I've come back off combat rotation feeling out of sorts. And the days spent there at our family cabin heal me. It simply knits my soul back together again."

Gabe sat there digesting her impassioned words. "I'd like that. I think my mother will be very happy to know I've got the right woman to share my life with. It will be a Christmas present a year from now they'll both be happy to receive."

He brought up his hand and kissed her palm. She had such long, graceful fingers. A healer's hand. "Well," Gabe murmured, "you're healing my heart Baylee-Ann Thorn." His voice deepened with emotion. "And I've served my country for many years. Now I want to live the rest of my life with you."

CHAPTER TWENTY-SIX

"OUR LAST PICNIC on the beach," Bay said sadly to Gabe as they walked along the beach. Earlier, they'd lain out their plaid blanket on the white sands in a secret cove near La Jolla earlier. They were the only ones in the cove. Tomorrow, she would be leaving for the East Coast for five months to expand upon her medical skills at another school.

"I know," he said, capturing her hand. The warmth of the late January sun beat down on Gabe's naked shoulders. He had been swimming in the ocean with Bay. The water was cold and they didn't stay in too long.

They'd used two boogie boards to surf the waves until their skin numbed and then it was time to get out. He pulled off his trunks and stood naked on the blanket, toweling off his wet body. He put on a dark blue T-shirt and picked up his black cargo pants after drying off his legs. He threw on his black leather jacket to ward off the cool ocean breeze. Sitting down, he pulled on a pair of warm socks and his combat boots.

Bay's hair was damp and hung in soft waves about her face as she jogged up to the blanket. Gabe tossed her a towel and she pulled the one-piece purple suit off her body and dropped it near his trunks. The wind made goose bumps stand out on her skin as she quickly dried off. Reaching down, she pulled on a long-sleeved red cotton turtleneck, jeans, red socks and shoes. Gabe handed her the dark green jacket and she gave him a grateful look of thanks.

Bay absorbed him as he quickly dried off his damp, short hair. Her heart expanded with incredible happiness to be here with him. Sadness accompanied it because her thirty days with him were at an end. Gabe was already training off and on with his platoon, so the one month with him meant almost daily separations. It was the way SEAL platoons trained, and families had to adjust to that tempo and pace.

Bay sat down next to Gabe, their knees touching each other. He looked so strong and capable, his shoulders broad, his chest wide and deep. In the water, as she'd discovered many weeks earlier, he was more dolphin than man. He'd taught her how to scuba dive, and she'd come to love it. The sun was warm, the sky a pale blue. It was midweek and the small crescent cove was devoid of people. The white gulls with black-tipped wings flew overhead, watching as Gabe opened the picnic basket and pulled out the food and a bag of chips.

"It's a perfect day." Bay sighed, opening the plastic container and picking up the tuna sandwiches. She glanced over and saw Gabe smile a little. Her heart felt heavy. Taking the bag of chips, she opened it and positioned it between them. "Do you think we'll manage to get some time to see each other while I'm here stateside?"

"We'll make it happen, baby. Next week, my platoon goes into the Chocolate Mountains of the Arizona desert for a month of battle rattle and EOD training. I won't be able to get away, but we'll have cell phone, Skype and emails." Gabe held her gaze. He saw the way her mouth flexed, the corners drawn in. He'd come to know many of Bay's quirks, her body language, in the past month. He knew she was withholding a lot of unspoken emotions when the corners of his mouth drew inward. Gabe reached over and tucked some drying strands of her soft hair behind her ear.

"The first month of my class will be grueling for me, too. I'll have weekends, but I'll be studying my butt off to get a handle on the course material and demands," Bay said before biting into the sandwich.

Gabe saw shadows in Bay's eyes as she ate. "We've been lucky to have this month."

"I know it." She sighed, giving him a tender look. "Every night in your arms has been a luxury I've never taken for granted."

Gabe felt his body respond to her yearning smile, the heat in her eyes for him. "A year from now, we'll have every day together. No more separations."

"I'm feeling very selfish right now. Maybe everyone who is in love feels this way." Bay picked up a chip. "I find myself wanting to stay here, Gabe, not go anywhere else. I've never felt like this before."

She wasn't really hungry, because tomorrow morning Gabe was going to see her off on a commercial flight to San Francisco. From there, she'd pick up another commercial flight into Boston, get a rental car and drive north toward Washington, D.C., where the advanced combat medical course was being held.

Moving his hand across her knee, he whispered,

"What you're feeling is what every husband and wife feel before separation. You're not alone."

Bay finished her sandwich and closed the plastic box, leaned across Gabe and placed it in the basket. "I wish I could clone you and take you with me." She grinned. "At least you have my afghan to keep you company. And I'll have the heart you carved for me." The soothing sound of the ocean waves crashing took away some of her anxiety. Gabe would be with his platoon and for the next month they'd be out on a desert training course in the Chocolate Mountains in Arizona, refining their shooting skills. Their platoon would work together once again, renewing their many skills as a flawless precision unit.

Gabe wiped his mouth with the paper napkin and dropped it into the basket. He studied Bay's profile. He felt no less torn by their coming separation, but right now he needed to be the stronger one. "Come here, baby." He brought her into his arms, cradled her head resting against his left shoulder. Kissing her cheek, Gabe rested his jaw against her temple as they watched the restless blue-green ocean. He felt Bay relax within his arms, her trust complete. "You know what today is, don't you?" he whispered against her ear.

"Our last day together."

Gabe smiled a little, hearing the sadness in Bay's lowered voice. "Didn't you know? It's All Hearts Day, too."

She snorted. "Hardly. That's February fourteenth, Valentine's Day."

"Oh," he said, grinning, "wrong day but right time." He released her and reached over into the basket. Gabe pulled out a small dark blue box. "I guess we'll have to consider this an early Valentine's Day gift for you…."

Surprised, Bay sat up between his open legs as he placed the box in her hand. Her flesh tingled. Sensing this was important, Bay eased out of his arms and faced him. "What's this?"

"Gotta open it to find out."

Bay frowned and stared down at the jewelry box in her hand. Her fingers trembled as she eased open the latch on the box. Inside were two rings. One was a simple gold band, a wedding ring. The engagement ring was set with four channel-cut blue sapphires, the color of her eyes. Her lips parted and she drew in a sharp breath of surprise. Lifting her chin, Bay stared into his smiling eyes. "Gabe…" She was at a loss for words, feeling such deep love for this man.

"Do you like them, baby?" Gabe asked.

"Th-they're beautiful," she managed, her voice growing hoarse.

Gabe picked up the box and pulled out the sapphire engagement ring. "Give me your left hand. Let's make this official."

Stunned, she lifted her left hand. Gabe gently held her hand and slipped the engagement ring on her finger. Bay stared down at the tasteful, classic ring now on her finger. Fighting tears, she blinked and then met and drowned in his warm green eyes. He was no longer smiling. As his fingers tightened a little around her hand, she saw the naked desire in his gaze. Her body responded just as hotly as she got to her knees and threw her arms around his shoulders.

Gabe brought Bay up against him, settling her

across his lap. "I love you, Bay. I wanted to give you the ring today before your left." He felt her tremble, her face buried against his neck. Her arms tightened around him and he smiled a little, feeling her trying to fight back her tears that wanted to fall. "When you get to missing me, you can have that ring sitting right along with that cedar heart I carved for you in your Kevlar vest. I'll be that close to you, baby. I'll be with you in spirit, watching over you...."

Bay felt hot tears squeezing beneath her lids as she clung to him. Right now Gabe was like a rock, steady and calm, while she felt her emotions bouncing back and forth between giddy happiness and desperate sorrow over their coming separation. She felt his hand move in a caress down her back and come to rest against her hip. She loved his ability to show her how he felt. Choking back a sob, Bay lifted her head from his shoulder and held his stormy looking gaze.

"You surprised me. You always do. I never expected this." Bay managed a one-cornered smile. Leaning upward, she captured his mouth. He groaned, his arms tightening around her, crushing her against his lean, powerful body. She surrendered to Gabe in every way. He eased her onto her back on the blanket and propped himself up by one elbow. No matter what they did together, whether it was going to a grocery store, seeing a movie, scuba diving off the kelp beds of La Jolla, his guardian energy always surrounded her.

Lifting his hand, Gabe gently threaded his fingers through her dry, soft strands. He saw the love burning in Bay's eyes, saw it in her well-kissed lips. He moved silky curls away from her flushed cheek. "You are my life," he told her huskily, kissing her brow, her nose, finally settling his mouth tenderly on her lips. Bay's hand came to rest on his shoulder. Her mouth was soft, searching, and he felt every ounce of her love in that kiss with him. He inhaled her warm breath deeply into his lungs and released his breath into her mouth.

Easing away just enough to hold her tearful gaze, Gabe whispered unsteadily, "We'll get through this together, Bay. We're strong people as individuals. Now we're twice as strong because we have each other." His hand came to rest on her flushed cheek. "I'm going to look forward to putting that wedding ring on your finger a year from now. And it's something we can look forward to, no matter where life takes us."

Gabe wanted to brand his belief into her heart and remove the sadness he saw in her expression. Moving his thumb, Gabe erased a single tear from the corner of her eye. "You're incredibly strong and resilient, Bay. And so am I. We've already weathered the worst. Now all we have to do is coast downhill for the next year." The last six months when she was once again in Afghanistan were going to be a special hell for them. Gabe would worry about her every single day, knowing she would be with either an SF or a SEAL team.

Bay reached up and grazed his cheek. "I know you're right. And I am strong. We've got so much to look forward to."

Gabe smiled a little. "Your mother is already in high gear with wedding plans. My mother has been talking with her about them. They're already fast friends. We'll let them dream for us, and that will keep them happy and help them not worry as much as they might."

Laughing softly, Bay agreed. "Let's go back to your condo. I want to spend the rest of the day with you, Gabe. Just you…"

He eased Bay up into a sitting position. "Anything you want, baby."

* * * * *

Don't miss Lindsay McKenna's sequel to this
Shadow Warriors story,
NEVER SURRENDER,
available July 2014 from HQN!

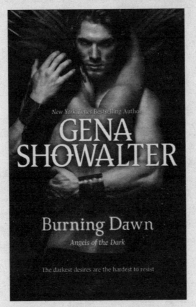

ALISON DELAINE

**brings you the thrilling tale of a hellion on the run...
and a gentleman determined to possess her.**

Lady India Sinclair will stop at nothing to live life on her own terms—even stealing a ship and fleeing to the Mediterranean. At last on her own, free to do as she pleases, she is determined to chart her own course. There's only one problem....

Nicholas Warre has made a deal. To save his endangered estate, he will find Lady India, marry her and bring her back to England at the behest of her father. And with thousands at stake, he doesn't much care what the lady thinks of the idea. But as the two engage in a contest of wills, the heat between them becomes undeniable...and the wedding they each dread may lead to a love they can't live without.

Available wherever books are sold!

Be sure to connect with us at:

Harlequin.com/Newsletters
Facebook.com/HarlequinBooks
Twitter.com/HarlequinBooks

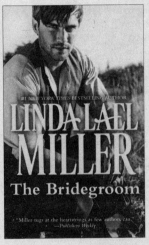

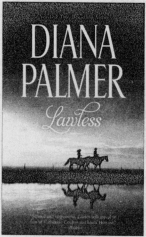

REQUEST YOUR
FREE BOOKS!

2 FREE NOVELS
FROM THE SUSPENSE COLLECTION
PLUS 2 FREE GIFTS!

YES! Please send me 2 FREE novels from the Suspense Collection and my 2 FREE gifts (gifts are worth about $10). After receiving them, if I don't wish to receive any more books, I can return the shipping statement marked "cancel." If I don't cancel, I will receive 4 brand-new novels every month and be billed just $6.24 per book in the U.S. or $6.74 per book in Canada. That's a savings of at least 22% off the cover price. It's quite a bargain! Shipping and handling is just 50¢ per book in the U.S. and 75¢ per book in Canada.* I understand that accepting the 2 free books and gifts places me under no obligation to buy anything. I can always return a shipment and cancel at any time. Even if I never buy another book, the two free books and gifts are mine to keep forever.

191/391 MDN F4XN

Name _____ (PLEASE PRINT) _____

Address _____ Apt. # _____

City _____ State/Prov. _____ Zip/Postal Code _____

Signature (if under 18, a parent or guardian must sign)

Mail to the Harlequin® Reader Service:
IN U.S.A.: P.O. Box 1867, Buffalo, NY 14240-1867
IN CANADA: P.O. Box 609, Fort Erie, Ontario L2A 5X3

Want to try two free books from another line?
Call 1-800-873-8635 or visit www.ReaderService.com.

* Terms and prices subject to change without notice. Prices do not include applicable taxes. Sales tax applicable in N.Y. Canadian residents will be charged applicable taxes. Offer not valid in Quebec. This offer is limited to one order per household. Not valid for current subscribers to the Suspense Collection or the Romance/Suspense Collection. All orders subject to credit approval. Credit or debit balances in a customer's account(s) may be offset by any other outstanding balance owed by or to the customer. Please allow 4 to 6 weeks for delivery. Offer available while quantities last.

Your Privacy—The Harlequin® Reader Service is committed to protecting your privacy. Our Privacy Policy is available online at www.ReaderService.com or upon request from the Harlequin Reader Service.

We make a portion of our mailing list available to reputable third parties that offer products we believe may interest you. If you prefer that we not exchange your name with third parties, or if you wish to clarify or modify your communication preferences, please visit us at www.ReaderService.com/consumerschoice or write to us at Harlequin Reader Service Preference Service, P.O. Box 9062, Buffalo, NY 14269. Include your complete name and address.

SUS13R

From #1 *New York Times* bestselling author

NORA ROBERTS

come two classic tales about finding the man of your
dreams right under your nose.

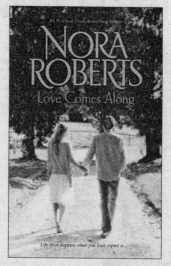

Life often happens when you least expect it...

Available wherever books are sold!

Be sure to connect with us at:

Harlequin.com/Newsletters
Facebook.com/HarlequinBooks
Twitter.com/HarlequinBooks

**A no-nonsense female cop reluctantly
teams up with the one man who makes her
lose control in a deliciously sensual new novel
from *New York Times* bestselling author**

LORI FOSTER

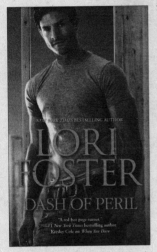

To bring down a sleazy
abduction ring, Lieutenant
Margaret "Margo" Peterson has
set herself up as bait. But recruiting
Dashiel Riske as her unofficial
partner is a whole other kind of
danger. Dash is 6'4" of laid-back
masculine charm, a man who loves
life—and women—to the limit.
Until Margo is threatened, and he
reveals a dark side that may just
match her own....

Beneath Margo's tough facade is a
slow-burning sexiness that drives
Dash crazy. The only way to finish
this case is to work together side
by side...skin to skin. And as their
mission takes a lethal turn, he'll have
to prove he's all the man she needs—in all the ways that matter....

Be sure to connect with us at:
Harlequin.com/Newsletters
Facebook.com/HarlequinBooks
Twitter.com/HarlequinBooks

HARLEQUIN® HQN™
™ www.Harlequin.com

PHLF857

LINDSAY McKENNA

77851	HIGH COUNTRY REBEL	___ $7.99 U.S.	___ $8.99 CAN.
77821	DOWN RANGE	___ $7.99 U.S.	___ $8.99 CAN.
77710	THE DEFENDER	___ $7.99 U.S.	___ $9.99 CAN.
77689	THE WRANGLER	___ $7.99 U.S.	___ $9.99 CAN.
77616	THE LAST COWBOY	___ $7.99 U.S.	___ $9.99 CAN.

(limited quantities available)

TOTAL AMOUNT	$ _____
POSTAGE & HANDLING	$ _____
($1.00 FOR 1 BOOK, 50¢ for each additional)	
APPLICABLE TAXES*	$ _____
TOTAL PAYABLE	$ _____

(check or money order—please do not send cash)

To order, complete this form and send it, along with a check or money order for the total above, payable to Harlequin HQN, to: **In the U.S.:** 3010 Walden Avenue, P.O. Box 9077, Buffalo, NY 14269-9077; **In Canada:** P.O. Box 636, Fort Erie, Ontario, L2A 5X3.

Name: _____

Address: _____ City: _____

State/Prov.: _____ Zip/Postal Code: _____

Account Number (if applicable): _____

075 CSAS

*New York residents remit applicable sales taxes.
*Canadian residents remit applicable GST and provincial taxes.

HARLEQUIN® HQN™
™www.Harlequin.com

PHLM0514BL